My first love
and other disasters

Also by Francine Pascal

The Fearless series

my first love
and other disasters

my first love and other disasters • love & betrayal & hold the mayo • my mother was never a kid

FRANCINE PASCAL

Simon Pulse
NEW YORK LONDON TORONTO SYDNEY NEW DELHI

alloy**entertainment**

Produced by Alloy Entertainment
151 West 26th Street, New York, NY 10001

SIMON PULSE
An imprint of Simon & Schuster Children's Publishing Division
1230 Avenue of the Americas, New York, NY 10020
This Simon Pulse paperback edition June 2014
My First Love and Other Disasters copyright © 1979 by Francine Pascal
Love & Betrayal & Hold the Mayo copyright © 1985 by Francine Pascal
My Mother Was Never a Kid copyright © 1977 by Francine Pascal
Cover photograph copyright © 2014 by Getty Images
For information about special discounts for bulk purchases, please contact
Simon & Schuster Special Sales at 1-866-506-1949 or business@simonandschuster.com.
The Simon & Schuster Speakers Bureau can bring authors to your live event.
For more information or to book an event contact the Simon & Schuster Speakers Bureau
at 1-866-248-3049 or visit our website at www.simonspeakers.com.
Cover designed by Karina Granda
Interior designed by Mike Rosamilia
The text of this book was set in Adobe Caslon Pro.
Manufactured in the United States of America
2 4 6 8 10 9 7 5 3
Library of Congress Control Number 2014931481
ISBN 978-1-4814-0168-5
ISBN 978-1-4442-9952-2 (*My First Love and Other Disasters* eBook)
ISBN 978-1-4391-0466-8 (*Love & Betrayal & Hold the Mayo* eBook)
ISBN 978-1-4391-0461-3 (*My Mother Was Never a Kid* eBook)
These titles were previously published individually.

Editor's Note

This collection of sizzling summer romances includes a bonus book: in *My Mother Was Never a Kid*, you'll get to meet Victoria when she's just turned thirteen and is having some seriously strange mother-daughter issues—and forms a friendship that transcends time!

Contents

my first love and other disasters

To my parents,
Kate and William Rubin

One

When I think about all the time I wasted last year moaning about how gross it was to be thirteen, I could kick myself. Thirteen turned out to be fantastic. It had to be. I mean, you finally make it. You're in the graduating class, and even if it's only the top of a bunch of little kids, it still makes you feel really special. Yes sir, thirteen was definitely first-rate. But fourteen? Forget it. It's the pits.

There are so many horrendous things about being fourteen that I'd have a fit if I had to name half of them. Just think about it. One day you're the biggest big shot in the entire middle school (among the girls anyway) and the next you're little Miss Nobody, which is exactly what everyone else in the whole high school seems to think about freshmen. At least that's the way they treat us.

Another drawback is how long it takes. Growing up, I mean. Except for times like Christmas vacation and summer, it seems like the years take forever to drag by. And for the plans I'm making, I absolutely have to be fifteen practically instantly. Especially seeing as how the person I happen to be madly in love with is seventeen. I'm definitely nowhere, sitting around being only fourteen, but it's absolutely hopeless—I mean, there's nothing I can do about it until I'm fifteen. Oh, sure, I'm getting there. But it's going to take me two more enormous weeks. I don't know how I'm going to stand the wait.

I probably forgot to tell you that there's another small problem, and that is that the love of my life has absolutely no idea that I even exist. But no sweat. I've arranged for our beautiful meeting to take place Tuesday at Howell's. I guess a shoe store for the orthopedically fashionable doesn't sound like the most romantic place for an encounter, but that's where he works on weekdays after school. The only other choice was his Saturday job—digging cesspools. Anyway, I'm not worried because I've worked out every single detail, so it can't miss. Theoretically. Of course in the real world, the one where practically everything I touch bites me, not only can it miss but it'll probably boomerang and come right back and hit me in the face.

No doubt it'll fail in some simple way, like I'll trip on my shoelaces. Big deal, so what if I'm not wearing shoelaces. I can always trip on somebody else's.

Or worse yet, I'll do what I did when my class went backstage at *I Love My Wife* last year and we met the whole cast.

I was so nervous and excited I thought I'd faint. Somebody said, "Victoria, I'd like you to meet Tommy Smothers—this is Victoria Martin." I smiled and said as sweetly as possible, "Hello, Victoria," and everybody cracked up.

Or what if it's something even more horrible? Suppose I'm standing there meeting the love of my life, and I'm smiling, and I don't know it but I have this black smudge across my nose, or worse, a crumb is stuck to my lip. Everything would be absolutely ruined. You know how it is when something like that happens, you can't even hear what the person is saying—all you do is stare at the crumb. But I think I may have that one beat because I'm bringing my best friend with me and she's going to be my crumb spotter, which will work out perfectly unless she starts laughing. We both do that at the most embarrassing times—crack up, I mean. But she's much worse than I am.

Anyway, about that dream guy of mine: After we get past that first meeting and we come to know each other, then I get right to work dumping the competition. But I don't do that here, in New York City—I do it on Fire Island. That's this super fabulous beach resort on Long Island where absolutely all the action is in the summertime. Anyway, *he's* going to be there for the whole summer and *she* isn't.

The first part is ready to move, but the Fire Island stuff could be sticky. I've got to get my parents' permission to be a mother's helper for the summer. For my parents that's the equivalent of asking them to let me hitchhike through Tasmania with the janitor. Still, I'm not discouraged because I know that the first time you try to get permission for anything new from your parents it always looks impossible, but if you keep at them long enough (and I've been at it all month long) they finally wear down.

So let's just say that I do get to meet him and somehow I convince my parents to allow me to go to Fire Island, then there's one more little side thing that I have to take care of.

There's this other boy, Barry. He's a complication. You see, I don't really know him, but he likes me. Which sounds peculiar, but it's one of those things where you can tell somebody's got a crush on you because they always turn up wherever you go, and you catch them staring at you all the time, and crazy things like that. Anyway, I have gotten friendly with him because it just so happens that he's a friend of Jim's, and he has a house on Fire Island, and I understand that Jim hangs out there a lot. I haven't figured out how to handle getting to be Barry's just-plain-friend-not-girlfriend yet. But I will.

Anyway, the first thing I have to pull off is the big meeting this Tuesday.

Now that you got that all straight, let me tell you a little more about the most important part—Jimmy.

Two

The first time I saw Jimmy I thought, what is everybody making such a fuss about? I mean, so okay, he's gorgeous-looking, so what's the big deal about that, and why is practically every single freshperson (I'm getting very heavily into women's lib lately) at Cooper High bug-eyed about him?

Actually, I figured that with all those girls dropping at his feet he had to be the most conceited, egocentric, me-me-me-type goon around. The kind I stay far away from.

Well, that was nearly ten months ago, and it's incredible but I think he gets better-looking every day. All I have to do is catch a quick peek at him in the hall or even from halfway across the gym and I'm positively knocked out. I don't know, maybe it has something to do with that number he does to keep his gorgeous straight silky blond hair from falling into his sexy hazel green-brown eyes. He kind of dips his head down and to the side a little and then flips it back. Two seconds later the gorgeous blond hair slides back down over his eyes again. I could watch him do that forever. In fact, one time I was doing just that when he looked up and caught me, and I had to pretend I was looking for someone in the row behind him. It didn't work so well because unfortunately, at the time, he was sitting in the last row.

Did I tell you that he's about six feet tall and he's got the most sensational body I've ever seen in my entire life? It's not all that different from everyone else's—I mean, it's got the same number of things—but on him it all seems to fit so perfectly.

I probably sound like I'm very superficial and that all I'm interested in is his looks. That's not true, because I know there's a lot more to Jim than just his looks. For one thing he's the kind of person everybody always wants to hang out with. And not just girls. Guys too. Maybe that's because he always looks like he's having such a good time. I suppose it's his smile. It's the catching kind. Makes you feel happy just to look at him.

He's been the president of his class for two years running, and the captain of the tennis team, so obviously I'm not the only one who thinks he's terrific.

One tiny little thing. He *probably* knows he's something special, but he'd have to be blind or a hypocrite not to. Actually, he just looks like he feels good about himself, and I don't think that's so bad.

Obviously I've completely lost my mind over him. And

like I said, he doesn't know I'm alive. But that's okay because Steffi (the friend I told you about) and I have decided that the situation is pretty viable (my mother's favorite word; no matter what you talk to her about, you've got to figure that somehow something in it is going to be "viable." It got so bad, I finally had to look it up).

Anyway, it's still definitely viable except for that one disgusting, ugly, grungy problem. Her name is Gloria, and she's been his girlfriend since the start of his junior year, which makes it almost a year that she's been going more or less steady with him. And that's not even the worst. Steffi and I did a little digging and we came up with a lot more bad news. Number one is that she's his sister's best friend. Number two, she lives in his apartment building. And number three is the real killer—she's sixteen. I would sell my kid sister's soul (and all the rest of her too) to be sixteen. But what's the use. Nobody's buying.

Even Steffi admits Gloria shoots a big hole in the viability angle. Especially when you see her and Jimmy together. She's always right there, hanging on to his arm like she was drowning. She'd better cool it or he's going to wake up one morning with one six-foot-long arm. I hate to think what his sweaters must look like. And she's a whiner—"Jim . . . my, I'm hungry—Jim . . . my, I'm thirsty—Jim . . . my, I'm cold—Jim . . . my, you promised . . ." She's not as bad as my sister Nina, but for a practically adult person she's pretty awful. And on top of that she's also one of those really girlish types of squeamish, too-too precious, dainty things that'd faint dead away if they saw one measly little worm. You know, the kind that's always wearing some guy's jacket or sweater because she's shivering, even in August. Very dependent type. You don't see too many of them around anymore since women's lib. She's the last of a dying breed, and we should probably preserve her. In fact, that would be a perfect solution. Have her stuffed.

Her and Norman. Norman's my sheepdog, and even though it's horrendous to talk that way about your own dog, with Norman it would probably be a month before anyone noticed the difference. It seems like all he ever does is sleep or watch Nina—that's my twelve-year-old sister—and me argue about whose turn it is to take him out.

We've had Norman forever, and for a long time we thought he had some kind of psychological block against showing affection, but now we realize that the only reason he doesn't give us those big leaping doggy greetings with all the kissing and tailwagging is simply because it takes too much energy. If he could figure a way to do it without getting up I know he would, because deep down he really loves us—except for that thing he has about us plotting to steal his food. My father says he's paranoid, but I don't think he's any worse than Nina when it comes to something she loves. First thing she does is spit on it. (That definitely discourages sharing.) She's a real winner, anyway. It seems like she's always hanging around, butting in, bugging my friends, tattling, whining, borrowing and never returning, and generally being a pain in the neck. She also looks like a troll—well, to me anyway, although she has nice greenish eyes if you can find them under her glasses. And they say she'll have pretty teeth when the railroad comes off. (I'm wired too, but not with tracks—the thin kind that's almost invisible.)

Listen, I know Typhoid Mary was worse, but she wasn't my sister. My mother keeps assuring me that it's natural for siblings to think they hate each other as kids but that there's really a deep well of love (her words) that we'll discover when we're older. She's probably right—when I'm about a hundred I should start liking Nina.

Actually, in this last year she's made two big improvements. One is her hair. It used to hang in strings like grunge. Then she made a brilliant discovery: shampoo. The second thing is her trick belch. You know what it's like to introduce some great guy to your sister and instead of "hello" she takes a monster breath and . . . well, that's the second improvement. Now she only does it around the house with family and close friends. She's still got a long way to go.

I probably ought to count my blessings. Steffi's brother still picks his nose and he's nearly fourteen.

Say I eventually do get Nina under control. That still leaves the real tough ones, Felicia and Philip Martin, terrific, fabulous, sensational people except when it comes to being my parents. The problem is so obvious to me. They take their job too seriously. I'm two seconds away from being fifteen, and they're still hanging over me, making sure I eat a proper breakfast, wear my scarf, my boots, my gloves, my sweater, and then there are all those watch-outs—watch the knife, your fingers, the bottom step, the car door, sharp corners, strangers, drafts, and fish bones. To be absolutely fair, I think they've got it together a lot this past year. Four different times in the last month neither of them warned me that I was going to tip over and crack my head when I leaned back on the dining room chairs.

I guess it's always possible that they've just stopped caring about my head, but I don't really think so. I'm an optimist and I think they were just going through a bad stage and now they're improving. Like now, they're actually considering the possibility of me being a mother's helper this summer out on Fire Island. I definitely know my mother's considering letting me take the job, because the last time we discussed it (actually it was the seventeenth time since April) she said, "We'll see." I know from way back that "We'll see" usually stinks, but I read it as a giant step up from "Are you out of your mind?" and "Absolutely not!" For my mother, even just considering the possibility is a huge improvement.

Naturally she still hassles me to do things her way, but now she's starting to listen to my side a lot more and even tries to let me make more decisions on my own. Even so, she has a long way to go—a lot farther than my father, who's pretty okay except when it comes to boys. It's like he thinks they're all out to steal his precious baby. When it comes to his darling daughters, he's just like Norman with his food. You should see the looks he gives them—the boys, I mean. Nickie Rostivo says it feels like my father's looking right through him. And Dad's definitely outrageous when it comes to any boy I show just the teensiest romantic interest in. Still, mostly he's pretty fabulous.

Anyway, back to sensational Jimmy. I think I'll start calling him Jim just to be different. I'm only just starting, so if I want him to notice me I've got to be special, which is a horrendous problem when you are as ordinary average as me. I'm sure just calling him Jim isn't going to make him stop dead and say, "Who is that mysterious average-looking girl who is courageous enough to call me Jim when the rest of the world calls me Jimmy?" Still, it's a start, and I need all the starts I can get.

Naturally I've been doing some dumb things like calling him on the phone and giggling. It's okay because I never say my name. I'd die if he ever found out.

Anyway, like I said, Steffi and I have a plan of attack that's really far out. We're going to go into the store where Jim works part-time and pretend I need a pair of shoes. You should see the shoes. They're great-looking if you happen to have hooves. Luckily, I've saved enough babysitting money so I could buy a cheap pair if I absolutely had to. I don't expect him to fall over dead at the sight of me; but at least I'll get to meet him.

I've created the scene in my mind a hundred times, and it always comes out beautiful. I go in there and there's nobody around but him, and he comes out and it's one of those things like in the movies, where his eyes and my eyes meet and we stand there held to each other while the electricity crackles around us. Then finally he pulls himself away and I sit down (I'm wearing my new Victoria's Secret nightgown) and he starts to take off my shoes and the touch of his hand on my bare foot stuns us both. (In dreams you don't have to wear peds to try on shoes.) So then he asks me what shoes I want and I tell him and he can't stop looking at me. Then there's a whole boring part where he brings out the shoes and tries them on me and that whole thing, and then finally when I'm about to leave (in this one I get stuck buying a really horrendous pair of espadrilles, but I figure I can always sell them to Nina), he says he has to see me, and he's shocked when I tell him that I go to school with him, and we plan to go out that Saturday night, and I can tell he's got to break a date with Gloria. Anyway, that's the dream.

Today is real life, and it's that Tuesday afternoon I told you about and I'm waiting for Steffi to buzz me from the lobby, and then we're going over to Howell's shoe store because this is the day that Jim works there.

My complexion looks sort of okay today. There are a lot of under-the-skin bumps that nobody else ever seems to see, but I do. Still, if nobody else can, I guess he won't, so it doesn't matter. I'm wearing Steffi's new French jeans, my cousin Liz's suede clogs (we traded—I gave her my old Adidas sneakers, which always killed my little toe anyway), and this fabulous Indian shirt I gave my mother for her last birthday.

My hair is only so-so because I didn't have time to wash

it, and it's been almost two days since my last shampoo so it's really disgusting. I washed my feet, anyway.

It must be three thirty because jerk-face just got home. That's Nina.

"You walk Norman!" I tell her first thing.

"Is Mommy home?" she answers.

"Walk him now!"

"Is Mommy home?" she keeps insisting.

"No."

"Up yours. I'll walk him when I feel like it." She's a monster when my mother is out. If my mother ever heard the language her darling twelve-year-old uses, she'd have a fit. I'm starting to tell her a few things when the downstairs buzzer rings. That has to be Steffi. I do a last check in the mirror, grab my father's velour jacket that fits me perfectly since my mother accidentally put it in the dryer, and race out.

Steffi is waiting in the front of the building. For some strange reason she's wearing her new jeans that she said she was saving for Myrl Weingard's birthday party next week. She's really got a fabulous figure. A lot of people can't wear tight jeans, but she looks great in them. She even combed her hair a little different. I have to tell her how terrific it looks with a side parting. And, my God, she's wearing eye shadow! And now that I come closer, at least half a bottle of my tea rose perfume that I left at her house last week.

Right at this second my feelings toward my very best friend in the whole world are very confused. I'm absolutely torn between hate and loathing. I can't believe Steffi would try to steal my boyfriend even before he's really my boyfriend. I'm probably jumping to conclusions and I really should be ashamed of myself. Steffi Klinger has been my dearest friend since we met in third grade. (It was really hysterical how we were both crazy about this jerky guy. . . .)

Oh, damn! How could she! Well, I'm certainly not about to blow my cool over a little competition. I've always heard that competition is healthy—for potato-sack racing. Not boys. I smile sweetly at her and decide to play it tricky. "Listen," I say to her, "if you're too busy to come with me today I can do it alone or we can make it for another day."

"That's okay," she says brightly. "I can come today."

"Or better yet, I can meet you later."

"Anything you like."

"Or you could wait outside."

"Sure thing."

"You mean you don't mind not coming?"

"I swear it's okay with me. Actually, then I can go home and change. I feel so jerky all dressed up like this, but my mother wanted to take some pictures for some special album she's doing and then I didn't have time to change. I'll probably get it all grimed up, and I wanted to save it for Myrl's party."

Suddenly I love her again.

"Don't change," I say.

"You don't think it looks gross in the middle of the afternoon? And I'm wearing eye makeup, too."

"You look beautiful."

"Really?"

"Absolutely."

"By the way, I owe you a new tea rose. I spilled the whole bottle on my foot. Gross, huh?"

Did I mention Steffi's the greatest friend in the world?

"You'll really knock them out in the shoe store," I say.

"I thought you wanted me to wait outside."

"Not a chance. I'd die if I had to go through it alone. You just have to be there."

"Great. I've been looking forward to this all day. I just know he's going to have heart failure when he meets you."

"You think so?"

"I know it. You look absolutely spectacular today."

"Quick. Let's go before I start to fade."

So we start to walk toward Broadway. Howell's is only about three blocks from my house. We're not even walking fast, but I'm starting to sweat just from excitement. Luckily, this blouse isn't clingy so you can't see that I'm dripping wet. Damn Secret.

Oh, God, I just remembered I'm going to get my period practically any minute! Now even my face is sweaty. Well, maybe the store will be air-conditioned and then I can sort of hang out near the front windows until I dry off. Unless of course I really do get my period, and then standing with my back to him would be a mistake.

Mostly when people think of Broadway they think it's all

theaters and hookers, but around my way, up in the Fifties, it's really okay. And when you go farther uptown it gets great. At least, I love it. You find all kinds of stores—great little clothes shops and markets—and it's always busy and noisy with a million things happening. And the people are outrageous. Not scary outrageous, just crazy and exciting. My father says there are more nuts per square inch on Broadway than on any other street in the world. Like the Lysol lady. She's some kook who runs around with a mask over her nose and mouth spraying Lysol all around her. Nothing else nutty about her. I mean she wouldn't bother anyone. She just likes things clean.

Anyway, in no time at all we're outside Howell's, and Steffi pokes me to look in the window. There he is. My Jim. He *is* gorgeous.

"Wait!" I grab Steffi just as she's about to open the door. "Let's say again what we're going to do."

"Relax," she purrs, "it's easy. All we do is go in and sit down, and when Jimmy sees you he'll come over, and from there on it's practically a snap. I mean, one look at those jeans and he'll be off the wall."

"You're the best friend I ever had, but what if he doesn't fall over dead for me?"

"He has to. I just feel it. I mean, you look totally perfect."

"Definitely."

"Should I have a shoe number to give him?"

"Ugh. They're all so ugly. Maybe those espadrilles aren't too disgusting."

"Okay, just remember 703."

"I got it."

"So come on. Let's go."

"Wait a sec."

"What now?"

"Maybe I should get the sneakers. At least they're not completely gross."

"Ugh, no. Sneakers are so unsexy. Stick with the espadrilles. At least they make you look taller, and he's probably six feet. Come on. They're beginning to look funny at us."

"No, wait . . ."

"Whaa . . . t!"

"I forgot the number."

"703. Now let's go." And she opens the door and shoves me in. Oh, God!

We're in the store and it's a lot smaller than I thought. There's no room to just stand there and dry off. There's also no Jim. Now Steffi jabs me in the arm and nods with her head toward the back room. And there he is, standing in the stockroom talking on the telephone. We're just standing there staring at him when Mr. Howell, the owner of the store, comes waddling over.

"Can I help you girls?" he says, leaning over and trying to catch what we're staring at.

"We—I mean, my friend . . . ," Steffi begins, still concentrating on Jim in the back. "Victoria, tell him about the shoes."

"Yeah . . ." This is going very badly. I certainly don't want

Old Man Howell to take my order. But I'm trapped. I can't just stand here like a jerk and not say anything.

"Well, girls?" he says.

"703," I say.

"Hey, Jimmy," he calls to Jim. "Enough with the girlfriend already. Get off the phone. I need you."

Jim looks really embarrassed and he quickly hangs up. Steffi pokes me again and says in a stage whisper you could hear four blocks away, "He's coming."

"About time," says Mr. Howell, and before Jim can even get into the front of the store he tells him to go down to the basement and get 703. "What size, honey?" Mr. Howell asks me.

"Six medium." I'm really more like six and a half or even seven, but I hate big feet, and besides, I plan to sell them to Nina anyway.

"In six medium." You can practically hear Jim moan as he heads for the basement to get my shoes. I don't even know him and he hates me already. I'm the jerk who made him drag all the way down to the crummy old cellar to get shoes. And I'm also responsible for making him hang up in the middle of a gorgeous conversation with his grungy girlfriend. Well, I'm not sorry about that.

Steffi and I sit down to wait. I'm beginning to think this was a dumb thing to do. I mean, the whole setting is so unromantic with Mr. Howell and this tiny store with all the ugly shoes and Jim having to disappear downstairs. It's all getting very messy. I wish we could get out of here, but we can't with

Mr. Howell standing there and just staring at us.

We wait at least a hundred years. Still no Jim. Now Mr. Howell goes to the back steps and calls down. "So, Jimmy, huh? Did you fall asleep down there?"

"I can't find any 703s, Mr. Howell," he calls back.

"Open your eyes and look near the boiler." This is mortifying.

Silence from the basement.

"So?" says Mr. Howell.

"I don't see them. I'm sorry, Mr. Howell."

"They're right in front of your nose on the side of the boiler."

More silence. I think I want to die. None of this was in my daydreams.

"Aiii, kids. You have to supervise everything. They wouldn't find their head if it wasn't attached." And with a lot of grumbling he goes to the top of the basement steps and shouts down, "Are you at the boiler?"

"Right," Jim shouts up. His voice is beginning to sound not so terrific.

"Now look on the right. You see those stacks of boxes near the window?"

"Yeah."

"So look."

"You want me to go through all the stacks?"

"You got something better to do?"

I hear what is definitely a moan from the basement, and

give Steffi a shove with my elbow and whisper that this is the worst idea in the whole world. "I've ruined everything. How am I ever going to face him again? It's over . . . finished. There's no hope." I'm moaning even worse than he is.

"You're right," Steffi says. She's the most honest friend I've ever had. That's the one thing I hate about her. "Keep your eyes on Mr. Howell," she says. "The minute he turns his head, we disappear."

I give her the gotcha sign and wiggle into my shoes. We get our bags in our laps and slide to the edge of our seats. But Mr. Howell's not letting go. He keeps us nailed there with his eyes.

There's a lot of noisy shuffling around coming from the basement but still no size sixes.

"You sure you take a size six? Let me measure your foot." And quick as anything he grabs one of those foot measures and advances on us. We both jump up, clutching our bags, and like we were attached, start squiggling away from him toward the door. He sort of slides around us and grabs a chair and shoves it into us from behind, pushing us down together on the same seat. Now he whips my shoe off and jams my foot down on the cold metal ruler thing. I guess maybe when you have such ugly shoes in your store you've got to work hard to make a sale. Of course it registers almost seven, but I don't care anymore. As far as I'm concerned my life is over anyway.

"I found them, Mr. Howell! I got them. The size sixes." And Jim comes charging out of the cellar.

Rats! Now he finds them! But it's too late because now Mr. Howell is going to say they're the wrong size and make him go back down and look for the sevens and naturally he's going to think I'm insane and hate me forever.

But it doesn't happen that way. All Mr. Howell says is, "You see what happens when you look with your eyes open?" And he grabs the shoes from the box and pronounces them "perfect, beautiful shoes—are you a lucky girl!"

"I'll put them on," I say, reaching for the shoes.

"No, no, dear, let the boy." And Mr. Howell nods to Jim, who sits down on one of those little seats with the slanted fronts for trying on shoes.

Remember that part in Cinderella where the mean stepsisters try to squeeze their feet into the glass slipper? That's nothing compared to what goes on with these loathsome espadrilles. Naturally Steffi is absolutely killing herself. She's so hysterical she keeps sliding off the chair and making all kinds of dumb snorting, giggling sounds.

I don't let him give up. I make some excuse about my socks being all bunched up and twist them around, adjust them, pull them up tight, and point my toes with all my might. The espadrilles slide beautifully past the toes and hit a brick wall somewhere around the middle of my foot about a mile from the heel. By now my dearest friend Steffi is totally convulsed on the floor. The rest of us pretend she's not even in the store.

"I think they're too narrow maybe, huh?" Jim is trying to

sound ordinary, like you do with regular normal human beings when they try on shoes that don't fit them.

At this point all I have to say is "Yeah, you're right, too narrow, thanks," or something like that, and pick up my imbecile best friend and walk out. And that's just what I'm about to do but I'm not fast enough.

"Don't worry, dear," Mr. Howell says with a sickly-sweet smile, "we'll get you the next size."

We're this little knot of people in one corner of an almost empty store and there's no way to get away. I see Jim roll his eyes and hear him make a soft groan when Mr. Howell says how he should go back down to the basement and find me the right size.

I absolutely cannot let him go back down to that cellar again for shoes I'm never going to put on once I take them out of the store. Besides, he'll despise me forever if I do. So with one horrendous shove I jam my foot into the shoe, which goes flying six inches into Jim's stomach, pushing him backward right off his seat.

"Perfect," I say through clenched teeth. "I love them snug."

You've got to picture Steffi still doubled over on the floor, Jim sprawled down next to her, and me on Jim's seat somehow with my leg sticking straight out in the air. It's too funny. Now Mr. Howell grabs the foot with the new shoe, gives it a this-way that-way squeeze, and pronounces it a perfect fit.

"I'll take them!" I say and start to pull it off.

You guessed. It doesn't budge.

"Write up the bill, Jimmy," says Mr. Howell, who's not taking any chances, "while I help the little girl off with her new shoes." And he starts to pull at the shoe.

Jim goes to the cash register to write up the sale. Naturally he's really confused because he doesn't know why someone would buy shoes that obviously are miles too small, and any fool can see they are the ugliest, grossest things ever made. How would he possibly know that I'm doing all this out of love for him? All he thinks is that I'm probably on a weekend pass from the nuthouse. Certainly Steffi looks like she is.

"Perhaps you would prefer waiting outside," I say to Steffi in a surprisingly controlled voice while I pinch her arm and nudge her toward the door. She can't exactly answer me, but she obeys and lurches into the street, in screaming hysterics. Very immature.

I, on the other hand, play it absolutely cool. In a flash I see that I can't get the shoe off without a lot of unattractive tugging and puffing, so I say, like it's practically an afterthought, "I think I'll wear it home."

"Here's the other one," Jim says, taking the second shoe out of the box.

"Thanks," I tell him, snapping the shoe out of his hand. "I can manage." He doesn't argue.

With what I hope looks like the greatest of ease, I begin to slip the second shoe on. I'm still toiling at it when Jim begins to wrap up my old shoes. He gives me some long, hard looks. Not those magical electric current things I dreamed about, the kind that pull you together and make everything zing. More like . . . yuck!

Well, nothing is perfect. I'm still working on the shoe when he finishes the wrapping. Now I figure I'll never get the back on, so I just stop trying and crunch down on it. At least I don't have to worry about it sliding off the front—not without a four-man pull team anyway. The worst may be over, so I'm feeling pretty cool. As Jim fills out the sales check, I busy myself studying the net weight on a can of tan Kiwi shoe polish.

"Uh . . . can you give me your name?" Jim says.

Dread moment, but I knew it was coming.

"Regina Goldin Vockwarger." You didn't think I was going to give my real name in a disaster like this, did you?

"Regina what?"

"Goldin Vartbarker."

"Vartwarker?"

"No, Vartrocker." It's the first actual conversation we've ever had, and I want it to last forever.

"Could you spell that, please?"

"Sure, W-A-R . . ."

"W?"

"Yes, *V* is pronounced *W* in Hungarian."

"You're Hungarian?" I can tell he's beginning to see me as a person now. Of course, it's the wrong person, but still . . . it's a start. He's probably saying to himself right now, "Gee, she's not so bad." From out of nowhere Mr. Howell jumps into our private conversation. "Who's Hungarian?" he wants to know.

"She is." Jim motions to me.

"What was that name, darling?" he asks, but I get very busy counting out the money, and as soon as he takes it I scoop up my shoe box and head for the door.

"Vartsugar," I mumble, trying to give a kind of Hungarian warble to my voice. And I open the door fast and zoom out.

The last thing I hear Jim say is, "She's nuts."

I don't know exactly where I screwed up, but I know in my heart it wasn't a total success. Probably more like a horrendous failure that I may never recover from. If only I could go back to where he doesn't know I'm alive.

Steffi comes back to my house and she tries to cheer me up, but I really feel heartbroken because when I looked at him today I knew this was something more than just a kid crush. I think I'm really in love with this beautiful guy, and it probably was dumb and silly and childish to go about it this way. I mean, this is too important for games.

I hope he doesn't remember who I was. But of course he will. He's not blind.

Steffi's all for trying it again, this time with a different approach, and she comes up with a couple of other ideas. In one I'm supposed to be taking a survey—you know, one of those house-to-house things, to measure the attitudes of teenage boys toward orphans or something, and the other is a whole big romantic thing where I pretend to faint in his elevator. They're pretty good ideas, especially the fainting one, but

I don't know, I'm beginning to think that sort of stuff may be kind of babyish. I don't say that to Steffi because I don't want to insult her, but I don't think I want to spoil what I feel for Jim with some contrived kind of setup. I tell her that if this thing can't start naturally and beautifully I'd rather just keep it inside myself. Of course she understands perfectly. Any best friend would.

Can it be that I'll have to suffer through one of those unrequited loves? That can happen—ugh. Sometimes you just love somebody and nothing can possibly happen. Like with old maids. I guess they probably loved somebody sometime in the past but they weren't loved back, or maybe the guy never even knew they existed and so they just spent the whole rest of their lives loving someone from far away.

That's not for me—I mean, silently worshipping some idol and just kind of drying up and shrivelling away to nothing without him ever knowing.

No way! Okay, so I don't make up some silly little scene. Still, I've made up my mind. I'm not the long-suffering type. I'm not going to tell anyone, not even Steffi. Then it doesn't look so much like a setup, but I intend to make Mr. Jim Freeman very much aware of me very shortly. Watch out, Gloria!

Three

Friday night I work on my parents some more about the mother's helper job on Fire Island this summer. I'd be working for Cynthia Landry, this woman who lives in our building. I've been sitting for her kids for almost three years now. Last year she got a divorce. It was really horrendous. David and DeeDee—those are the kids—were very upset. It's not like you could tell by just looking at them, but it seemed that they were always crying about something. Both of them. They would just burst into tears for nothing. All you had to say was, "David, it's too late to watch TV," or just disagree with him about any little thing, and boom, he would start bawling. It was truly horrific since neither of them are babies. David's almost eight now and DeeDee is five. It could really upset you, except I knew that it was a reaction to what was happening, so I tried to be extra nice. I felt bad for them.

Divorce is such a scary thing. I don't know how you feel, but anytime my parents have an argument I practically hold my breath. I guess divorce is the worst thing next to something horrible happening, like one of them dying. (I'm very superstitious. I have to knock wood when I even think something awful like that.) Just the thought of my father moving away and my mother not loving him, maybe even hating him, makes my stomach sink.

Cynthia hates Jed—that's her ex-husband. He moved to California and he hardly sees the kids anymore. When they broke up, people were saying he was playing around with Cynthia's best friend, Amy. I don't know all the juice. All I know is that Amy didn't leave her husband to run off with Jed, but Charlie the doorman (he knows everything) says Cynthia doesn't talk to Amy anymore, and he says they were practically like sisters. Like Steffi and me, I guess.

It's a funny thing, but I used to think they had a fabulous marriage and I used to babysit a lot for them, so I knew what they were like together. It really looked fantastic, I mean they hardly ever argued, and mostly they helped each other and did things together even, like cooking. He liked to mess around in the kitchen and make bread and things like that. I don't know. I even used to hope that my husband (if I ever get married, which I'll probably do when I'm about twenty-seven or so, but I want a career and I want to live with a few people first so I can make the right choice) would be a lot like Jed.

Ugh! He turned out to be such a creep. I don't blame Cynthia for hating him. But that's what makes me so nervous. Not that my parents fight a lot, because they don't. But neither did Cynthia and Jed, and look what happened to them. You can't ever tell what's really going on with your parents. One day they could just come in and announce that it's over, for some dumb reason, like they're incompatible or unfulfilled, and that's that. I mean, there's nothing in the world you can do about it. It's not like a Disney movie where the kids come up with some outrageous plan and then in the end they get the parents back together again. Baloney. It never happens.

Like with Steffi's parents. Everything was great, and then they got a divorce and it looked like there wasn't even a reason. Steffi said there absolutely wasn't anyone else involved, and she and her brother did all sorts of things to try to get them back together, but it didn't make any difference. They had made up their minds. Kids never really have anything to say about family things like that. Whatever your parents decide, no matter how gross or how much it hurts you, forget it, they get to make the decision and that's that. I don't think it's fair at all. But a lot that counts! I mean what a kid thinks.

Anyway, David and DeeDee seem to be pretty okay now. I guess they'll get it together, but still I feel bad for them. I would just love to be their mother's helper for the summer, and I know Cynthia really wants me to be. I get the shivers just thinking about how sensational it would be living on Fire Island this summer. Not only would I be near Jim, but I'd be practically living on my own. Sure I'd have to take care of the kids, but I don't mind that, and then on my time off I'd be on my own—me and Jim. Oh, I don't think I ever wanted anything so much in all my life!

I have to make my parents understand how much it means to me. My mother is still saying "We'll see" about the job, but I have to get a definite answer one way or the other soon because if I don't Cynthia is going to get someone else. It just so happens that Steffi's mother said she could go, so if I can't I guess then maybe Cynthia would ask Steffi. I would hate that. I know that's sour grapes and Steffi is really my best friend, but between you and me, I would hate Steffi if she took the job, which of course she would because, after all, why shouldn't she? Naturally I would tell her that I didn't mind, and then she would probably say, "Are you sure?" and I would say, "Absolutely," but I would absolutely hate her and my parents and Nina, too, because she'd probably think it was hysterical that Steffi was getting my job.

No matter how much I want it to be the best, I guess this summer could just possibly be the worst summer of my entire life, which is a pretty awful gift for somebody's fifteenth birthday.

Did I forget to mention that? I turn fifteen on Sunday, and that's when I make my major, final, desperate, dying-gasp plea for the Fire Island job—at my birthday dinner.

Four

I have nothing to wear.

"I have nothing to wear!" I have to scream because I am buried four feet into the bottom of my closet hunting for some scrap of something to wear out tonight for the big dinner with my parents and the gnome, who unfortunately insisted on coming along even though she hates Italian food, especially since I believe I may have mentioned to her sometime or another that it all has squid and octopus in it—alive! She still practically gags at the thought of Italian food, but no, she wouldn't stay home tonight. She knows this is when I plan to talk to my parents about the summer and she wants to make as much trouble as she can. This is going to be a tough fight, all uphill, and I have to look just right, kind of sweet/cute but also old/sophisticated, and I can't find the right dress to wear. It's got to be a good dress, but not my best in case I have to throw myself dramatically out of my chair and pound the dirty floor in a tantrum.

Amazingly, I just found a great skirt I haven't seen since I accused my sister Nina of borrowing it and lending it to one of her friends who I was certain had lost it. So, big deal, she didn't. She does enough other awful things, so she could have done this too. Actually, if my closet were neater it would have been hanging up, and then she'd have seen it and certainly would have borrowed it and lent it to her friend, and they're so jerky they absolutely would have lost it, so you see I wasn't wrong in accusing her.

"Victoria, come on, move it! The reservation's for seven thirty."

My mother is standing in the doorway. I can hear her but I can't see through all this junk.

I push through all kinds of hanging things, past clumps of dusty shoes, and shopping bags stuffed with scraps of suede from when I was going to make a patchwork skirt, and wool from my crocheting projects, and old letters from summer camp. I'm a saver, sort of. Now I'm peeking through at my mother, who is getting more aggravated than she sounded.

"I have nothing to wear." That wasn't my mother.

"Put on your navy blue dress."

"Gross."

"Or the beige pants. I haven't seen you wear those in ages."

"They're in the laundry."

36

"Since January?"

"Well, they're at the bottom."

"Ugh." That wasn't me either.

"No jeans, please. This is a good restaurant."

And with that irrelevant information, she leaves the room.

Now, I want you to know that I'm not just being difficult. I actually have nothing to wear. Sure there's a lot of bulk in my closet, but it's all horrendous. Like for example, the navy dress. I can't imagine why I was so crazy to buy it, it's positively disgusting and I look like a giant baby doll in it. My knit skirt hangs down half a mile longer in the back than in the front, and my red dressy sweater itches. Most of my clothes are just nowhere, full of lumps and bumps in all the wrong places, and I'm really in the mood to make a big thing about my wardrobe with my mother, but the plain fact is I can't risk angering her tonight of all nights. She absolutely has to let me go to Fire Island. Period.

I kind of have it worked out in my mind how to do it. We're going to this terrific little restaurant in the Village called Trattoria da Alfredo. The food is out of sight, but the best part about it is that it's very small and sort of quiet. A perfect place to put the squeeze on somebody. I know just how it's going to happen. I start asking them about the mother's helper job, and they're not hot for the idea but I keep at it, and then my father says to lower our voices and we start to whisper louder, and then people start to turn around. You know how adults get very patient with kids when other people are listening? I mean, they just can't say, "I said no, and I don't want to hear anymore," like they do at home. They have to pretend to listen and consider it and then give a reasonable answer. I really have them with their backs to the wall, I hope. I'm preparing for an all-out blitz tonight, the kind that takes everyone's appetite away (except, of course, Nina, who could eat through an earthquake).

Five

It happens exactly like I said only a little different. First thing my father says is "No, and I don't want to hear about it anymore."

Of course this is a very bad start, but I push on. I give them the business about how I'm fifteen and they still treat me like a baby. That's an old argument so they know how to answer that easily. Even *I* know how to answer that. All you say is "When you can't take no for an answer, that's acting like a baby so we treat you like one."

Then I give them the business about how every other girl in the entire high school is going to be a mother's helper this summer and before they can say anything I rattle off six names ending with Laura Wolfe, the only one I absolutely know is going to.

Up to now the toad has been gorging on fettucine. Now suddenly she zeroes in to destroy my life. "Uh-uh," says Nina, "Laura Wolfe is going on a camping trip with her parents."

"She is not, smarty, she's going to be a mother's helper for the Kramers out in East Hampton, so there." I could kill her, I swear it.

"Uh-uh." She shakes her dumb head, and the strings of the fettucine hanging out of her mouth swing back and forth.

"She is so!"

"Nope."

"Is so, creep!"

"Mom!"

"Jerk."

"That's enough!" hisses my father. "I don't care what Laura Wolfe or anyone else is doing with her summer."

"But she is, Daddy," I insist. "I know because she said . . ."

"Well, she isn't anymore because her sister, Linda, is in my class, and she said . . ."

"Did you hear your father?" Now my mother's in it. And suddenly the couples at the next table are all dying to hear about Laura Wolfe. "And, Nina, for God's sake, swallow that food. How many times do I have to tell you not to eat spaghetti with half of it hanging down to your chin!"

"I can't help it," she whines, "it just slips out."

"Roll it on the spoon the way I showed you," my father tells her.

"I did."

"If you did it properly it wouldn't fall out of your mouth like that. Do it like this." And my mother starts rolling up a spoonful of spaghetti on her spoon and then pops it into her mouth perfectly. "You see? It's simple. Now let me see you do it."

"I don't have a spoon," says Nina.

"Why are you telling me you rolled it when you don't even have a spoon?"

"I did but it dropped."

Naturally everybody at the surrounding three tables starts hunting for Nina's spoon.

"Ask the waiter for another one," my mother says, embarrassed and completely out of patience.

"I know Laura Wolfe is definitely going." I have to get them back on the track.

"Laura who?" my father says, as if he never heard the name before.

"The girl who's going to be a mother's helper."

"Uh-uh," says my gross sister, and she's got a new batch of spaghetti dropping out of her mouth.

"Shut up!" I tell her.

"How many times do I have to tell you not to say shut up to your sister!" my mother snaps.

"Then make her mind her own business," I say.

"Why do we always have to have these arguments over dinner?" my mother says. "I look forward to a pleasant meal with my family and this is what it turns into."

"Girls," says my father, "enough, you're ruining your mother's dinner. I don't want to hear anything more about Laura Wolfe or what she's doing for the summer. Do you understand?"

"And you," he says to Nina. "Don't order spaghetti anymore if you don't know how to eat it."

"But I don't like anything else."

"Then stay home," I tell her.

"Mind your own business, Victoria, I'm talking to Nina," my father says.

"She's always minding my business, and besides, just because of her I didn't even get to ask a very important question. It's not fair!"

"Okay, Nina, be quiet," my father says. "Now what's your question, Victoria?"

"Can I?"

"Can you what?" He turns to my mother in exasperation. "Can she what?"

"Can she be a mother's helper," my mother says.

"Well, I don't know." Good sign that my father didn't say absolutely no. "Maybe she's a little young. Maybe next year. What do you think, Felicia?"

Lovely. He's sticking with it. Now she can't say "Your father doesn't want you to," or something like that. It's very bad when you get in the middle of one of those things and then each one keeps blaming the other and you never get the right answer.

"I don't know, Phil, you may be right."

She throws it right back to him.

"If that's what you think, dear."

He grabs it and shoots it back to her. I've got to get it away or they'll just keep passing it back and forth forever.

"Liz started when she was fifteen," I volunteer. Liz is my cousin from Philadelphia, and she really did start last year.

"That's true," says my father, like it's maybe not such a bad idea to do, especially since his favorite sister, Liz's mother, let her do it. "It worked out okay, didn't it?"

"I think so," says my mother.

"It was perfect," I pipe up. "Liz said she really learned a whole lot that summer." You bet she did. But I'm not crazy enough to say *what* she learned.

"Except, now that I think about it," my mother says, "there was some problem about the people leaving her alone for a weekend. I think they went away or something like that. I know Dinah"—my aunt—"was very upset about that. Fifteen-year-old girls shouldn't be left alone with small children overnight."

I swear to them that Cynthia Landry—wonderful, mature, responsible Cynthia—would never go anywhere and leave me alone with the kids overnight. I tell them how she really needs me because now that she's working she has to have someone with the kids.

"Will she be going into an office every day?" my mother wants to know.

I tell her no, mostly she works from home. But she'll

probably be going into the city maybe about three times a week. And then I make a big thing about how Cynthia and the kids really want me, especially because I've been baby-sitting for them for almost three years and the kids are crazy about me. I can see that they're considering the matter seriously and that it's looking good. Even Nina is minding her own business. Maybe she ate some octopus. I keep my fingers crossed.

They kick it around awhile, and then they ask me a million questions. Practically Cynthia's whole family history and where on Fire Island and what kind of a house and on and on, and then right in the middle of dessert they decide. Of course they want to talk to Cynthia and drive out and see the house and all that, but so far the answer is yes.

I practically die, I'm so excited. I jump up and hug and kiss both of them. Now the other people and even the waiters are all smiling. Everyone wanted me to go. I almost expect applause, they're all so pleased.

"But . . ."

I knew it! The big "but." Probably my mother will have to come along too, or maybe Nina, or maybe they'll hire a mother's helper for *me* or something grotesque like that, I just know it.

"But," says my mother, "we must be absolutely certain that Mrs. Landry knows that we don't want you to be left alone overnight with the children."

"That's very important, Victoria," my father says. "Mrs.

Landry must understand our feelings on that. It's far too big a responsibility for a young girl to have."

"I'll tell her you said so," I say.

"We'll bring it up when we have our talk with her," my father says.

"Please, Daddy, let me tell her."

"I think it's better if we do it ourselves."

"Please, I want to try to handle everything myself. I want her to see that you think I'm responsible enough to make my own arrangements. Then she'll feel better about trusting me."

"That's a good point, honey." Sometimes my dad's absolutely perfect. "She's right, Felicia," he tells my mom. "Let her make her own arrangements. She knows what has to be done."

This was even better than I expected, and I grin like a fool—right at Nina.

Actually, talking to Cynthia myself may be a little tricky because, you know, I don't want to sound like I'm telling her what to do. I can't say to her, "Hey, you can't stay out overnight," like I'm her mother or something. Still, I don't really think she would do it, so it probably won't even come up. If it does—well, I'll just have to figure a way to handle it when it happens. Anyway, it's nothing to worry about now. The main thing is that I'm going. I can't believe it. I'm really going to be on Fire Island with Jim for an entire summer. Wow! Fifteen is going to be a great year!

Six

My job is supposed to start on the Friday of the July Fourth weekend, but Cynthia asks me if I'll help them move out on Wednesday. Sure, I tell her, and I can hardly wait to start. I'm supposed to get twenty-five dollars a week and Mondays off. That's probably not a terrific salary but it's great for me. Actually, I'd do it for practically nothing just for the chance to be on my own on Fire Island near Jim.

Moving day is really hot, almost ninety-four degrees, and we're all stuffed into this Volkswagen, and there's no air-conditioning, and DeeDee's got poison ivy from the trip to the house last weekend, and she keeps crying how it itches, and Cynthia says don't scratch it. She's got some medicine to put on it but DeeDee says it doesn't help. And every time she scratches it David says, "DeeDee's scratching, Mom," and Cynthia says,

"Don't scratch," and DeeDee says, "But it itches," and then ten minutes later they do the whole thing again. It's funny to hear someone else doing the kind of thing Nina and I do. It's not so bad when you're the one doing it, but if you have to just listen, it can drive you up the wall. Then the kids keep asking if we're almost there and can we stop for some kind of Texas hot dog in some special place, and Cynthia says, "We'll see."

But they're not so dumb. They keep asking please because they know what "We'll see" means. I wouldn't mind stopping off for something either, but naturally I can't say anything because I'm the employee, a flunky, sort of, and can't really ask for things. This is the first time in my life I ever worked for anyone like this except babysitting, and that's different. You really have to do what your boss tells you, and you can't say "How come?" or "I'll do it later," or anything. Like when we stop and Cynthia tells me to take DeeDee to the bathroom and then run across the street and get David a candy bar. Or when DeeDee asks for something, Cynthia says, "Victoria will get it." And they're always asking for something—the kids, I mean—and if they don't get it they whine and cry, and DeeDee even once held her breath for God knows how long. I don't remember them doing those kinds of things when I babysat for them. And we're not even on Fire Island yet.

Somewhere around Bay Shore we have to unload everything and drag it all on the ferry. DeeDee says she can't carry anything because her poison ivy itches. David says he's not going to get stuck carrying everything, and Cynthia says

Victoria will carry DeeDee's things. Everyone else makes two trips from the car to the ferry, and I make four, but I don't care because I'm so excited that I would have carried everything all by myself.

The ferry ride cools us all off. The kids and I sit on the top deck and Cynthia sits downstairs. I put my head back and figure I'll pick up a little quick burn on my cheeks. The air smells salty and the wind whips my hair straight back. I'm going to love this place.

"Victoria," Cynthia calls from the lower deck, "are you watching the children?"

I wasn't but I jump up and search around quickly, and lucky for me they're right there standing at the railing.

"They're okay, Cynthia," I call down the stairs. I sit back down and don't take my eyes off them until fifteen minutes later when we dock. I'm just not used to what I have to do, but I guess I'll learn in a couple of days.

There are no cars allowed on Fire Island so we have to pile all our stuff on rented wagons—the kind that kids play on, only bigger. It turns out that no matter how we arrange it we can't get it all in four wagons, so we have to leave a load of baggage with the man who rents the wagons. No problem, Cynthia assures everyone, we'll be able to pick up the rest of the stuff when we return the other wagons. By now I've got a pretty good idea who "we" is.

Each one of us grabs a wagon and follows Cynthia in a line down toward the house.

From the back Cynthia looks like she could be my age. She's the delicate type, very petite. I'm only five feet five inches, and she's got to be at least two inches shorter, and she probably weighs only about 105 pounds, but she's not skinny— she's got a terrific figure. A lot of curves with the tiniest waist. I think she's very pretty, with greenish eyes set wide apart, and a real short straight nose, not pug. There's nothing special about her mouth, except that when she smiles she does show very white straight teeth. What I like best is her hair. It's dark, dark brown and naturally curly, and now, in the sun, with all the curls flying loose, it has a red sparkle. Not that I have any chance to admire it, not with two kids getting unhappier by the minute pulling wagons. DeeDee breaks first.

"It's too heavy," she wails from about twenty feet back.

"Victoria," Cynthia calls to me without stopping, "please take some of DeeDee's things and see if you can fit them in your wagon."

My wagon is already the fullest, jammed with all the heavy things. I couldn't squeeze in another toothpick. I fix it so that DeeDee walks alongside me and I pull my wagon with one hand and help DeeDee with the other. I've heard a lot about Fire Island, but this is the first time I've ever been here. It's not at all what I expected. We're in a town called Ocean Beach, and it's fairly well built up, no apartments or hotels, but lots of small wooden houses all close together. There are no side-walks, only narrow boardwalks and lots of trees and bushes lining the sides.

I love it here already.

"DeeDee, please don't sit in the wagon," I say. "I can't pull you and all the stuff. My arms are breaking." Not only isn't DeeDee helping me pull her wagon but now she wants to ride in it. I have to ask her again nicely please not to. "My arms are breaking. C'mon, DeeDee, please."

"I'm tired . . . and itchy." She pouts. I can see she's going to start crying any second, and I don't want to start anything the first day, so I let her climb on top of the pile of stuff in her wagon. Just when I feel that I can't go another inch, I see Cynthia turn through a creaky old wagon-wheel gate about ten houses up. DeeDee jumps off the wagon and runs ahead.

Somehow I drag myself and the two wagons up to the house and collapse on the front steps. I love the place. It's the cutest one on the street, all white shingles with red trimming and geraniums in every single window box. It looks like a doll-house.

"Victoria, why don't you start carrying in some of the stuff while I make us all some nice cold lemonade," Cynthia says. She leaves her wagon in front of the house and disappears through the front door. The minute she's gone, DeeDee and David shoot off toward the back of the wagons. Nothing to do but start unloading all this junk. Ugh.

"Where should I put these things, Cynthia?" I ask, my arms loaded with clothes.

"David will show you," she calls from what must be the kitchen.

50

I go back outside and start calling David, but he's nowhere around so I go back into the house to tell Cynthia. I find her sitting in the kitchen drinking lemonade.

"I can't find David," I tell her.

She looks annoyed right away and asks me did I try the backyard. I say I didn't, but I called loud and he would have heard me if he was anywhere around.

"You can't let them just wander off by themselves," she says to me, getting up and going toward the backyard. She sticks her head out of the screen door and calls the kids, and, my luck, they answer right away.

I can see she thinks I didn't look or something.

"I guess they were probably hiding on me." And I smile to show her that it's okay, but she looks like maybe she's wondering if she didn't make a monstrous mistake with me.

"When Victoria calls you, you come, hear?" she tells them.

"We didn't hear anybody calling," David says, shaking his head in all innocence, and DeeDee sees what he's doing and starts to shake her head too.

"I even went outside—where were you?" I ask them.

"It's not important," Cynthia cuts me off. "But next time," she tells them, "you answer when you're called. Now get a move on and help Victoria unload."

"I'm itchy," DeeDee whines. Boy, she better get over that poison ivy quick.

"All right, then don't carry anything. But show Victoria where things go and don't disturb me—I have some important

51

calls to make." And she plops herself down in one of those swivel chairs by the phone and starts dialing.

DeeDee and I go out to get our belongings. David has already brought in his load and dumped it in the middle of the living room. I grab a couple of armfuls and follow DeeDee upstairs. There are these bedrooms on the second floor, all just adorable, freshly painted in sunny colors with starchy curtains on all the windows.

"Where's my bedroom?" I ask DeeDee.

"I'll show you," she says, and starts running up another flight of steps. It's a short steep flight and you come up right in the middle of a small room. It reminds me of a tent, and I love it. The ceiling is sloping and sort of low on the sides, but I can stand up almost straight in the center with no trouble. It's a cozy room and not jammed up with a lot of extra things. There's a neat-looking bed with a sort of antique-looking metal headboard and a nice old wooden dresser. I guess maybe it's a little too small to be a dresser, but it's perfect for most of my clothes, and besides, I can hang up the rest in the closet. I don't see a closet, but they have a perfectly good metal rod behind the dresser that gives me plenty of room to hang my stuff, and then I can see exactly what I want without having to bother opening a door. It's a little warm in here now, but that's probably because the window has been shut. It's a nice little window like on a boat, and it doesn't need a curtain or even a shade because it's too small for people to look in, which makes it very private. I love it. I love it all.

"I love the room," I tell DeeDee. "It's so cozy and perfect."

"It used to be a storage closet," she announces and starts downstairs.

"Victoria!" That's my employer calling me, so naturally I answer right away. When my mother is doing it I don't even hear her until the fourth call.

I follow DeeDee down to Cynthia's room. Poor Cynthia is sprawled on the bed with a wet rag on her head, looking awful. She motions me closer. It's like one of those big dying scenes in the movies.

"Honey, I've got a terrible headache." It seems like an effort for her just to talk.

"Can I get you anything?" I ask.

"Do you want my Teddy to stay with you?" DeeDee asks.

"No, darling." Cynthia manages a weak smile. Then she tells me that she's taken some painkillers and the best thing she can do is rest and try to sleep. Would I please take the kids and go down and get the stuff we left with the wagon man, and while we're there could I please pick up a couple of items from the grocery store.

"Maybe you'd better give them lunch before you go," she says, "and take the dollar on the kitchen table for an ice cream treat for all of you."

"Could I have a double, Mommy?" DeeDee asks.

"We'll leave that to Victoria to decide," she says, and I kind of like that because it shows she trusts my decisions.

"Close the door on your way out, please," Cynthia whispers, sinking fast.

We aren't even down the stairs when DeeDee starts pulling on my jeans.

"Can I?" she asks. "Can I? Please?"

Now that's the big difference between me and a real mother. A real mother would definitely look at her and not have the vaguest idea what she's talking about. "Can you what?" she'd ask. But of course I know exactly what she wants. She's asking about the double scoop. Another thing—Cynthia would certainly say to her, "We'll see," and make it all hinge on how she eats her lunch. But I always hated when my mother would make one thing hang on another, and I swore I wouldn't do that with my own kids, so I might as well start practicing right now.

"Absolutely," I tell DeeDee. "You can have whatever two flavors you want."

Naturally the kid's stunned.

I find David and fix them both tuna sandwiches. David wolfs his down in two seconds, but DeeDee just sits there staring at hers.

"Come on, DeeDee," I coax her. "At least finish half."

"I don't want to," she says, shoving it away from her.

"Do you want something else?"

Naturally I could threaten to take away the second ice cream, but what for? That'd be just what mothers always do, and I want to try out some of my own ideas about raising kids.

"Are you sure you're not hungry at all?" I ask her one last time.

"Uh-uh, I'm all fulled up."

You have to trust what a kid says; after all, she knows if she's hungry or not better than I do. "Okay," I tell them, "then let's get going."

We get the empty wagons and David shows me how to pile them all on my wagon. We start walking toward the docks. I can see that DeeDee is unhappy. I think it's because she wants a ride, so I ask her if she wants to sit in the wagon, but she shakes her head no.

"What's the matter, DeeDee? Come on, you can tell me."

"Am I still going to get the ice cream?" she asks, about a millimeter away from tears.

"Of course you are. Just like I promised. A double scoop." Poor kid's not used to trusting mother figures. I'm going to be the best mother in the whole world.

"I want it now."

"It'll taste better when you're hungry."

"But I *am* hungry." Instantly her nose is red, and the tears are streaming down her cheeks. "I didn't have any lunch," she wails.

I think I've been had by a five-year-old. "Okay, okay . . ." What can I do? I really did promise.

"Now," she says, all smiles, "you said I could ride on the wagon. Put me on."

I'll get her.

The little monster climbs up on the wagon and off we go toward the ice cream shop. It's down near the ferry dock. All the action is around there. Cute boutiques and grocery stores and even a pizza place. I keep my eyes open for The Dunes, the place where Jim works, but I don't see it. David and DeeDee never heard of it, but that's probably because they're too little.

The ice cream is sensational, best I ever had, but I guess the price must have gone up since last year because I have to kick in fifty cents. I don't mind, though, especially since I know Cynthia's having a terrible money problem. She's trying to sell the Fire Island house, and I heard that they may have to move from their apartment in the city. Everyone says it's because Jed doesn't pay anything. He's truly disgusting to walk out the way he did and then not send money, not even any for the kids. That really stinks. I feel very bad for Cynthia.

We return the wagons to the rental place and pick up the one we had to leave there. Another ferry is pulling in and the kids want to watch, so we walk out on the pier. And then I hear a guy's voice not two feet behind me say, "Hi, Victoria."

Seven

It's Barry, that guy I told you about, the one who's always staring at me, from school, Jim's friend.

"Oh hi, Barry," I say, giving my mouth a quick wipe for any stray cone crumbs, pulling in my stomach, smiling, and trying inconspicuously not to notice if Jim is anywhere around. With another couple of seconds I could do a fast fix on my hair, which probably looks like rat tails hanging from my head. But I guess it's okay, because I don't see Jim around anyway.

"Hey," Barry says, coming over to us, "I didn't know you were going to be out here." And he looks so nice and smiley that I think it's not going to be hard making friends with him. Actually, he's a lot cuter than I thought he was in school. Maybe it's that terrific tan he's got. It goes great with his wavy black hair. He just looks different out here. I always thought of him as a string bean, kind of tall and skinny, but he's not really skinny, he's slim, and he's got a fairly nice build. Don't get me wrong; he's far from gorgeous—his nose is a little biggish and his smile doesn't dazzle like Jim's, but his eyes are soft brown and friendly, and he's got a shy, sweet look about him that makes me feel totally relaxed.

Another thing, Jim is so perfect that I sometimes think I would probably feel kind of clunky next to him, but with Barry I feel pretty. Prettier than Barry, anyway.

A wide grin crosses his face and he asks, "How long are you here for?"

"All summer," I say. "I'm a mother's helper."

"No kidding. Are those the victims?" He winks at David and DeeDee.

"Right," I say, and introduce him to the kids.

"How do you do, David," he says, solemnly shaking DeeDee's hand, and she practically falls down giggling. And then David gets into it and shakes Barry's hand and says *he's* DeeDee, and then Barry says no, *he's* DeeDee, and then I get into it and we're all bowing and shaking hands, and the kids are hysterical, and in two seconds we're all old friends. He's cute. Barry, I mean. Nice cute.

I don't want him to know how much I know about him, so I have to ask him what he's doing out here, and then he tells me all the things I already know and one extra. The best one. That ferry I mentioned? The one that's just about pulling into the slip right this minute? Well, Jim is on it. How's that for timing?

Now, of course, I've got to find a way to fix my hair. Inconspicuously. I don't want Barry to think it's because of Jim.

"DeeDee, honey," I coo to her, wiggling my finger for her to come. "I just want to fix your hair a little," I tell her. Of course she's going to say no, and then I'll tell her, "See, I'm going to fix my hair too."

"Okay," she says, screwing up the whole plan. It's too late to change plans, so like a fool I add, "See, I'm going to fix my hair too."

"So what?"

"And then I'll fix your hair."

"I wanna go first."

"And so you will." I smile down at her, frantically brushing my hair. "Right after me, you go first."

She's so confused she doesn't even make a fuss.

"Look," I tell the kids, "the ferry's docking."

The four of us stand there, watching the people coming off the boat. Everyone is loaded down with tons of luggage and backpacks and things. It's the opening of the season, and people with houses are moving all their things out. My heart is practically pounding out of my chest knowing I'm going to see Jim. I'm getting worse every day.

There he is. And . . .

"There they are." Barry pokes me to look at Jim leaving the ferry with this horrendous growth hanging off his left arm. Barry waves at them!

"Hey! Jimmy! Gloria! Over here!"

"I didn't know Gloria was coming out here too," I say very casually.

"She's just here for the day," Barry says, and looks at me kind of surprised. "Don't you like her?"

"Are you kidding? I think she's . . . she's . . . something else." I'm smart enough not to say what. Actually I despise her type of girl—as I told you—the cutesy cheerleader kind with the slippery blond hair that hangs a mile down their backs and the dimples that simply look like cheek holes to me.

A lot of the little kids in school are impressed just because Gloria is captain of the cheerleaders. They think she's a real big deal, and at the ball games you're always hearing them saying did you see what Gloria did with her hair, or get a load of those boots Gloria's wearing, or something about her eyes. You'd think she was the only person in the world to have blue eyes. In my opinion, one look in those eyes and you think nobody's home.

Anyway, here they come. I don't think Jim's going to recognize me from the shoe store because, after all, there are probably lots of customers going in all the time. Why should he just remember me? I wasn't in there that long, and most of the time he was down in the basement anyway. I hope like crazy he doesn't remember me. I don't think I was at my best that day.

"Gloria?" Barry grabs one of Jim's bags from her.

Obviously *he* doesn't think nobody's home behind those

eyes. "Do you know Victoria Martin? Victoria, do you know Gloria Donovan and Jimmy Freeman?"

And like I never laid eyes on either of them before this minute, I say, "Hi." Please, God, don't let him recognize me.

"Hi," Jim says, and he does one of those double takes and looks kind of puzzled, but I keep very cool and look at him like I'm a completely new person. I give him a wide, open kind of smile—slightly upturned face, merry eyes, absolutely nothing to hide. It works. I can practically hear him say to himself, "Naaw, that can't be that nut from the shoe store."

As for Gloria the Magnificent, she can't even squeeze out a "hi." All she can manage is a sickly dumb smile with those stupid cheek holes. Naturally every tooth is perfect.

"How's it going, buddy?" Jim says to Barry, giving him one of those affectionate back slaps.

"Okay," Barry says, "still pretty quiet, though."

"But picking up a little, right?" Jim kind of motions in my direction. At least I think that's what he's doing. Obviously Barry does, too, because he gets real embarrassed-looking and says, "Yeah, I guess so."

And Gloria looks annoyed. Great! I guess he did mean me.

"Been getting in any tennis?" Jim asks, and Barry says he's been waiting for him, and Jim says, "Well, buddy, here I am."

And that's the feeling you get, that it's all about to start because *here he is.* Jim is definitely a mover type, and people like to move with him. Like now, with Barry, Jim's the one who sets the time and date for their tennis game even though

61

it's Barry's court. But that's the way it is: Jim calls the shots, and people just kind of want to go along with him.

Everyone's always talking about how some politicians have charisma. Well, I'm not exactly sure what it is—charisma, I mean—but the way everyone is so attracted to Jim I think he must have tons of it.

"Victoria . . ." DeeDee is sniffing and tugging at my shorts. "My ice cream is melting all down."

"Who is *that*?" Gloria says, looking at DeeDee like she was some kind of bug. I admit she looks pretty disgusting with chocolate ice cream all over her face and running down her arm and dripping off her elbow. Still, I don't like Gloria's tone.

"That's DeeDee," Barry says, "if you can find her under all that ice cream. Victoria's a mother's helper."

"Who are you working for?" Suddenly Gloria is all interested.

"Cynthia Landry," I tell her.

"I know her!" she squeals.

"Come on, DeeDee," I say, paying no attention to Gloria, who obviously can't wait to unload on Cynthia. "I'll wash you off in the water fountain."

"No," she says, "I want to do it myself."

Gloria can't hold it in. "Boy," she chirps, "poor Cynthia. She had a real rat husband who played around with everyone and ran off to California. Was he gorgeous! Looked like Al Pacino."

Gross! No wonder Cynthia hates Jed. It's horrendous to think everyone knows your whole life's story and how your husband was playing around. He really was disgusting. And so is Gloria for gossiping around like that.

"That's what a lot of people are saying." I sniff. "But of course they don't know the real story, so they just keep repeating the old gossip."

That ought to shut her up.

"Cool! I'd just love to know the whole story," she says. She's so dumb she doesn't even know when she's being put down. How can Jim stand her?

"Hey, the Landry house is in Ocean Beach too," she says, and then turns toward Jim. "Isn't that nice," she purrs, giving him a brilliant smile. "You'll be real close neighbors."

"I don't know how close we'll be," I say as nonchalantly as I can manage.

"Well, I do," she says, really snotty. "The Landry's house is on Evergreen, right around the corner from Jimmy boy's. Actually, Cynthia offered *me* the job this year, but I said no. I would have considered it if gorgeous Jed was still there, but I make it a policy never to work for divorced women. They stick you with the kids twenty-four hours a day because they're always running around. Besides," she says, sending the last bullet directly into my brain, "she was paying peanuts."

"That's really good news!" Barry cuts in. What's good news? That she's paying me peanuts? "All three of us are going to be together this summer," he continues, and he's really excited. Jim doesn't dare say a word with Gloria staring at him.

"It sounds so cozy, maybe I should plan to spend a little more time out here too." Gloria says that last line right in my face. God, I loathe her!

"Jimmmmmy." There goes Gloria the whiner again. "I'm positively exhausted. I simply must get to the house. Are you coming?"

"Yeah, sure," Jim says, grabbing up his gear. Then he says to me, "You know, I know you from somewhere."

"It must be from school," I say weakly. I'm in absolute, stark terror.

"No, not school," Jim says thoughtfully. "Maybe with Barry. Or—no . . ."

He'll never let go.

"Jim-my!" Gloria whines.

"Okay . . . ," he says. "I was just trying to figure out how I know Barry's girlfriend."

Barry's girlfriend! That's disaster if he thinks I'm Barry's girlfriend. I have to set him straight right now.

"I think there's some misunderstanding. . . ." I want to do it gently because after all he is Barry's friend, and besides, I don't want to hurt Barry. "Barry and I . . ."

"Jimmy, c'mon . . ."

"Okay . . . ," he says, but he's still looking at me.

"I'm hungry."

"Hungry!" he says like he just discovered the wheel, and points to me.

"No, thank you. I just ate. Well, I'll see you all around sometime," and I grab DeeDee and call David, who's been lost in a comic book all this time, and take about two giant steps when a hand grabs my shoulder.

"You're the Hungarian who went home with tight shoes!" Jim is on the other end of that hand.

"The Hungarian?" Barry and Gloria say it together like a vaudeville act.

"Oh man, you should have seen her and her friend . . ." And he practically doubles over in hysterics. He starts laughing so hard he can barely tell the story. Frankly, I didn't think it was funny at all.

Finally he gets the whole story out, and the three of them are cracking up. I ask, kind of cold, "What's so funny about being Hungarian?"

"Hey, nothing . . . we weren't laughing because you're Hungarian . . ." And he practically falls on the ground, he's laughing so hard.

Anyway, one thing and another and they finally pull themselves together and Jim grabs his stuff, which of course had fallen all over during his little story.

"Hey, see you around," Jim says to me. Then to Barry, "You really picked yourself a winner, chum," and he chuckles good-naturedly.

I can do without the whole thing. I am not Barry's girl-friend. "I am *not* Barry's girlfriend," I say to all three. "I practically only met Barry for the first time today. So I couldn't possibly be Barry's girlfriend, and furthermore, I'm not even Hungarian. My friend is."

And as if it didn't matter at all, Jim and Gloria say, "Sure, that's terrific," or something like that. "See you later," they say, and while my brain is seething, the love of my life takes off with the love of his life, and I'm left alone with David, DeeDee, who just dropped her cone on my left shoe, and lover boy Barry.

"You shouldn't tell people I'm your girlfriend. That's ridiculous, we only practically just met." I'm not trying to sound angry, but I'm really ticked off.

"I didn't exactly say you were my girlfriend, more like . . . that . . ." I hate to make him struggle like that, but damn, it's not *fair*.

"More like what?"

"That . . . you know . . . more like I liked you."

Well, I can't exactly hang him for liking me. At least someone does.

"Actually . . ."

Now he's really stammering. "It's more than that. More than like . . ."

Now I'm the one staring at him.

". . . I love you."

No way!

"You can't love me!"

"But I do."

"But you can't!" I know this is a ridiculous argument, but he can't. "You hardly even know me."

"I know you better than you think. I've been watching you all year."

See, I told you he was always following me around and staring at me.

"And I know I'm deeply in love with you."

Oh, God, he's deeply in love with me. Is he crazy or something?

"I think you're the most beautiful girl in the entire school."

He's really making me nervous now.

"I can't think of anyone but you. You've become the most important person in my life."

And when I get nervous . . .

"We have to be together."

. . . I laugh.

And of course I crack up. I know it seems like the meanest thing in the world, but I swear I'm not laughing at him, I'm just laughing because I'm nervous and I can't handle the situation. It's horrible but he naturally thinks I'm laughing at him. Now he grabs me by the shoulders, and his face is two inches from mine, and he looks crushed, and I feel terrible, and I want to cry but I can't stop laughing. I try to tell him that I'm not laughing at him, but every time I open my mouth to get the words out I become so hysterical I can't talk. All I can manage is half of "I'm sorry," which he probably can't even make out.

Now he turns away from me, and I'm afraid he's going to cry. Just like that, the laughing jag disappears and I'm back in control. First thing I tell him is that I'm sorry and that I wasn't laughing at him, I just wasn't expecting anything like that and he threw me, and more "I'm sorrys" and "please forgive mes" and "I feel horrible," but it's like he didn't hear anything, because when he turns back to me he's really angry.

"Forget it. It's my problem." And he starts to walk away.

"No, wait," I grab his arm. "I really am sorry. Please . . ."

"I told you, forget it. It was a mistake. I shouldn't have told you. What a jerk I was." And I can see he's really hurt. If I can love Jim without even knowing him, why can't Barry love me? Then I think, suppose I told Jim and he laughed in my face . . . I think I'd just die. Oh, God, I feel horrible. He shakes my hand off his arm. I keep apologizing, but it's too late.

"Don't tell me how you're so sorry, just don't tell me anything. I suppose you think it's funny . . . well, it isn't. It hurts. . . . It hurts a lot." And while he's still talking, he starts to walk away.

"Please, wait . . ."

"Good-bye."

And he's gone.

I feel like a monster. I absolutely hate myself, and now I'm the one who feels like crying. I'm so ashamed.

"I'm sorry . . ." DeeDee puts her arms around my leg and kisses my kneecaps, "I didn't mean it. I'll never do it again."

I bend down to ask her what she did, but all she does is shake her head and look as if she's going to cry. Boy, we're a great group today.

I ask her again and this time she says she doesn't know.

"Then why are you sorry?" I ask.

"Because," she says, "I don't want you to cry."

Oh, God, she thinks I'm upset because of her. Naturally I hug her and tell her she had nothing to do with it, and besides, everything is fine now and I feel great. Funny, isn't it? When you're little like that you think everything that happens has to do with you. I can remember when I was really young, if I heard my parents arguing in their room I was always certain it was about me.

We pick up the things from Cynthia's list at the grocery and the drugstore and start back to the house.

All the way home I can't help but feel miserable about what happened with Barry. I swear I'm going to make it up to him somehow. I can't love him, you know. If you don't love someone you just can't make yourself. But at least I'll show him that I appreciate the way he feels about me and that I understand and that it makes him really special to me . . . always. I'm absolutely going to spend the whole summer making it up to him. Not that I expect it to take the whole summer.

Still, you have to realize that it's only partly my fault that it worked out so bad. After all, that was a heavy thing to lay on someone, especially when they didn't expect it at all. It's not my fault he fell in love with me. I certainly didn't make him do it. I didn't even know he was doing it. Sure, I shouldn't have laughed, but you take your chances when you spring something like that on someone you hardly know. And then the part about letting Jim think I was his girlfriend—that really bugs me. That was really gross of him—not that I'm saying what I did was right—still, he wasn't so right himself.

Even so, he's really a pretty nice guy, and it would be nice to be his friend. Not only because of Jim, but because he's definitely a nice person with a good sense of humor and cute and . . . I don't know, he's just a good type to have for a friend.

On the way home David sees one of his friends and wants to go back to his house, but I have to say no because I don't know if I have the authority to let the kids go off on their own like that. David gets a little aggravated and starts crying, and then DeeDee says something, and he kind of kicks her, not a bad one, only on her shoe, but she gets hysterical. It's sort of embarrassing because I think everyone thinks I probably hit them, and of course I would never touch them, ever.

I try to explain to David that it's my first day and I don't really know the rules but he's going to be there for the whole summer and there'll be other times and so on, and I almost feel like a mother. I know I sound like one. What's really funny is that I think someone said something just like that to me a couple of years ago at camp. I don't remember what the situation was, but I know it didn't help then and it doesn't help now. All the way home David won't even talk to me.

Turns out he could have gone with his friend, which makes him even angrier, but I was afraid to take the chance. But everything gets better anyway because I play a couple of games of War with David, and Sorry with DeeDee, and then the three of us play Monopoly, and then DeeDee gets upset about losing and throws the board in the air and all the pieces go flying. David runs off to tell his mother, who says it's time for DeeDee's bath anyway, and to me, "Victoria, see that they put that game away properly, please." Suddenly David gets a bad stomachache and has to go to the bathroom, and DeeDee goes up to get ready for her bath. It doesn't take me that long to pick up the pieces, and by the time DeeDee is ready for me to shampoo her hair I've finished. The game will never be the same. When the kids are in their pj's, Cynthia says they can watch TV until eight and then to bed.

I figure that later on, after they're in bed, if Cynthia isn't going out I'll take a walk down to the dock and see what's doing. It probably takes a while longer for my room to cool off because it gets the afternoon sun, so it's still a little warmish up there, but that's okay because by the time I'm ready for bed it will probably be perfect. I throw myself together a little bit and go downstairs. Cynthia is on the phone so I just sit down and grab a magazine and wait.

"That's out of the question," she's saying. "No!" She sounds furious. I hope it isn't about me. Whoops, I sound just like DeeDee. "Absolutely not, Henry. I won't permit you to see them and I don't want you to call anymore. . . . I certainly can, they're my children. . . . He's your son, you see what you can do with him."

Of course it has to be about her ex-husband, Jed. Maybe she doesn't want the kids to see him.

"Well," she snaps, "until he does there's nothing more to

71

say. Please don't call here anymore." And she hangs up.

"Damn that man!" she says, and I hear her throw something like a pencil against the wall. Well, at least it wasn't about me. I figure now's not the time to ask to go out, so I just sit there pretending to be reading. Finally she sits down next to me. She's still angry.

"If Henry Landry—that's the children's grandfather—calls, I don't want you to let him talk to them."

"You mean you don't want me to let the kids talk to their grandfather?" It's not like I mean to question her, it's just that I want to be absolutely sure what she wants me to do. Because, after all, it is their grandfather.

"That's right. You just tell him they're not home and that I said not to call anymore."

"Even if they are home?"

"Yes, Victoria, the whole point is that I don't want him to be in touch with them at all. At least not until his son pays some of his bills."

"Oh, I see." But I really don't. I can't believe she's not going to let the kids speak to their own grandfather. That's horrendous.

"I suppose as long as you're going to be involved in this mess you should understand it a little better." And then she tells me how Jed took off for California (of course, she doesn't say anything about how he was playing around) and how he never even calls the kids and now he's even stopped sending money. She does design displays for stores, but it doesn't pay all that much money, and now they're going to have to sell the house on Fire Island, and the kids really love this place. Worse than that, she thinks she'll have to move out of the city because it's too expensive, and then it means she'll have to do more traveling to her job and she won't be able to spend as much time with the kids, and now that they don't have a father they need her even more than ever.

"I suppose we really shouldn't have even come out this summer," she says, "but I knew it would be the last time for the children on Fire Island, and they suffered so much this past year I wanted to give them the best summer I could." She looks so sad.

"That's really terrible," I say. "I mean him not helping out at all. It's like he doesn't care."

"He's impossible, and the truth is he really doesn't care."

"Can't you make him pay? Take him to court or something?"

"It's very hard because he's way out in California. If he were in New York I could haul him into court and they would make him pay. They have ways of taking part of his salary. I've talked to him, pleaded with him, everything, but all he does is hang up on me. I know his father has some influence over him, so I thought if I refuse to let Henry—that's his father—see the kids, even if Jed wouldn't do anything for his children, at least he would do something for his father. I'm hoping Henry will be able to do something with Jed. Henry is very fond of the children, but I feel he's also somewhat responsible for his son's behavior. I don't know . . ." She puts her head in her hands, and I know she's trying hard not to cry in front of me. "Maybe it's not the best way, but I've tried everything else . . . Anyway"—now she sort of pulls herself together—"that's what I want you to do. If Henry calls, tell him no and not to call anymore. If he gives you any trouble just hang right up."

It blows my mind just thinking about hanging up on somebody's grandfather. I could never in the whole world hang up on my grandfather, and I would hate anyone else who did. Maybe if I just let the kids answer the phone . . .

"What if David or DeeDee picks up the phone?" I better straighten this out right away.

"I'm going to tell them not to answer the phone."

"But won't they want to know how come?"

"I'll deal with that. In the meantime I don't want them to know anything about what I told you. Victoria, I'm sure you understand how important it is that they don't know even one thing about the situation. They're much too young—they'd never understand."

"I won't say anything, I swear."

"I'm counting on you."

I just know I'll lose it if he calls. What a drag. I guess she sees it on my face because she says, "Don't worry about it, Victoria—he's probably not going to call anymore. After all, I asked him not to, and he's a pretty decent man. A lot better than his son, I might add."

"I guess he probably won't," I say, but I know I'm going to die every time the phone rings.

"Listen, honey, I'm going out for a while. After a day like today I need a little relaxation . . . moving day is always a nightmare. But you were a great help. You did a terrific job."

"Thanks."

"No, thank *you*."

I told you she was a terrific person. We really get along sensationally. "By the way," I ask, "do you know where The Dunes is?"

"Sure, it's just past Ocean Beach toward Cherry Grove. That's where I'm going tonight."

"You are?" I ask, a little surprised.

"Yes, it's a bar and a restaurant, and sometimes they turn it into a disco. Everybody goes there. But I think the crowd is a little old for you."

"Oh no, I wasn't planning to go, I just know someone who's working there. He's a waiter."

But Cynthia won't let go of the subject. "Well, where do you know him from?" she asks.

"From the city," I answer. I really wish she'd drop it.

"The city. I see. Victoria, please sit down for a minute. There's something I want to discuss with you."

I know a lecture's coming. God knows why, but I know it in my bones. Naturally I sit right down. I hope I have a tissue in my pocket in case she makes me cry.

"Don't look so scared. There's nothing wrong."

It's worse than I thought.

"I only wanted to give you a little advice. I know this is your first time on your own and problems are bound to come up, so I want you to know that you can come to me anytime about anything. Kind of look on me as your summer mother. Okay?"

"Sure, that'd be great." I told you she's really very nice.

"Another thing. While you're living with us you're my responsibility and I take that very seriously. So remember, if I'm your summer mother that makes you my summer daughter, and I think I'd better warn you about something. There are two discos out here, The Dunes and The Monkey, and they're both really a couple of years too old for you. Especially The Monkey. I know a lot of teenagers go there. But it's a pretty raunchy place, if you want the truth. Anybody who goes in there is expected to know the score—if you follow me. So be careful about that place. Be careful about where you go and who you see and everything like that, okay? And one last thing—your curfew. It's pretty safe out here as far as crime goes, this being an island and all, so I think your curfew can be a little later. How's one o'clock on the weekends?"

"Terrific!"

"Okay, that's set. But please remember I expect you to be on time."

"Oh, I will. I promise."

"All right then, that's it. I'm off. Watch TV if you like, or I have a new *Vogue* in my bedroom if you want, and if you get a chance, could you please throw in the laundry? The whites are separate and don't put any sweaters in the dryer. Thanks a lot. You're a doll." And she's off.

It's okay that I'm not going tonight. I look gross anyway. I have to wash my hair, and besides, I'm really exhausted. I get the laundry from upstairs. Turns out to be two big laundry bags full. I guess Cynthia's been so busy getting packed and ready to go she didn't have a chance to do anything else. I don't mind doing laundry—it's an easy job. I separate the whites and colors, and it looks like maybe four loads. I probably have time to do most of them. I'd like to do something really terrific my first day so I start putting in the laundry and by about one a.m. I've finished all the laundry, washing, drying, and folding everything except the stuff that has to be ironed. I pile everything on the couch and chairs in the living room and go off to bed.

It's still very hot in my room, but that's because it's especially hot tonight. But I'm too tired for it to matter, and next thing I know it's morning and DeeDee is crawling in my bed.

Eight

"C'mon, Victoria, let's go to the beach." DeeDee is pulling on my arm, but for a minute I don't even know where I am. Then I remember.

"What time is it?" I mumble.

"The big hand is on the four and the little hand is right next to the seven, but not on it yet."

I work it out and groan. "Oh, God, it's twenty past six. DeeDee, it's too early, go back to bed."

"I don't want to. I'm hungry. Mommy says you're supposed to fix me breakfast and I'm hungry."

"But it's not even seven." I'm trying to be reasonable and nice at the same time. Very hard so early in the morning.

"But I'm hungry." DeeDee is being neither.

"Okay, five minutes more."

"Now!"

Monster. I sit up, bumping my head on the ceiling. I guess it's a little lower on the sides than I thought. It takes me a while to get up and get it all together. With my eyes half shut I creep downstairs and into the kitchen.

"What do you eat for breakfast?"

"Pancakes."

"Forget it! What else?"

"Or eggs and bacon or sometimes Mommy even makes waffles. . . ."

"What else?"

"I dunno . . . cereal, I guess."

"That's it." And I go to the pantry and pull out three different kinds of dry cereal.

"I want Sugar Pops!"

Naturally we don't have any Sugar Pops. I try to sell her on one of the others, but she only wants the dumb Sugar Pops, so I fix her scrambled eggs, which she pushes around on her plate until they finally slip into her lap. That's the end of breakfast. I guess she wasn't so hungry after all.

"Why don't you watch some TV for a while and then we'll get dressed and go to the beach."

"I can't."

"Why not?"

"There's no room to sit," she says, pointing to all the laundry still piled up all over. I guess Cynthia got home too late to bother with it. I clear a little spot for DeeDee and put on the

TV and sneak upstairs to get back to bed, but David hears me, and now he wants his breakfast, and we go back down and go through the whole breakfast thing, only he insists on a peanut butter sandwich and swears he has one every morning.

No point in going back to bed, so I get into my bathing suit and straighten up my room. I tell the kids that if they want to go to the beach they have to make their beds. They both say they don't have to make their beds. Then we have this little thing about how their mommy never makes them make their beds so why should I. I guess they're right, so I make their beds while they get into their bathing suits, and we all head down to the beach.

The beach is fabulous, with white clean sand and roaring white water, and absolutely empty except that way down you can see someone who looks like maybe he's fishing. David takes off as if he was shot out of a cannon and races across the sand right into the water. Brrr!

"Wow!" I say to DeeDee. "Does he always do that?"

"Uh-uh, my mommy never lets him go in the water like that unless a grown-up is with him."

"Oh, God!" I shoot down after him. I race into the water even though it's unbelievably freezing. He's already over his head. I can see he's a pretty good swimmer for a little kid, but still he's way too far out, so I call him and wave my arms, and I know he sees me, but he doesn't pay any attention. So I have to swim after him. When I get close enough, and I'm really angry now, I call him and tell him to get right back inshore. Now! He says something that sounds like, "Aw, damn," and heads back.

"You're never to go in the water without me!" I scold him. "You understand? I'm not kidding around either." He really scared me, so I'm sort of sharp with him.

"I thought you were coming with me." He's so full of it.

"I didn't even know you were going. Come off it, David, just don't do that again. Next time you want to go in the water, tell me first so I can go with you."

"I want to go now."

"Well, you have to wait. We're not even settled yet—besides, I want to sit down and warm up a little in the sun."

"When can I go?" he asks.

"In a few minutes," I tell him, and DeeDee helps me spread the blanket down. The minute I lie down, David wants to know if we can go swimming again. Then every sixty seconds, like clockwork, he says, "Now?" It's hopeless.

"Let's collect some shells and then we'll go. How's that?"

"I wanna, I wanna." DeeDee jumps up.

"C'mon, David," I say, and I get up, brushing the sand off me. David has been jumping around so much that the sand was flying all over. He didn't do it purposely but it's all in my hair.

"Then can we go swimming?" he asks, and I tell him absolutely. We head down the shoreline toward the fisherman, our heads bent as we look for treasures. Every time DeeDee finds any kind of shell she has to show me. I can tell she really likes me. And I like her too, except I think that maybe they're both a little spoiled. Still, she's really very cute, with blond curly hair and chocolate-brown eyes. She's got the kind of lips that look like she's wearing lipstick, they're so rosy. Her cheeks too. She's truly adorable, and I think she knows it.

As we get closer to the figure on the shore, we can see that he *is* fishing.

"My grandpa is the best fisherman in the whole world," David says, and for the first time since we left New York DeeDee agrees with him.

"And sometimes he even takes us fishing with him," says DeeDee, "and then we catch great big fish." And she spreads her arms as wide as they will go.

"You never caught a big fish," David says, and she says, "I did too," and he says, "You did not," then they do that uh-huh, uh-uh thing, and I start pointing at the fisherman and shouting, "I think he's got one!"

I don't really think he's got one, but I have to change the subject. As soon as we get up to the man, DeeDee tells him how her grandfather is such a great fisherman, and the man is very nice, and he smiles and says he bets he is, and then the three of them gab on about fishing and the kids really seem to know what they're talking about. Even DeeDee. They must have spent a lot of time with their grandfather, which makes me feel bad since they're not going to be allowed to see him or even talk to him. I know that Cynthia's right to be angry because her ex-husband is really a creep, but maybe it's wrong for her to take it out on the grandfather. After all, it's not his fault that his son is so disgusting. At least I don't think it is, or maybe Cynthia's right, maybe the old man can do something to make Jed start paying again. I don't know, but it makes me feel awful, I mean really sad, and not just for the kids but for the grandfather, too. I can just imagine how my grandpa would feel if he wasn't allowed to see Nina and me.

The fisherman lets David and DeeDee hold the line for a few minutes, but they don't get anything, and after a while we walk back to our towels.

"He's okay," David says, nodding back at the fisherman. "But my grandpa is much better. My grandpa woulda caught maybe ten fish by now, right, DeeDee?"

"Yeah, maybe eleven. Do you know my grandpa?" DeeDee asks me.

"I don't think I ever met him," I say, and then just because I want to change the conversation, I ask David if he wants to go swimming. The water's great to look at but it's freezing. Still, even that's better than talking about their grandfather.

I can see David's a terror in the water. You have to watch him every second because right away he goes too far out, and then it's unreal when you tell him that's enough swimming for now. His lips turn bright blue, but still he says he's not cold, and then he pretends not to hear you, and then the worst is when he makes believe he's drowning. First time he did it I almost jumped out of my skin. I swam out to him with all my might and grabbed him and started pulling at him, not exactly like in the life-saving class at school but good enough to get

83

him back to shallow water, and then he starts laughing like crazy and I could have *really* drowned him. I told him that if he ever did that again I would tell his mother and he wouldn't go in the water for the whole summer, and besides, I would quit. I was really mad. In fact, I was practically in tears. I guess he saw how upset I was because he swore he would never do it again. I made him swear to God and cross his heart on his mother's life and all that, and I made sure he didn't have any fingers crossed, and I think maybe he means it.

At about noon we head back to the house for lunch. There's a note from Cynthia saying not to disturb her because she has a headache. I hope she's not coming down with anything, because that's what happens to me when I get sick. Sometimes I start off with headaches. Anyway, the note says I should give the kids lunch, put the laundry away, and then there's a list of things for me to pick up at the store.

I give the kids tuna salad sandwiches and do their dishes and whatever was left from Cynthia's in the sink.

After I put the laundry away (the kids tell me where everything goes) we all go down to the dock where the stores are to do the shopping. DeeDee tells me her mother always takes the wagon to the store, and the list is pretty long so I take one. Naturally DeeDee and David ride in it while I pull. Like I said, they're a little spoiled, but it's not too bad, and besides, I don't want to start off pulling rank on them too much. I want them to get used to me first.

Of course, the minute we get in sight of the dock they

want ice cream. So we stop in for that delicious ice cream, and gross!—there's Barry working behind the counter. What's he doing here? He turns red like a beet when he sees me. I'm really surprised to see him working. I thought that all rich kids ever do is go boating and play tennis.

"Hi," I say, and give him one of my nicest smiles. I still feel pretty bad about what I did say to him on the pier. I guess I always will. "I didn't know you were working here."

"Only part-time," he says, "three afternoons a week." And then he says hi to the kids and gives them a nice smile. He barely looks at me and starts concentrating on the vanilla ice cream.

"I want the jumbo double scoop!" David says.

"Me too! Me too!" DeeDee starts jumping up and down.

"Uh-uh," I say. "I don't have that kind of money. Besides, I didn't even ask your mother if you could have ice cream anyhow."

"Mommy always buys us a double scoop after lunch. Right, DeeDee?" David says, pushing DeeDee.

"Yeah, always," she says right on cue. I know they're both full of it, but they're making such a fuss I figure I'll treat them, so I say okay.

Barry starts to scoop the ice cream and they keep changing flavors so they end up with almost four different scoops apiece. He only charges me for singles anyway.

"How do you like it so far?" he asks me, and I can see he's not so angry anymore.

85

"Pretty good," I tell him. "I really like it."

"Where are you?"

"Over on Evergreen."

"Yeah? I know where that is."

"Right after Seaview," I say.

"There's a yellow house with turrets on the corner."

"Right," I say. "That's practically across the street from us. We're in the white house with the red shutters."

"Yeah, I think I know it."

That's it. Now we have nothing in the whole world to say. Maybe I should start the geography lesson again.

"Would you like to get together sometime?" he finally says. "We could play tennis—just as friends, I mean."

I wince at that.

"Do you play tennis?" he asks.

"A little."

"Well, we could play a couple of sets. . . . Or there's the disco where a lot of the kids hang out. . . . We could go there."

"Sure, that would be nice."

"Should I call you?"

"Sure." What else can I say? I mean, he's being so nice and friendly, especially after the embarrassing time yesterday.

I give him my number and tell him thanks for the extra ice cream and head off in the direction of Cherry Grove.

Fire Island is great. You can never get lost. All it is is a long skinny strip of sand off the coast of Long Island. The Atlantic Ocean is on one side and the bay is on the other. If The Dunes restaurant is on the way to Cherry Grove, there's no way you can miss it. You just keep walking and you have to hit it. The kids aren't too hot to go but I make a deal with them. It's really very simple—they sit in the wagon and I pull. By the time the summer ends they'll probably forget how to walk and I'll have grown gorilla arms.

The Dunes is a big outdoor-indoor restaurant right on the beach. It's busy and there are a lot of people sitting around eating. There are some women and a few kids, but mostly there are men. I already know that Cherry Grove is a big gay hangout. These two guys, friends of my parents, have been coming out here every summer for years and my parents always spend a weekend with them. Naturally my folks are planning to come out this summer, and I'm not looking forward to that. I'm sort of a different person out here already. It's like this is kind of my place and being somebody's little girl out here is going to bug me. I just know it. Well, I've got a good four weeks before my parents come to worry about it. Anyway, I look around but I don't see Jim, but of course he could be inside, so I tell the kids not to move and I go inside to see if I can find him. He's there. The first waiter I see.

I work my way around to his table and come up from behind and tap him on the shoulder.

"Hi," I say, and I can't believe I'm doing it. I mean, this is so unlike me. Mostly I plan things for a hundred years in advance, and then at the last minute I lose my courage and think of a million reasons why I can't do it.

"Hey," he says, turning around. "How you doing?" And I can see he's surprised to see me. But he gives me such a nice smile that my knees begin to wobble.

"Okay. You working here?"

"Right, uh . . . er . . ."

"Victoria." I don't know why I did that. I'm sure he knows my name.

"Sure, Victoria, I didn't forget." See, I told you. "How's Barry?"

"Gee, I don't know. I haven't seen him in ages," I lie.

"We played tennis this morning."

"Yeah, he told me." Oh, damn. "Ages ago."

Jim kind of chuckles and so do I, and then I ask him what's to do here and where do the kids hang out and he says mostly at night everyone goes to The Monkey, a disco.

I tell him that I have Monday nights off and maybe I'll drop by The Monkey. "Will you be there this Monday?" I ask as offhandedly as you can possibly be asking someone for a date.

"Probably," he says, and I manage to say, "Maybe I'll see you there." And then he says he has to go, and I say, "See you later," and I'm so excited I almost walk into the wall.

I can't believe I did it. I actually did it. I got to see Jim and practically have a date with him. And I did it all by myself. He didn't even help.

I'm flying. The kids are outside, right where I left them, driving some old lady crazy. They're saying curse words back and forth to each other and going hysterical, and the lady keeps saying how that's not nice and nice children don't talk like that and on and on, and the more she tells them not to, the dirtier they talk, and it's so embarrassing I don't even want to go over and get them.

"DeeDee!" I call from a pretty safe distance. "David! C'mon."

But they're having too good a time shocking the lady, so I have to go over and practically drag them to the wagon. David is smart enough to keep his mouth shut, but DeeDee lets fly with one last zonker that nearly knocks the poor lady off her seat. It is a little too much for a five-year-old.

I pile them both in the wagon and zoom off along the beach. Now, you have to appreciate something that I didn't understand until I got to Fire Island. You know, a lot of people don't wear bathing suits on the beach. But nobody told me, so here I am walking along the beach pulling these two dead-weights and at first I'm not even looking around, I'm just pulling with my head down and my mind on Jim, then I catch a look at this guy and I'm past him before I realize he's naked, and I stop dead (really cool, huh?) and slowly sneak a look. And my jaw drops. Almost everyone is naked, guys and girls, and because there's no one else there I have to say it to David and DeeDee. "Look at those people."

And they look and then David says, "What about them?"

"Are you kidding? They're naked, that's what's about them."

"Victoria?" Now David's going to ask me about them, and I don't know what to say. I hope he doesn't ask me something physical, because now that I'm looking around I don't think I want to go into the whole anatomy thing.

"Can we go swimming now?" Huh? Unbelievable! He doesn't even care. It has to be because they've been coming out here all their lives and naked human beings are common sights to them. Completely natural. Well, let me tell you, *I'm* freaking out. I'm trying to be cool, but, wow, will you look at all those penises! Crazy thought: Do my parents go naked when they come out here? I'm so busy watching and planning what I'm going to write to Steffi that I run us, the wagon and all, into the water four times.

The closer you get to Ocean Beach the more crowded the beach gets and the fewer naked people you see, and by the time we're into the middle of Ocean Beach there's only one or two and they're girls and only topless. I wish Steffi was here.

We swim for a while and get back to the house by four. Cynthia is out on the deck sunning herself. I guess she's feeling better.

I get up to my room and it's boiling hot. I think DeeDee must be wrong, that it would be too hot for a closet. I guess it's terrific in the winter. There's a whole pile of DeeDee's dresses and a couple of David's things on my bed with a note from Cynthia that says if I wouldn't mind pressing these clothes when I got a chance she'd really appreciate it.

I roll up the laundry because I'm just too exhausted to do

it today, but it's a problem finding a space to store it. I told you it's a very cozy room and there's not a whole lot of extra space. I end up putting it on the corner of my bed with my tennis racket and my blow dryer.

Dinner is super. Cynthia is a fantastic cook. She does something to the hamburgers with Worcestershire sauce and butter and herbs that's the best I ever had. She says it's from Craig Claiborne or somebody. She's sort of a gourmet cook. I'm really lucky because I love the way she cooks.

"Listen, Victoria," she says to me over dinner, "please don't rush with that ironing. It doesn't all have to be done tonight. Just do as much as you feel like and you can finish the rest at your leisure." Then Cynthia says she has to go get dressed. She's a little excited because she has a date with this man she met last night at The Dunes.

"That's all right," I say. "I don't mind ironing. Besides, I hate to just sit and watch TV. I like to be doing something." That's not exactly true, but I want her to see that I'm not lazy like last year's mother's helper, who, she keeps telling me, was practically comatose.

I'm a lousy ironer, so it takes me until almost one o'clock in the morning to finish all the stuff, and I'm dripping wet when I do so I take a shower and practically fall into bed.

Then I remember that I absolutely have to write to Steffi tonight if I want her to get the letter before she leaves for her camping trip. Besides, I have a million crucial things to tell her, except that when I actually write the letter it takes me two full pages of really tiny writing just to get through the part about work. I just stuff what I wrote into an envelope, turn out the light, and dive into the bed.

Suddenly I'm wide awake. What if what Gloria said was right? Is this a terrible job? Is Cynthia taking advantage? But she's not. I just know it. Cynthia's very nice in a lot of ways, even though I can't think of exactly what ones they are this very minute. Maybe this is what it's really like being a mother's helper. Not that *I* do all that much. Still, it's sort of more than I expected—maybe because it's new and I don't have the hang of it yet.

Boy, if my mother knew all the work I was doing, she'd faint.

Nine

It can't be morning yet. It can't be. But it is because
DeeDee is climbing all over me, pulling at the covers and telling me she's hungry. I try to tell her that she's big enough to get
a glass of juice for herself and watch TV until I get downstairs.
But she says she can't squeeze the juice herself and I remember
that Cynthia likes to have freshly squeezed orange juice in the
morning.

"How about a glass of milk instead?" I ask her.

"You said juice."

"Milk's better."

"I want juice."

There's no way. Once DeeDee makes up her mind, that's
it. So I drag myself out of bed and go downstairs to fix her
breakfast, which she leaves over half of anyway. I turn on the

TV and curl up on the couch and try to sleep a little more. No luck. David's heard us, and now he wants his breakfast too. I think maybe these kids could do a little more for themselves, but I guess that's up to the mother.

There's the cutest note from Cynthia that says how she had a great time and she got in late so we should go to the beach without her. It's written like a please-excuse-Cynthia note from school. See, that's one of the nice things about her—she's got a terrific sense of humor.

We do the beach bit again, and today there are a few more people on the beach. I guess it's beginning to fill up for the Fourth of July weekend. There are some other mother's helpers with kids, and we all kind of sit close by and the kids begin to play together, and then we start to talk and a couple of them are kind of nice girls and we'll probably get friendly.

One girl, Dana, is tall, with a great figure and legs that look like they go on forever. She's got long hair, sort of light brown with blond streaks, and the nicest smile. I know I'm going to like her, and besides, she's new like me. She takes care of two kids too, but one is a two-year-old baby and the other is a five-year-old girl like DeeDee. In fact, Leah—that's the kid's name—and DeeDee get along fine together.

The other mother's helper is from last year, and her name is Anita. She has reddish-brown hair so short and curly that it almost looks kinky, and she's so cute and little she could pass for fifteen but she's actually seventeen. She's got only one kid and he's almost eight, so she really has it easy, and besides, she says, they have other help in the house so she doesn't even have to do anything but take care of Scott. And she says she gets forty dollars a week. Even Dana gets more than me. Not that much—thirty dollars—but still . . . it's okay with me because I know Cynthia's not being cheap. Not deliberately, anyway. She just can't afford to pay anymore.

"I knew the girl who worked for the Landrys last year," Anita says. "And she says Mr. Landry was always trying to flirt with her. Can you imagine trying to make out with your own mother's helper? Isn't that disgusting?"

Ugh, we all say. "I'm really glad he isn't around," I tell them. Anita goes on.

"And she said Mrs. Landry wasn't so great either. She didn't do a whole lot."

"I heard about that girl last year," I say. "Her name was Christie, right?"

"Yeah," Anita says.

"Cynthia—that's Mrs. Landry," I say, "she said that Christie was really lazy with a capital *L*. All she wanted to do was sit around and polish her nails."

"That's all I want to do too," Dana says, and we all laugh because she's right.

Then we all compare our jobs, and it turns out that mine is the worst. Far and away. But I don't let them see how bad it really is because I'm sort of embarrassed. Besides, it's not as though Cynthia is mean or anything like that—in fact, she's probably a lot nicer than the woman Anita works for, who sounds like a real bitch. The trouble with Cynthia is that she's used to having a housekeeper, so it's just natural for her to leave the work to someone else, and besides, she's probably very depressed and not herself because of the divorce and all her troubles.

Then there's something else. I'm really sort of stuck. I don't want to just quit because then I'd have to leave Fire Island and Jim, and also it'd be like admitting to my parents that I just can't hack it. And of course I'd have to tell Cynthia, and I don't think I'd have the nerve unless she really did something awful to me. In the meantime I'm just going to let things go the way they are and keep my eyes open in case something else comes up. According to Anita, after two weeks all the mothers hate their helpers and all the helpers are ready to switch. I think I'll just wait and see.

"I don't care how much she makes me work, I really like Cynthia," I tell Anita and Dana, and I find myself feeling bad because I don't want people not to like the person I'm working for. It's just that she's having a hard time now, and I tell them what a pig Jed was.

"Cynthia's really pretty," Anita says, and we decide that she's one of the best-looking mothers around. And I don't know why, but that makes me feel good. We're on the beach for three hours, and Dana and I sit there listening to the stories Anita tells us. She knows all the juice and there's enough dirt to bury the whole island. The stories are all about adultery. It's like nobody's happily married. Always when I hear all these stories I go home and worry about my own parents. Except that's impossible, I just can't picture my mother fooling around. And my father! I practically break up trying to picture that. Listen, I have enough trouble thinking about them doing it together.

We rotate lying in the sun. One of us watches the kids while the other two gets a tan. Dana is on watch now.

"Gorgeous!" Dana says. "Absolutely knockout stuff." Anita and I pop right up. Gorgeous can only mean a guy.

"Where?" Anita says, grabbing for her sunglasses. They're prescription glasses and she's practically blind without them. But she pretends they're only sunglasses.

"There," Dana says, pointing to two surfers right in front of us in the water. It takes me two seconds to realize they're Jim and Barry.

"They're both cute," Anita says, "but the blond is sensational."

Naturally she's talking about my Jim. He really does look like an advertisement.

"I know them," I say as casually as I can. And they both nearly jump out of their skins. They have a million questions, and I can tell from the questions that Dana really digs Barry, which sort of surprises me a little. I don't tell how Barry feels about me.

We watch the guys surfing, and it's funny but they're both a lot like the way they surf. I mean their personalities. Barry's pretty good, but he doesn't seem to take it too seriously. He looks as if he's having a lot of fun. Even when he falls off he seems to be laughing. Another thing: He's so busy surfing that he doesn't seem to be aware of the people on the beach. He's just having a great old time.

But Jim knows he's got an audience (I guess someone who looks the way he does always has an audience) and he's playing to them. I don't mean he's not having fun, but you can tell by the way he stands on the surfboard that he wants to look his best. And boy, he sure does. Dana's right. He's gorgeous. And he's a very good surfer, too, his blond hair whipping back, his arms straight out as though he's flying, and a big happy smile on his face. I wish he really was my boyfriend. I'd love that more than anything else in the world. And I'd love everyone to know.

Suddenly it seems all the mother's helpers who normally detest the water are nagging their charges to go in. Me too. Except I don't have to ask twice because David is always ready. Even DeeDee wants to go in.

Like lemmings we all head toward the water. Counting the kids, we must be about fifteen. There are so many of us bobbing in the water that if the guys still want to do serious surfing they'll have to move farther down the beach. I guess the temptation of all those cute girl lemmings is just too much, because pretty soon we're all fooling around on their surfboards and nobody's taking anything seriously. Except dumb me, I always take Jim seriously. Kind of cuts into my fun but I can't help it. That's just the way I feel about him.

Jim shows David how to hold on to the board, and I feel super because he picked my kid. That must mean something.

By the time we finish with the water and head up to our blankets Jim has a group of female admirers around him you wouldn't believe. Actually it's disgusting, except he doesn't seem to think so. In fact, he looks like he can hardly tear himself away. When I see how popular he is it makes me think I'm probably wasting my time. I'll never get him.

Out of the corner of my eye I see Dana talking to Barry. I told you she liked him. And he seems kind of interested in her, which is a little annoying, particularly since he's supposed to be so crazy about me. Not that I really care because he definitely isn't my type. It's just that he made such a big thing about how he felt about me. Sometimes guys really give me a pain.

"Hey, buddy," Jim calls to Barry, "I gotta get back. Are you coming?"

"Sure thing," Barry says and grabs his board.

"See you around," Jim says, and he gives everybody one of his big heart-stopping smiles. Then he sort of points at me and says, "At The Monkey, right?" And I nearly drop dead.

"Take it easy." Barry waves, and they both go off down the beach.

The other girls drift off to their own blankets, and I just stand there staring.

"Wake up," Anita says.

"Did he point at me or did he point at me, huh?" I ask them both, and I'm positively hyperventilating.

"He definitely pointed at you," Dana says.

And then I ask them about six more times if they're absolutely certain it was at me, and they swear it was, and I still can hardly believe it. I would go on about it for another half hour except that Dana has a million questions about Barry that I have to answer. Like I said, she's interested in him. I tell her everything I know about him except how he feels about me, which he probably doesn't anymore anyway.

"Are you going to The Monkey later?" Anita asks me as we break up and head back to our houses.

"Are you kidding?" I say. "There's no way I'm not going to be there tonight."

"See you later, then." They both wave and go off.

Ten

We're pretty late getting back for lunch. Cynthia probably couldn't wait for us so she left a note saying she went to the Youngs' for lunch and would I pretty please make the kids tuna sandwiches and see if I can't sort of straighten up the house a little because some friends are coming for cocktails. P.S., she says, the vacuum is in the pantry closet, and so is the mop. Good-bye afternoon for me.

But I don't mind because if she's having company, it means she'll be home tonight and I can get out for sure. Fantastic!

After lunch David goes to his friend's across the street and DeeDee is so tired from the beach she takes a nap. Lucky for me, because it's going to take me a while to get things in shape. There's another note from Cynthia on the kitchen table that says only to change her sheets, everyone else's is clean. I start on the downstairs first so I can be sure that's ready for the company. I'm just starting to drag the vacuum up the steps when the phone rings. At first I leap for it, but then I remember about the grandfather and I just stand there and let it ring. But—I know this is a long shot—maybe it's Jim. Maybe he asked Barry for my number and . . . no way. Still . . . I answer it.

"Hello?" Very sweet, warm, intelligent person of at least sixteen. That's me.

"Cynthia?"

"No, she's not home. This is the mother's helper."

"Mother's what?"

"The mother's helper. You know, I take care of the kids and . . ."

"Great little kids, aren't they?" whoever he is says, cutting me off right in the middle of my sentence. "Best in the world. How about putting David on?"

"David's not home. Who is this please?"

"What about DeeDee?" he says without answering my question. Except I think I know the answer already. "Isn't she home?"

"She's sleeping," I say. "Is this Mr. Landry?"

"How'd you know?" And he gets a suspicious tone to his voice.

"Cynthia said you might call."

"What'd she tell you?"

Now I'm his enemy and that makes me start to fumfer all over the place.

"Nothing . . . except she said . . . uh . . . she thought it would be better if you didn't . . . I mean . . . she said . . ."

"She don't want me to talk to the kids, right?"

"Well . . ." Even though he's not exactly sweet and gentle the way I expected, still it's hard to tell him he can't talk to his own grandchildren. And he seems to be reading my thoughts. He says, "Look, honey, those kids are my flesh and blood—she ain't got no right to do this."

"I'm sorry, Mr. Landry, but I'm only the mother's helper."

"Well, listen here, mother's helper or whatever you are, you get that little girl awake and let her talk to her grandpa. You hear me?"

This is terrible. Cynthia said I should hang up, but I can't slam the phone down on someone I practically know, especially a grandfather. "Please, Mr. Landry, can you call back when Cynthia is here?"

"That won't do me no good; that girl's too sour. I ain't saying she's wrong about that boy—a rotten kid Jed is sometimes—but she ain't got no right doing this to me and the kids. I'm their grandpa and we got a right to be together. You got a grandpa?"

"Yes, sir."

"You love him?"

"Oh yes, definitely. I love him very much."

"What would you think, somebody steps in there and says

you can't see him and they've got no good reason?"

"Cynthia thinks maybe you could talk to your son about the money."

"I talked to him about that more'n she has. He's just a downright nasty boy and I'm ashamed of him. If I had a penny more on my Social Security, I'd pay it myself."

Now I feel even worse. I mean, the poor man has no money. I think maybe Cynthia is wrong about doing it this way. But what can I do?

"Please, Mr. Landry, I don't know what to do. I have to do what Cynthia told me. Maybe you could call when she's home."

"No good. Tell you what, just wake DeeDee up and let me talk to her."

"I can't, Mr. Landry. Please don't ask me to do something like that."

"But you know it ain't right what she's doing. I'm an old man . . . uh, what'd you say your name was?"

"Victoria."

"Victoria, you sound like a nice girl. Let me tell you, I ain't so young anymore and maybe I don't have too much time left. I don't mean I'm sick or anything, but I'm past seventy and . . . tell you the truth, honey, those kids is all I have. And I'm the only grandpa they have. . . . Well, there ain't much in my life I'm so crazy about, but those kids, they're special. I guess I love them more than I do . . . well, anyone."

When I hear his voice break I start to fall apart myself.

Nobody has ever talked to me like that before. I mean, I never had the power to say yes or no like this. It's terrible. I hate it.

Right in the middle of everything DeeDee comes down from her nap, still half asleep and creeps onto my lap and snuggles up. She's soft and all warm from sleep and so lovable.

"Who's that you're talking to," she asks, and I cover the phone, but it's too late.

"That DeeDee?" Mr. Landry asks in a loud voice, and suddenly he sounds so excited. "DeeDee, it's Grandpa!"

Well, forget it. I'm not going to do something I know is really wrong just because someone tells me to. And in a giant burst of—I don't know, maybe courage or maybe the opposite, maybe I'm too weak to stand up—I put the phone to DeeDee's ear.

And her face lights up. "Grandpa!" And then to me, "It's my grandpa!" And then back to the phone. "Grandpa, I told Victoria all about you and we saw a fisherman today and he wasn't half as good as you, and I told him how my grandpa is the best fisherman in the whole wide world and David said so too. . . . I miss you too. . . . When are you coming out to see us? . . . How come? I want you to come today. . . . I want you to come tomorrow, then." And then she turns to me and says, "My grandpa can't come out this week, that's what he said. . . . How come, Grandpa?" She's back talking into the phone and they go on for a while, and she's so cute, and she tells him all about every single thing that happened since she came out here. I mean everything, like what she ate for breakfast, and he asks her lots of questions, and you can tell he's really interested in everything about her. And then they say, "I love you," and they throw kisses and finally they say good-bye and the call probably costs him a fortune. I know people get very little money on Social Security, so I guess he'll have to do without something else to make up for talking to his granddaughter. I'm in a lot of trouble so I'm building up his case. First thing I have to make sure is that DeeDee doesn't say anything to Cynthia.

"You really have a terrific grandpa, DeeDee," I start off.

She loves that and she tells me all the things they talked about on the phone, which of course I just heard.

"Do you have any special secrets with your grandpa?"

"What's a special secret?"

"Something you have that nobody else in the whole world knows. I have one with my grandpa."

"What about?"

"I can't tell you. Then it wouldn't be my special secret."

"I want one too." And she wants one so much she's beginning to pout. So I give her one.

"Okay, DeeDee, that phone call from your grandpa, the one just now, that's your special secret. Now, remember, don't tell anyone else."

"'Cept my mommy. But not David."

"Not even your mommy if you want it to be a special secret." I feel so low tricking a baby like this.

"Not even my mommy?"

"Right. Not even your mommy. And you know what happens to people who keep their special grandpa secrets at the end of the summer?"

"Uh-uh." And her eyes get twice their size. These kids can smell a prize a mile away.

"They get a prize."

"A kangaroo?"

"Maybe so."

"Oooh." And she jumps up and down and claps her hands.

"Are you going to keep the special grandpa secret?"

She thinks hard for a minute and says, "I'll ask my mommy."

I try a different approach. "DeeDee, if you tell your mommy about your grandpa calling, my grandpa is going to be very upset and I will be too because then you won't be a member of the Secret Grandpa Club and then you won't be able to come to the meetings or get the button or anything." I can see I'm getting to her. She's a little confused but the button's got to get her.

"I want the button," she finally announces. What did I tell you?

"Then don't tell Mommy."

"Let me see it."

"If you don't tell Mommy."

"Okay."

"My grandpa is going to be very happy, and me too."

"Victoria?"

"What, sweetie?"

"I want my button."

"I'm going to write away this very afternoon."

"I want it now." And she screws her face up like she's going to cry.

"I have to write away, DeeDee. Look, I don't even have mine yet."

"You promised."

"I know and I'm going to do it right now. See?" And I take a scrap of paper and start to write some gibberish.

"Maybe if I ask my mommy she can call on the phone and then they can bring it over today."

"They don't have any phones, and besides, if you tell your mommy anything, all the buttons will turn green and melt away." She's pushing me. If it was Nina I'd tell her *she'd* turn green and melt away. It's so much easier with a sister.

"I swear I won't tell, ever, ever. . . ."

"That's fine. Now let's finish cleaning up for the company."

"Send the letter." She says it like a midget general. Now that I've created a button monster, I'm not about to screw up, so I put the letter in an envelope and tell her I'm sending it special delivery. That sounds okay to her and we—well, not exactly we, more like I—finish cleaning. I hope I do a good enough job, because I never really cleaned a whole house like this. At home the most I do is some dishes, and when they really bug me enough, my own room. I finish just before Cynthia comes home and am I pooped. Cynthia says I did a terrific job. She tells me to start dinner for the kids while she throws herself together for her company.

While she's talking to me, DeeDee is whispering in my ear how I should ask Cynthia if I can go to the post office. The kid's developed a button fixation. I don't know if this is going to work.

"DeeDee, DeeDee darling," Cynthia says. "What's all the whispering about?"

Before DeeDee can open her mouth, I jump in with how we have a special secret. I do a lot of winking and smiling at Cynthia and make her promise not to ask anymore. Of course, she goes right along with it, and in the adult-pretended-interest way she says, "It's wonderful," and starts upstairs.

"And I'm gonna get a button too, right, Victoria?" DeeDee the button maniac says.

"That's terrific," Cynthia says, and disappears up the stairs. So far so good. It's horrendous having your entire career in the hands of a five-year-old.

Cynthia's company comes at five, and it turns out to be Eva and Ron Thompson, the people Anita works for. Anita told a whole juicy adultery story about them, and I can't keep from gaping at them, especially her. After they have a couple of drinks (this is going to shock you) I think I see Cynthia and Ron Thompson giving each other little special looks. Wow! This is a weird place.

I feed the kids and it's almost seven and Cynthia and her guests are still having cocktails. Now another couple from down the street comes over, and it's sort of turning into a party and Cynthia looks hot to get rid of me. So she says when I put the kids in bed I can go out for a while. Super!

I dive into my makeup. I don't need too much, because I'm really getting a great tan, but I do my eyes and put on my fabulous new lipliner with the pale gloss on the inside. A final touch or two and down I go.

Cynthia is so involved she doesn't even see me come downstairs, but I don't want to leave without letting her know so I sort of stand around waiting to catch her attention. Finally she sees me, so I give her a little wave and start out the door.

"Victoria, honey," Cynthia calls me, "wait a sec, will you?"

I stop at the door.

"Honey," she says, coming over to me, "I hate to do this to you, but I think there's been a change in plans and we might go over to the Thompsons' later for some drinks, so I don't think you'd better go out."

"But I told some people . . ." One look at her face and I know it's no use.

"I'm really sorry, dear, but . . . maybe tomorrow. Tomorrow night for sure."

There's nothing I can really say. I mean, she's paying me to take care of the kids, and if she decides to go out I can't tell her not to. Still, that seems sort of mean because she isn't even sure if she really is going. She only said they might. Maybe they're not planning to go for a couple of hours. I wouldn't care if I could only stay for a little while.

"If you're not going for a while," I say, "I could be back in an hour, even less."

"No, dear, I don't like to be tied down. Come on, Victoria. Don't look so unhappy. You have a whole summer ahead of you."

That's the same garbage I told David. There's no point in standing there with my face hanging out, so I go back upstairs and I cry.

Well, that's not so peculiar considering I'm very disappointed, and besides, this was practically a semi-date with Jim and now it's going to be like I'm standing him up and that's certainly going to be the end of me. Can you picture anyone standing Jim up and getting another chance? Never.

There's got to be a way to get out tonight.

Eleven

I must have fallen asleep because next thing I know it's midnight and the house is quiet. I'm still dressed so I slip out of bed and creep downstairs to see what's up.

The living room is empty, so they must have all gone out. I check on the kids and they're sleeping fine. Cynthia's door is open so I go in to get the new *Vogue* she said I could borrow. I'm not in the least tired. Just miserable.

I'm two steps into the room when I see Cynthia is in her bed sleeping. She didn't go out after all.

Damn. I could have gone. She really stinks. Maybe she came up to tell me and saw me sleeping and figured I wouldn't want to go. Still, she could have waked me and asked. She must have seen I was dressed. I think she's kind of selfish. She probably didn't even think about me at all. Maybe I'm not so crazy about her anymore. If I tried hard enough I could probably hate her guts. She ruined my entire summer. Maybe my entire life. Damn her!

Maybe I should wake her up and ask her if I could go now. Ten after twelve isn't that late for a disco. Nah.

She'd probably say it's too late to be going out. "What would your mother say?" or something like that. Besides, I wouldn't have the nerve to wake her up to just ask her if I could go dancing. Even if it is just probably the most important night of my life.

I'll never be able to sleep tonight. I just know it. There's no way . . . unless. I know this probably sounds really sneaky but suppose I just went out without saying anything. It's not like I'm not doing my job, because Cynthia's home and the kids are sleeping and everything is under control. I could go for just a little while and be back and nobody would know the difference.

I'm not saying it's the best thing in the world to do, but it certainly isn't going to hurt anyone except me if I don't do it.

If I keep analyzing it I'll never do it. So I stop analyzing, fix my hair, put on more gloss, and tiptoe down the steps like a thief, feeling awful. The house is deadly quiet. I turn the door latch as delicately as I can so there'll be no thunderous click to wake the house up. It works. I'd probably make a great burglar. Anyway, I'm out and my heart is pounding.

Twelve

I don't have any trouble finding The Monkey. Halfway down to the dock, I can hear the music. It's almost twelve thirty, but the place is packed and the overflow is hanging out all over the front steps and into the street. Mostly everyone is wearing jean shorts and T-shirts, which is perfect. At least I guessed right, and I love my top—it's sort of a camisole with laces up the front. Very sexy. Last time I wore it, my father made me put on a shirt underneath. But that's the great thing about being out here. I'm on my own, and I think it looks just fine without anything underneath.

I kind of hang back a little—maybe I'll see someone I know. I hope not Barry.

"Vicky! Hey, over here!" It's Dana. Great!

"Hi!" I call, and head toward her.

"I figured you weren't going to show. What happened?" she says.

"Cynthia took forever to decide she wasn't going out."

I look inside at the people. There must be a hundred of them all jammed together, drinking and laughing and dancing on the tiny dance floor. "Boy, this is wild," I exclaim.

"Is this your first time here?"

"Yeah. It looks great."

"C'mon, let's go in."

The music bombs your ears and the lights spin around so fast that you couldn't tell if your own sister was here. Boy, what a thought. It's hopeless to try to find Jim until the lights slow up. Somebody taps me on the shoulder, and when I turn around it's some guy I don't know. He makes a *dance?* sign. No point in talking—you can't hear a thing anyway. I nod yes and we squeeze our way onto the dance floor.

Like I told you, I'm a pretty good dancer. It's the one time I feel like I've got it all together—when I'm dancing, I mean. I wish I could feel this way all the time.

The next record is Joni Mitchell singing "Court and Spark." She's so cool. Now, before I can make my way back to Dana, some other guy asks me to dance. He's kind of cute but too tall for me. I hate to slow dance with a real tall guy. It's so boring to stare into the middle of a T-shirt.

The lights slow down and I find Dana. She's with Anita.

"I heard my people were at your house," she says. "What do you think of them?"

"She's gross, but he's kind of cute in a goopy sort of sweet way."

"Right," she says.

"This is going to make you laugh," I tell her, "but I think Cynthia has the hots for your boss's husband."

"Ron? You have to be kidding! He's so . . . like, shy."

"That's what you think. You should see him come on to Cynthia."

"Good. I hope so. She deserves it—Eva, I mean. You know what she did to him tonight? She . . ." But the music starts blasting and you can't hear. A guy asks Anita to dance, and then someone puts his hand on my shoulder, and when I turn around my knees almost crumble.

"Victoria?" It's *him*. He smiles at me and motions to dance. I don't even look around at Dana. I'll apologize later. I just follow him through the crowd onto the dance floor.

I can't believe he's asked me to dance. And it turns out he's a great dancer and it's like we've been dancing together forever—I mean, we just fall into this natural rhythm. I can tell he knows it too. We can't talk because of the music, but we dance the next two dances even though someone else comes up and asks me. He shakes his head no to the guy, and I do too.

Three dances practically wipe us out, and he takes my arm and leads me toward the door. I'm soaking wet. And more excited than I've ever been in my life. I'm so knocked out at the thought that I'm with Jim that I can hardly catch my breath, and that's not just from dancing either.

We get outside and he keeps going past the kids hanging on the steps, and toward the dock. I think I would follow him anywhere. Just the feel of his hand on my arm makes me tingle. We don't talk until we get to the end of the dock, and then he stops.

"Want to sit here for a while and just cool off?" he asks, sitting down on the edge of the pier and making room for me.

I should say, "Yes, good idea," and sit next to him, but all I can manage in my stunned condition is a smile as I sit down.

He takes a joint out of his shirt pocket and lights up. Then he takes a couple of drags to get it going and hands it to me.

I'm not a pot smoker. For one thing, my parents are always warning me how it's illegal and if you get caught terrible things can happen to you. And for another, I don't trust it. Some people feel really cool and great, but some of them get nutty giddy and absolutely anything cracks them up. Other times they just sit there and cough their heads off. Also, it's tough enough for me to handle what's happening sober. But stoned? Forget it.

"You're a sensational dancer," he says to me, and he turns and looks down at me with just a little bit of a tiny smile. I smile a thank-you, and it's funny but we both keep looking at each other and wow!—it feels to me like we're almost touching.

"And you're pretty, too," he says.

This time I manage a thank-you and even more.

"You're a good dancer too," I tell him.

117

"And am I pretty, too?" he says, smiling his usual beautiful up-the-corner smile with white even teeth that you can see into. He flips the end of the joint into the water, then very gently he brushes a straggly strand of hair out of my eyes. And the smile gets smaller and more private, and we sit there silently looking at each other, and I don't even feel that we have to talk. He moves closer and his thigh brushes against mine, and the feel of this touch zings through my body and makes me shiver a tiny bit.

"Cold?" he asks.

"A little," I lie, because how else can I explain the shiver? He puts his arm around my shoulder and gently pulls me closer to him. My head is against his chest and he feels warm and I can hear his heart beating. It's going pretty fast. I think mine must be too. I'm staring down at the water, but all I can think of is should I say something or should I just sit there and let him hold me like this. I only practically just met him. I mean, this is the first time I've ever been with him alone like this. While I'm in the middle of the big decision, he says my name softly, and when I look up to answer him, he kisses me.

His lips are unbelievably soft, and as he bends down to me he pulls me up toward him. And what starts off as a light kiss grows stronger and harder until our lips are pressed against our teeth and I feel his mouth begin to open and I pull back a tiny bit, not far, but enough so that he sees I don't want him to do that. Still kissing me, he leans back on the dock and pulls me down with him. Anyone else tried this the first time and

I would just push him away, but I don't move. The tops of our bodies are still facing the way we were when we were sitting. Now Jim rolls over toward me and with one arm pulls me close to him. I don't even pull away. It's like I'm not inside myself. All I want to do is be near him.

He takes his lips off mine and lifts his head and leans on one elbow. His face is only inches away from mine and he looks very serious.

"Is something wrong?" he asks me, really concerned. I must look scared because I am, a little.

"Uh-uh." I shake my head. "It's just that . . . I don't know. I guess I didn't expect this . . . I guess."

"Me neither," and he smiles and I think he's got the most trusting face I ever saw.

He kisses me again, and this time I feel more relaxed, like I know him better. I'm feeling really happy and good, and then I begin to get sort of lost in the kiss, in his closeness, and when his mouth opens against mine I let mine open too. He puts his tongue against my teeth and I don't know what's the matter with me, I never kiss this way with anyone. But I do with Jim, and then I even let him put his tongue inside my mouth and his hand runs down the side of my body, sort of over my hip and down the side of my leg and I don't do anything. I mean, I don't stop him and I don't even want to.

The way he touches me doesn't feel like other guys who just want to grab you: It's like he's caressing me and it makes me want to caress him but of course I don't. No matter what,

I don't think I ever could. My eyes are always closed when I kiss, but now I open them a tiny bit just because I have to look at him. His eyes are closed, shut tight, and he's got blond eyelashes. I didn't know that. Suddenly I become tense because the hand that was caressing my side is moving up under my arm and I'm afraid he's going to try to touch my breast. Besides, I'm very ticklish. He feels me jump a little and his hand moves away, down my side again, and he pulls me closer and moves his face down to kiss my neck and that makes me really shiver. Nice shiver. I know this is too much but I can't stop it. I can, but I don't want to. It's the first time in my whole life I ever felt like this.

Now he brings his lips back to mine and we're kissing, and I'm kissing just as hard as he is and my arms are around his back and I'm holding him tight and I feel like I don't care what happens.

His hand comes up under my arm again and he lets it brush lightly over my breasts, and my head is buzzing but I don't even stop him, and now his hand covers my whole breast and I can't think of anything else except what he's doing and that I'm letting him. How could I let him do this? What's the matter with me?

The awful thing is that it feels good. I won't let him go any farther, and I'm beginning to tense up waiting for him to try. But he doesn't, and I kind of let myself relax and he kisses me and I kiss him and our whole bodies are tight together and I'll worry about everything later.

We kiss like this for a long while, and then I feel him push his legs into mine and I feel something against my thigh and I know it isn't his keys and I feel kind of scared because maybe this is getting out of control. Maybe I won't be able to stop him. But I can because it's Jim and I know him, and besides, everyone says he's a terrific guy and he would never do anything like push himself on someone who didn't want him to. He's not like that, I just know it. But still I feel a little scared, so I pull back slightly and he pushes against me kind of hard, and I open my eyes and pull my face away from his, and he looks at me and sort of swallows hard and takes a couple of breaths and gives me an it's-all-right smile and goes back to gently kissing me.

But it doesn't stay that way long and we're back to holding each other tightly, and now his hand is working around my camisole straps and I should have worn the damned T-shirt underneath like my father said. Oh, God, what a time to think of my father. That does it. I push his hand away and he puts it back the minute I push it away.

"Please . . . ," I say, "don't do that."

He moves his hand away from my straps and slides it down the side of my leg to the top of my thigh. Now I really push it away.

"Please . . . ," I say again, and he starts to kiss my neck and my ear, and then his hand is on my breast again, but I already let him do that so I can't say no now. Besides, that's not so bad, I think. Sometimes his hand skips off the material and onto my bare skin and I get goose bumps. It slips off more and more and I know he's trying to put his hand under my camisole and I know I shouldn't let him, but it all happens so gradually, and by the time I put my hand on his to pull him away he's already holding my bare breast and it's too late. So I let him. And then he pushes off the shoulder strap and I keep my eyes tight shut because I don't want to see myself undressed like that. He lifts his head slightly and I know he's looking and I feel ashamed, but I think of the naked people on the beach and then it's not so bad. Now his hand starts to slide down across my stomach, and I grab it tight.

"No, please, I don't want you to do that," I say, louder than I expected.

"Don't be afraid," he says, and starts to kiss me more.

"Please . . ." His hand slips out of my grip, but I push it away again.

"It's okay," he says.

No, it's not. But I don't say that. I just keep pushing his hand away every time he puts it anywhere under my waist-line.

He puts it.

I push it.

He puts it.

I push it. This goes on till I think I might start to laugh, except I'm beginning to get kind of angry. Now I pull up my shoulder strap and sit straight up. "I don't want you to do that," I say, and it's really crazy because here it is, my body, and he's annoyed that he can't do what he wants to it. Unreal. And he really is annoyed, like it was his.

"I'm not doing anything. I'm just touching you." He lies as if I don't know what he's trying to do.

"Then please don't touch me."

"Don't be afraid."

"I'm not afraid. I just don't want you to do that."

"You mean this?" And he puts his hand on my waist.

"Not that."

And he moves his hand farther down my leg and says, "This?"

And I say, "You know where," and he says, "No, show me," and I say, "I'm not going to because you know," and he says no, really he doesn't, and this stupid conversation goes on and we discuss my body like it was a map and he can touch here and he can't touch there and it turns out that he owns the entire northern half down to somewhere around Tennessee and I own the rest. For now, anyway. And it turns into a sort of cute conversation and I don't know why but I don't even really feel embarrassed.

Then I say I have to go, and he pushes me back down and starts to kiss me again and we neck for a while longer, but he tries all the same stuff I told him not to again, and finally I get up and say I really have to get back.

He sort of pulls himself together, facing the water, and shoves his hands into his pockets. Steffi and I have discussed this a million times about how boys put their hands in their pockets so you can't see they have an erection.

I sort of sneak a peek, but it works—the hands in the pockets, I mean—I don't see a thing.

We start walking up the dock toward the shore, and I'm hoping Jim will want to walk me home, and lucky me, he does. Except all the way home he keeps stopping to pull me to the side of the walkway to kiss me. A couple of times people come by and he doesn't even stop, and I can hear them giggling about us. If only someone from school could see us. Someone like Gloria.

I try to keep away from the lights because I must look a mess. My hair is a horror and my face feels like somebody walked on it. We kiss good night in front of the house, and then he says he'll call me tomorrow night. Isn't that the most fabulous thing in the whole world? Jim wants to see me again. I think he must really like me. He writes down my phone number and then he goes.

I watch him until he's out of sight, which only takes half a second because the street is pitch-black. It's got to be at least two in the morning, and I'm probably the only person awake on the whole block. It's dead quiet. Not a light on.

Up till now I haven't let myself think too much about what a disgusting awful underhanded thing I was doing—sneaking out, I mean—because if I really thought about it I know I wouldn't have done it. And I know I absolutely *had* to because it was crucial—I mean, not even just for my whole summer but maybe even for my whole life. I guess that sounds a little much, but still it *was* very important to me. Suddenly all my reasons sound crummy. How come it's all falling apart now just because I'm scared? And I am, too. In fact, I'm having a fit at the thought of trying to get back into my room, especially since it means tiptoeing up two flights of creaky stairs.

I take off my sandals and gently, very gently, turn the handle on the screen door. Again I gently squeeze down on the handle, turning it quietly all the way to the left and push. Nothing. Wrong way, dummy. I wipe my sweaty palm on my jeans and grab the handle again and this time turn it all the way to the right and push. Still nothing. I'm not in a panic because no one locks their doors on Fire Island. So it must be just a little stuck. Probably because of the heat and the dampness and all.

It's going to be tough shoving it hard enough without making any noise. I put my shoulder against the door and start pushing with my whole weight. It doesn't move. Now I wedge my feet under the porch railing and with both hands, using the railing for leverage, push the door. Nothing happens. If I didn't have to worry about making a noise I could just get back and ram it the way they do in the movies. Even though I'm getting very sweaty and very nervous I calm myself enough to try thinking straight. First thing I've got to find out is exactly where the door is actually stuck, top or bottom.

I check the top first. No problem there. And the bottom seems pretty free, so that means it must be caught in the middle, which is a funny place for a door to be stuck . . . unless what's sticking it isn't just sticking . . . it's locked. Help! I can't believe it. They absolutely never lock their door. Unless . . . oh, no! I did it myself when I turned the door latch sneaking out. I wasn't opening it, I was locking it!

Suddenly I'm so panicked that I have to sit down just to catch my breath. It's horrendous. I can't believe that I'm actually stuck out here and there's no way I can open that door.

Then it hits me. The windows!

I jump up and run around to the kitchen window, which I know was open all day long. I'm right, it's still open, except that I can't get to the stupid thing because the goddamn screen is on and the only way to get past the screen is to take the whole thing off and there are some dumb things holding it from the inside. It's hopeless. I'm finished. It's all over.

The almost summer of Victoria Martin.

Fired after three brilliant days.

And shamed.

The whole thing is so grotesquely embarrassing. And then, on top of everything else, my parents will have to know. How could I do such a dumb thing? And then be jerky enough to get caught.

I'm crying. Well, naturally, what else am I going to do?

All I figure I've got are two choices and they both stink. First one is I can stay here until the morning. But that's no good because it's going to be a mess when DeeDee comes in to wake me up and I'm not there. Besides, then they'll think I stayed out all night long, which is worse than waking Cynthia up now—and what difference does it really make? Either way I've had it. So I take choice Number Two. I ring the bell.

Do you know what it's like to ring a doorbell at two in the morning when the whole world is sleeping? It sounds like a nine-alarm fire.

I make a quick try at coming up with a plausible story but nothing sounds even half good so I decide to tell the truth, if she's even interested by then.

I can see the lights going on in Cynthia's bedroom, then the hall light, and then she's at the door. This is so awful.

"Victoria!" she says, opening the door. And boy, is she stunned and confused. "Victoria! What are you doing out here?"

"I don't have a key," I say, postponing the inevitable.

"The door isn't locked."

"Yeah, it is." Wouldn't it be nice if she just forgot everything else and we stood around and talked about the locked door.

"But we never lock the"—she didn't forget—"door. What are you doing out here anyway?"

"Well, it's sort of a long story."

"Why don't you just come in here and start telling me?" And there's a whole big change in her tone. Not good, either.

We get into the living room and I pick the worst chair in the room and sit at the edge of it. She sits opposite me. If only there really was something easy like a nine-alarm fire.

"Okay, Victoria, let's have it from the beginning. What are you doing out at two thirty in the morning?"

"I don't think it's two thirty yet."

"All right," she says, looking at her watch, "out at two twenty-five in the morning, when you're supposed to be home in bed? I mean, what *is* going on here?" By now she's really rolling and nothing's going to stop her. "You know you have a one o'clock curfew, and what's even worse, you just take off in the middle of the night without a word to anyone. I can't believe you'd do such a thing! It's so dishonest. Victoria, what's got into you?"

"I'm sorry," I say, because I really am.

"Where were you?"

"Out."

"Out where? With whom? What's going on? Don't make me pull it out of you. For goodness' sake, I think I deserve a proper explanation. After all, I am responsible for you while you're living in my house."

I start to answer but she goes right on. "What if I weren't home? Would you have just sneaked out and left my children alone? How can I believe that you wouldn't? After this, how can I believe anything you say or do?"

"I'm really sorry," I say, "and I would never, ever, go out and leave the kids alone. I made sure you were in bed way before I even thought of going. I was only out an hour and a half."

"Where were you?"

I try to answer her, but the minute I open my mouth I start to cry.

"All right, Victoria, calm down and tell me everything. I'm

not a monster. If it's possible to understand, I will. Now please start from the beginning."

"Well . . . it's this boy," I begin, and it's really rough. "I know him from the city and I like him . . . a lot. Actually, I think I love him . . . except naturally he doesn't know it because we only just met. I guess it's all pretty dumb, isn't it?"

"Not really," Cynthia says, and it's crazy, but I think she might understand. "Go on, Victoria, let's hear the whole thing."

"There's another complication," I tell her. "He already has a girlfriend, but she's really awful except she's very pretty. I personally don't see it but almost everyone else seems to think she's absolutely beautiful. Anyway, he can't be all that nuts about her because he's definitely interested in me. That's why I *had* to go out tonight. I've been working up to this since before school ended, and finally, today, he asked me out. Sort of."

"What do you mean 'sort of'?"

"Well, it wasn't exactly a formal date. It was more like asking me casually if I was going to be at The Monkey tonight. But I could tell that he was really saying that he wanted me to come, so I *had* to be there. It was my big chance."

"And I said you couldn't go."

"But you didn't know how important it was."

"Then why didn't you tell me?"

"I didn't feel right asking you to change all your plans just for me, and besides, I guess I was kind of embarrassed about asking. Then I fell asleep and when I woke up you were asleep and I felt funny about waking you, and besides, I didn't expect to stay out that long. And there were some other things I didn't expect to do either."

She looks a little alarmed, so I reassure her that I didn't mean that I had sex with him.

"Absolutely not," I say. "I just got sort of carried away. But I didn't think I would because—well, I never did before. But that's the way it's been with Jim. All the things I plan and figure out for myself fall apart the minute he comes into the picture. I can't understand why that happens."

"I don't think I can tell you why, but I can swear it happens and not just to you," she says.

"You too?" I can't picture Cynthia being out of control.

Cynthia stops for a moment and looks hard at me as if she's deciding whether she can trust me. "Yes," she finally says, "with Jed. All the time, but it's over now."

"I'm sorry," I say.

She shrugs and throws out her hands like, *What are you going to do?* "I guess it was the hardest time of my life," she says. "I let it happen. I let myself be the victim, sitting around in misery and tears waiting for the next blow. And they came. One woman after another. Finally one day I started to get angry and then I got furious, and I realized, my God, I'm finally alive. I threw him out, and even though it was like tearing something out of my body I survived it. And I'm okay now. I'm still angry, but I'm not bitter. Bitter is just more self-pity and that's not for me anymore."

See how you don't know about people? I always thought of Cynthia as sort of nice but she's definitely a lot more. She's sensitive and understanding and a whole different person to me now, and I like her much more and I even respect her. I feel like we're friends, really and truly friends.

"Even though your situation with Jim is different," she tells me, "in one way it's the same: You're being the victim. Don't let it happen."

I say I'm not going to, but I'm not really sure because I don't feel angry or anything like what she feels about Jed. All I feel is in love with Jim. And I want very much to stay out here, and if only she'll forgive me I wouldn't care how much work I had to do or anything.

"All I can do is advise you about your love life," she says, "but when it comes to your job, that's a different story. There I can lay down the law. You did a lousy thing tonight, and the only way I would even consider allowing you to stay on is if I have your solemn word that this kind of thing will never happen again."

"Oh, it won't! I swear!" More tears. I can't help it, I'm a very emotional person. Besides, these are sort of happy tears. I think I'm out from under.

"Well, I hope I'm not making a mistake. . . ."

"You're not. I promise!"

"Okay, then. We'll forget the whole thing."

"Thank you, Cynthia. I really appreciate—"

"I don't know how much you're going to appreciate it when

DeeDee starts pulling at you at seven in the morning. You know it's after three. We better get to bed."

"Thanks, Cynthia . . . a lot." And she turns out the light and we both go to bed.

She's really a terrific person. I don't know how fast I'd be to forgive someone who did such a sneaky thing to me. She's sensational and so understanding.

On the other hand, I hear it's pretty hard to replace a mother's helper after the season starts. And DeeDee does get up kind of early.

I shoot upstairs. Reprieved!

Boy, this room will be so terrific in August! I know I keep saying that, but I know everyone will be so jealous when we start to get those cold nights. Right now, of course, it's stifling.

I throw off my clothes and plop down on the bed. What a night! I wish Steffi were here so I could talk to her about it. Except maybe I wouldn't talk about everything. Now that it's over, I'm beginning to feel a little funny, sort of embarrassed and—I don't know—maybe I shouldn't have let him go so far on the first date. Except Cynthia didn't seem all that surprised. Oh, God, it really was the first date and I let him put his hand under my clothes. Oh, I'm beginning to feel awful. Why did I do that? It was all right to do some necking, but that was really heavy petting, and now he probably thinks he can make out with me anytime he wants. I wish I didn't let him put his hand under my clothes. I don't know why I let him. I never let anyone before. Oh, it's so embarrassing. How am I going to ever face him again? He must think I'm really easy. Steffi would too, if I told her. But I'm not going to. I'm not going to tell anyone else. But what if *he* does? Suppose he tells Barry?

Maybe he went back to The Monkey and maybe he's telling his friends now and they're all laughing and talking about me the way they do about Sheila McCauley, who's known for being . . . friendly with the boys. I'd die if they talked about me like that. I'd never go back to school or anything, ever again.

Jim wouldn't do that. He's not that kind of guy. I know it, I think. I hope. Boy, that would really be low.

Even though I don't think he would be that low, still it takes me forever to fall asleep because I can't keep my mind from thinking what if he was a bigmouth, and then I keep tracing it down to how it even got back to my family. I'm an expert at self-torture. The last thing I remember is dawn.

Thirteen

It doesn't make any difference to DeeDee that it's Sunday. She's in there pulling on me before seven, same as usual. No fighting it, so I struggle up. I must be getting used to the room because this is the first morning I don't bump my head on the ceiling when I sit up. I bump my knee.

Among the piles of dirty dishes there's a note from Cynthia saying we should not wake her up because she's exhausted from all the nighttime activity, but she'd love it if I could just straighten the living room a tiny bit. She always leaves the cutest notes, like this one starts off, "Help! Help!"

I give DeeDee her usual breakfast, which she wastes half of as usual. No matter how little I give her she leaves more than half. While she's eating, I start to clean up the living room. It looks like the party Cynthia had the night before was great from the horrendous mess they left. In the middle of cleaning up, David comes down and I give him his peanut butter sandwich and go back to work. The kids watch TV for the next couple of hours until I finish everything. I want to do it right because I'm really sensitive about what Cynthia might think of me, especially after last night.

After breakfast I start to get the kids into their bathing suits when the phone rings. Don't let it be Mr. Landry, please.

It isn't. It's my mom. We have a sort of strange conversation. At least from my end it's a little weird. Naturally she wants to know all about my job, and if she called yesterday I would have given her an earful. I had planned to do some fancy moaning about all the work Cynthia dumps on me, but after last night's horrendous fiasco I play it very cool.

"Cynthia's terrific, really, Mom," I say. "I'm crazy about her kids, too. It's the best summer job I ever had." That's a little overboard, seeing this is my first summer job. "I love it out here. Everything is absolutely perfect, really super. Boy, it's just great. I tell you this is fantastic, sensational—"

"Victoria?"

"Yeah, Mom?"

"What's wrong?"

"I must be getting my period," I say, thinking faster than I ever thought in my whole life.

"Are you sure that's all it is?"

"Well . . ."

"Well, what?"

135

"Well, I didn't think it was going to be so hard," and even though I said I wasn't going to let it happen, everything starts running out of my mouth—all the things that Cynthia makes me do. (If you can't complain to your mother who can you complain to?) I go on and on about the laundry and the dishes and the cleaning and everything, and I can tell my mother is absolutely on my side. In fact, she's so much on my side that she's beginning to hate Cynthia and in two seconds she's going to tell me to quit and come home. Well, I certainly don't want that, so I do a fast double about-face and go right into how, of course, Cynthia is right there working along beside me, she and the kids, and by the time I finish I make it sound as though all I do is sit around polishing my nails while everyone waits on me.

"It sounds terrible," my mother says, not one bit fooled. "But if you're so anxious to stay, try it for another week. And don't be shy, Victoria. If you think she's being unfair, tell her."

My mother makes it sound so easy, but it isn't like that when you're a kid *and* an employee. I tell her I'll talk to Cynthia, but I know I'll never have the guts.

Then my mom tries to make me feel better by telling me how lucky Cynthia is and she bets that I'm doing a terrific job.

And I do feel better because except for mistakes like last night I really am doing a pretty terrific job, and even though it's hard, it makes me feel kind of proud. If only I could handle the other part of my life the way I clean the house, I'd be in business.

"I love you, Mom," I tell her.

"Love you too, sugar. Now what's up for this afternoon? Are you going to the beach or does she have you scrubbbing the walls?"

I laugh and tell her that we were just getting into our suits.

"Have you been swimming yet?"

"Are you kidding? David is a water demon. We go in four, five times a day."

"Don't forget to take those vitamin pills Daddy gave you, and watch out for the sun, and . . ."

And she's off and rolling again. The rest of the conversation is filled with warnings to watch out for this and that and news of everyone back home. (What big things have happened in four days?) Plus not to forget that it's really very important to Daddy about me staying alone overnight. Did I talk to Cynthia about that? I lie and say it's all settled. I promise myself to bring it up in the next couple of days for sure. Then she says how I should make sure to write a nice long letter to Nina.

Sure thing. "Dear toad, . . ."

After I hang up from talking with my mother, I take the kids down to the beach. Funny, I really wasn't homesick until that telephone call, but just talking to my mother suddenly makes me feel very alone. Maybe it's because even though mostly it bugs me to pieces, still it's kind of nice having someone worrying and caring so much about you. Isn't it ridiculous?

I miss my mommy. Oh, God, I sound just like DeeDee. The thought tickles me enough to make me feel better.

By the time I get down to the beach Dana and Anita are already there, and of course they're dying to know what happened to me at The Monkey last night. Naturally I don't tell them anything much. I pretend that Jim and I danced and then went out to the end of the pier to talk. They both think Jim is something else and want to know all about him and when am I going to see him again. That's a little tough to answer, but I tell them probably tomorrow. That's Monday, my day off.

"Where's he taking you?" Dana wants to know.

"Well, we're not sure yet," I tell them, "but we might have a picnic dinner and then hit The Monkey later." That's not really a lie because if we do go out together tomorrow he'd probably love to do that.

We chat for an hour or so while the kids play around, and then it's time to go home for lunch.

There's a beautiful four-hundred-page thank-you note waiting for me on the kitchen table. Four hundred pages of explicit instructions. First, though, she says I did an A-job and she's going to love me forever for saving her from waking up to such a huge mess and that she's off to the Hendersons' for a brunch party and not to wait for her for lunch. Then she says a couple of things about what to feed the kids and would I please get a few things started for dinner. She tells me exactly how to clean the chicken and prepare it for the oven and how to do the vegetables and clean the shrimp and make the salad (she must be having company) and everything. She must have taken twenty minutes just to write the note.

DeeDee goes in for a nap and David eats his lunch watching TV. It looks like rain. Just as well because dinner is going to take me a while to get ready and at least the kids won't be hassling me to go to the beach.

The phone rings. I leap for it because it has to be Jim. It isn't. But lucky for me, at least it isn't Mr. Landry again. It's Barry.

"I looked for you last night at The Monkey," I say. I want to find out if he was there and if he saw Jim.

"We had company last night," he says. "My cousins from Connecticut came, so I had to hang around. Were you there?"

Obviously he didn't speak to Jim yet so he doesn't know, or maybe he did speak to Jim and Jim didn't say anything because of the way Barry feels about me. "For a while," I tell him.

"How'd you like it?"

"It's okay." I'm not feeling as cool as I sound.

"Hey, listen, if you're off tomorrow, do you want to come over for some tennis?"

"In the afternoon?" Jim works till five so I might as well.

"Around two," Barry says.

"Sure, that'd be great."

"Yeah?" Like he's really surprised. I guess he still likes me. Poor Dana.

"Sure," I say, and he tells me where his house is and how to get there.

I tell him I have to run to close the windows because now the rain is really coming down. Too late. The whole side of my bed is soaking wet. I don't know how so much rain came in that tiny window. I change the sheets and hang the blanket up to dry and come back downstairs to finish cleaning the shrimp. Gross. There must be fifty of them. It'll take me forever.

The phone rings again and I almost tell David to pick it up because my hands are gloppy from the shrimp, but then I remember Mr. Landry and dry them off and answer it myself.

"Hello?" I say.

"You the mother's helper?" It's a man's voice. I know exactly who it is and my stomach sinks.

"Yes, it's me, Victoria."

"Right. Listen, Victoria, how are my grandchildren?"

"Fine, just fine."

David strolls in to see who I'm talking to. "Who's that?" he wants to know.

"Nobody," I tell him. "It's for me."

"That David you're talking to?" Mr. Landry asks, and I'm not about to lie so I say yes, it's David.

"Please let me talk to him." And I can't really say no. After all, I let him talk to DeeDee, and besides, I already decided that I'm not going to do what someone says if I think they're absolutely wrong. Of course, now I have to think of a story for David so that he doesn't tell his mother. She'd really be furious if she ever found out. But I have to take that risk because the

140

kids have to be able to talk to their grandfather, especially if they love him the way David and DeeDee love theirs. I don't usually make big important decisions like this, I mean with adults involved, so it's kind of scary.

"David," I say, "I was wrong. It's for you."

"For me?" He jumps up and runs over to the phone. "Hello? Grandpa!" Then to me, all excited, "It's my Grandpa." See, they really do love him a whole lot.

". . . Yeah, I'm okay. When are you coming out? . . . How come not for so long? . . . But you said you were going to take us fishing. . . . But you said . . . I don't want to go fishing with Victoria. I want to go fishing with you. . . ." And he looks like he's going to cry. "Please, Grandpa, I miss you. . . ."

Oh, I feel awful.

"Can I come see you? . . . How come? . . . Mommy could take me. She's going into the city Tuesday and then she could take me to your house . . . I don't know, she has an appointment, I guess . . . she said she has to make an early train . . ." Then he turns to me. "What time is Mommy coming home Tuesday night?"

"I don't know," I tell him. "Late, I think. Why?"

"Victoria says late, Grandpa . . . You will? . . . Oh boy, terrific." And he starts jumping up and down. "Victoria! My Grandpa's gonna see me on Tuesday!"

Oh, no! "Give me the phone for a minute, David," I say. "I want to say something." And I practically grab the phone out of his hand.

"Mr. Landry? Don't hang up, I have to talk to you." And then I turn to David and say to him, "I forgot to tell you but Steven from across the street was here before and he wants you to come over."

"Tell my grandpa to come out early," he says.

"I will. You better get over to Steven's because he wanted to show you something."

"What is it?" he asks.

"He didn't say what it was but he said he would let you hold it." God, I hate to lie. Still, it was good enough to make him shoot right out the door.

"Mr. Landry, Cynthia's going to be very angry that I even let you talk to the kids, but when she finds out that you're coming out she won't go to the city at all and then she's going to be furious with me."

"We won't tell her."

"I can't do that. That would be really dishonest and I don't think that's fair."

"All right," he says, "I won't come." I'm surprised that I convinced him so easily, but he must be a really nice person if the kids love him so much, and they do.

"Thanks a lot, Mr. Landry. I'm really sorry that it has to be like this. If you hold on one sec I'll get David and you can tell him yourself," and I race across the street toward Steven's house and practically run smack into David on his way home.

"Nobody's home," he tells me.

"Come on, quick, your grandpa's still on the phone and he wants to say something to you."

And we both run into the house and David picks up the phone and says, "Hello," and then he holds the receiver out to me and says, "There's no one there."

And I take it and, sure enough, there's a dial tone. We must have got disconnected, or else that nice old man purposely hung up so he would stick me with having to explain why he can't come Tuesday.

"We must have got cut off," I say. "But he wanted me to give you the message that he's afraid he can't make it for Tuesday."

"How come?" And David's really disappointed.

"He has to go to the doctor."

Now he's worried. "Is Grandpa sick or something?"

"Oh no, he's absolutely fine, but he has to take his friend who's very, very sick."

"Mr. Whiteman?"

"Uh-uh," I say with a shake of my head. "This is a friend you don't know. But your grandfather said he knew that you would understand and not to say anything about his call to your mother because he wants to surprise her when he comes out."

Boy, he's really crushed, and he keeps asking me things like maybe he can go into the city and then he can go to the doctor with his grandfather or maybe his grandpa can come out after he takes his friend to the doctor, and then a million questions about how come he can't come out on Wednesday and then Thursday, and the kid is really and truly disappointed. I feel like a rat, and on top of all that, Steven wasn't home and now he wants to know what Steven had for him to hold.

"I think it was his new book on Vitamins and Children's Growth."

"That stinks. I don't even want to see that dumb book. He's a jerk."

"I told him you wouldn't care." But he doesn't even listen because he's back into the TV.

I go back to the shrimp, which look like they had a few baby shrimp while I was gone. It takes me another hour and a half to finish cleaning and deveining the shrimp and I'm halfway into chop ping the onions and crying my eyes out when Cynthia comes in. DeeDee hears her and comes downstairs. I go into the living room, and while Cynthia's talking to DeeDee I give David a little poke and remind him not to say anything about his grandfather's call because of the surprise.

Cynthia comes into the kitchen and makes a big fuss about how great I cleaned the shrimp and how I'm the best shrimp cleaner in the country, and I told you, she really is appreciative about things. So would I be if somebody cleaned a truckload of shrimp for me. As soon as I finish the onions, she says, leave the rest to her (except that it's all done) and would I please take the wagon down to the grocery store and pick up some beer and soda.

"David! DeeDee! Go help Victoria with the soda," she calls to them just as I'm about to slip out of the house. I don't know why she thinks they're such a help. I wish I could tell her it's easier to get it without them.

No luck. Naturally they jump in the wagon like always. It's not bad going there but coming back with the kids and the soda it's horrendous. I have to figure out a way to get them to walk sometimes.

The phone rings just when we get back, and I dump my packages down and grab it. It's got to be Jim.

"Hello? . . . Is Victoria there?" It's him.

"Hi," I say, "it's me."

"Yeah, well, I'm working now so I have to make this fast. Something's come up so I won't be able to see you for a few days, but I'll call you sometime around the end of the week. Okay?"

"Sure." I'm disappointed but he *did* call even if it was to say he couldn't see me. That's a whole lot better than not calling at all. I told you he's a very considerate person.

"Well, see you around," he says.

"Okay, see you." And we both hang up.

It's not so bad anyway, because I probably wouldn't be able to get out tonight so it's just as well. He called. That's really what counts.

The company turns out to be two other women and one guy and the food is delicious. The kids and I eat first in the kitchen and then after I put them to bed I come down and do

145

the dishes for us and for the company. It's only seven people but it feels like a million dishes because they don't have a dish-washer.

Cynthia offers to help, but she's a little tipsy from the drinks so I just tell her, don't worry, I can handle it myself. She looks a little surprised, then says, "You're a doll," and goes back to some crazy game they are playing, a kind of porno-charades that they think is the funniest thing since the belly button.

I think maybe after the dishes Cynthia is going to suggest that I can go out for a walk, but she says she's probably going out, so I get into bed with a book and before I know it my eyes are starting to close. Tomorrow's my day off and I'm going to sleep till twelve. At least. Hooray!

Fourteen

"No, DeeDee, it's my day off," I tell her when she starts climbing in my bed, but a lot of good that does. She says she's not hungry, she just wants to sleep with me. I can't throw her off the bed so I move over and she squeezes in, and that's not easy because it's a very narrow bed and I'm always hanging off. I try to get back to sleep but she keeps jumping around and telling me how she'll be very quiet and how she's going to sleep and all that, so finally I get up.

"Now let's eat," she says, and as long as I'm up I might as well give her breakfast.

David comes down the usual time, and I remind him not to say anything to DeeDee about the phone call because she's too young to keep a secret. He likes that. I thought he would. Actually, she's terrific about her own secret grandpa thing.

And I know she didn't forget because all she wants to do all day is go get the mail.

Cynthia's still sleeping and the kids want to go to the beach and so I figure I might as well take them. I guess you can call it the high cost of sneaking out.

The usual group is at the beach and they're surprised to see me.

"Hey," Dana says, "I thought you have Mondays off."

"I do," I tell her. "But I wasn't doing anything this morning so I figured I might as well bring the kids to the beach."

Dana and Anita say I really shouldn't do that because I could screw it up for everybody, but I tell them that Cynthia is really very nice to me and so it's no big deal to me, and besides, it's not as though she asked me.

Anita wants to know what Cynthia does that's so great, and I tell them I can't think of anything specific right this minute but she's a very appreciative person, and I'm about to tell them about the notes, how cute they are, but then I think maybe they won't see them that way so I just say, "I don't know . . . things."

We chat about this and that, but I don't mention going to Barry's house today because I know Dana sort of likes him. Funny, I'm not even very excited about going. It's practically that I feel I have to. Still, it did kind of bug me a little that day he was paying so much attention to Dana. You know, the day he and Jim were surfing. Maybe I just don't like to lose any of my admirers.

I get back with the kids at about eleven thirty and Cynthia had to go pick up her shoes (her note says) and she'll be back in a second.

She must have got held up, so while I'm waiting, I give the kids lunch and do her morning dishes. She doesn't get back until almost two because that dumb guy at the shoe store didn't finish fixing her shoes and she had to wait all this time while he did them because he closes in the afternoon and she needed them for work tomorrow. I can see she was really aggravated to hold me up like that but I tell her it's all right. I was only going to play tennis and he'll wait.

I love the tennis clothes almost more than actually playing. I have this terry cloth skirt that's really cute. I just wish my knees weren't so bony and stick-outy. I should wash my hair, but I don't feel like it, and besides, it's only Barry.

His house is beautiful. He must be really rich because it's like one of those houses you see in magazines and it's right on the water with a beach in the back and a tennis court in the front. Barry is rallying with some kid, a girl about Nina's age. He stops as soon as he sees me and comes over to the gate door.

"Hi," he says.

"Hi." I smile. "Hey, don't let me stop your game. Go on, I'll sit here and watch for a while." And I throw my stuff down on a wooden bench.

"That's okay, we were just killing time. You want to hit some balls?" He completely ignores the girl.

"What about her?"

"That's nobody," he says, almost surprised that I mentioned her. "That's just my sister." And then he shouts to her that we're going to use the court—just like that. She shrugs and starts to walk over toward us.

"Can I have winners?" she asks.

"Hey, Kathy," Barry says impatiently, "don't bug me. I told you I was going to use the court all afternoon."

"Can I watch?"

"Oh, for God's sake! Do you have to?"

"I won't say anything. I'm just gonna sit here and watch."

"Let her watch," I say, "I don't mind." Amazing how easy it is when it's not *your* sister.

"Yeah, wait till you see what a pain in the neck she is!" He says it like she's not even there.

"Is it okay if I move your stuff?" Kathy asks me. She's tough like Nina. You can insult Nina and say anything you want right in front of her, and nothing, she never even gets embarrassed.

"Beat it, Kathy," he tells her.

"It's a free country. I can stand where I want." And she puts her hands on her hips and just stands there. I think this kid must be taking lessons from Nina. Now he's the one who's getting embarrassed.

"Hey, Barry, it's okay with me, really." I jump in, trying to save the situation. "Let her watch."

"See, even she doesn't care, big shot," Kathy says, and she really is a pain. I think I'll have no trouble creaming Barry, he's so thrown, but he blitzes me anyway. He's a fabulous player. We rally a few times and you can see he's trying to hit balls that I can return, which is very nice of him, and he's so good that they come in straight and I'm hitting them with no trouble at all, or hardly any. We don't even see when Kathy gets bored and leaves.

After a while we both start clowning around, imitating ballet dancers and ninety-year-old people playing tennis. Then Barry does a zoo thing where he's a monkey and a chicken, and I know it sounds like the dumbest thing but it's absolutely hysterical. I laugh so hard I keep collapsing on the ground. Finally I have to run off the court because if I don't I swear I'm going to wet my pants—I mean, he is so wild. I think he could be a comedian.

"How about a swim?" he says, coming over to where I've thrown myself down on the grass trying to catch my breath.

"Yes, help," I gasp and we both head for the pool.

It's terrific being with Barry when he doesn't push all that heavy stuff on me. In fact, I laugh more with him than with Steffi even, and she and I spend half the time being hysterical about something or someone. It's as though Barry is an old friend—I mean that's how comfortable I feel with him. I love to have boys for friends, but it's always hard because mostly they don't want to be just friends. Too bad.

The inside of his house is even better than the outside. It's all bright green and white, and it looks clean and crisp. I love it. I change into my bikini and head for the pool. It's in the back of the house on a wooden deck facing the ocean. The water is bright aqua and so delicious-looking. I dive right in.

You know how in all the ads the girls look so fabulous after they come out of the water even with dripping hair? Not me. I look like real people do when they're wet, only worse.

Kathy comes out with a friend and we all play some dumb kid games in the pool and have a great time, chasing each other and diving in and all that. At one point I'm "it," and I'm tearing around the pool chasing Patty, Kathy's friend, and she's screaming, and I'm just about to grab her when out of the corner of my eye I see a figure. A girl's figure. A great girl's figure and long blond hair, and I stop midair.

"I win! I win!" Patty shouts, and I know without looking that I lose and it isn't the game.

"Hi, everybody," says Gloria, and my heart actually stops for a second and then starts pounding so hard I can hardly hear myself think.

I turn around and look and there she is, looking perfect. Her blond hair catching the sun makes her look like one of those religious pictures where there's a halo of light around the angel's head. Even if I'm going a little too far, still she looks fabulous. Her bikini is a light blue velour that probably matches her vacant eyes.

And right behind her is Jim. What a blow. So that's the special something that came up. It's not that I thought we were going steady or anything like that, but . . . I don't know, I guess I just didn't expect to see Gloria out here. I can hardly bring my eyes up to his face, I feel so embarrassed. He should be just as embarrassed as me except when I do look at him he isn't at all, but he does look surprised to see me.

By now my face is so burning red that all I can do to save myself is jump into the pool. I dive and I'm in such shock that I do a horrendous bellyflop. Why do I always look bad when it's so important to look good? Anyway, I keep swimming around, stalling for time. I hear Barry calling my name, but I pretend I don't. What if I just stayed here . . . forever? After a while I'd be a curiosity and people would come over to Barry's just to see the girl in the pool. I'd get my name in the *Guinness Book of Records*.

"Victoria!" It's Barry calling me. I'm floating with my eyes closed, but he knows I can hear him, so I turn around and swim toward his side.

"I'm going to put up a barbecue," Barry says. "Can you stay?"

This whole thing is bad news and I know I should get out fast but I can't. I want to be with Jim, even if Gloria is here too.

"Sure," I tell Barry. "I'd love to." And I pull myself out of the water. "It's great," I say to Gloria in my friendly, outgoing voice.

"It looks terrific but it kills my hair." She doesn't even sound bitchy like the last time I met her. "I have the same problem as you do," she goes on. "My hair looks horrible when it's wet." I was wrong.

"Anybody want a Coke?" Barry asks.

"Yeah, I'll take one," Jim says, and Barry goes in the house to get them. "How do you like it out here?" For a second I don't even realize Jim is talking to me. It's like he hasn't seen me since the first day at the pier. Like there was no night on the pier. I guess it's because of Gloria.

"I love it out here." I play along.

"How's Cynthia?" Gloria asks, and her voice actually is rather pleasant. I wonder why I hate it so much.

"She's terrific," I tell her. "Really super and I love the job."

"I'll just bet," she says, really snotty.

"Where are you staying out here?" I ask, and she practically laughs in my face.

"You have to be kidding. Where do you think I'm staying?" And she looks at Jim and nods toward me and shakes her head like I'm some kind of a moron. Jim doesn't say anything but he looks very uncomfortable. How am I supposed to know who she's staying with? But she obviously wants me to guess, so like a dope I say, "Relatives?" And she cracks up.

"I don't know. . . ." She's full of giggles, burying her head in Jim's chest. "Are you my relative?"

I don't believe it. She's just putting me on.

"Hi, cuz," she says cutesy-poo-like, poking Jim in the stomach with her little finger.

"Yeah . . . ," Jim says, blushing a little but still kind of enjoying it.

Unreal! She's not putting me on. She really *is* staying with him! All I can think of is that she's only a year older than me and she's practically living with someone. So what if it's only for a couple of days, that's still pretty wild for only a high school junior. That's all she is, you know, a junior. I'm stunned but I disguise it with a real cool face and a kind of *that's nice, so what else is new* look. I'm not about to give her the satisfaction of knowing that she's blowing my mind.

"Sor-ry, didn't mean to shock you," she says right into my hopeless see-through face. What I'd really like to do is let her know what her lover boy has been doing before she got here. But I can't because it's not so great for me either. I don't say anything but I give Jim a look like he's a real two-timer. And he reads me so perfectly he takes off. Right into the pool.

I figure since my hair looks horrible already, as Gloria so kindly reminded me, I have nothing more to lose, so I jump in after him. Anything is better than standing there listening to that.

I know that it's rotten for him to do that to Gloria, but I'm the one who feels lousy. After all, it's not so bad for her—she doesn't even know. How could he do that, pretend to be so interested in me when all along he knew he had this relationship with someone else?

I'm swimming around thinking all these angry thoughts and I don't even notice where I'm going so, sure enough, I swim right into his feet. It's always like that with me. I mean, it might be sort of romantic if I accidentally swam into his arms, but his feet? I'm hopeless. Anyway, we both come up out of

155

the water, and he sort of grabs me around the waist and says, "You okay?"

I picked up a mouthful of water that I don't feel like spitting out right in front of him so I just nod my head, okay.

He smiles at me. A private, warm hi-there-honey smile that makes my whole body woozy. Boy, he just knocks me out. I wish he didn't because I'm beginning to think maybe he's not so great. "Sorry for that," he says, nodding back toward Gloria.

Maybe he was trapped into having her out. I mean, maybe he promised a long time ago, before me anyway, and now he couldn't get out of it. It could happen that way, you know. I decide that that's exactly what did happen, and I smile.

Mistake. I still had a mouthful of water. Beautiful the way it comes running down from between my teeth and down my chin. But Jim's not turned off.

"Looking good," he says and starts to laugh. Nice like. *Very* nice. I sneak a look over my shoulder to see if Gloria is watching and she is. But so what? There's no law against talking, is there? Still, I cool it a little and start swimming around.

After a while we come out of the water and Gloria must sense something because she's really icy to me. Maybe she just plain doesn't like me. That's okay with me. I don't like her.

I head for the bathroom to make repairs on this gross hair and Gloria follows me. I don't actually turn around to see her, but you know how sometimes you can practically feel somebody behind you? Especially if it's someone you don't want to be there?

Barry's sister, Kathy, gives us directions to the bathroom and hands me a blow dryer. Hint, hint.

"Want me to help you with your hair?" Gloria asks me, and I try not to look stunned.

"Yeah, sure, if you don't mind."

"No problem," she says. And she plugs it in and starts doing my hair. I'm probably going to end up looking like I was plugged in but I'm lousy at saying no.

"What do you think of Jimmy?" she asks.

"Okay, I guess," I say.

"That's all? Boy, he'd be crushed to think there was somebody who didn't think he was gorgeous."

"Well, he *is* very good-looking."

"Nobody knows that better than he does."

"If you think he's so stuck on himself, how come you're always hanging out with him?"

"Well . . . ," she says. And for the first time her eyes don't look so vacant and she doesn't seem quite so sure of herself.

". . . I guess, maybe, I'm sort of stuck on him too." She waits for me to make a comment but I can't think of anything nice to say, so she goes on.

"A lot of girls are always throwing themselves at Jimmy." Now she snaps off the blower and looks straight at me. "And he's always nice to them but they don't really have a chance.

We've been going together for almost a year now and it's a pretty solid relationship."

I don't say anything because I don't want to hurt her, even if I'm not exactly crazy about her.

"It's tough to keep a good thing going when all sorts of girls are always getting in the way," she continues. "But he's only human, you know, so naturally he's going to respond . . . sort of. I don't really feel that threatened. Still, I could do without the interference. I suppose if he wasn't so gorgeous it wouldn't happen—but then if he wasn't so gorgeous maybe I wouldn't like him so much."

All I can think of is that no matter how blue those eyes are or how silky that hair is, I'm glad I'm not Gloria.

But I know what she means. Turns out that fancy hot-stuff Gloria is hooked even worse than me. Worse because she knows something funky's going on but she's so knocked out about him that she just sticks around and takes it. I don't think I could ever do that. Don't get me wrong, I don't think what Jim's doing is so great either—I mean, seeing another girl while he's supposed to be going steady. Still, it's probably hard for him to break away from Gloria because it's been so long now.

"One time," Gloria says, and she sounds sort of sad, "way in the beginning when we first started dating, we went to an opening of this off-Broadway play and some guy thought we were movie stars, which freaked us both out. When we told him we weren't, he said we should be and that we made a perfect couple—I mean, we looked so right together, what with the same color hair and all that. Maybe that's not so good. Maybe I'd be better off with someone a little more ordinary. Probably be a lot easier."

It's like she was talking to herself, so I just sit there quietly looking in the mirror.

"What do you think?" she asks me.

"I don't know. I guess you can't always help who you fall for."

"Save the Ann Landers bit," she says. "I meant your hair." Just when I was beginning to like her a little she goes back to the old Gloria bitch. "Well, do you like it or not?"

"Oh . . . it's very nice." I wish I was gutsier. It looks awful and I'm sure she did it on purpose. "That's okay," I say. "I'll finish up."

"Sure 'nuff," she says, and dumps the blower in my lap, still roaring and plenty hot, and disappears.

I finish up the best I can and go back outside.

Barry is fooling around, trying to light a fire, and everybody is telling him how to do it and naturally no one knows what they're saying. I just sort of melt in with the crowd. Jim gets us all beers and I sip on mine. I don't like beer—in fact, I really hate any kind of alcohol. It tastes awful. A couple of times on holiday dinners at home I've got a little giddy on wine but that's all. I guess I'll never be much on drinking unless they come up with something that tastes a whole lot better than Scotch. Ugh!

"I'm going to ride some waves," Jim announces after a while. "Anybody coming?"

Gloria takes it as a personal invitation and whines, "Ohhh . . . Jimmy, it's too cold. Brr . . ."

She's too much. It must be ninety.

"I'll pass on it," Barry tells Jim. "I want to get this fire under control."

Now Jim looks at me. And Gloria looks at me. And Barry looks at me. My mind is racing around in a quick think. I know exactly what I should do. A lot of help that is.

"Sounds good to me," I say, doing the exact opposite, and he says terrific, and before anyone can add another word we both turn and race off toward the beach. I don't care so much about Gloria but I feel a little bad for Barry. I know I didn't come here as his girlfriend, but still I wouldn't want him to think I'm trying to get a thing going with Jim right in front of him. After all, all I'm doing is going for a little swim. Oh, who am I kidding!

The water is sensational. It's rough and the undertow is strong but the waves are just perfect for riding. I think Jim is a little surprised at how good I am in the water, especially after someone like Gloria. Bearing that in mind, I show off a little and scare myself half to death a couple of times. I'm actually risking my life to impress Jim. I must be nuts or really crazy in love with him.

We have a super time and he shows me how to ride the waves with our arms around each other, and then he rides the waves with me sitting on his back like I'm on the surfboard. It feels like we're only out there twenty minutes or so, but from the looks of where the sun is it must be a lot longer. We're exhausted when we get out of the water and both of us collapse on the hot sand.

"You swim like a fish," he tells me. What he doesn't know is that I'm not all that good but I never worked so hard at anything in my entire life. It shows what you can do if you really knock yourself out trying. Funny, but in this relationship I seem to be surprising myself all the time.

"Maybe we should go back," I say presently. I start to get up but he pulls me down. "I think the food's probably ready by now," I add.

He starts to kiss me but I pull away and look around, especially back toward the house. Thank goodness nobody's in sight.

"I really think we should get back," I tell him. "Besides, somebody could be looking. Gloria or somebody."

"Sure," he says, "no big deal. Let's go back."

Then I think maybe he gave up a little too easily. I must be really freaking out. I don't know what I want anymore.

When we get back to the pool nobody's around, so we head toward the house. I get a sinking feeling that it's really late. I mean, we must have been fooling around out there for probably a couple of hours. It feels sevenish.

From the pool you have to go through an enclosed patio. Bad news. The clock says almost seven thirty. I can't believe we were out that long.

"Hey, Barry! Gloria?" Jim calls their names as we walk into the den. "Where is everybody?" Barry's sister is sprawled on the couch with her friend, watching TV.

"Oh boy, are you two in trouble," she says, the typical brat sister. I shouldn't have wasted my time being nice to her. I can tell she's even worse than Nina.

"Barry around?" Jim asks as though she hadn't said anything.

"Uh-uh." She's an expert. She's going to make him crawl for it.

"Where is he?" Jim finally asks.

"Out," she says, and doesn't even look away from the television.

"What about Gloria?" You can see he's really getting teed off.

Kathy shrugs.

"Now look," Jim says, snapping off the TV. "Talk! Where'd everybody go?"

"Barry's out at the ice-cream shop. He said he was going to work a couple of hours and Gloria said that she's going home and to tell you . . ." And she stops and smiles up at him.

"Tell me what?" he says, falling right into her trap. Even I can see it's going to be fatal.

"Turn the TV back on first," she says, still with that disgusting grin.

He turns it back on.

"She said to tell you . . ."

"Yeah?" he says.

"Drop dead!" And both she and her friend crack up and practically fall on the floor in hysterics. Best day they've had since the cat was run over.

Jim charges out of the door and I follow him. "Monsters," I tell him. "I know because my sister's just like that."

"I can't stand that kid," he says, and I can see he's aggravated and it's probably not about Kathy. Probably about Gloria. This whole thing is really a mess now. It's not exactly fair because mostly we were just swimming. Oh, who am I fooling. It was awful.

Then he surprises me and instead of going after Gloria he asks me if I want to go over to The Monkey for a while.

I don't know. It's so bad already I don't suppose it's going to be any worse if we go over and have a few dances. So I say yes.

The Monkey is one of those places that is always jammed.

It's not even eight o'clock and you can hardly squeeze in the door. I spot Anita and Dana and they see me and we wave. I'm glad they see I'm with Jim because I told them I would be anyway. At least one thing worked out.

Jim leads me to the dance floor and we start to Hustle. They have "Don't Leave Me This Way" on and it's one of my favorites. I know this whole thing's not exactly working the way I planned, but still, I'm not complaining. I am actually out on a date with Him. I've been waiting for this night since I first saw him last September. He's different than I thought he was but I still think he's outrageous and I really am crazy about him.

The next record is real slow: "You Make Me Feel Brand-New."

He holds me close and we barely move. My head is against his chest and he smells sort of salty and nice. I hope Anita and Dana see us. After all, he is horrendously handsome. Oh, God, everybody's going to just die when we get back to school this fall. Imagine me being Jim Freeman's girlfriend. I'll go to all the tennis matches and sit in those special seats right behind the team. That's where their girlfriends sit and everybody knows it and looks at you. And then we'll eat together in the lunchroom. Anybody on the varsity team always gets to sit in this side section of the lunchroom that's just reserved for them. It's not really reserved but that's just the way it works out. It will be so fantastic, and then maybe I can even get Steffi a date with one of his friends, and then if they like each other we can double-date. Oh, this year is going to be the greatest in all my life. I just know it.

I'm so into these gorgeous thoughts that I'm not even aware that Jim is holding me tight and whispering something into my hair. Then I lift my head and I bump his chin a tiny bit, which catches the tippy edge of his tongue and makes him pull back just a little. These things never happen in movies, do they?

They probably don't even happen in real life except to klutzes like me.

"Let's go sit on the pier," he whispers and starts to move me off the dance floor. But I stop him and tell him we only just got here and it'd be fun to dance a little longer.

"We'll come back later." Now he's sounding very insistent and I'm beginning to feel very confused. The first thing that comes to my mind I really don't like but there it is. Looks to me like he's in a mighty big hurry to get out there on the pier again, and I know it's not just to talk. That thought gives me a funny feeling. I'm not really sure what it is but I know it's not so good.

He smiles and gives me a sexy little wink and says, "Come on, I won't bite you." And it's very tempting, but something happens inside my head and I just don't move. He looks surprised and I guess I am too.

We're standing there in the middle of the dance floor and he's saying come on, and I'm saying I don't really want to right now, and this goes back and forth and finally he walks off the floor. I don't want to just stand there, so I follow him to the bar where everybody is standing three deep. I feel bad and very embarrassed, very depressed, like I could cry any minute. But I don't. I just stand there next to him and we both pretend we're watching the dancers.

He's still next to me so maybe it's not so bad. I turn to look at him, but he pretends he doesn't see me and just stares straight ahead.

Maybe he really does want to talk. Maybe I insulted him by not even just going with him to chat for a while. No wonder he's angry. It was really babyish of me to think that all he wants to do is make out with me. How are we ever going to have a relationship if I don't trust him? That's it.

"Listen, Jim," I say, "I'm really sorry I acted that way. If you want to go . . ." And right in the middle of my apology he takes off. He just walks away. I watch him and I can't believe my eyes. I run after him and grab his arm. "What's the matter?" I ask, my voice trembling. "Can't you even tell me what's wrong?"

He shakes my arm away and stares hard at me. "Come back in a year or two," he says. "You have a lot of growing up to do." And he turns away and goes up to another girl, a pretty blonde, and pretty soon they're dancing. My throat chokes up and tears fill my eyes. I'm in the middle of a crowded disco but now I don't see anything or anyone. I can't just stand here with tears running down my face. I've got to get out of here but I can't even see enough to find my way out. Naturally I don't have a tissue so I have to wipe my eyes with my sleeve so anybody watching me must know I'm crying. Who cares? As soon as I can see in front of me I push through the door. I hear Anita calling me but I don't even turn around. I just keep walking until I'm out of the door and down the stairs, and then I start running and I'm really crying.

I hate him! I hate him with all my heart. How could he do that to me! Finally I'm crying so hard I have to sit down on a bench on the side of the walkway, and I just sob like I haven't done since I was really little. I've never been so unhappy in all my life.

And there's something else. I've been a terrible person. I'm really surprised at myself. I'm not at all like I thought I was going to be. I would hate it if someone else acted the way I did—to Barry and even Gloria, I mean.

I can't believe how bad I feel.

I get back into the house and thank goodness everybody's sleeping, so I just go up to my room and get into bed and turn out the light. I wish I was home. I hate it here.

Fifteen

Tuesday morning is crazy busy because Cynthia has to make an eight o'clock ferry to be in the city for an eleven o'clock appointment. She overslept so we all end up flying around the house trying to help. The rushing pays off because she just barely makes the ferry. Actually, they hold it a couple of seconds for her. The kids are jumping up and down, shouting, "Wait! Wait!" while Cynthia races down the dock. One of the men gives her a hand and she leaps on. We stand there waving until she's far out of sight.

I hope she doesn't run into my parents. I told you we live in the same apartment house, and it could be embarrassing since I never spoke to Cynthia about the sleeping-out business. I'm going to but I'm just waiting for the right moment. She probably won't see them anyway because she said she was only stopping off there to pick up something and then going right on to her appointment.

In all the furious activity I didn't have any chance to think about yesterday. Ever since I got up this morning I've had a sort of heavy feeling, and now that everything's quieted down and I start thinking about how horrendous yesterday was, I almost feel sick. I practically wish I'd never come out here. Maybe I can't really make it on my own. All I know is that I keep doing things that make me feel terrible the next day. There must be something awful wrong with me if that keeps happening.

In all the rushing to get Cynthia on her way, the kids never did eat breakfast, so I fix the usual when we get home. They're just finishing when somebody knocks on the front door. We don't even have a bell and the door is always unlocked (almost always). That's one of the special things I like about Fire Island, you never even think about being scared. It's really open and very safe.

DeeDee jumps up from the table and runs to open the door. I hear a happy squeal and I can't figure out who's there, so I poke my head into the living room and get a big shock. It's an old man, with lots of white hair, dressed in a suit and tie. He has DeeDee in his arms and, right away, the first think I think is, Damn it, it's Mr. Landry, and I want to sit down and cry because everything is just so awful and now this.

"Is that Victoria?" Mr. Landry asks DeeDee, and she nods and says to me, "This is my grandpa," and gives him a big squeeze with all her might, and he laughs and gives her a big kiss on the cheek.

All this time David was upstairs changing into his bathing suit, but when he hears who's here he comes charging down the stairs two steps at a time and practically jumps into his grandfather's arms, which happen to be completely filled with DeeDee.

"Hold it! Hold it!" Mr. Landry says, and with a lot of laughing and hugging he struggles free. You can see he loves it.

"Grandpa! Victoria said you couldn't come," David cries. "She said you had to go to the doctor with your friend." David sounds like he's practically accusing me of something.

"Is that what she said?" Mr. Landry acts surprised. The rat. I can't believe he's going to stick me with a bum story. "I guess she just wanted to surprise you," he says. I know the kids love him but I don't think I'm so crazy about him.

"I didn't tell anyone about the phone call, Grandpa," says DeeDee, "and Victoria says I'm going to get the button."

"The button?" he asks.

Naturally he doesn't know anything about the special grandpa club button. Still, you'd think he'd play along. But all he says is, "Never heard of it." He's really beginning to bug me.

"Where's your mother?" he asks, looking around like he didn't know she was going to the city. The kids tell him where she went.

"Looks like I missed her," he says, "but I'll catch her when she comes home." Then to me, "When's she coming home?"

"Dinner time, I guess," I say.

"Shame," he says, "but I gotta leave around five. It's okay, though, I'll catch her the next time." Damn. He sneaks out here when he knows Cynthia's away, spends the day with the kids, and then disappears and sticks me with explaining to their mom.

The kids keep bugging him to eat something, and finally he says okay, he'll have some coffee. All the while he keeps asking what train Cynthia is making and trying to figure out what ferry she'd be making if she was going to get home for dinner. I think he's kind of nervous about being here.

After his coffee he plays with the kids and he's really terrific with them. He makes them laugh with some crazy imitations of a barnyard and what happens when Cornelius's cat gets into the chicken coop. And it really is funny. Even I laugh.

What isn't funny is how he jumps when Steven from across the street comes in. Then I realize that he's afraid about Cynthia. I don't know how come I didn't see it before, but he's so crazy about the kids that he takes a chance and comes all the way out here just because he has to see them and all the while he's really scared about meeting Cynthia. It takes a lot of guts to go somewhere where you're not wanted and you could even be thrown out. Cynthia would do that. She's that angry about her ex, Jed.

Anyway, it's terrible to see a grandfather have to sneak

around just to see his own grandchildren who love him. And it's not as though he's a bad man. At least I hope he isn't. I mean, think about it, suppose you get an old man who's a criminal. He's probably someone's grandfather. Anyway, anyone can see Mr. Landry isn't a criminal.

The big excitement is when he tells them that he's going to rent a little dinghy and they're all going fishing. They positively go bananas and it takes us ten minutes to calm them down. I get DeeDee into her bathing suit and they get their towels and life preservers and they're ready. Mr. Landry says he's going to buy some sandwiches and they'll have a picnic on the boat.

I figure that since he's on Social Security he probably doesn't have all that money, so I say, "Why don't I make the sandwiches here?" and for the first time he looks a little grateful. I suppose maybe he thinks I'm on Cynthia's side and he doesn't trust me too much. I'm not so crazy for him as a person, but as a grandfather he's terrific.

Mr. Landry doesn't want to change at the house so he stops into the pizza bar and puts on his fishing clothes and packs his regular clothes in a brown shopping bag. He ends up looking like one of those old New England fishermen. He's even got the hat with the flies stuck on it.

Anyway, I walk them down to the dock, where he rents a little sailing dinghy because all the fishing dinghies are already out. People go fishing really early. The boat's a perfect size for the three of them.

They go off, and I realize that the kids haven't argued once since their grandfather came. He must be magic because mostly they can't be together for two seconds without fighting. Just like Nina and me.

Nothing to do but go home. Just as I get to the house the phone is ringing. I make a run for it. Maybe it's Jim. Maybe he reconsidered. Even if I did act a little immature last night, still, that's the kind of thing people can talk over and straighten out. I grab the phone on the fifth ring. At least I don't have to worry that it's Mr. Landry.

"Hello," I say. Let it be Jim.

"Victoria? It's me, Anita."

"Hi, what's up?"

"That's what I was going to ask you. How come you weren't at the beach this morning?"

"Yeah, well . . . DeeDee had a sort of stomachache so we hung around here. She's okay now."

"Good, 'cause we were wondering if something was wrong. You left so fast last night. I mean, I called you but you just kept going." I know she's fishing for the story of what happened with Jim, but she's not going to get anything from me. She's okay, Dana is too, but they're not my good friends. I only just met them, so I don't expect them to stand up for me or anything like that. But I don't like the idea of them gossiping about me either.

"Gee, I'm sorry," I say, "I didn't hear you calling me. I had to rush because I forgot that I promised Cynthia I'd be home by nine thirty. There was something urgent she had to do and she needed my help."

"Well, we thought something was wrong because you left alone." She's dying for the real story but she's never going to hear it from me.

"Yeah, I know, Jim was really upset but I told him to stay and dance. I think I'm getting a little tired of him anyway."

"Yeah?"

"Sort of. . . . What's up, anyway?"

"Nothing much. I was just wondering if you're going to be free tonight."

"I don't know. Why?"

"Dear old Ron just called from the city and he's got some business thing so he's staying over, and lover boy is out of town so Eva is stuck home. I thought maybe I'd go down to The Monkey tonight. Wanna go?"

"I don't know yet. Cynthia's in town, too, and I don't know what time she's coming back."

"Sounds cozy."

"What do you mean?"

"You know, Ron and Cynthia both in town together."

"Yeah, sure." She's really beginning to bug me, so I tell her I have some things I have to do and that I'll call her later, and hang up.

Well, I have a whole day to sit around and be miserable about yesterday. I probably sound like it's not so bad, but really it's horrendous. I can't see how I can face any of those people again in my whole life. It's even terrible what I did to Gloria. She never did anything to me except be Jim's girlfriend, which isn't something you can exactly blame her for. And Barry. How can I be so awful to hurt him again after what I did the first time! And Jim? He's not a whole lot better than I am. We make a great pair except that I don't really think we're ever going to be a pair again. I think he's going to go right back to Gloria, and I bet she'd take him back. When it comes to Jim, she's really got it as bad as me.

I sound like I have it all figured out, but I absolutely don't except for maybe one thing. I think I'm still so hooked on Jim that I would do almost anything to get him back, and if it means trying to act more mature, I guess I would do that too. That's all I've been thinking about since last night.

I actually sit on my bed most of the afternoon and even cry because I feel so unhappy. I probably should have gone to camp like I did last year and then I wouldn't have all this trouble. In camp you can be a little kid again. They do all the thinking for you. I'm beginning to think this being on your own, like now, is for the birds. Not really, but it is tough to be able to do practically anything you want. There's just too many ways to make mistakes.

I would call my parents but I couldn't tell any of this to my mother. She'd probably be shocked and maybe she'd tell my father and then I'd really die. I could send a letter to Steffi, but she's away with her father on a camping trip, and anyway, I don't think I want to put everything down in a letter. It'd be too depressing. I didn't commit a crime or anything like that, but you know what? I feel like I'm in one of those old movies where this rat of a girl, the trampy siren, steals the heroine's boyfriend (not that I see Gloria exactly as a heroine) and the rat steps all over everyone and you really hate her and that's just what I feel like.

I can hardly believe that's me because I always see *myself* as the heroine. In my fantasies the Glorias are bad and I'm terrific. In my dreams *I'm* the one who gets the boy because I'm so wonderful and good. But this time I got him because I'm really bad. Except maybe I didn't exactly get him anyway. I'm confused.

I don't even feel like lunch, and when the phone rings I practically jump out of my skin. It's got to be Jim. I pick it up and say a really little "Hello."

"Victoria? It's Cynthia."

Uh-oh.

"Everything okay? The kids okay?"

"Everything's great. Were you on time for your appointment?" Oh, God, I hope she doesn't ask to talk to the kids.

"Right on time," she says. "Thanks for your help."

"I almost died when the boat started to move out." Maybe I can keep her mind off them.

"Me too, but I made it. Listen, honey, I've run into a little problem and I need your help."

My help. First thing I think of is more shrimp. "Sure," I say. What can you say when someone asks for your help.

"I may have to spend the night in the city because there's a late appointment I should keep."

Oh, no! I'm torn. I promised my parents that I wouldn't stay alone overnight with the kids, but it would work out so great if she didn't come home tonight. Mr. Landry could spend the day with David and DeeDee and then he could go home and I could invent some Big Secret Day or something and they'd keep quiet about their grandpa and then maybe that would be the end of it. I mean, he would have seen the kids and that would keep them happy for a while, and then there wouldn't have to be any horrendous scenes when Cynthia came home. Maybe Cynthia could straighten things out with Jed and nobody would have to know what happened until everything was okay again. And anyway, it would only be this one time that she would sleep out, and my folks wouldn't ever have to know. I know it's the wrong way to do things, but I'd go nuts if I had to face any more problems right now.

"It's okay with me, Cynthia," I tell her. "Don't worry, I can handle things here."

She gave me a few instructions—who to call if I need any help and how to lock the front door. I can tell she's absolutely delighted about the arrangements and is so hot to get off the phone that she doesn't even ask anything else about the kids. Except by now I've got it together and I could tell her how David and DeeDee are across at Steven's. It's awful how if you lie once it seems you have to keep on lying. You always have to cover it with another one. I'm never going to get myself in a hole like this again. Boy, will I be glad when this day is over.

I wonder if Anita is right. About Ron and Cynthia having an affair, I mean. It fits right in with the rest of this mess.

I get back to thinking about last night and make myself even more miserable about Jim. It can't just end this way. I have to see him once more. And I don't care how. I decide I'm going to call him as soon as he gets off work about five. Then I think about how badly it's all been going and how gross I acted and finally I guess I just cry myself to sleep.

Sixteen

The next thing I know, someone is shaking me awake. I open my eyes and squint up and it's Cynthia, and for a minute I don't know whether it's morning or night. I can't figure out what she's doing waking me up, and then I remember about Mr. Landry and the kids and I nearly panic.

"Victoria," she says, standing over me. "What's going on here!" I can see she's angry. "Where are the children?"

"The kids?" I sit up. I search around frantically for something to tell her and then see it's not nighttime.

"How come you're home so early?" Now I'm really confused.

"You're damn right I'm home early," she says, and she's not just angry, she's furious. "Why didn't you tell me your parents didn't want you to stay alone overnight? I asked you if it would be all right. Why didn't you tell me?" And she charged on without even letting me get a word in. "What a damn embarrassment to run into your mother in a crowded elevator and have her inform me that I cannot leave you alone here at night." Cynthia continues. "Why did you lie to me?" Oh, no! They *did* bump into each other. Just my luck.

"I'm sorry . . . I didn't mean . . ." I start to apologize but she cuts me off.

"Where are the kids? Are they at Steven's?"

"What time is it?" I've got to get myself together.

"What difference does that make? Where are they? Tell me this instant!" Now she's in a panic.

"It's okay, Cynthia, they're okay. They're with their grandfather." You can't fool around when someone thinks their kids are missing.

"What do you mean they're with their grandfather? Where? What's going on here?"

"He came to visit them . . . and . . ."

"Their grandfather came out here and what—he's with them here, or took them away? *Tell* me." She looks like she's going to explode.

"Well, he didn't actually take them." That sounds like he stole them or something.

"He's got them, hasn't he?"

"Well, yes, but—"

"You let him take my children! How dare you decide such a thing when I told you I didn't even want him to talk to them on the phone!" She comes toward me like she's going to attack me and I move back.

"Where are you going?" she demands.

"No place. I'm really sorry. . . ." I never in my whole life had anyone outside my family yell at me like this and be so angry. I know I'm going to cry any second.

"How dare you disobey me with my own children! Who do you think you are?!" Now she's practically screaming at me and I'm too scared to cry. Please, God, let her calm down.

Just like on command she stops and says in a quiet, mean voice that practically spits at me, "Where are they now?"

"Fishing." I manage to get it out in a very small voice.

"At six o'clock!" Again she's screaming. "Are you telling me they're out on the water at this hour?"

"I don't know. . . . They're probably on their way back."

"They damn well better be." She spins around and says, "Come with me." And she pounds down the stairs.

I don't even stop for my shoes. I just race after her. That was rotten of Mr. Landry to keep them out so late. Why did he have to do that? I knew I didn't like that man. Boy, he doesn't care about anyone but himself. And after I was so nice to him. He really stinks. I can hardly see the stairs because now that she's stopped yelling at me I'm crying.

Cynthia doesn't even stop at the door, she just pushes through and lets it slam in my face. I follow her but I manage to stay behind her. I'm afraid she'll start screaming at me in the street. She is steaming mad. We get to the dock and I don't see the kids or Mr. Landry anywhere around. We look for the woman who rents the fishing boats, but there's nobody on the pier.

"Well"—Cynthia turns to me—"now, where did they go?" As if I would know.

"Maybe he took them for something to eat or something . . . ice cream! That's it. He must have stopped in . . . with them."

It has to be because they never let anyone pass that store without buying them a cone. I run on ahead to the ice cream store but I can see they're not there. Barry is alone behind the counter. My heart sinks.

"Barry?" I pull open the screen door and poke my head in. "Did you see David and DeeDee?"

He's surprised to see me. "Who?"

"You know, the kids I take care of."

"Oh, yeah. . . . No, I didn't see them."

"They were with their grandfather. They must have come in here."

"I've been here since eleven this morning and they haven't come in."

"Oh . . . ," and I can't help myself. I start to cry again right in front of Barry.

"Hey, what happened? Are they missing or something?"

"They were with their grandfather. . . ."

"Hey, come on, nothing to cry about. If they were with their grandfather"—and he comes out from behind the counter—"they're fine. I bet he took them for something to eat."

By now Cynthia is here. "Well," she says, "where are they?"

"Barry says maybe Mr. Landry took them for something to eat," I say.

"Yeah," Barry says, sticking up for me.

"Have you seen them?" Cynthia asks Barry, and he says no, and then her whole expression changes and she looks scared instead of angry. Then she says, "Maybe they never got back. Maybe they're still out there and something's happened." And without another word she shoves the screen door open and races out and toward the pier. Barry and I run after her.

There's still nobody on the pier. It looks as though all the sailing dinghies are in, but there are so many you really can't tell. Still, the woman wouldn't have gone home if one of her boats was still out.

"They must be back because the woman wouldn't have gone home with one of her boats still out, right?" I say to Barry more than to Cynthia. I'm sort of afraid to talk to her.

"That's right," he agrees. "She wouldn't leave until all the boats were in." But Cynthia looks like she's not about to trust either of us.

"Who owns the boat rental?" Cynthia asks Barry.

"Mrs. Randolph and her son Charlie," he says. "They live across there over the grocery store." He points to an old wooden two-story house. Before he even finishes showing her, Cynthia starts running across the street.

"I'll just die if anything happens to them," I say to Barry. "It's all my fault." I'm feeling almost sick to my stomach.

"What do you mean?" he says. "I thought they were with their grandfather."

"They were, but they weren't supposed to be. It's a long story, but Cynthia doesn't want them to see their grandfather."

"Is he a bad guy or something?" Of course Barry is confused.

"No, nothing like that. It has to do with her ex-husband. He owes her money so she said his father can't see the kids—oh, it's all a big mess."

"She sounds nuts not to let the kids see their own grandfather."

"I know, but that's the way she wants it, so I guess I should have listened to her. After all, they're her kids. Oh, I don't know. I wish I'd never come out here. . . ."

"Hey, come on, they'll turn up." He's really a very nice guy, which makes me feel even worse because I was so awful to him.

"Hey, look," he says, pointing out on the water. "There's a small sailboat coming in toward shore." It has to be them. Please, let it be them. We both run to the end of the pier. As the boat comes closer, we can see that there's only one person in it. Even close I can tell it's only Mrs. Randolph alone. She pulls the boat up to the pier and Barry runs over to grab her line.

"Mrs. Randolph," Barry shouts to her, "did the man with the two little kids come in yet?"

"They sure didn't," she answers, and my heart falls three

feet. "That's who I was looking for." And she climbs up on the dock and ties up the second line. "They're almost two hours late and I was getting worried. They got whitecaps out there now, you know."

This is becoming a nightmare. Cynthia comes running up to us out of breath, saying she can't find the woman, and we tell her this is Mrs. Randolph, and then she finds out that the children and their grandfather are still out there. Mrs. Randolph leaves out the part about the choppy water, but Cynthia's face turns white anyway, and she grabs my shoulder as if she's going to faint. Mrs. Randolph says she thinks they'd better alert the police and the Coast Guard, and then she tries to calm Cynthia by saying they probably ran aground around the cove. Lots of people do, and there's no danger because they can walk to shore from there. That helps Cynthia a little but she's still frantic. Mrs. Randolph takes Cynthia back to her house to call the Coast Guard, and Barry tells me to wait here while he locks up the store and gets his speedboat, and he runs off.

I wait alone at the end of the pier and start thinking how all this is my fault. Then I start thinking about David and DeeDee. If anything ever happened to them . . . but I can't even finish the thought because it's so horrendous. I'm glad I at least made them wear life jackets, and then I remember that Mr. Landry didn't have one and I think, gee, he's pretty old and if the water is rough . . .

In the middle of all this I start thinking about how angry

and disappointed my parents are going to be about the business of me staying alone with the kids. They may even make me come right home. It probably won't make any difference—coming home, I mean—because Cynthia's certainly going to fire me anyway.

I'm so involved in thinking about all this mess that I don't even see Barry pull up in his speedboat.

"Hey, Victoria! Over here," Barry shouts from the boat, and when I turn around, my stomach does another drop, which brings it about to China. Jim is with him. Right now he's the last person in the world I want to see.

Barry puts out his hand and I grab it and jump in. I try to give Jim a casual "hi" but only half of it comes out words and the rest gulp. He's busy throwing lines and pushing the boat away from the dock and the other boats, and Barry is steering and I kind of creep into a corner and hope nobody notices me.

Mrs. Randolph is right, the water is awfully choppy and we're bouncing up and down, banging hard every time we hit the water. Naturally I pick the worst seat, and every time we hit the water a cold spray smacks me in the face, taking my breath away. Barry turns around and waves me up with them. Hanging on to the rails for dear life, I creep up to where Barry and Jim are and squeeze between the two front seats. At least there's a plastic shield that keeps off most of the spray. Barry shouts something to me, but the noise of the motor and the splashing is so loud I can't make out what he's saying.

I finally understand that he wants me to let go of the wheel. I can always count on me to do the dumb thing. Barry is breaking his neck trying to steer the boat in all this mess, and I have the wheel in a dead man's grip. I let the wheel go and grab on to Barry's arm, which also makes steering impossible except I have to hold something. Jim pokes me and points to a metal bar right in front of me that I can hang on to.

It becomes even rougher as we get farther from shore, and all I can think of is those little kids and how scared they must be and poor Mr. Landry—how awful he must feel because he really loves them so much.

Still hanging on to the metal bar, I let myself slide down to the floor with my back against the instrument panel. This way I end up facing Barry and Jim. They're both standing there. Barry is steering and Jim is squinting into the wind, searching the water. The wind is whipping their hair back and they're both wearing sweatshirts, the kind with the hood except the hood won't stay up.

Boy, Barry is a nice guy. I didn't even have to ask him anything. As soon as he saw something was wrong he jumped in to help. I mean, he didn't have to go out searching himself, but I guess that's the way he is.

I suppose it's pretty nice of Jim, too. Except I don't think of Jim as nice like Barry, which sounds peculiar. But I don't mean it as a criticism of Jim, it's just that now that I know them both a little better, I think Barry may be a nicer guy. I still dig Jim much more.

"They didn't say anything, just that they were going to try for flounder," I tell Barry.

"That means middle fishing," he says to Jim, and he heads the boat out toward the center of the bay.

It's so rough now that it feels like we're in the middle of a squall.

"Hey, buddy," Jim shouts to Barry, "this could be really dumb."

"What do you mean?"

"Going out in all this," Jim says. "It's getting too rough for this size boat. We should head back."

"We can't!" I say first to Jim, then again to Barry, and I'm practically pleading. "We have to find them. Don't you realize they're just two little kids and Mr. Landry, and he must be at least—I don't know—almost seventy. And I don't even think he has a life jacket."

"Hey," Jim shouts to me above the wind, "I know it's serious, but I'm just saying we can't handle it."

"We have to," I say, mostly to Barry.

"No, we don't," Jim tells me, "that's what they've got the Coast Guard for. They know what they're doing. They have the equipment, the power boats and helicopters and everything. We don't belong in this thing. All we're going to do is get ourselves in trouble."

Suddenly he got to be forty years old. I can't believe he's acting so awful.

"You could be right," Barry says, "but I'm willing to take

the chance. I figure it's safe enough to take a couple of fast swings around the area."

Hurray for Barry!

"They're probably holed up along the shore somewhere and we're risking our lives for nothing." Now Jim sounds almost nasty, but it's two against one so there's nothing he can do about it. For the first time since I've known Jim I feel angry at him. Even what he did last night didn't make me feel this way.

Barry steers the boat in big circles, trying to cover as much of the bay as he can. No luck. The sea keeps getting choppier and now it's starting to rain. It really is a squall.

"Look," Jim says, "I told you you're not going to find them. Come on, buddy, let's head back. This is crazy."

"Please, Barry." I practically beg him. "Just a little longer."

"It's getting very hard to handle the wheel," he says, and I can see it is because every time we hit a wave both of them have to hang on to the wheel for dear life.

"Maybe we should head back."

"Smart boy," Jim says, pleased that he won.

Gross. How could he be pleased that he won such a horrible kind of argument!

"How come," I say to Jim, "if the Coast Guard is so great, we haven't seen any of their boats, and no helicopters or anything else?"

"Believe me, they're out here," he says, "looking in the right places. They do these kinds of searches twenty times a week."

"Maybe," I say, "but if we haven't seen them yet, they're not looking around here, and if the kids are here they're not going to find them. Barry?" I turn to him. "Can't we just look around this part once more?"

"Okay, we'll head for that tower over there," he says, pointing to a lighthouse on the mainland, "and then we'll circle back around that cove. Okay, Jim?"

"What am I supposed to say? It's your boat," he says, and he looks really annoyed.

Barry heads the boat across the bay toward the tower, and we all keep looking around, trying to spot the kids and the old man. It's getting harder and harder to see because the rain is coming down heavy now and the sky is black.

I see a piece of wood in the water and my heart stops. Maybe it's part of their boat, and I point it out to Barry (absolutely not to Jim) and he says, no, it's only a log.

"I told you we're not going to find them," Jim says to me. "We're only one little boat on this whole great big bay. No way we can find them if they're even out here. They're probably back on shore and we're risking our necks for nothing. God, what a dumb idea."

All the while he's talking I'm busy searching the water. I don't even look at him. I may not ever look at him again in my entire life.

"Come on," Barry tells him, "it was worth a try. The more people looking the better the chances of finding them."

"Baloney. They're back at the dock," Jim says, and I pray like crazy that this time he's right.

A bolt of lightning cuts through the rain and I jump six inches off the floor. I'm terrified of lightning on the water. I'm about to ask Barry what would ground the lightning on this boat, but I'm afraid he'll say "us," so I just swallow the question. I always knew I should have listened in that damn science class.

Just as we're making the last turn I think I spot something.

"Wait! Wait!" I'm shouting and pointing over the side. "Over there!" But over there keeps changing because the boat is rolling so much. Whatever I saw is gone.

Barry circles the area I was pointing to, but there's nothing there. The rain is coming down in sheets now, and Barry turns the boat lights on—not that it helps us see, but at least other boats can see us.

We search blindly for another ten or fifteen minutes and don't see a thing. I've never felt so bad in my whole life.

"Hey, look!" Barry suddenly shouts, pointing to something off the right side of the boat. "There *is* something there!"

It takes all three of us to turn the boat and keep it heading into the wind. Whatever's in front of us now isn't very far away, but the going is so rough we can only inch along. A couple of times we lose sight of the thing, but Barry keeps the boat straight on forty south on the compass. We're practically on top of it before we see it again.

It's the boat with the kids and Mr. Landry!

I don't even bother saying, "I told you so," to Jim. I'm so

relieved to see them, even Mr. Landry, that tears well up in my eyes and I practically begin bawling out loud.

The kids are huddled together in front of the mast in the cockpit, in water almost up to their waists. Mr. Landry is at the tiller trying to steer but doing nothing but spinning in circles. The sail is torn and flying in all directions. That must have been why they got lost. A sailboat's useless without a sail.

The kids go crazy when they see us. They start jumping up and down and waving, and we shout to them to sit down, but they can't hear us over the motor and the storm. We motion wildly for them to sit. Mr. Landry gets the idea and with one hand still on the tiller leans way over and pulls them down.

Barry motions for Jim to take the wheel and tells him to head off the bow of the other boat. He's going to make a grab for their mast.

Mr. Landry sees what we're trying to do. He moves to the mast and wraps one arm around it and holds out the other to Barry.

Jim swings the boat around twice, but both times it's too wide and they miss each other. I hold on to Barry's leg so he can lean out farther.

Again Jim makes a pass at the little boat, and this time Barry grabs Mr. Landry's hand. But a wave hits our boat and it breaks their grip. When the wave hits the dinghy it catches Mr. Landry off balance, and we all watch in horror as he slips off the narrow deck and into the water on the opposite side of their boat.

I can hear the kids screaming and I start to scream myself. Barry grabs one of the lines and dives off after Mr. Landry. The kids are hysterical and hanging over the side. I know they're going to fall in any second.

"Head into their boat," I shout to Jim, "and I'll try to jump in."

"Take the line with you!" he calls to me as I crawl along the side of the boat up to the bow.

I take a line and wrap it around my waist. I don't even know why or how it'll help, but it seems like a good idea. I turn back to Jim and he's nodding his head yes. It must be right.

We head in toward the dinghy and I set myself to leap. I have no sneakers. It's slippery. I don't have a life preserver and I'm scared to death. But I have to get to those kids because if I don't do it fast they're going to be in the water.

Our boat's coming in closer. I can't wait too long to jump because one big wave can take us past their boat in a second and then we'll have to make an entire turn, which could be too late.

The little dinghy is still pretty far away but I'm so afraid of another wave that I let it come only a tiny bit closer and make my leap.

It's got to be the biggest jump I ever made in my life. I feel like I'm flying, and then I hit their deck and slide right into the mast. I made it!

In two seconds I'm in the cockpit and I've got both kids down with me and I undo the line around my waist and wrap it around the mainsail cleat. There's a jerk and we go flying after the bigger boat. We're attached.

Meanwhile, Barry's got the line around Mr. Landry and he's hanging on to the side of our boat. "I'm going to bring him over to my boat," he shouts up at us. "You'll tip if we try to get in."

And with his arm under Mr. Landry's chest, he gets him over to the speedboat. Mr. Landry looks so limp it's scary, but I tell the kids everything's okay, he's going to be fine.

Barry and Jim manage to get Mr. Landry into the boat, and he collapses into a heap in the cockpit. Jim doesn't lose any time getting us out of there, and even though it takes us almost an hour to get back to the pier and we're sitting in waist-high water, we're dumb enough to feel that we've made it. In fact, we're all smiling. Even Jim.

Wouldn't you know it, just as we're getting in, the rain stops and it's practically calm by the time we reach the pier. It probably looks like the whole thing was a snap.

The pier is jammed with people. Practically all of Ocean Beach is down at the docks. Cynthia is right in front and she's crying and laughing, and when we hand the kids up she nearly devours them with hugs and kisses. David will be complaining about that for the next month.

Even Mr. Landry isn't in as bad shape as I thought. They have to help him onto the pier and he looks weak and exhausted, but he can stand on his own two feet. Not so steady, but he's standing.

I dread the moment when Cynthia calms down and sees me and Mr. Landry. I can tell Mr. Landry dreads it too. Everybody is jumping around and making a big fuss, and even the Coast Guard is there. They're using walkie-talkies and calling in all their boats, and it turns out they even had helicopters out looking for us. And everybody wants to know what happened and everyone's talking at once so nobody knows what actually happened, but we're all happy and smiling and exhilarated.

Barry and I try to help Mr. Landry because he really is wobbly. The kids see us and run to him. "Grandpa! Grandpa!" they both shout and start pulling him by the hand and hugging him.

Cynthia just stands there looking at him. God! This is going to be horrendous.

The kids keep pulling at Mr. Landry, and he keeps shaking his head no and urging them to go along with their mother and saying he'll catch up later.

All the time Cynthia just keeps staring at him. I can't believe she's going to be so mean to that poor old man.

"Henry," she finally says, and you can't tell from her tone if it's good or bad.

"Hello, Cynthia," Mr. Landry says, and you can see he's really embarrassed and very uncomfortable. He mumbles something about how it turned out to be quite a mess and how he's really sorry for it, but the kids cut him off, shouting how he's the best sailor in the whole world.

"Oh, Mommy," David says, "you should see how Grandpa steered the boat even with those big waves and he wasn't afraid of anything. Right, Grandpa?"

"Well, David," Mr. Landry says, "now that it's over I gotta admit it was a little hairy there for a while, but you and your sister were so brave I knew we'd make it."

"We were scared when you fell off, Grandpa," DeeDee says, hugging his legs. "I was crying, and you were too, David."

"You fell overboard?" Cynthia asks, horrified.

"I was not crying," David says, sounding like his old self.

"You were too," DeeDee says.

"Well," he says, "that's only because it was Grandpa and I thought he was going to drown and that's why."

Cynthia stands there with her mouth open while Barry tells her the story of how Mr. Landry climbed up on top of the boat and hung off trying to reach him and how he'd slipped. Barry leaves out the whole part about how he saved Mr. Landry's life.

But Mr. Landry puts that right and shakes Barry's hand and thanks him and then hugs him and everybody smiles and it's hero time and you should see Barry's face. Is it red!

Cynthia keeps watching Mr. Landry, and there he is with the kids hanging off him, dripping wet and looking sort of frail and really old, and finally she comes over to him and puts her arm around his shoulder and says softly, "I'm glad you're safe."

"Thanks," Mr. Landry says, smiling, and all the time his

eyes are full of tears. "I'm sorry, very sorry, Cynthia . . . and you, too"—and he looks at me very apologetically, except he can't remember my name—"uh . . . mother's helper . . . very sorry for what I did . . ."

"Forget it, Henry," Cynthia says before I can say anything. "I was a fool to tell you to stay away from your own grandchildren. I don't know what I thought I was accomplishing." Then she stands back and looks at him. "What a mess! We have to get you into some dry clothes."

"Oh, that's okay," he says. "As soon as I get back to the city—"

"Are you kidding? You're not going back to the city like that."

"Sure I am, it's not so bad. A little damp here and there."

"Henry," she says, "I'm not going to hear another word. You're coming back to the house with us, and we're going to round up some clothes for you, and you're going to take a good rest—for about a week."

"A week!" DeeDee exclaims. "Whee!"

"Hey, that's neat," says David. "We can do lots more fishing."

"Well, Cynthia," Mr. Landry says, and you can see he's so close to tears he can hardly talk, "if . . . you're sure . . ."

"I am absolutely sure, Henry, absolutely." And she gives him a hug and a big smack-type kiss on the cheek. The kids are jumping up and down, out of their heads with joy. Mr. Landry is all smiles.

Me too. I couldn't bear the thought of anything else bad happening to that old man.

"I think we all deserve a little celebration," Jim pipes up. "How about it? A drink for the heroes." And then he looks at me. "And for the heroine."

"Hooray for the heroine!" Barry shouts, and now my face gets all red.

Barry asks everyone to be quiet, and then he tells how I jumped across to the dinghy to get to the kids before they fell in and he makes it sound like Wonder Woman at work. When he finishes everyone says, "Hooray!" and I think I'm going to die of embarrassment.

I don't believe this whole scene, but I have to admit it feels great.

"Thank you," Cynthia says to me, "for what you did . . . for all of us." And she looks like she's going to cry, and I feel like I am too.

"I'm really sorry, Cynthia," I say. "You were right to be angry with me. If I didn't go against you, none of this would have happened."

"Maybe not," she says, "but the more I think about it the more I feel the mistake was mine. I made a bad decision and expected you to carry it out. It wasn't fair to you, to the kids . . . to anyone."

"All along I felt bad about doing it behind your back," I say to her. "I'm sorry about that."

"Well, when you think about it," she says, "blindly following a bad decision is a lot worse." Cynthia looks really pleased with me and I feel terrific.

It's turning out to be a sensational day and I feel proud. I hope it doesn't show too much in my face.

"You *should* feel proud," Cynthia says, smiling at me.

There goes my see-through face again.

"How about it?" Jim says. "Should we head for The Monkey?"

"Not me," Barry answers. "I just want to get home and get these wet clothes off. If you want to come with me"—and he looks mainly at me—"I can offer you some iced tea."

"I'll pass on the iced tea, thanks anyway," Jim says, and then turns to me. "How about it? You want to hit The Monkey for a while?"

He's asking *me*. Jim actually wants *me* to come with him. All my plotting and planning, all that's happened, finally pays off. I can't believe it.

"Thanks," I tell him, actually both of them, "but I think I should go home with the kids. After what they've been through today I think I should stick with them."

"Sure thing," Barry says. "You have a raincheck for any-time you want."

"Thanks," I tell him, "and thanks for helping me. Both of you. It would have been a disaster if you both hadn't been so together." But I'm looking directly at Barry as I say it.

Then Cynthia thanks them both and Mr. Landry thanks them again and Cynthia thanks me again and this could go on forever except, thank goodness, DeeDee starts jumping around a lot saying she has to make pee-pee and everyone laughs and we all start back.

All five of us tramp into the house, all wet and sandy, and the phone is ringing. David picks it up.

"It's your mommy," he says and hands it to me.

This is going to be rough.

Seventeen

I'm out in rough water swimming as hard as I can to reach a buoy that keeps moving and bobbing away from me. I'm just about to grab it when something small and soft slides into my hand and pulls at it. I think it's a fish and try to get my hand away, but the little something holds tighter and tighter. I jump up and, of course, I'm in my bed and the little fish is DeeDee, who stands there at the side of my bed, holding my hand and grinning her cute smile with the missing teeth.

"Oh, God, DeeDee, not yet," I moan, covering my face with the pillow. I feel her creeping under the covers, and I know sleep is hopeless. She's like a jumping bean in bed.

"Where are the hands?" I ask the same question every morning.

"The big hand is on the twelve and so's the little one."

"Can't be," I tell her.

"How come?"

"Because then it would be twelve o'clock."

"Oh."

"Go look again, okay?" And she runs down the steps while I hide back under the covers. Something about the day feels strange. DeeDee comes back all out of breath.

"Now, little cookie, where is the big hand?"

"On the one."

"That sounds right, now what about the little hand?"

"It's stuck on the twelve."

Crazy! I bend over the side of my bed and look out of the window. It does look different and it's noisier, and I think DeeDee's right. It's twelve. I can't believe it. The little monsters let me sleep till noon.

I jump out of bed, almost knocking my head on the ceiling. I'll never learn.

"What happened?" I ask DeeDee. "Where is everyone?"

"Everybody's sleeping except me and you. Was your mommy mad at you last night?"

Oh, she must have heard me on the phone with my mother.

"Well she was a tiny bit angry at first," I answer. More like out of her head furious, but I don't tell DeeDee that. For a full five minutes my mother did a nonstop number on how my not staying alone overnight had been the most important condition of the job and how could I completely disregard their rules? Obviously I was too young for such a responsible job.

Then she went into how I probably shouldn't be out there all by myself and was working herself up to how maybe Cynthia ought to look for someone else, and somewhere in there she had to stop for breath, and that's what I was waiting for.

I started talking and told the story right from the beginning. When I came to the part about Mr. Landry visiting the kids and how they were almost lost in the storm, she was stunned. Then Cynthia got on and told her how I jumped in the boat and saved the kids.

I love to hear the story even though it changes every time someone else tells it. Naturally it gets better.

My mother was very impressed, and then we had to wait while she recounted it all to my father, and then I got back on the phone and they asked me a million questions about the rescue and everything.

In the end they understood. My father agreed that there were extenuating circumstances and mostly I had made some good choices and they were very proud of the way I handled myself in an emergency.

"But please, Victoria," my mother ended up saying, "next time you get in over your head, remember we love you and care about you, and all you have to do is call us and we'll help you."

So it ended up that they were pleased and proud of me, and when your parents feel that way about you nothing can be too wrong with the world.

"Anyway, DeeDee," I say, and give her a kiss on her tiny nose, "they're going to come out and visit us this Sunday."

She loves that idea, and when I tell her they're going to bring her a surprise, she can't wait.

"Can we go to the beach today?" she asks, folding up my pj's until they're practically small enough to put in my wallet and then stuffing them under my pillow. She's a terrific help.

"Sure thing. Right after we eat."

"Is he going to come?"

"Who?"

"The boy in the living room."

"What boy in the living room?"

"The one from yesterday," she says.

Can't be. But it has to be. DeeDee doesn't play tricks like that. "Why," I ask, "didn't you say something before?" I guess I sound sort of aggravated because she screws up her face as though she's going to cry and says, "You didn't ask me."

"You're right. I forgot." And I give her a hug.

"I love you, Victoria," she says, and gives me a big wet kiss on my cheek.

"I love you, too," I say and hug her again. I think she's getting to be less of a monster. I hope.

When the love scene finishes, I ask her which boy is in the living room.

"The big one," she answers. No help. To her, both Jim and Barry are big. But I know it has to be Barry because Jim wouldn't come here. That's not like him to just pop in. He's sort of a big-shot type, and I know he'd expect me to meet him somewhere or better yet come over to where he was. It must be Barry. Great. Maybe he'll come to the beach with us. He'd probably be wonderful with the kids. Then I let my mind dance around a little. What if it's Jim? I guess that's like all the dreams I had coming true—and on my terms too. What a thought!

I send DeeDee downstairs to tell whoever it is I'll be there in a second, and then I race down to the second-floor bathroom and brush my teeth, wash up, and comb my hair the best I can. Nice, if you like rat tails.

I take my time walking down the bottom flight of steps. Can you imagine if it really was Jim? That would be like saying he was very interested in me. What a fantastic summer this could be! The three of us could hang out together. Jim, me, and Barry. You know, I really like Barry a whole lot now that I've got to know him better. I probably *like* him even more than I like Jim. But that's not the point. My feelings for Jim are completely different.

I hear DeeDee regaling whoever it is with a wonderful tale of how my mother was angry with me last night but now she's not and did he know that when she, DeeDee, wakes me up in the morning sometimes I curse?

I move a little faster. God knows what else she'll decide to tell him.

No question about it. I want Jim Freeman to be standing in that living room. My luck, it'll be Steven.

But it isn't. It's Jim. Excellent!

"Hi," I say, smiling like crazy.

"Hey." He smiles back. "You snuck up on me. I was listening to some very interesting stories."

"Oh, God, DeeDee, don't you dare." And I pretend to be horrified. I know I told you he was handsome, but I think he got even better-looking overnight. The sun has put white streaks in his straight blond hair and turned his skin this absolutely fantastic apricot color. He's positively gorgeous. The kind of person people turn around and stare at.

"Come on, DeeDee." He picks her up in the air and she squeals with delight. "You and I have a few things to talk about."

"No, you don't." I laugh. "DeeDee, don't you tell him a thing."

"Oh, yes," he says, and we play this back and forth, and DeeDee loves it, but I can see she's trying like crazy to come up with something, so I cool it because she really could produce a few beauts.

I take DeeDee into the kitchen and set her up with a tuna sandwich, and when I come back into the living room Jim is sprawled out on the couch looking through the sports section of the *Times*. So far he hasn't said why he came by. As soon as he sees me he puts the paper down and says, "So what do you want to do today?"

Like a dummy I answer, "I don't know . . . I have the kids, you know." I guess with Jim the terms have to be his.

"Are you stuck with them all day?"

It's a funny thing, but I haven't been feeling my usual

uptight heart-racing kind of thing with him today. In fact, something's bothering me but I don't know what it is.

"If you put it that way, I guess so."

"That's okay. Why don't we all go down to the beach this afternoon? I know where I can get a kite. I bet the kids would love that."

"Are you kidding? They'd go wild. They love kites."

"Terrific. I'll get the kite and meet you down at the bay beach in about three-quarters of an hour."

"No good," I tell him, "the kids hate the bay beach."

"Well, just tell them that's the only place I can fly the kite." And he starts to open the screen door. "See you at one thirty."

And he's out of the door.

"Wait! Wait up!" I run to the door and shout.

He stops and turns to me. "What's up?" he says.

"It won't work. DeeDee's terrified of the bugs and things on the bay beach. She absolutely won't go."

"Then you want to forget the whole thing?" Suddenly he's angry. And I know he's talking about a lot more than the kite and the beach. And then it hits me what's been bothering me about him since yesterday, maybe even from before that but I guess I didn't know. I think he may be a little spoiled.

Actually a lot spoiled. Spoiled rotten, I think that's what they call it. I told you how he was so fantastic-looking, really gorgeous, and that he has a very charming personality—you know, charisma and all that. So naturally with that combination people are always fighting to be with him and catering to him, and by now he's come to expect it all the time. He's the guy in charge of all the hanger-on-ers, and it bugs him if someone doesn't do things his way. Like now about the beach or even yesterday when we were searching for the kids. As soon as he saw he wasn't in charge he didn't really want to be part of it, and it had nothing to do with his being afraid of the storm. He is definitely not a coward. It's worse.

He's arrogant. We bruised his ego, Barry and I did, just because we didn't let him run the whole show. The fact that we were trying to actually save people's lives, little kids'—that was secondary. The big thing to Jim Freeman was who's running things, and if it wasn't going to be him—well then, forget it, and that went for the kids, too.

I don't know how he and Barry could be such good friends. I mean, they're so different. Like yesterday. Barry didn't even give a thought about his boat or himself or anything. All that mattered was finding those kids.

Funny how I guess I never looked much deeper than Jim's good looks. I suppose I'm pretty much like everybody else that way, but now, knowing what kind of person he really is, I'm beginning to think that maybe he isn't so gorgeous after all and that I don't want to go to the beach with him today—or any day.

He's still standing there, good old arrogant Jim, waiting for my answer, and you can tell just by looking at that confident face that he expects me to crumple up and practically beg him to let me go with him to the bay beach.

"Okay," I tell him, "then let's just forget the whole thing."

Beautiful. For half a second even his suntan turns ashen, but Jim Freeman types recover fast.

He shrugs a kind of *your loss* shrug and turns and starts walking down the street.

Watching him walk away, I have a sinking feeling in my stomach, and I almost want to call him back but I don't. Am I making a mistake? God, I hope not. I let this great thing walk out of my life when I could absolutely have him (nobody's going to believe it, anyway) and I don't do a thing. This just isn't me.

Or is it?

Because it feels right.

I walk back into the house and sit down on the bottom step and try to decide whether or not to cry. After all, it's not every day you fall out of love for the first time. It's not such a bad experience. Disastrous, but not really too bad. So I decide not to cry.

And I make another decision.

I go right to the phone and I'm just about to dial when I see this note propped up against a little vase on the table. I open it. It's from Cynthia. I didn't even know she wasn't home. It's another one of her cuties. It asks me "pretty please" will I give the kids and Mr. Landry lunch and put in a load of laundry and then there's a shopping list for when I get back from the beach and could I be a "positive pussycat" and iron her white pants outfit. If the "best little shrimp cleaner in the country" wants to clean the shrimp in the refrigerator she has no objection. The note ends saying I'm a doll and she's over at the Walkers' for the afternoon. It's signed, "Love ya to pieces, Your Summer Mother."

It takes me about ten seconds to decide what I'm going to do. I grab the pen next to the phone, turn Cynthia's note over, and *the new me* writes:

> Dear Summer Mother,
> Could you pretty please hem my pink skirt and my black pants and I'm missing four snaps on my white blouse, two buttons on my jacket, and the zip on my red shorts is stuck. Could you do them before the weekend? I would be forever grateful if you could spare an isty-bitsy 45 minutes every evening to help me with my logarithms for extra summer credit. Love ya!
> Your summer daughter
> Victoria

Now I dial, and as I listen to the phone ringing at the other end I begin to feel very happy about a lot of things and more excited than I expected about making this phone call.

Yes, going to the beach with *someone* today is definitely a terrific idea, but Jim just happens to be the wrong person.

"Hello," the right person's voice says.

"Hi, Barry. You dried out yet?"

love & betrayal & hold the mayo

One

This has to be the most exciting year of my life. For starters I finally made it to sixteen. Mathematically that should take only sixteen years, but with overprotective parents like mine, it seems more like thirty. Still, in the end they really came through. They gave me the most fantastic surprise Sweet Sixteen party.

My best friend Steffi helped them with the guest list, and what with friends and friends of friends and crashers, we had almost sixty people. My mother and father made all the food themselves, and it was fabulous. And the incredible thing was that I never saw them doing a thing. Even El Creepo (that's Nina, my thirteen-year-old sister) helped. Nobody seemed to know exactly how she helped, but it didn't matter, because the very best thing she did was to go away for the whole weekend.

Do you know what it's like *not* to have your thirteen-year-old sister at your Sweet Sixteen? It's the best present in the world.

The party was a sensational success. Everybody in school was talking about it for weeks. My father is a lawyer, and one of his clients is a music arranger for the Rolling Stones, and we had their brand-new record, autographed by the arranger himself. It hadn't even been released yet. It was the sensation of the party.

So was Jenny Groppo and her latest love, Robert Boyer. That's her fourth steady this year, and it was only May. She's probably going to have a thousand husbands before she's finished. Anyway, she and Robert sneaked off to one of the bedrooms to make out (guess which bedroom the dummy picks?) and, of course, you-know-who walks into his own room and turns on the light right in the middle of some heavy stuff. That was last month, and my father is still recovering.

Now the second fabulous thing is starting. I'm packing my trunk to go away for the whole summer. I'm going to be a camper-waitress in a summer camp in the mountains in Upstate New York. Being a camper-waitress means that you wait on tables and get to be involved in all the camp activities. For all that, your parents have to pay only $740 out of the usual $1000 fee and the camp pays you a big $260. I know it's not a whole lot of money, but Steffi says the place is terrific. She knows because she's been going there for the last five years. It's called Mohaph. Sounds like an Indian tribe, but it's not—it's named for the owners, Mo, Harry, and Phil.

The job is a snap. All we have to do is set the tables and serve three meals a day. We don't wash the dishes or anything like that. Steffi and I figured it all out. You know how kids don't like to sit at the table too long, so they jam the food down real fast and then they're gone. We figured that each meal should take tops forty-five minutes from beginning to end, so that's forty-five times three, or two hours and fifteen minutes of work a day, and then freedom!!! After that we can do whatever we want. Can you picture it—two hundred miles from home, completely on our own, with the easiest work in the world? And getting paid for it! I can hardly wait.

Another great thing is that I practically don't have to wait. I mean, we're leaving next week. The season doesn't actually start for another week, but we're going to get there early for a training period. Can't imagine what kind of training anyone needs to serve dinner to a few kids. I could do it with my eyes closed.

There is one small drawback. My parents thought the place sounded so great that they signed up El Creepo as a camper. It's a pretty big camp, though, so if I'm careful maybe I can keep far away. Except we're not even there yet, and she's giving me trouble already. I leave a week before she does, which means that anything I don't take with me she'll wear. I can't fit all my things into one trunk, but the idea of her dancing around in my best clothes sends me right up the wall. Of course I can tell her not to touch my things, and of course she'll say she won't. In fact, she says she never does, but that's baloney. The minute

I leave this house, she's into my wardrobe. Not only does *she* wear my things, but then she has the gall to lend them to her gross friend Annette, a greasy-haired beauty who probably hasn't had a bath since Christmas. Just thinking about them almost makes me want to stay home. If only I could electrify my room. I wouldn't even mind barbed wire.

I had a thing with her just last week about my fabulous new bathing suit. It's a one-piece, white with gold threads running through it, cut high on the thighs and off one shoulder. Very sexy. Anyway, I've worn it only a couple of times. I was saving it for camp. I folded it very carefully, and every time I looked at it, it seemed to be slightly different. I don't know, it just looked like someone was messing with it. Naturally I asked Nina, and naturally she swore she never touched it. The minute you ask her anything she always swears on everybody's life she's innocent. I try never to stand too close to her when she does that because, for sure, one day a bolt of lightning is going to get her. Anyway, I asked her nicely, and she denied it completely, but something about the way she said it made me suspect her.

"Look, jerk"—I stopped being so nice—"I know you've been at my bathing suit. And if you touch it once more, I'll destroy you, Creepo!"

"I never touched your lousy bathing suit," she lied, "and if you don't leave me alone, I'm going to tell Mommy! And don't call me Creepo!"

"Try and stop me, Creepo."

"It makes me crazy when she lies straight out like that. "Oh, sorry, honey," I said, not so accidentally knocking a pile of her newly folded underwear to the floor as I turn to make my exit.

"Mom!" she shrieked, like she was being murdered.

And my mother and Norman, our giant sheepdog, came running. They almost collided at the door, and Norman went bounding into the fallen laundry, sending it flying in all directions.

"What's going on here?" my mother said, throwing up her hands and not waiting for an answer. "Can't you girls get along for five minutes without fighting? For God's sake, Nina, how many times do I have to tell you not to throw your clothes on the floor?"

"She did it!" the little ghoul said, pointing at me.

"Prove it," I answered, staying very calm.

That did it. She went right into her crying act. She must have the most highly developed tear ducts in the world. She cries at least four times a day. She doesn't even have to have a reason—all she needs is an audience, preferably my parents, who are the biggest suckers in the world when it comes to their baby.

She did the entire number about how I always blame her for everything; I'm always picking on her, and on and on. Naturally I denied everything, because it wasn't true. She's the one who makes my life miserable with her borrowing and lying and snooping and everything. We had this big argument with my mother in the middle and of course she took Nina's side because she said you can't just run around accusing people without any proof, and on top of that said I owed the creep an apology. Of course I didn't want to give her one, but my mother said I had to or I was grounded for the whole day.

There she was, the little creep, really winning, standing there in her room changing her clothes and telling me that I better apologize fast because she was in a hurry. And she had me, because my mother was standing right there, waiting. All the while she was unbuttoning her shirt and smiling that vomit smile, just waiting for me to start crawling.

I figured I'd make her pay for the next hundred years, but I was trapped right then, so I started to say how maybe I had misjudged her, and she was lapping it all up and asking for more when she began pulling off her shirt.

"She's so mean to me, Mommy," she said, "and I never even touch anything of hers."

The biggest out-and-out lie of the century. And on and on she whined about how cruel I was to poor little innocent her. She pulled off her shirt and let her skirt drop, and my mother and I were standing there with our mouths hanging open. There she was, perfect little Saint Nina, standing there without a stitch on except for the outline of my one-shoulder bathing suit suntanned onto her skin.

It turned out to be a glorious day. For me, anyway. Nina spent the rest of it in her room, contemplating the disadvantages of messing around with her big sister. She probably didn't learn anything except to cover her tracks better.

But that still doesn't help me with my problem now. I'm not going to think about it anymore. With luck, she'll get the flu for a week, and all she'll borrow will be my nightgowns. I decided to hide my best nightgown behind my chemistry books.

Even though I'm very excited about going, there are a couple of things that make it sort of hard to leave. One is Todd Walken and the other is Judy First. Todd has been my boyfriend for the last three months. He's terrific, and I like him very much. In fact, I more than like him, but I don't think I'm in love with him. At least not the way Steffi is in love with Robbie, the guy from camp. Actually, I don't think I've ever been in love that way. Steffi's just totally gone on Robbie. Not even interested in anyone else at all. She must write to him at least twice a day, and she doesn't even care if she never has another date with anyone else. I know I don't feel that way about Todd, but I am very attracted to him, and I certainly like him more than anyone else at the moment. But I know that the minute I get on that bus, Judy First is going to move right into my territory.

She's been dying to get near him all winter. She must have asked him to ten different things at her parents' club and anything else she could think of. But he always said no because I was around. As of next week, I won't be. Personally, I have nothing against Judy First. If Todd likes dumpy dodos with bananas for brains, dyed hair, and no personality, he's welcome to her. Wait till he tries to drag that klutz around the dance floor. Of course, there is one thing she seems to do very well, and often, and with anyone. If that's all he's interested in, he's going to have a wonderful summer.

Steffi says there's no point in working myself up since the only way to solve the problem is to stay at home, and I'm certainly not going to do that.

Boy, I really hate that Judy First.

Why do they always stack up two good things and then make you choose? How nice it would be if everything were like this—would you like to spend the summer chatting with Nina or be a waitress in a summer camp? That's the kind of choice I'd like to have.

It's nearly impossible to decide what to take with me, particularly when everything I own is absolutely terrible. I must have the ugliest clothes in America. Even the things I pick out myself turn awful after a couple of weeks. Fortunately, Steffi has some great things, and we're the same size. That's very important in a friendship, you know. And the best part is that she hates her clothing too. So we switch. I probably should be packing her trunk and she mine.

Every few minutes my mother comes in to tell me not to forget my heavy sweaters and my down jacket. And my rain boots. I can't believe her. She must think I'm going to the North Pole or something. I nod my head yes, but I'm definitely not taking my rain boots. When will she ever learn that I'm not ten anymore? Never, I suppose. Funny, but sometimes when I hear my grandmother talking to my mother, it sounds like she's talking to a little girl. I suppose if someone is your child, they're always your child in some ways.

My aunt Laura gave me a beautiful case just for makeup for my birthday. I figure my makeup will fill that plus a couple of shopping bags, and then I can buy things up there if I need them.

Besides leaving Todd and my family, I'm a little nervous about the camp. I know I have Steffi, but she's been going there for a long time, so she knows everybody and I know only her. What if I don't like it? I can't change my mind and just come home. I guess if it was awful I could, but when I take on something it's very important to my parents that I go through with it to the end. My father, especially, is very firm about not being a quitter.

I'm going to miss them very much. Even though you're sixteen, you can still get lonely for your parents. I know I did last year at Fire Island, especially when there was any trouble. I guess it's natural to worry about something new. And I'm good at worrying. I hope there aren't too many disgusting things, like bugs and wild animals. I've always lived in the city, so the only animals I'm comfortable with are dogs and cats.

I am also going to miss Norman very much. Norman has been our family failure. Nina and I took him to a dog-training course when he was a puppy. He was beyond a doubt the sweetest dog in the class. He loved all the other dogs, even

221

the most vicious ones. And he did get his diploma, but there was no question that he was simply pushed through. You can say "heel" and commands like that until you're blue in the face and get no reaction, but there are certain words he understands perfectly—go out, eat, cookie, cake, bread, lamb chop, steak, ice cream, and get off the bed, Mommy's coming.

This is the first summer both Nina and I have been away at the same time. My parents are going to miss us terribly, especially when it comes to walking Norman.

"Who's going to walk Norman in the mornings?" I asked over dinner the other night.

"Daddy is," my mother shot back instantly. Then, in a sweeter, softer voice, she said to my father, "Well, darling, you have to get up at that time anyway."

"But not on the weekends," he said, and then matching her for sweetness said, "Mommy will walk him on the weekends."

"But I like to sleep late on the weekends, too," she said very reasonably.

By now Nina had stopped eating her meatloaf, which happens to be her favorite dinner, to pay more attention.

"Then maybe you want to walk him a couple of mornings during the week," my father suggested.

"I walk him every afternoon when you're not home." My mother's face was getting a little stiff. "Maybe you'd like to come home early a couple of times a week and walk him?"

I don't know if it was the meatloaf, or that he sensed the conversation was crucial to his future, but Norman pulled all one hundred and twenty pounds of fur and dog up from his favorite resting place under the table and stood alongside Nina, his chin resting on the table.

"You know, darling," my dad said, trying a smile, "I can't be stopped in the middle of a brief to come home and walk the dog." Feeling he'd scored a good point, he looked to Nina and me for a little agreement. Neither of us was stupid enough to take sides or to disturb the flow. This was too beautiful to end too quickly.

"Who's going to walk him at night?" Nina stoked the fire a little.

"Eat your salad," my father snapped at Nina, who hasn't eaten salad in thirteen years.

"Sure, Daddy," she said, actually spearing a tiny piece of lettuce with her fork. "Don't you think you should walk him at night if Mommy walks him every afternoon?" That would teach him to mess with Nina.

"But I walk him every morning," my father defended.

"But not on the weekends," my mother attacked.

"We could share the weekends," he offered.

"Oh, and what about the nights?"

"That's not fair," my father said, and that's when Nina and I cracked up.

"Good Lord," my mother said, "where have I heard that before?" And we all cracked up.

That's the terrific thing about my parents. They have a sense of humor. They seem to have developed it fairly recently.

Seems to me they took everything so seriously when I was younger. At least everything about their children. They're still heavily into the parent thing, but they're getting better at it. Better and worse. My father is still terrible when it comes to boys. I dread bringing home a date, because I can see that my dad doesn't like him before he comes in the door. It's like he's guarding the palace. Most of the time I think he would like to throw all of the guys into a crocodile moat. A lot of them probably belong there.

Most guys I know are either creeps or semicreeps. I guess there are a couple of okay ones around. Todd, for one. But even Todd can be a pain sometimes. Especially when we go out at night. We have a great time. He's a terrific dancer with a great sense of humor, smart, fun, and everything, and then suddenly at the end of the evening he turns into Dracula. Sometimes I feel like I ought to get myself one of those big wooden crosses to keep him away. It's not that I don't like fooling around, but unless you're really in love with someone, I can't see me getting that involved. I don't know how I'd feel if I were in love, but so far it hasn't happened.

We have to be at the bus station by 7:45 a.m. For some reason it's a group activity. That means not only my parents but El Creepo and Norman.

"Are you wearing jeans?" That's me, asking my mother.

"Don't start, please." That's my mother answering.

I have to explain a little about my mother. She's very pretty and very young-looking. Which is good. I mean, it's ideal to have that kind of mother, but sometimes I'd like her to look a little more like everybody else's mother.

There's some last-minute craziness because Nina says it's my turn to walk Norman, but my father says it's obvious that I'm too busy, and Nina says something stupid like I'm always too busy, just to have the last word. My father is in no mood for her nonsense and tells her simply to walk Norman. She grumbles, whines, moans, and does the full Nina act, even throwing in a couple of quick tears. It's a tired act and nobody is impressed. Certainly not Norman, who simply waits at the door for the loser.

By 7:30 we're still not out of the house, and now it's getting frantic.

When we finally arrive, the bus station is jammed. It looks like a billion different camps are leaving this morning. It takes us forever to find our bus, and then I don't see Steffi. One bad thing about Steffi, and her mother, too, is that they're always late. Incredibly enough, they've never missed a train or a plane, but it's always a sweat at the end.

I look around but, naturally, I don't know anyone. My mother gets busy looking for the person in charge. She's always very big with people in charge. It's as though, if she makes herself known, they'll know they'd better take good care of her child. Let them know someone cares. In this case, the man in charge is Uncle Roger, and I'm introduced to him like a six-year-old. Nobody really has anything much to say to Uncle Roger. The message has been delivered. This camper-waitress has a family, and a dog, and you'll be held accountable for anything that happens to her.

It's time to get on the bus. I'm starting to get in a small panic because Steffi isn't here and I'm having trouble saving her a seat. Somehow, everyone seems to want that particular seat.

Big parting scene, hugs, kisses. Norman, in a frenzy, knows something unusual is happening and is pulling, not in any special direction, just pulling. That's a hundred and twenty pounds of pulling.

Steffi finally arrives. There's all kinds of squealing and hugging and kissing. Obviously my friend Steffi is very popular. Strangely enough, this makes me a little uneasy. Not that I'm jealous, that's not it, it's just that she's the only one I know at camp, and I'm not anxious to share her with a million other people.

And that's what happens right away. I'm saving her a seat next to me, but though she dumps all her stuff on it, she whispers that she's going to sit with Ellen Rafferty for a bit. Ellen lives next door to the famous Robbie in Connecticut, and Steffi's dying for information. I can understand. I really can.

The bus pulls away, and my wonderful parents, fabulous sister, and adorable dog get smaller and smaller and farther away. Two minutes into the summer and I hate the whole thing, because my best friend is sitting next to someone else. Can you be sixteen and six at the same time? The only thing left is a few tears, which I could easily work up. I don't, though.

Instead I bury my head in my new book, but that's all I can do because I have to keep my eyes closed. I get nauseous if I read in a car or a bus.

Funny how people look when you meet them for the first time. After you get to know them, they never look the same again. Right now I look around and everyone seems sort of formal and cold, like they could never be my friends. They all look much older, too. That's possible, because camper-waitresses can be as old as seventeen. I hope I'm not the youngest. I can see right away that one girl looks, at most, twelve. There's always someone who looks so young, and then you find out that they're really seventeen. Even when they're twenty-five, they still look like kids. I don't think I'd like that. Life's hard enough without having to explain all the time that you're really not twelve. This particular girl seems pretty nice and she's sitting right across from me, so I figure I'll act a little grown-up and try being friendly.

"Hi, I'm Victoria Martin," I say.

And she smiles and says she's Annie Engle.

I go on with the usual things about how this is my first year up here, and how I'm sort of nervous about it.

"It's my first year too," she says, and she is so natural and easygoing, I hit it off with her right away. She's got a nice inno-cence about her that's really adorable, and I know we're going to be good friends. With some people you can tell right away.

"Naturally I'm a little nervous about the work because I never waited on tables before, but the way my friend Steffi and

I figure it, it's going to be a snap," I say. "Have you ever done this before?"

"You mean wait tables?"

"Right."

"No, I think I'm too little."

"Hey, don't worry," I tell her. "I don't think it makes any difference if you're short."

Surprisingly, she gets really indignant. "I don't think I'm so short."

We're not even out of Manhattan and I've had my first failure. I'm the Norman of the camp set. "I didn't mean it that way." I start falling all over, trying to ingratiate myself. "I always wanted to be petite. It's so cute." Once I start burying myself, there's no stopping me. "Tiny hands and feet."

Now she's really insulted. "I was next to tallest in my class last year."

I'm beginning to get a sinking feeling about my new friend. "What class was that?" I ask.

"Sixth grade."

No wonder she looks twelve.

I go right back to my book. Things are tough enough without latching on to a twelve-year-old. They must have put her in here just to trick me. Like a decoy. God, I hate this place.

I'm sitting there with my eyes closed, turning the pages at the proper time, when I sense someone looking over me.

"That's a great way to read a book if you don't like it," the guy leaning over me says in a friendly voice that has the little bumps and chuckles running through it. I like him before I can even twist around to see his face.

He pulls back and stands up straight. I was right—he is nice, tall and lanky, with silky straight brown hair that hangs over his forehead and always will. He's got a nice face. It's not gorgeous, but lively and smart, with a few freckles sprinkled across the top of his nose to give him a casual, easygoing look. He must be at least six one. Probably a tall twelve-year-old.

"I'm Ken Irving. I work in the front office."

"Hi, I'm Victoria Martin and I'm going to be a waitress."

"You mind?" he says, sweeping Steffi's stuff to one side and sliding into her seat. "You're going to be a waitress, huh?'

"Is that bad?'

"No, it sounds great, I guess."

Suddenly I'm nervous. "What do you mean, you guess?"

"Hey, I didn't mean anything." I can see I've thrown him off balance, which I didn't mean to do. "This is my first year here so I'm just guessing at everything. Waiting tables sounds terrific."

I smile to let him know everything's all right. "You think so?"

"Are you kidding? It's great. I guess." Now he's smiling back, and I have to smile too.

Waiting on tables, what could be so great about a job like that—except if it's your first adult job? Not like babysitting or mother's helper or some other kind of gofer kid job. Being a waitress is the real world, and so it *is* great. Naturally, I don't tell him all that. He'd think I was off my nut.

"What are you going to be doing in the office?" I ask him.

"I'm not even sure. So far all they told me was that I'd be answering phones."

"Boy, that's a snap. How'd you get such an easy job?"

"The usual way."

"From an ad in the paper?"

"Are you kidding? That's the easy way. We had to get my mother's cousin Caroline's daughter to marry Mo of Mohaph's son. Then Caroline put in the fix, and, voilà, here I am. How'd you get your job?"

"Obvious," I tell him. "I'm Mo's son."

And we both laugh. I like Ken because he's one of those people you feel comfortable with instantly. It's as if we're old friends after five minutes. Only trouble might be if he tries to make it more than that. Right now, I don't feel like it. I can sense a little something else from him, but not from me, not yet, anyway. Good friends, that's all.

And we're gabbing away a mile a minute, having such a good time that I don't even see Steffi come over. Ken sees her first, and he gets a funny look on his face. Uh-oh, looks like I won't have to worry about Ken bothering me. I think he just got zonked. Too bad, but I know there's no chance for him against Robbie.

"This is my friend Steffi," I say. "This is Ken . . . uh . . ."

"Irving," he adds, not taking his eyes off Steffi.

"Hi," Steffi says, open and friendly as always. And not noticing a thing.

Now, straight off, I want to make it clear that I don't have any real interest in Ken Irving. None at all. Not even the slightest bit, though I like him as a friend. A lot. But no other way. However, it does make you feel a little frumpy, dumpy, gross, and highly rejectable when, after spending fifteen minutes dazzling someone, one look at your best friend and he forgets you ever lived. And she isn't even trying. This is not my day. In fact, what with Judy First probably making out with Todd the minute I got on the bus, this may not be my summer. But I'm not going to let it bother me. After all, it's only my whole life.

While Steffi chats with Ken, I sit there not allowing the destruction of my entire summer ruin a lovely bus trip. Just as I'm being overcome, Ken reluctantly tears himself away from Steffi and goes back to his seat. And Steffi turns to me.

"He's cute," she says. "Do you think he likes you or what?"

"Or what what?" I kid her. That's her new thing, every-thing ends in "or what?" Last year it was "you know." When she gets these things it can sometimes take months to get rid of. And they're very catching.

"Seriously, Torrie, I really think he likes you."

Even smart people can be so dense sometimes. "He *is* cute," I tell her, "but it isn't me he likes."

"Come on, all he did was say three words to me."

"Sometimes you don't even need that," I tell her.

"Oh, Victoria, you're so romantic. You read too much. It doesn't happen like that. Whammo, and you're in love."

231

"How did it happen with Robbie? Didn't you know the minute you saw him?"

"Not really. At first I thought, gee, he's cute. Then after a couple of minutes talking to him, I thought, gee, he's smart and nice and even better-looking than I thought. By the end of the first date I thought he was gorgeous and brilliant and the most exciting guy I'd ever met. And when he didn't call me the first thing the next morning, my stomach got so knotted up I couldn't even eat breakfast or talk or even think. It was either a twenty-four-hour virus or I was in love. Since I didn't have any fever, it had to be love."

"You see too many movies."

We both laugh, and then Steffi gets serious. "Wait till you meet him, Victoria, he's so terrific you're just going to love him. I've never met anyone like Robbie before. He's not like any of the people we know at school. Most of them are just stupid kids.

"I mean, all they care about is making out. But Robbie's different. He's a real person. He cares. Not just about the people close to him, but everybody. Whole countries, the world. If something happens in Afghanistan, it really matters to him. And he's ready to pitch in and help or donate something or write a letter or whatever. He's the kind of person who could be president. I mean it, he's so special. I really am in love with him, Torrie."

I never heard Steffi talk that way about a boy before. Even her voice has a different sound to it. You can probably hear the love. I'm really happy for her and I tell her so. "I can't wait to meet Robbie. I like him already," I say, and I mean it. Anyone who's that important to my best friend is going to be very important to me, too.

Steffi goes back to her daydreaming about Robbie, and I sit worrying about the summer, watching the countryside zip past. The sight of green meadows begins to relax my fears. I've lived in the city all my life, and I still get very excited when I get into the country; show me a brook and I go nuts, or those farmhouses that look like the ones I used to draw in fourth grade. And the sight of a herd of cows just hanging out in somebody's front yard still knocks me out. Steffi spends every summer up here, so she's not nearly as impressed as I am. I think she'd rather stick with her Robbie fantasies than listen to my babbling about the beauties of nature, so I just stay quiet and take it all in. It's hard for me to imagine what it would be like living in any of these small towns we're passing through. Sometimes I think it might be a nice life, sort of easy, in a place where everyone knows and cares about everyone else. Somewhere warm and friendly and safe, with lots of country fairs and hay rides. Or maybe it's only like that in the movies. Come to think of it, it might not be so great having everyone know everything about you. You can get lost in a big city if you want. Still, I think I might like to try a small town for a while. Maybe after college. Just to find out what they do in between hay rides and country fairs.

I'm so busy planning the rest of my life that I almost don't notice that we've turned off the main road and are on a single-lane country road. Everybody is grabbing stuff off the racks and putting things together.

"Another five minutes," Steffi says, stuffing her jacket into her overnight case.

"I'm so excited," I tell her.

"Me too. You're going to love it, Victoria. It's going to be our best summer. Nothing but fun from early morning to late, late, late, late as you want at night. Nobody's going to be standing over us. We're on our own."

"Excellent! I just hope I can handle the work, though. I've never waited on tables before."

"Are you kidding or what? It's a cinch. It's not like you're serving real people in a restaurant. These are just kids. You just shove the food in front of them and they eat it in two seconds and then you're finished. Free! Nothing to do for the rest of the day but lie around in the sun, swim, curl our hair, polish our nails, and dress for fabulous parties every night. The hardest thing you'll have to do is fight the boys off. They're going to just love you, Victoria. Wait'll you see." With that, the bus pulls up to a big iron gate and stops.

"Are we here?" I ask.

"Yup, this is picturesque Camp Mohaph on Mohaph Road. High on Mount Mohaph above beautiful Lake Mohaph. Remember from the brochure?"

"It's beautiful," I say, and it is. We drive through the high iron gates up a winding tree-lined gravel road, and at the very top of the hill stands the camp. It's divided into two circles of bunkhouses, one for the boys and one for the girls. Both are fantastic. It looks more like a hotel than a camp. I thought they said it was an old camp, but all the bunks look brand-new.

From the bus, if you look down behind us, you can see the lake. It's small but sparkling, with a tiny island right in the middle (Mohaph Island, I guess) crowded with weeping willows that drip their long branches into the water. Along the banks there are acres of green lawns carpeting the hills, and in the distance you can see the playing fields, a playground for the little kids, and a gigantic pool shining aqua in the sun. Steffi's right. I'm going to love it here.

The bus pulls into the parking lot, and we all grab our stuff and, loaded like packhorses, slowly make our way out of the bus. Uncle Roger leads the way. The closer we get, the better it looks. The bunks are glossy white, so freshly painted they look almost wet. Each bunk has different color shutters. On the girls' side, wonderful violets, soft mauves and pinks, with an occasional splash of burgundy. On the boys' side, the bunks are also sparkling white, but the shutters are in the more traditional browns, grays, deep blues, and reds. I love it all.

With Uncle Roger in the lead, we all start moving toward the bunks.

"I hope it's the one with the mauve shutters," I whisper to Steffi. "It's my favorite color."

"Actually, these are for the campers. Ours are further back." For some reason Steffi seems a little uncomfortable.

"Great," I tell her. "More privacy." And I mean it. I'd hate to be in the first row with all the little kids.

Uncle Roger turns around and holds up his hands for us to stop. "Waitresses can head over to the right," he says, pointing toward a big, beautiful building, almost like one of those New England meeting halls.

"Fantastic," I tell Steffi, "it's the best one of all."

For some reason Steffi is hanging back a little. Almost like she's trying to keep away from me. Maybe she's worried that I'll be disappointed because it's not one of the little bunks. I try to reassure her. "Steffi, I love being in the big building away from everyone else, and we'll have the whole place to ourselves. Just waitresses. Fabulous."

"It's not that building." She sounds positively glum.

"Big, small, it's all the same to me."

She mumbles something I don't catch and heads around the back of what everyone is referring to as the social hall. That's where they hold all the dances and entertainment. Terrific, we'll be close by the fun place.

I accidentally drop my backpack and bend down to pick it up; when I get up again, I see Steffi picking up speed, and without a backward glance, she disappears around the back of the big hall. She's acting strange. I hope it isn't anything I've done.

I turn the corner of the building, but I don't see her. She's vanished—I must have come around the wrong side of the building, because there's nothing here but a couple of rundown old ramshackle buildings in the middle of what looks like a rubbish dump.

The buildings themselves must be old storage shacks that they don't use anymore. Half the shutters are falling off on the one closest to us, the front steps are broken and what remains of a front porch just barely clings to the building. Could our bunk be in the wooded area behind these shacks? It must be. I hope it's far enough away from the mess. I pick up my backpack and start walking around the back of the shack.

"Victoria . . . Torrie . . . here." A tiny voice comes from inside the first shack. Then a head sticks out. Steffi's head. Then I see the rest of her.

"What are you doing in there?" I ask.

She comes out of the shack, gingerly moving her feet around, searching for a fairly safe spot on the porch, smiling the weirdest smile I've ever seen. Sort of what "I'm sorry" would look like if it was written in lips.

I open my mouth to say "What's up?" Then it hit me. Suddenly I know exactly what's up, and it's not good.

"Oh no, Steffi, I can't believe it . . ."

"I'm sorry, Torrie, I swear it didn't look this bad last year. I remember it as sort of quaint and charming."

"Yeah, like the Black Hole of Calcutta."

"Do you hate me or what?"

"I'll tell you when I see the inside."

I make my first mistake. I bound up the stair and right

through the porch. And I mean through it. My foot sinks down up to my ankle and sticks there.

Steffi helps me pull it out. I don't say anything. With one slightly scratched leg, I make my way to the doorway. And just stare. There's only one thing I can think of to say. And I turn to Steffi to say it, but I don't. Her eyes are afloat with tears. Nothing running down her cheeks, but one word from me would start a cascade.

"I just wanted you to come so badly. And you never asked me what it looked like. If you did I would have told you, I really would have."

"Let me look again," I say, and go back to the doorway. That was my second mistake. Looking again. It's even worse the second time. I'm mesmerized by its awfulness. Eight terrible iron cots, most of them bent out of shape, with legs that don't exactly touch the floor on all four corners and sagging hundred-year-old mattresses that look like someone bought them at the prison rummage sale. Each bed has a small cubby next to it. And I mean small. Three shelves on top and a tiny cabinet underneath. Perfect to hold everything for a short weekend. A single naked bulb (probably no more than forty watts) hangs down in the middle of the room with a broken piece of chain dangling from it. No problem reaching it if you're over six three.

You can't lie to your best friend. "It's the worst, ugliest rathole I've ever seen," I tell her.

"Sure, it needs some work, but if we all pitched in we could do it in no time."

"Certainly—by Christmas."

"Come on, Victoria. All it takes are some pretty curtains, maybe a cute bedspread, and some throw pillows. We could even get some pictures and posters. Maybe my mother could send me my Stones poster. We could hang it right over this rough spot," she says, indicating a gaping hole in the wall the size of a bowling ball.

But Steffi is only warming up. She's got a million ideas on how to turn this dump into Buckingham Palace, but I've stopped listening. Instead I'm hunting for the showers. But I can't find them, mainly because they aren't there. The only thing in the back is one crummy toilet with a cracked seat, guaranteed to pinch you every time you use it.

"It's positively primitive," I tell her.

"It's the country."

"What country? Where's the showers?"

"Just outside."

"How just?"

"A little way . . ."

"Stef . . . fi!"

"Three blocks away. But they're very tiny blocks Victoria. I know it's not perfect, but . . ." There's no way to finish that sentence.

I look around once more. It's dark and ugly. And then I look at my best friend Steffi, and I feel dark and ugly because I'm giving her such a bad time. Okay, so it's not great, but we could fix it up, and besides, what with all the parties and great things to do, we're hardly ever going to be in the bunks anyway.

"My mother had some material left over from my curtains she could send to me," I say.

Suddenly Steffi's whole face lights up, and she runs over to me and hugs me. I hug her back, and everything is terrific again.

Then we both start to giggle. "It's the pits, isn't it?" she says, beginning to crack up.

"You think it's that good?"

"Nothing a demolition crew wouldn't cure."

"Or a bomb."

"I think they've tried that."

"Well," I say, looking around, "which bed do you think is the best?"

"The least horrendous or what?"

"Yeah."

"Well." Steffi starts walking around the room, inspecting all the bunks. "This is a tough one, but I think it would be terrible to be under the hole."

"You mean the rough spot?"

"Yeah, the rough spot. Anyway, wise guy, I think that side near the bathroom is the worst. This side has the most light."

"Mainly because the shutter is broken and hanging off."

"When it falls off, you'll really have some nice sunlight. Anyway, it seems to me that far and away the best bed in the bunk is . . ."

And just as Steffi is announcing her choice and pointing to

the bed in the far corner nearest the door, a very pretty blond girl sweeps in and, with one quick survey of the room, flings her stuff down on the very bed Steffi was pointing to.

"That one!" Steffi finishes too late.

"Are you referring to my bed?" the yellow-haired girl asks, in an accent that's a cross between phony American and phony British and sincerely unpleasant.

"It's okay." Steffi smiles. "Hi, welcome to the Black Hole of Calcutta. I'm Steffi Klinger, and this is my friend Victoria Martin."

"I'm Dena Joyce Fuller," she announces, with such aplomb that I feel we should applaud.

There's a tiny silence. She seems to be waiting. Maybe she thinks we should applaud, too.

Before anything more can be said, another girl comes in and, while Steffi and I stand there, grabs the second-best bed, and within ten seconds, four more girls race in, and the next thing we know we're stuck with the only two beds left in the bunk. One is next to the toilet, and the other is under the hole in the wall.

We both shrug and move to the closest bed. There's no real choice, since they're both such beauties. I end up under the hole. I hope nothing big crawls in while I'm sleeping.

There's a lot of introductions around, and with the exception of Dena Joyce and maybe Claire, everyone else seems pretty okay.

There's a Liza from New Jersey who Steffi knows from last

year. They were in the same bunk. And the Mackinow twins—I'll never learn to tell them apart. Alexandra from Boston, who looks very nice, and Claire, who's got a black mark against her from the beginning. She's a friend of Dena Joyce, a Miss Perfect type. I can tell already we're not going to hit it off.

Before anyone can unpack, the PA starts screaming a frantic announcement. "Attention all camper-waitresses. Attention all camper-waitresses."

"My God!" I say. "What's wrong?"

"It's nothing, take it easy," Steffi says. "It's only Edna at the office. She always makes everything sound like a five-alarm fire."

"You should hear her when she's really excited," Liza says, and then she starts laughing about some time last year, but it's cut off by the rest of Edna's announcement.

"All camper-waitresses report to the flagpole. Immediately. Right this minute! On the double! Let's go, girls! Ten . . . nine . . . eight . . . seven . . . Move it, girls! . . . six . . ."

"Hurry, everybody!" Steffi shouts, flinging her bags on the bed, grabbing my hand and yanking me out the door. "It's the gargoyles."

"Oh, no," Liza moans, flying after us. Now everybody, even the cool Dena Joyce, is beating it down to the flagpole, wherever that is. Steffi's got my hand, and I never saw her move so fast.

From all directions, the sixteen camper-waitresses come running. All the while the shrill command of Edna can be heard over the pounding, panting girls. I'm dying to ask Steffi what's going on, but I'm running too hard to get out the words. There's such a mob behind us that we're almost rammed into the flagpole.

"What's going on?" I finally find enough breath.

"Later, Torrie, later. For now just stand next to me with your hands at your sides."

"Is this a joke, Steffi?"

"No, no. Not in the front line," she says, pulling me into the second tier behind two of the tallest girls in the group.

"I can't see," I protest.

"Neither can they."

Just then all sound stops. It gets so quiet you could hear a pin drop. That's even quieter than you think, since we're standing on grass. I can't see past the girl in front of me, but I see everyone else turn their heads toward the side nearest the administrative offices. I see them following something with their heads until the whole group is looking straight forward.

I peek around between the two giants in front of me. Oh, God! I'm sorry I looked. I pull back and turn my shocked face toward Steffi.

"Nothing's perfect," she whispers, and snaps her head forward again.

So do I, only now for some reason the girl in front of me has switched places with her partner and I have no trouble seeing what had to be the gargoyles.

Without hesitation, a broad-shouldered, two-hundred-pound monster lady, a hands-down winner for prison matron of the year, introduces herself.

"Welcome," she spits out at the quaking group. "I am Madame Katzoff, and this"—pointing to a skinny little man next to her, dressed for riding in jodhpurs and boots and riding crop—"is Dr. Davis." The only thing Dr. Davis is missing is a monocle—otherwise he's a perfect old-movie Gestapo officer.

He smiles, and we're all ready to turn in our mothers.

"Who are these people?" I ask Steffi, but all she does is gulp.

Maybe they're just passing through.

"You!" Madame Katzoff shouts, and it looks like she's pointing in my direction. "You!" Again, but this time the shout has a built-in growl. Poor "you." whoever that is. I look around.

But everybody is looking at me.

I look at Steffi, and she nods her head yes.

My God, I'm you. Someplace way back in the bottom of my throat I find enough of a squeak to answer, "Yes, ma'am."

"If you have any questions, ask me. That's what we're here for. Right, Dr. Davis?"

He does another one of those terrifying smiles, cracks his crop against the ground, and nods his head. For some strange reason he doesn't click his heels.

"Now, your name?"

"Victoria Martin."

With that, Dr. Davis consults a chart he has, and stretching up on his toes, he whispers something to Madame Katzoff.

"Thirteen."

"Huh?"

"You," she snaps, "you're thirteen."

"No, ma'am, I'm sixteen."

"I know that, but your number here is thirteen. We don't use names. Now, thirteen. What is the question that was so important as to hold us up for a full . . ."

Dr. Davis supplies the time. "Four minutes."

In all my entire head there is not one question. So I just shake the whole stupid thing and say, "I'm sorry, ma'am, but I forgot."

"That will cost you a fifty-cent fine," she says, and goes right on.

Fifty cents! What is that all about?

"Let me read you a few of the rules and regulations that are going to make summer at Mohaph a joy for everyone," she continues. "Dr. Davis and I think the best way to start any day is singing. Don't you agree, girls?"

"Yes, absolutely," lots of heads nodding in agreement. It sounds okay to me. Maybe I misjudged them.

"Good," Madame Katzoff says, flashing a carnivorous smile. "Then be here lined up in front of the flagpole every morning . . ."

All right.

". . . at six thirty. In your uniform, with the caps. Following the flag-raising and the camp song, there will be daily instruction and appointment of volunteers."

"Appointment of volunteers?" I whisper to Steffi, but I've lost her. She won't even look at me. Before I can poke her, Madame Katzoff launches into a list of our duties.

"Each waitress will have two tables . . ."

Not so bad.

". . . of twelve kids and three counselors."

That's thirty humans!

"She will be responsible for seeing the tables are wiped clean and set, the trays are washed, the glasses sparkling, and the Batricide room is spic and span. . . ."

"Steffi, what's the Batricide room?"

"The kitchen after we disinfect it."

"There will be fifty-cent fines for the following infractions of the rules," the matron, I mean, Madame Katzoff, continues, and for the first time both she and Dr. Davis smile. "Lateness, talking back, peanut butter and jelly on the tables or chairs, spilling, dripping, unpressed uniforms, missed curfews, smoking, drinking, sloppy bunks, oversleeping, undersleeping, bikinis on the soccer field . . ." and on and on she goes. I panic.

"I'll never remember all that," I whisper to Steffi.

Without moving her lips she says something that either sounds like, "Everything's going to be all right," or "We'll never make it through the night."

In pure Steffi style I ask myself, "Could this be a horrendous mistake or what?"

Two

Okay. It's not exactly what I expected, but there are some good things about it. For one thing, I have my best friend with me for the whole summer. The rest of the camp is beautiful, I love the country air, Madame Katzoff isn't my mother, Dr. Davis isn't my doctor, and nothing larger than a mouse or a bat could possibly get through the hole in the wall over my bed. And I don't have to worry about them because, as I've been assured a thousand times, they're more afraid of me than I am of them.

These are some thoughts jumping around in my head while I try to unpack my things. It's not an easy job, because there is no possible way to jam everything into the tiny cubbies alongside our beds. Everyone has the same problem, so we all arrange to leave most of our clothes in suitcases at the foot of our beds, which leaves about an inch and a half of floor space in the bunk. There's sure to be a lot of knocked knees and stubbed toes this summer.

In a way it's kind of cozy fitting everything into this little space. Luckily, I brought up a couple of new posters and remembered to throw in some thumbtacks. First thing I do is hang one of them over the hole above my bed. It may not be strong enough to stop the rodent invasions but at least I'll hear them, which will give me time to move my head so they don't drop down on my nose.

"You're not going to leave that vomitous thing up on the wall, are you?" That, of course, is Dena Joyce talking about my Stones poster.

"Not if everybody hates it. I thought it was pretty hot. What do you think, Steffi?"

"I like it. Liza?"

"Really hot. I have the same one at home."

Dena Joyce turns to her honcho, Claire. "Do you like it?"

"Yuck . . . it's the pits."

One for Dena Joyce.

Now she turns to the Mackinow twins. They shrug their shoulders, sort of agreeing with her. They're funny, the twins—okay, but kind of like sheep who follow whoever gets to them first. Most twins like to be different, but not the Mackinows. They seem to do everything the same, even dress alike. Now Alexandra has the deciding vote. I'm not taking any chances. I get to her first.

"What do you think, Al?"

"It's okay with me."

That makes it even. I really do want to be nice since we have to live together all summer, so I suggest we toss for it. Dena Joyce says heads and wins.

Later Steffi tells me that Dena Joyce always wins. She's that kind of person. She's awful, but she always gets her way. You know how you see that happen in movies? The bad person always seems to get her way.

I take the poster down, and now I have that huge hole again.

"That's better," Dena Joyce says, rubbing it in.

I'm stacking that up in the back of my mind for sometime in the future when I can pay her back. And I will, too.

That day, after dark, Steffi and I are alone on the porch. She's sitting on the railing, risking her life, and I'm balanced on the only step that's still in one piece.

"Are you sorry you came or what?" she wants to know.

"Absolutely not," I tell her, and I mean it. "It's going to be great once we get things under control."

"You're the best, Torrie. You really are. I guess I just didn't remember how, well, not perfect it was. All I remember is Robbie, and he *is* perfect."

"When is he coming?"

"In two days."

"Friday?"

"Yes, he's coming up a couple of days early because he knows I'm here. Oh, Torrie, I'm so nervous. I haven't seen him in six months. That's a lifetime. Anything could have happened. Maybe he won't be attracted to me anymore. Oh, God, I shouldn't have cut these bangs. He probably hates bangs."

"Steffi, you're crazy. Those bangs are terrific. He's going to love them. I can tell from that letter you let me read that he wouldn't care if you had two heads and both of them had bangs."

"You think so?"

People become so different when they're in love. Normally Steffi is pretty sure of herself, but when it comes to Robbie, she's a mess. I guess when you love someone the way she loves Robbie, you always worry you're going to lose them. I've had crushes on boys, but I've never been in love like that. I worry so much normally that I'd probably be a basket case if I ever fell in love.

I don't know how she's going to survive the summer. He isn't even here yet, and she's falling apart. Well, at least I'm here to help her. That's what best friends are for, right?

"For starters, the bangs are great, you look even better than you did last summer. Don't you remember how that guy on the bus, Ken, went gaga for you?"

"Did you really think so or what?"

"Absolutely."

"He was sort of nice, but I hardly even look at boys the way I used to since Robbie. I practically look at them like brothers."

"I don't think he wanted to be your brother."

"No chance of anything else." She shakes her head. "Torrie?"

"Yeah?"

"Can I dribble on about Robbie for a while?"

"No longer than a week."

"Forget that he's the best-looking guy you ever saw outside of a movie. He's sexy and he's fun, and best of all, he cares. He's the first one to jump up when anybody needs help. Torrie, he's like a hero in a movie. I can see him saving people's lives all the time."

"He sounds so great, I know I'm going to like him a whole lot."

"I want you to. You two are the most important people outside my family in the world. Sometimes I worry that you won't like him, and then I don't know what I'd do."

"Are you kidding? I like him already."

"Is he really as gorgeous as everyone says?" Dena Joyce says, carefully coming out on the perilous porch. Obviously, she's been listening. "Come on, Steffi, let's hear it. I'm really interested in Robbie Wagner. *Very*." She sounds almost hungry when she says the last very. I personally will kill her if she goes after Robbie. I really will.

"John Travolta is almost as good-looking," Steffi says, without even a trace of worry. It's like a fat little lamb walking into a wolf's den. I wouldn't trust Dena Joyce with Frankenstein.

"He's just great," my lamb friend goes on.

"Really?" says the wolf, practically salivating.

And Steffi launches into a description of Robbie that makes him sound like every girl's dream come true. Certainly it's Dena Joyce's dream, and she's probably going to try to make it come true, but she hasn't got a chance. He really is in love with Steffi. I've seen some of his letters, and it's serious.

Still, Dena Joyce *is* very good-looking, the cheerleader type, long blond hair, blue eyes, good figure, just the way a sixteen-year-old girl is supposed to look but never does. Except Dena Joyce does.

Steffi's no slouch in the looks department either, but she looks more like a real person. Her hair is a rich, dark brown, almost the same color as her eyes, and even without rouge she has rosy cheeks all the time. Her features are small, not perfect, but soft and nice. Sometime in the last three years she picked up five extra pounds and they stuck. I kind of think they're in the right places, but she's always fighting them. So far they're still there. Oh well, it's a lot better than my problems.

I have long blond hair, my eyes are sort of greenish, I'm five five, and I weigh one hundred and ten. Sounds pretty good, huh? It probably would be on someone else, but on me it just looks like me. It just doesn't come together like it does on Dena Joyce.

I would worry if Dena Joyce was interested in the boy I loved. But not Steffi. She rattles on about Robbie and doesn't seem to notice old D. J. drooling.

The conversation moves on to work, and Dena Joyce loses interest and goes inside.

After a while the lights go out in the bunk, and Steffi and I sit outside a while longer. It's only a quarter moon and very dark. The sounds of the country are nice. I wouldn't like to meet the noisemakers personally, but all together they sound good. I guess it's mostly crickets. I don't think snakes make any sound, or even mice or rats. . . .

"What kind of animals are around here?" I ask Steffi.

"Not many. Sometimes you see a little garden snake or one of the ones that swim. And one time they caught a rattler near the pool. Last year we had a mouse in the bunk, and they say there are bats living in the rafters in the rec hall . . ."

"Bats?"

"Oh, don't worry, Torrie, they're just the ordinary ones. Not the Dracula kind."

"Nice."

"And of course, raccoons and stuff like that. And spiders. Last summer we found the most gigantic—"

"I'm going to bed." And leaping across the broken boards and jumping inside the door, I hear Steffi in her most reassuring voice, "Gosh, Victoria, don't worry. They killed it."

"With what, a cannon?" I hate the country.

It takes me hours to fall asleep. There is just enough light for me to see the hole above my bed. It's not the most comfortable position for sleep with your head twisted up and sideways, but that's the only way I can keep a watch out for the invaders.

253

There's not much of me they can get, since I'm wrapped in my blankets up to my eyeballs. It's a little warm, but well worth the discomfort.

Here I am, just where I begged to be. It's all my parents' fault. Don't they know how to hold on to a position? If they didn't want me to go, they should have made sure I stayed home. God, they are so weak-willed it's infuriating.

And on top of everything, that boy in the bus really dug Steffi. In other words, he didn't like me.

Last thing I remember hearing is the sound of someone sucking her thumb. Either it's a thumb-sucking bat or somebody's got a very embarrassing secret. I'm sure it's not Dena Joyce; it must be Claire.

Of course I have a nightmare. I'm camping out on the ground in the jungle in shorts with no blanket or flashlight. I wake up in a sweat. Before the full terror hits me, Edna, the lunatic lady from yesterday, is screaming over the PA system.

"Let's go girls. Up and at 'em! Up, up, up . . . everybody up!" And then the most horrendous bugle blast imaginable.

We all leap out of bed, racing in all directions, bumping into each other, rushing to get someplace, but nobody knows where.

Except Dena Joyce. She's the first in the bathroom, first at the sink, first at the toilet, and first in front of the mirror. Amazing!

The rest of us dummies begin throwing on our uniforms,

backward, upside down, and inside out. All the while Edna screeches on.

In less than ten minutes we're all dressed, most of us unwashed and uncombed, but ready. Heading out of the door is the messiest group of waitresses, with the exception of D. J., perfect in her uniform, hair combed, teeth shining.

We make it on the double to the flagpole, assume our positions of yesterday, and wait for the gargoyles. I had forgotten how horrendous they were, but the sight of the two of them marching toward us reminded me.

We're sixteen half-dressed waitresses, shivering half from the chill morning air and half from plain old terror.

"I forgot to tell you not to put the pins in your hat," Steffi whispers to me.

"It's okay, I don't have any pins."

"Thank God."

"Tell me."

"We have to sing. Remember the camp song they told us about yesterday?"

"Why do you need a hat to sing?"

Suddenly she stiffens up and without answering me whips her head straight forward. Madame K. and the good doctor have arrived.

"Okay, girls. The flag."

With that, two girls, I guess old campers, walk to the flagpole. Carefully they take the folded flag and attach the two ends to the pulley. To the accompaniment of the bugle we all sing something about raising the flag once again at the break of day. I still can't figure out what the hats have got to do with anything.

We hear a pep talk about how wonderful camp is, how lucky we are to be chosen, and what a wonderful summer we're all going to have. Coming from anyone but the gargoyles I might buy it, but I just don't trust . . .

"Let's hear it, girls!"

Steffi whispers, "Just watch me." Most of the girls are old campers and know what to do. They raise their right arms above their heads and drop their hands onto the tops of their hats. We, the new girls, follow and watch silently as (like they say in the books) they raise their voices in song. And their hats.

Hats off to Katzoff and Da-vis,
They lead a wonderful team,
Rah, rah, rah! . . .

Three stanzas. I don't believe it!

Here we are, sixteen normal teenagers, singing and tipping our hats like idiots. Steffi is afraid to look at me. She should be.

Marching single file, still stepping to the inspiring beat of "Hats Off," we head toward the mess hall.

The mess hall is in a big white building at the far end of the campus, near the administration building. The eating part is one large room divided in half by a trellis-type wall covered with artificial philodendrons, thousands of shiny green leaves that look like someone oiled each and every one of them. Probably a perfect volunteer job for a camper-waitress.

The whole place sparkles with cleanliness. Each side has about fifteen or twenty tables, some round and some long rect-angles. All are covered with shiny green plastic tablecloths, the same color as the leaves.

All the tables are numbered. Mine are seventeen and nine-teen. They're in good places, not far from the kitchen. I just can't wait to get started.

We get to look at the kitchen, and it's empty and spot-less. No problems here. I can just picture how smoothly this is going to go. We'll just shoot through the whole thing, in and out in under an hour.

They let us do a little practicing with the trays. Even though they're a little heavier than I expected, still I feel very comfortable holding it. It's going to be terrific fun, I know it.

"That's great," Steffi says, when I show her my tray-holding method. "Someone show you that or what?"

"A friend of my mother showed me. She was an actress when she first came to New York, and they do a lot of wait-ressing."

Now Alexandra and Liza come over, and they want a demonstration too. I show them the trick of balancing the tray on one shoulder so that it rests on the palm of your hand. They all try it, but it's harder than they expected. I've been practicing for weeks, so I've got it down pat.

I'm off to a very good start, I can tell. Sure, I'm a little nervous, but I know it's going to be great. I just can't wait.

Steffi was up at five this morning. It's Friday, the big day. Robbie is finally coming. The bus won't arrive until eleven a.m. but it's taken Steffi all morning to prepare herself. First she had to try on everything in her wardrobe. Naturally she hated everything and finally ended up wearing a combination of my shorts, Liza's blouse, Alexandra's belt, and one of the twins (horrible to say but I still can't tell them apart—maybe it's really only one person breaking through the sight barrier) lent her a small suede vest. It looks great over the white blouse. The only thing I'm not crazy for are the shorts, but that's probably because they're mine.

Once she got the clothes under control, she moved on to her hair and makeup. She did at least fourteen different styles and ended up with the original one, long and softly curled at the ends, with one side pulled back. Except for the bangs, it's exactly the hair style she's been wearing for the past year. A quick hour to choose the nail polish and apply. By ten thirty she was ready. At ten forty-five she decided my shorts were wrong with the vest. At 10:55 she changed every stitch.

It is eleven now, and she completely loses her cool and changes back to the original outfit, half dressing, half running to the parking lot. Her vest is on inside out and the zipper stuck open on my shorts. Fortunately, the bus is a few minutes late.

By the time the Greyhound pulls into the campgrounds, everything has been pulled into place. Now the zipper is closed—forever. Nothing matters except that Robbie is here. Well, almost. He still isn't off the bus.

I move back so Steffi can have the field to herself. I step away, just beyond the parking lot, far enough to be out of the picture but close enough to be able to watch, like it was a movie. It's very romantic. I can't wait to see Robbie, to see them together. After all the messing around with the preparation, Steffi looks beautiful. A lot of it is her excitement and anticipation; it makes her face absolutely glow. It's hard for me to imagine someone making such a huge difference in your life. I've had lots of crushes but nothing that starts so far down and comes out all over. It's great.

Steffi is all by herself out there, just like it *was* a movie and she's the star. The bus is more than half empty. I can see people inside getting up and reaching above the seats for their luggage. With the tinted windows it's hard to tell which one is Robbie. I'll just have to wait and see.

It rained earlier this morning, but now the sun is strong and there's enough breeze to spread the wonderful fresh country smells. It's not hot enough to make you sweat, and the breeze isn't strong enough to mess your hair; it's a perfect summer day. Perfect for meeting someone you love.

The first three people out of the bus are girls. The next person is an older man and then . . . Robbie. It has to be. I can tell from Steffi.

Even though her back is to me, I know it from the way her body stiffens and gets alert. For an instant Robbie doesn't see her. He's expecting her to be on the other side where the rest of the people are. He searches them.

He's too far away for me to tell much. But I can see that he's probably terrific-looking, tall and slim, with a model's body—very sexy.

As soon as he spots Steffi he drops his bags and walks right to her. She's still nailed to the spot, but now she's tilted her head up to him. It's only a few steps away, so he's there in an instant, slipping his arms around her waist as she flows in and up against him. It's all one move. Steffi lifts her face to meet his and then her arms are around him, and from the angle of their heads I can tell they're kissing, and the kiss goes on and they move closer to each other, and I can practically feel their closeness. Now he takes her face in his hands and looks down at her, then kisses her cheeks and her forehead and then down again to her mouth. And stays there. Their bodies are pressed together, tenderly and lovingly.

Wow! I can hardly believe it's only my friend Steffi. It really is like a play. She seems so much like a woman, I feel I don't even know her. Maybe I won't with Robbie. Maybe she'll be so different with someone she loves, it'll be like she's outgrown me.

I'm so stuck in those stupid thoughts that for a minute I don't even hear her calling me. Finally my name breaks through, and I drag myself out of the fantasy I've been watching, throw on a smile, and head toward them, taking a new look at my old friend. She's beaming.

"Victoria," she says, putting out her free hand to me. I take it, and now we're on two sides of Steffi. Me holding her left hand and the great Robbie attached to the right one.

"My two closest friends," she says. "Robbie, this is the fabulous Victoria. And Torrie, this is some guy I picked up at the bus stop."

Now my smile is true, and I take my first close look at Robbie, the wonderful, the spectacular—

Oh . . .

Suddenly it's as if everything stopped dead and opened up, and I fell out. The air is humming and buzzing around me, or is it only inside my head? I catch his eyes, and it's like I touch an electric current and got locked into it. My God, Steffi! Surely she can see something's happening, but she doesn't seem to, because someplace way back on the surface I hear her chattering on. I feel like I've been caught in a laser beam, something that stops me from moving or feeling anything. . . .

"Victoria." It's Steffi's voice coming through.

"Hi." I jump in immediately, staring right past Robbie's ear.

He puts out his hand. "Good to meet you."

I don't dare look at him. I'll never be able to pull away. I don't know what's happening, but I hate it. *Stop it, Victoria!*

He's talking. Something about how he's heard so much about me, and on and on, and all the time I'm smiling a goofy

261

smile that's directed somewhere between Steffi's face and Robbie's shoulder. Back and forth I go. Is he ever going to shut up?

Finally he does, and then they wait for me to take my turn. I say the same sort of thing about how much I've heard about him. I take myself right up a blind alley, and then a weird silence falls and Steffi jumps in, and with a pull on Robbie's hand and with a kind of loving shove to me, gets us moving.

I keep falling behind, and Steffi keeps bringing me up alongside them.

"We've got some beauties in our bunk. Something called a Dena Joyce. The pits, right, Torrie?"

That's easy. "Right," I say.

And for some reason, Robbie directs his next question at me. I miss the question because I'm bending down to tie my sneaker. Unfortunately, I'm wearing slip-on sandals. They both stop and watch me dust my sandals.

"How do you like being a waitress?" he says to the top of my head.

I look up. They're both looking down at me, my best friend and the boy she adores, loves, worships, and will probably even marry one day. He repeats the question. I should look at him to answer it. But I know once I look at him, once I fall into that magnetic field again, I'll never get out. I've never felt such a strong pull to anyone ever. I don't even know what it is, it's so enormous. All I know is that it's not funny.

"Steffi loves it," I say. "Right, Stef?" That's the perfect

answer. It turns it all back to Steffi, where it belongs.

"So far it's pretty simple, since nobody's here. I don't know what's going to happen tomorrow when the kids get here. I'm a little scared."

I'm still bending down messing around with my shoes, the same stupid smile still pasted on my face. Now I look up at Steffi, who is directing her conversation to Robbie, who is looking at me without a smile. It's probably only for a second, but it feels much too long. So long that I know I have to get out of here—and fast.

"Hey, I almost forgot. I have to fly. I volunteered for leaf waxing this morning." And, like I was a starter in a foot race, I shoot off, running at top speed.

"Leaf waxing? What's that?" I hear Robbie ask, but I'm out of earshot for Steffi's answer. I can't really remember if I made it up or they really have it. I'll volunteer anyway and see what happens.

Three

I get back to the bunk out of breath but safe. I walk in to find D. J. alone, with her nose in Steffi's cubby. She doesn't even have the courtesy to jump when I catch her.

"Looking for something?" I say, like they do in the movies. At least that's what I mean to say, but I'm so crazed that it comes out "Looking for someone?"

"In a cubby. Really, Victoria, what's your problem?" And slowly, without one iota of embarrassment, she stands up, closes the cabinet door, and turns to me. "Did you get to meet the great Robbie?"

I can feel my face turning tomato-red. Dena Joyce has already turned the tables. There she was sneaking through Steffi's cubby, which is an absolutely disgusting thing to do, and instead of her being the guilty one, she's caught me doing something worse. In a second she knows something's up just from the color of my face.

"Not bad, huh?" she winks, and gives me a smile like we're both in on something.

"I barely saw him. He's okay, I guess—no accounting for tastes, right? I mean, good-looking isn't everything. Or even being tall and well-built."

Please someone stop me!

"Frankly, I go for an entirely different type. I'm not so crazy for that very dark hair, especially if it's very straight and shiny. I like curly blonds. And light eyes with dark hair doesn't turn me on. He probably lifts weights to get those kind of muscles, and you know what happens if you miss even one day, it all falls apart."

Anyone!

"Turns to mush right in front of your eyes. Naw, he's nothing much. Far as I can see, anyway. I mean, he's probably okay if you like that type. I suppose Steffi thinks he's cute. I mean, I know she does, but it beats me. Boy, is he ordinary. Just plain old nothing much."

Help!

"Absolutely nothing much. Even less. A minus, you know, a hole, a gap. It's like there's nobody there . . . you know . . ."

"Wow!"

"What do you mean, 'wow'?"

"I never saw anybody hit that hard that fast. Wow!"

"I don't know what you're talking about. I told you he's nothing special. He's . . ."

265

"Don't worry, Victoria, I'm your friend. You can trust me."

I'm lost. If D. J. is my friend and I have to trust her, it's all over. Then I remember that she really can't get inside my head. At least I can lie. I still have that left. So what if she doesn't believe me? Nobody ever believes her, and she gets by. "You can think what you like," I tell her. "It's all ridiculous, since I have had a steady boyfriend for the last two years back home."

"Sure."

"Besides, let's talk about you. What were you doing in my friend's cubby, anyway?" Now I've got her.

"Was that hers? Gee, I thought it was mine." She doesn't even make any attempt to give me a reasonable lie. And she seems to be enjoying it all. "Just like you with Robbie," she says.

Here she is, boldfaced lying, and I'm the one who's uncomfortable. We could all take lessons from Dena Joyce.

No point in continuing this, so I just turn around and get busy with my own things. It's almost time to change for lunch. In fact, if I hurry I can get out of here before Steffi comes back. I certainly don't want to see her with Dena Joyce around. I've got to pull myself together, or at least go someplace where it won't all show.

How is it that everyone can always read me so perfectly? Steffi's got to know there's something wrong. She has to. You just can't fool your best friend since the fourth grade. Especially if you have a face like mine. I need those Dena Joyce lessons.

"Torrie?"

Too late, Steffi's back.

"I'm so glad I caught you. We've got to talk."

Oh, God. She knows.

"Privately," she says, motioning her head at Dena Joyce. "Come on, walk with me."

"Believe me," D. J. singsongs to Steffi, "the last thing I want to hear about is your marvelous Robbie. I've heard plenty from your very best friend here. Haven't I?" That last bit directed to me.

"We better hurry, Steffi," I say, grabbing my friend's arm and pulling her toward the door. "We only have about fifteen minutes before lineup."

She follows me out of the door, slightly confused. "She got a problem or what?" she asks. "What was that all about?"

"You better watch out for her. She wants everything that isn't hers." It really is the truth, but in this case it's not perfectly accurate. Still, it's pretty good thinking. In fact, it's Dena Joyce thinking. Now if I can only handle what's coming now half as well.

Steffi and I are very close friends. She's the most important person to me apart from my family, and we never lie to each other, but this time I have to. It would be the end of the friendship if she even suspected I could possibly betray her. I know I wouldn't, but even just feeling strange about Robbie is so terrible. Actually, I don't even know what I feel about him, but something happened out there. Something outside my control. I mean, he knocked me out. That's it. My best friend's boyfriend knocked me out. Maybe that sounds stupid, but something happened between us. Well, maybe not between *us*. It didn't have to happen to him too. Just me. Oh, I don't know. Maybe it was nothing. Maybe it was just something I ate. Whatever it was, Steffi has nothing to worry about. I plan not even to look at him. I'm staying as far away as humanly possible and then some.

"What's up with you, Torrie? You didn't hear a word I said. I'm asking you a very important question."

"No!" I answer, even though I haven't the faintest idea what she asked me, but I'm not taking any chances. "Absolutely not. Not one bit. Never! No!"

"Huh?"

"I said no. N . . . O!" I practically bark it out.

"You don't think he's a little nice or what?" She's absolutely crushed.

Oh, I should have listened. "Oh, Steffi, of course I do."

"Then why do you keep shouting on when all I asked you was whether you thought Robbie was a nice guy?"

"Oh, I thought you were asking about Dr. Davis." There goes my Dena Joyce again. It's getting to be a habit.

"Dr. Davis? That monster! Are you nuts or something?"

"Sorry, Steffi. I guess I'm just starting to get nervous. You realize those kids are coming up tomorrow?"

"So?"

"Well, there are so many. . . ."

"What about Robbie?"

"Right."

"Right what? Torrie, what's the matter with you? Do you like him or not or what?"

"I do."

"No, you don't."

"I swear I do. I think he's terrific, and gorgeous and nice and—"

"You hate him. I can tell. You can't lie to me, Victoria. I know you too well."

"Honest, Steffi—"

"He likes you."

"He doesn't—"

"Yes, he does. He even said so. In fact, he was very interested in hearing all about you."

"No."

"What do you mean, no? Why shouldn't he? After all, you are my best friend. I want to know all about his friends."

"Well, that's nice. So what do you think about . . . uh, Dr. Davis?"

"I'm seriously in love with him."

"Dr. Davis?"

"No, silly. Robbie. And I want to know what you think of him. I guess all that counts is that I love him. Still, I'm really curious why you seemed so cold to him."

I can't believe she read my reaction as cold. If it was any hotter I'd have exploded. This situation is really out of hand—I mean, I just can't stand around talking about Robbie. Something's going to show. I don't know what's happening—all I know is that it's not good, but instead of feeling bad, all I feel is excitement. It was bad enough when I was with him, but now it's even worse just thinking about him. And all Steffi wants to know is why was I so cold to Robbie?

So I tell her the truth. "I don't feel cold toward Robbie. Not at all. In fact, I took to him the first time I saw him. He's exactly the way you described him." The truth is good up to a point: "And I know we're all going to be good friends." But no further.

"Really, Torrie? I hope so, because that's what I want."

I do her another D. J. and describe the wonderful summer we're all going to have together.

No way. I intend to avoid Robbie every chance I get. When I think about him, I almost hate him. In fact, that's just what I have to do . . . hate him. I don't like Robbie Wagner. Not one bit! No way! No how!

"After lunch I said we'd all have a Coke together."

"Gee, Steffi, I'm sorry but I can't."

"How come?"

"I promised Alexandra I'd do her nails."

"That's okay, we'll do it after dinner tonight."

"Actually, I was planning on writing some letters . . ."

"I knew it! You don't like him."

". . . but they can wait. Hey, I'm looking forward to it. A great idea . . . a Coke. I'm thirsty already."

"Torrie, I don't know what's cooking with you, but something's weird, and since I'm supposed to be your best friend, why don't you try to tell me?"

"I miss Nick."

"Who?"

"I mean Todd. I really do, Steffi. Maybe I'm in love with him. What do you think?"

"If you were, you'd know it, Torrie, you wouldn't have to ask. I don't have a minute's trouble about Robbie."

I really can't bear all these Robbie conversations. Everything turns into Robbie. "What if something happened? I mean, what if you just stopped loving him?"

"That's impossible."

"Suppose he stopped loving you? It could happen, couldn't it?"

"I guess it could, but I can't even think about it. It's too terrible. I don't know, but right now I think it would destroy my life."

"Come on, Steffi, you're only sixteen. This isn't the last guy you're going to be in love with."

"It might be, Torrie. Robbie is the kind of person I could end up spending my life with."

"You mean you would marry him?"

"If I had to decide right now, absolutely yes."

Suddenly I feel like I'm going to be sick if we go on with this conversation one more minute. Luckily, Edna on the PA system saves me.

"Let's go, waitresses! Lunch call! Hurry . . . hurry . . . hurry! Ten . . . nine . . . eight . . . seven . . . Move it, ladies, flagpole time!"

And the stampede begins again, this time with Steffi and me in the lead. Nobody is ever late for flagpole. Nobody. Ever!

Somehow I manage to get through the rest of the day without seeing Robbie and Steffi. Now all I have to face is tonight. I promised we'd all have a Coke after dinner. I'm beginning to work up to a major sickness. It's a toss up between lockjaw (which of course would be very handy for turning down a Coke) and some vague allergy that would make me itch all over. I start scratching right after lunch. Incredibly enough, nobody asks me what's the matter. It's almost dinnertime and I have red lines all over my legs and arms. Still nobody seems interested. Not even Steffi, who is so busy floating on air that she doesn't even know anybody exists.

"Don't forget about the Coke tonight, Torrie."

Unfortunately for me, she hasn't quite forgotten everything.

I tell her I can't wait, and I hope that this terrible allergy (lockjaw is too hard to pull off, what with the clamped teeth and all) lets up. She wants to know what I'm allergic to, and I resist the temptation to say Robbie Wagner. "I think it's something I ate for lunch or maybe some plant or something. Nobody ever knows with allergies."

"Maybe you should go to the nurse."

"I already have, and she said I should try to get to bed

early and she gave me some stuff to put on." You see how one lie leads to another. It's like that Shakespeare thing about the tangled webs we weave when first we practice to deceive. It's too late with me. I've finished practicing. I'm from the Dena Joyce school of professional liars, top of the class.

Four

Tonight is the first night we're going to be formally meeting the boys, the junior counselors, the staff members—everybody except the counselors, they're not here yet. They ride up with the kids tomorrow.

Preparation starts for the big night at about four in the afternoon. Sometimes I think that's the best part of any party, getting ready. It all sounds so terrific when it's in the planning stage. It hardly ever works out that way. Even your clothes. You think you put together this fabulous outfit, a little something from everyone, and it looks terrific in your head, but somehow when it gets on your body it loses its magic. And then every little thing seems crucial, like even the color of your nail polish is going to matter. Probably nobody notices, but you can't take that chance. You need every advantage you can get, at least I do. But not tonight.

It's really tough to dress down, to try to look lousy. Lots of times I end up looking that way, but I don't know how to start off trying to look awful. It's harder than you think. I'm certainly not going to choose things that don't match or make me look fat or short. As a sacrifice, and to show myself that I'm really serious, I dress from head to toe in my own clothes. I hardly recognize myself. It's absolutely horrendous, but it is easy, and I'm the first one ready. By at least two hours.

"Hey, D. J., I love those velour shorts. They are hot!" Claire, Dena Joyce's best, closest, and probably only friend in the whole world, says. She holds up fabulous mauve shorts with pink satin trim. "Mind if I borrow them tonight?"

"Oh, honey, I'd love to but I can't. They're not really mine. They're my cousin's and I promised her. . . ." It oozes out so sweet and drawly, Dena Joyce almost sounds Southern. And it's absolutely untrue. So far, every stitch anyone wants to borrow belongs to that famous cousin. She's just plain selfish, but Claire gobbles up everything D. J. says.

"Hey no, D. J., I wouldn't want you to do anything like that. Gee, I know what it's like when you have to take care of somebody else's things . . ." And on and on Claire dribbles, practically apologizing for asking. It's really gross to watch.

"Honey," Dena Joyce says, reaching over and lifting the belt Claire has lying on her bed, obviously the one she was about to put on. "You don't mind, do you?"

"No sweat." She practically licks Dena Joyce. It's *dégueulasse*.

That's a French word that means disgusting, but sounds even worse, and it's perfect for Claire. "I like this jumpsuit better loose like this." And she sort of twirls around modeling what looks like a sack. "What do you think?" she asks the queen.

We're all watching, waiting for her to tell Claire, the balloon person, how marvelous she looks when she looks like a blimp.

D. J. takes a slow, long look at Claire. "No good, honey, you gotta put something around your middle. Otherwise," she says, snapping the perfect belt around her own waist, "you look like a glob."

"I don't think I have one," Claire says, like she really doesn't.

This is very hard to watch. If it was anyone other than jerky Claire I would jump in, but she deserves it for being such a nerd. I just can't believe someone could have so little character. It makes you want to throw up.

But Dena Joyce is perfect. All she does is shrug her shoulders, like too bad but it's not my problem, and turn away. Back to her curlers.

Eventually one of the Mackinow twins comes up with a belt that works okay. I swear to you D. J. actually stops and checks it out, just to make sure she definitely has the best one.

"What do you think?" Steffi keeps asking me, every time she puts on something else.

"You look so fabulous tonight it doesn't matter what you're wearing. Did you do something different with your makeup?" I ask her. "A new blush?"

"No."

"It's something."

She smiles. And suddenly I know what it is. She's beaming. It's that love thing again. Too bad they don't have a counter of it at Bloomie's.

Finally we're all ready. Except for me, they all look great.

I suppose my mother would go bananas if she saw the bunk. Every bed has at least three rejection outfits on it. The floor is covered with shoes, curlers, hot curls, and blow dryers. Every flat surface is jammed with makeup bottles, jars, tubes, compacts: I would guess there was an easy thousand dollars' worth of eye shadow and face goo of every kind around, stuff to make your face peel, stuff to stop it from peeling, softening, hardening, opening pores, closing pores, special liquids that do everything except make you look older, which is what we all want. Steffi once used her mother's youth cream and worried for a whole day that it would make her look too young.

We head off in a troop to meet the enemy, the friendly enemy. Most of the time too friendly.

You can hear the music blasting before you're halfway there. It feels good—it's the first real sounds of home.

It's always horrendous walking into those things, even in a safe group like we are. I wonder if Dena Joyce has these regular human feelings. I can't picture her being nervous about meeting a boy.

"They're probably all jerks, what do you think?" Alexandra

is walking with Steffi and me. She's a wreck too, you can tell.

"I know one that isn't," Steffi says, winking at me.

"Nobody could accuse Robbie Wagner of being a jerk. Ever!" Alexandra agrees.

"And that other guy from the bus?" Steffi pokes me. "Remember him? He was cute."

"Except he was madly in love with you," I remind her.

Right away Alexandra wants to know who, what, and where. So Steffi tells her about Ken. She was really impressed with him. I thought he was okay, but not that good. She probably liked him because he was obviously so gaga about her.

I personally hate him.

"Sounds like everybody's there already," I say, trying to move the conversation off Ken.

"Get a load of D. J." Steffi pokes me. And sure enough, there's good old Dena Joyce pulling out ahead. She's got to be first in everything.

"She thinks if she gets in there first she'll get the best one, like she did the first day with the beds," Steffi says, laughing.

"Right," I tell her, "but you better move it because the best bed this time happens to be none other than Robbie Wagner."

Steffi laughs and pretends she's making a run for it; Dena Joyce actually speeds up. Allie and I crack up.

"What's so funny?" one of the twins wants to know.

Before we can answer, her echo joins her, ". . . so funny?" They're really strange those twins. It's like they're Siamese but

278

they're not joined where you can see. They're stuck together at the mind, which is barely big enough for one anyway. It's the same person stamped out twice.

So I answer the closest one. "Nothing," I say, and continue to be hysterical. I still haven't forgiven them for the poster bit on the first day.

With Dena Joyce in the lead, Claire following respectfully a few steps behind, and then the rest of us, we go up the wooden steps of the social hall. The music is so loud inside they don't even hear us. Before they see us, we get a couple of seconds' free look at twenty-five boys, all brand-new. Excitement and terror.

Now someone spots us. You can see the word spreading through them. We keep heading in. They've become one large moving blur engulfing us.

"Smile, Torrie," Steffi whispers to me. Then I realize how tight my face is. It probably started off as a smile then froze into something horrendous. Something you practically have to chop off.

"Steffi! Over here, Steffi!"

I'd know that voice anywhere. It's coming from over my left shoulder, but I don't dare turn. Steffi starts to pull me toward the voice, but I say, "In a minute," and she heads off into the crowd. Now I'm alone. I make a quick search for Alexandra, but I can't find her. I'm on my own. Help!

"Hi," a nice voice says, and when I look up I see it's Ken from the bus.

"Oh, hi. How you doing?"

"Great . . ." He searches a second for my name, then, "Don't tell me. I remember. Steffi!"

Jerk.

"Steffi's friend," I say, as nicely as I can with one more try at being cute.

"Right." He smiles. "Steffi's friend." And he joins in the joke and he is nice. I get a quick sense that he's taking another look at me.

"Victoria," he says, and I think he likes what he sees.

"Right." I smile a real smile back and point to him and say, "Robbie!"

I can't believe my ears. Did I say that?

The instant it leaves my lips, the second the smile leaves his. I'm horrified. I really never meant to say that name. It jumped out of my head. I know his name is Ken, and I certainly know he isn't Robbie. Oh, God, I'm going crazy.

He recovers first. "Okay, now we're even." And he's back to smiling.

"Ken Irving," I say, to show him that I really do remember him. "How's the telephone business?"

"Great. I've disconnected twelve people in only three days. What's up with the waitressing? I haven't seen any of you girls in the mess hall so far."

"We don't start until tomorrow, when the kids come up. All we've been doing is learning the rules. You wouldn't believe how complicated it is. I'll never remember it all."

"So big deal. So you forget something. Don't be so nervous about it. After all, it's only your first time."

"Have you seen the gargoyles yet?"

"Unfortunately, yes."

"Would you like to make a mistake in front of them?"

"I don't think they'd do more than shoot you."

All the time we're talking, I'm watching Steffi and Robbie out of the corner of my eye. They've been dancing, a slow dance, real close. When the music ends they begin to make their way over to us. They're holding hands. I'm looking right at them, but I blur them out as they come closer.

"Hi," Steffi says, then I see her struggling for Ken's name.

"You remember Ken from the bus?" I say.

"Right, Ken Irving," she says, and Ken Irving beams. He's been remembered right down to his last name. This boy could never be interested in me. Then she starts to introduce Robbie, but it turns out they know each other already. In fact, they're sharing a bunk.

It's happening to me again. I'm . . . I don't know . . . upset by Robbie. When he's near me he seems to take over everything. It's really terrible, and I don't know how to deal with it. I know I've got to start by getting away from him; then I can think out a plan of action.

I barely wait for the new song to begin. "I love this song," I say, looking directly at Ken, who is hopelessly lost in something Steffi is saying. He doesn't even see me, but Steffi does, and before I can stop her she says to Robbie, "It's your favorite, too. Torrie, show him that new step you were trying yesterday."

And she pushes me onto the dance floor. Of course, he has to follow. But I stop it.

"I can't," I say to both of them (still not actually focusing on Robbie). "I twisted my ankle."

"I didn't know," Steffi says, concerned. "When?"

"Just before."

Steffi looks at me in a funny way, like something's up, but I just go right on. "I gotta get something to drink. I'm dying of thirst. Anyone want anything?"

"I'll get it," Robbie says. "You should get off that foot."

"No," I say, taking full control of the situation. "It's better to walk it out."

"But not dance it out, huh?" Steffi's looking at me really strangely, but I pay no attention. I have to do it this way.

"Three Cokes?" I say, and head off without waiting for an answer.

I don't care what happens, I am *not* going to get involved with my best friend's boyfriend. No matter what, I swear I will absolutely not go near him. I swear on our friendship. All the way over to the other corner where they're giving out the drinks, I keep telling myself that this is the way it has to be. I have no choice. It's simple. I'm just going to walk away whenever he's around. I'll find reasons. They may not be fabulous, but it's better than what would happen if I stuck around. I know it. I can't control it any other way. I never had someone be so totally awesome in my life before.

"Torrie!"

Steffi comes up behind me, pulling me out of my daydream/nightmare.

"That's okay," I say, "I can carry them."

"What's up?" she says. "What's all this business about your ankle? There's nothing wrong with your ankle. You're not even limping. What's going on, Torrie?"

"Nothing. I really did hurt my foot, but it feels better now. I told you I had to walk it out."

"You're full of it. You just don't like him. That's what it's all about. I know it."

"You're wrong. I think he's terrific."

"You hate him. I can tell. You were practically rude to him. I can't believe you'd be like that to someone who's so important to me."

"That's not true."

"It is, too, and you know it."

Here we are, the two best friends in the world, and we're fighting over something that isn't even real. I've got to stop it.

"It's because of Ken." I have to say something, anything.

"What do you mean? How can it be because of Ken? What's he got to do with your being so awful to Robbie?"

All the time she's asking the question, I'm thinking like mad for an answer. Then I find it. "I really didn't mean to be rude to Robbie," I tell her. "It's just that I think I've fallen in love with Ken, and he's all I can think about."

First I'm fighting, now I'm lying. It's really gross what's happening.

"I didn't want Ken to think I wanted to dance with Robbie because he'd just asked me to dance, and I got so nervous I had to say no, so . . ."

Just looking at Steffi's face tells me this is a stupid lie, but it's too late.

"So," I dig myself deeper into the hole, "I couldn't very well dance with Robbie, could I?"

Steffi looks at me; she's angry. I've known Steffi Klinger since the third grade. We used to have little fights, nothing serious, when we were really young, but we haven't had even a real disagreement since we got into seventh grade. I've seen her angry, but never at me. I just stand there because all the baloney is finished. This is really intense.

"I don't know why you're lying to me. And I don't know why you don't like him, unless, and I think this is crazy, you are jealous of him or what?"

"Jealous of Robbie?"

"With me, I mean."

I don't believe it. I'm saved. She gave it to me herself. I know it's more lies but it's the only thing that's going to work. It's bad if I like him too much and bad if I don't like him enough. This is the only way out. So I take it.

"Well . . . I guess he *is* going to change our relationship."

"No he's not. Sure, maybe I'll be spending more time with

Robbie, but we'll still have a lot of time together. After all, we'll be living together in the same bunk. We'll be spending more time together than we do at home, right?"

"I guess so, still . . ."

"Really, Torrie, and besides that, we'll all be together, all three of us."

Now it's getting bad again. I have to stop complaining. "You're right, Steffi, I guess I'm just not used to you having someone special, but really, when I think about it, I guess it's no different from the time I spend with Todd when we're in the city. Actually, you *should* be able to spend time alone with Robbie. I do with Todd, right?"

"Sure, a little, but most of the time we'll all be together."

Not if I can help it, but I don't say anything else. Enough. I'll worry about the togetherness later.

"Torrie, you're my best friend and you're very important to me, but gee, you can't do things like this. You know we have that pact that we tell each other when something's wrong. It would have been terrible if we lost our friendship over something like this. Something that could have been straightened out so easily."

I tell her she's right and how I feel so much better.

"Come on, Torrie, let's get back. They'll think something's wrong."

"Steffi, I know you're right about everything. And I feel so much better now, but I just don't feel like going back in there." And that's the truth, and Steffi sees it and tells me it's

285

okay, she'll tell the boys my ankle was bothering me.

"You're my best friend, Torrie. I hope you'll be my best friend for always."

"I really love you, Steffi."

She smiles at me. "See you later," she says, and turns to go up the steps to the rec hall. "Take care of that ankle."

"Hey, gimme a break," I say, but she's already inside the screen door.

Okay, it's not perfect but I can work with it. The most important thing is to stay far away from Robbie Wagner and keep close to Steffi. It's a trick, but it has to be done.

I go back toward the bunks. The air is nightime sweet, filled with the scent of honeysuckle and grass. If only I didn't have this huge problem I really could be happy here. Tonight anyway. Tomorrow is another story.

Tomorrow the kids arrive. They're supposed to come here about eleven a.m., in time for lunch. It will be the first meal we've ever served. We're all pretty nervous, especially since the gargoyles will be watching. Worse than that, they'll be eating there too.

I'm so lost in my problems that I don't even notice that I walked almost all the way back to my bunk with nothing but a flashlight, all by myself through the jungle. Well, compared to New York four trees is a jungle.

I keep shining the flashlight directly in front of me and walking fast. If I weren't up to my eyebrows in all these other humongous things, I would have been scared to death to walk all by myself. It's wonderful how horrible things become okay next to horrendous things.

I'm the first one back and I hop right into bed so I can be asleep when the rest of them get there. I don't want to answer any questions. Especially from Dena Joyce.

The last thing I remember is pretending to be asleep.

Five

We're all up by six thirty. Everybody's a nervous wreck, even the invincible Dena Joyce. And the day doesn't help. It's been raining all morning, not heavy, just a drizzle, but it's cold and gray and everything in the bunk feels and smells damp. All the talk has been about lunch—the first meal. Our big test. It looks like Claire is the most nervous, but inside my head I know I'm miles ahead of everyone else. Just the thought of remembering all those orders, balancing everything, and doing it all fast enough to serve lunch for thirty people (even if twenty-four of them are just kids) spins my brains and gives me a terrible whooshing feeling in my stomach. A little of it leaks out in a low moan.

Nobody can even eat breakfast, and since then we've been just sitting around waiting for the big moment. The kids arrived early, about ten thirty, and everything is different. The noise of all those kids settling in fills up all the empty sound space. I like the company. It brightens everything just to hear the excited activity.

"Ten minutes to blast off," Alexandra announces. Of course, we've all been ready for hours. Then it comes.

"Attention all waitresses! Attention all waitresses! Report to the main dining room on the double. Let's go, girls, move it!" And on and on she goes in that hysterical World War III shriek. Boy, do we move it. Faster than the first day to the flagpole.

Again the stampeding herd barrels down to the mess hall, hands on their hats, flying across the grass. I catch glimpses of kids coming out on their porches to watch the whir of waitresses.

From the distance I can see the gargoyles waiting in front of the mess hall. Madame Katzoff holds her hands up and we all screech to a stop.

"This is it, girls," she announces. "I hope you're ready. We're counting on you. Isn't that right, Dr. Davis?" And the little doctor smiles his assistant-to-the-killer smile, and everyone shivers.

"Yes, we're counting on you," Madame Katzoff continues, "and watching you. Now, let's hear it, girls. What are you here for?"

"To serve!" we all shout.

"And how are you going to serve?"

"Perfectly!" we answer as we've been trained.

"To the tables!" she shouts, and we all race into the dining room.

This is the first time all the tables have been set up. Going to be a lot of people, much more crowded than I expected. Jammed is more like it.

We already know which are our tables and head right for them. Even though I'm nervous, now I'm beginning to get excited.

I have the two youngest groups. One table of six- to seven-year-old girls and one of the same-age boys. They have to be the most adorable.

I start setting up my tables. They're a little crowded, but the kids are small, it shouldn't be too bad.

I don't know why, but it seems to be taking me longer than anyone else to set up. Maybe it's because Dr. Davis is watching me. He's making me so nervous that forks and knives keep sliding out of my hands.

"How you doing?" Steffi says, coming over to my tables.

"Are you finished already?" I ask her, and fall into a real panic.

She shakes her head. "I think my tables are smaller. I'll give you a hand." And she grabs some plates and starts helping me.

"How many do you have?" I ask, stooping down to pick up the same fork for the third time.

"About thirty."

"Me too."

"You're just jumpy today. First day and all."

"Yeah." But it's her first day too. I don't know why I'm such a mess.

Finally we finish. Actually, it looks pretty good. In fact, I add a little touch for my kids by folding the napkins a special way so that they look like birds. Well, sort of.

"Trays, girls," Madame Katzoff commands, and we all rush over to the stack of heavy metal trays. Everyone takes one.

Somehow Steffi and I are last to get the trays, so we get the worst ones. Mine is crooked with a bubble right in the center that makes everything sort of slip to one side. Hers has a bend along the edge, the perfect place for a glass of milk to slide off. There is one tray in perfect condition. Claire gets it but it's just a matter of time before good old D. J. wheedles her out of it.

"Here, Claire, you take the lighter one," D. J. says, handing Claire an identical tray, only not as new and perfect and certainly not one ounce lighter. Dopey Claire says thank you.

Now we're all prepared, trays in hand, standing at our tables. It's very quiet and everything looks great. All we need are the kids.

I can't wait to meet mine. I love them already. I've pictured this day a hundred times. They'll march in, in double file, holding hands the way little kids do when they cross city streets on class trips; it's always so cute to see the tiny ones hanging on to each other. That's the way they'll come in, excited and happy. It's their first day and everything is going to be new for them so they may be shy and a little nervous, but I'm going to make them feel comfortable right away. I'll make some kind of announcement about how I'm Victoria, their waitress, and to ask me anything they need and I'll see that they get it. Anything, because they're my kids.

Then I'll take their orders. I've been practicing a kind of speedwriting so that I can take the orders fast. And I also have this method where I write down the seat numbers so that I don't have to ask who had what; I can just give it to the right person. And then I'm going to give them special personal treatment, like if one kid hates hot cereal, I'll make a point to remember and give him an egg or something else. I intend to be the best waitress in the whole camp. My kids are going to love me.

God, I can't wait. I know it's going to be terrific. It has to be, because what with this awful Robbie thing the rest of the summer is going to be very hard. At least I'll look forward to working.

Suddenly everyone gets alert. We can hear the kids in the distance. They're marching up to the mess hall, singing. Fantastic!

We all start to crowd up around the windows when Madame Katzoff announces stations.

We race back to our tables.

"Trays up!" she commands. Madame Katzoff never speaks, she commands.

We tray up and wait at attention.

They've stopped singing. We can hear them assembling

outside the building and now they're marching up the steps. Sounds like a lot of them.

Suddenly the double doors swing open and a million campers explode into the dining hall. Involuntarily we all pull back as they rush in, over, around, and through the tables and chairs. Alexandra is practically knocked over, Steffi is bumped into a chair, and I'm pinned against the wall. It's like a madhouse with the shouting and pushing and shoving, grabbing seats, changing them, rechanging them and all the while counselors trying to make some kind of order and then finally settling for saving themselves.

It's an invasion but it only lasts a few minutes. And then just as suddenly as it started it's over and everyone is seated. I look at my little kids and I'm scared. They're all over the place. All my beautiful settings are scattered and the bird napkins look like they've been bombed.

It's hard to decide which table to start with; it's bedlam both ways, but I choose the girls' table because, I don't know, I guess I'm just more comfortable with my own kind.

"Hi, everybody, I'm Victoria, your waitress."

Nobody even looks up, they're all so busy shouting at one another. In fact, they don't even seem to hear me. I try again, this time a little louder.

"Hi, everybody. I'm your waitress, Victoria."

Still no response. Not even from the counselors. They're both too busy trying to make some order. It's madness with everybody jumping up and down again, changing seats, talking and shouting all the while. Two kids are crying, and one is under the table. This table is hopeless so I try the other one with the boys.

It's no better, maybe worse, except for one little boy sitting very quietly with the saddest face I've ever seen.

"Hi there, I'm your waitress, Victoria." I flash my big smile and shout.

The sad little boy looks up at me, confused. Of course, he can't hear what I'm saying.

One last try, this time at the top of my lungs.

"Hi, there," I give it all my power, and then suddenly, just like an E. F. Hutton commercial, the whole place goes dead quiet, but it's too late for me. "I'm your waitress, Victoria," I shout into the silence.

And the entire dining room turns to look at Victoria, the waitress. I stand there horrified for what feels like a month, and then somebody starts to laugh, and soon the whole place is roaring, and a second before embarrassment turns into tears, the real reason for the silence speaks up and everyone turns away from me.

"Welcome, campers," Madame Katzoff announces from the head table. Through my blurred vision I can see something that looks like a smile on Katzoff's face. For only a second and then it's gone. She tells everyone how delighted she is that they're here and lots of other baloney, but nobody messes with her. They all stay at attention until she finishes and then it's right back to bedlam.

"Victoria!" the blond counselor for the girls' table calls to me.

I grab my tray and race over.

"Hi," she says, "I'm Carrie." She smiles and introduces me to Anna, the other counselor, who barely looks at me. Then she goes around the table telling me the names of all the kids. They're my kids and they look terrific.

Okay, so it started off badly—more like horrendous. So what? Now I'm going to show them what I can really do. I don't think anyone else prepared for this thing the way I did. I got it all down; all I need is to do it.

"Hey, everybody, we've got a great soup today, clam chowder," I announce.

And they really respond—almost everyone at the table wants some. Fantastic. I feel like I've just made a big sale. Eleven soups.

"Be right back," I say and rush right off to the kitchen.

We have this arrangement where the waitresses line up in front of the windows to the kitchen and wait for one of the cooks to pass them their orders but when it comes to the soups you get it yourself.

It works out perfectly because there's a line at the window already, so I go right around and through the swinging doors into the kitchen.

It's wild in there. Everyone is running around grabbing plates and shoving them out to the waitresses. It's a little tough to find an opening to get through to where the soup pot is, but

I wait a few seconds and then dart across. Sort of like crossing a super highway. And almost as dangerous because the floor is really slippery from spilled food.

I get to the soup and wait for someone to ladle it out for me.

But no one seems to even notice me.

"Jesus?" I say to the littlest cook. I think that's his name but he doesn't answer so I try "Iago," but still nothing.

"Can somebody give me the soup? I have eleven orders."

"Get it yourself, kid. That's what the ladle's for," the one who wouldn't answer me shouts, pointing to the gigantic soup ladle.

I don't understand how I'm going to be able to do this because there isn't even any place to rest the empty soup bowls or anything. But I've got eleven people waiting so I have to figure out something. And then I remember that I completely forgot to take the orders from the other table. I don't know whether to go back and get them or get the soup.

I decide to bring out a few soups and then take the other order. I'm hopelessly confused already.

I find an empty corner on one of the counters and put the bowls down and start to fill them. The soup is boiling hot, and by the time I get it over the floor to the counter where the bowls are stacked, I've spilled half.

"Hey, blondie, why don't you try holding the bowls near the pot," Jesus, or whoever, shouts in my ear, and of course, I jump and there goes the rest of the ladle.

"Oops, I'm sorry," I say, grabbing a napkin to clean it up,

but Jesus has the mop and with one long sweep shoves the puddle of clam goop under a counter.

"Just get the soup and get out. You're in everybody's way."

"I'm hurrying, but it's just that . . . ," but he's gone back to his mashed potatoes.

I load up the tray, but I can only fit three bowls on it because of the bubble. I've been practicing carrying a tray since I've been here, except I never had any real food on it. Especially not steaming soup.

The whole trick is to tuck your hand under the center of the tray and let the back of your hand rest on your shoulder. I think.

"Move it there, kid," Iago shouts, pushing past me. A spurt from every bowl leaps up and onto the tray. Forget it, I'll just carry it in two hands in front of me.

I make it back to my table and everyone is jumping all over the place.

"What took you so long?" Anna asks me.

I start to explain but she cuts me off. "Just give out the soups, will you? Everyone's starving."

"Come on, Anna, it's her first day." The other counselor, Carrie, is very nice and even gets up to help me. Meanwhile the boys' table is shouting for me to take their orders. Please don't let them order the soup.

Carrie writes down the rest of the orders at the girls' table while I get the orders from the boys'.

"How's the soup?" I ask-answer.

"Yeah," the other counselor says, "how's the soup?"

"Terrible, the worst, horrendous, and it doesn't even taste good," I say, and puff out my cheeks like you could throw up from the thought alone. Instantly everyone loses interest. It's the best move I've made all day. All day? All week. Ever since I've got here things have been going downhill. Even on the bus it was starting to slip. This is the first positive step I've made. I would smile but I don't want them to think I'm kidding about the soup.

Carrie pokes me. "Hey, Victoria, I've got the orders."

"Thanks, Carrie, I really appreciate it."

"That's okay. Here it is . . . two veal cutlets, plain, no tomato sauce, mashed potatoes on one and fried on the other. Six regular veal cutlets, two with fried potatoes, three with mashed potatoes, and one with no potatoes. Four chef salads, two with Russian, one oil and vinegar, and one French . . ."

"Hey, Victoria." It's Anna from the other table. "What happened to the rest of our soups?"

"Sorry, I was just taking these orders."

"Victoria!" That's from the boys' table. It's the JC again. "How about taking our orders? We're starving."

"In a second."

"They're already on their soup and you haven't even taken our orders. What's up?" Now the senior counselor joins in. They all start shouting at the same time, and my brilliant plan of speedwriting goes down the drain.

I start to scribble things down, but they go too fast.

Everyone seems to be eating the veal, but nobody wants it the way it comes, and then they all want something different with it.

"Don't we get any rolls or something?" someone else shouts out.

"What about some water?"

"And butter!"

"Coming—coming," I say and rush off. I would really love to run right out of the door and never come back. I can't do this. I just can't. I look around and everyone else seems to be handling things okay. What's wrong with me?

Just when I'm rushing toward the kitchen I spot Robbie coming in my direction. That's just what I need. But he's heading someplace else. He gives me a smile that sinks my stomach, and passes.

I get at the back of the line for the food, then I remember I still owe them seven soups.

"Should I get the rest of the soups or stay here and get the food?" I guess it's stupid to ask Alexandra that, but I don't know what to do.

She says, "Huh?"

"I'm making a mess of everything. I just can't do it."

"Sure you can. It's really hard the first day, but you'll see. It'll get better. You'll get the hang of it."

"What should I do about the soups?"

"Go get them. I'll hold your place."

"Thanks, Al, I'll do it as fast as I can."

I run back into the kitchen and start ladling out the other soups. I find a way of piling them to get six on the tray at once. In fact, I'm sort of pleased with myself. Maybe it's not hopeless.

Very carefully, I carry the tray into the dining room and over to the table. I stop behind Anna and start to hand out the soups. Just as I'm serving, Madame Katzoff rises and the whole camp leaps to its feet. Including Anna, whose shoulder sends my tray sailing up, out of my hands. Soup bowls spin off in all directions.

"Watch it, you jerk!" Anna shouts, but it's too late. The next instant she's coated with white clam goo. I grab a napkin and start wiping her off, but she fights me and only makes it worse. Little minced clams cling to her eyelashes, potato chunks dot her brown curls, and lots of just plain soup drenches her T-shirt and shorts. She looks terrible. And she looks like she's going to kill me. I edge away from her, but some of the clam slime gets caught under my shoe and I start to slip. I grab the nearest thing to steady myself. It happens to be Anna.

Together we swing sideways, way out to the end of the table like we're dancing, and then there's a scramble of legs and arms flying and we're on the floor. It's so embarrassing I don't even feel the bang of my bottom hitting the floor. But Anna feels hers.

"You stupid ass! Are you trying to kill me or something? You are the worst, clumsiest waitress in the world! You should be fired!"

"I'm really sorry," I say, trying to help her up, but she shoves me away and, grabbing a chair, starts to lift herself up. It doesn't work, and the chair turns over and she goes back down into the clams, even angrier.

Meanwhile I move back into the crowd of kids. No way to get lost in a mob of three-footers. We're causing such a commotion that counselors from other tables come over and soon everybody's walking in clam goo and then a couple of little kids start to write in it with the backs of their forks.

Almost instantly, the kitchen clean-up squad come out with their mops. Anna, in a rage, storms out of the dining hall.

In no time they put the place back in order and everyone is starting to shout orders at me again. I hope they're going to wait to the end of the day to fire me. I mean, they've got to fire me. I'm the worst waitress in the whole country. I can't understand why I'm such a terrible failure. Even Claire is doing okay. At least she isn't swimming in clam chowder.

There's no time for too much inner misery because the outside stuff is even worse. At least I'm off the hook for the soup.

Nobody wants soup—ever! Well, at least not from me.

I finish taking the orders and hurry back to the line. It's even longer now. My table, my people, my kids, the ones I really wanted to love and to give the best special service and everything, are doomed—under my special care they'll probably starve to death.

"Hey, it's the clam kid," Jesus shouts when he sees me, and

the rest of the kitchen turns around and it's all the big joke. Only trouble is, it's me that's so funny.

"May I please have—"

"Let's hear it, baby. Fast, speed it up, kid! There's hungry people out there and I've got a hot date this afternoon."

I start to read off the orders, and then I get to the ones Carrie wrote down, and I can't read a word. It's all chicken scratch.

"Come on, baby. I haven't got all day."

But I can't read it. "Could you just start on those and I'll be right back?" I shoot to the table without waiting for an answer.

My heart drops when I pass Steffi's table. I'm lost. They're eating dessert!

By the time I get back to the kitchen window, Jesus is shoving plates of veal out at me. I grab as many as I can, piling them on the tray so that I get eight on at once. That's pretty good stacking.

Feeling a little better, I spin around and head forward. As I do, one full plate of veal flies off my tray and lands neatly in the giant trash can. I give a quick look around. Nobody saw. That's it, gone—plate and all. I keep moving. Seven's not so bad either.

"Who had the veal without the sauce?" I ask the boys' table.

Nobody can remember. Well, they're only seven years old. What can you expect? They're just little kids.

"How about the veal with the sauce?"

They all raise their hands and start shouting. "Me . . . me! Me!"

I know I got some orders for the veal without sauce, but what can I do? Even Carrie is beginning to look at me funnily. I've been doing everything else wrong, why not this, too? I grab the three sauceless veals and race back, shove them at Jesus for saucing, grab what he has, pile them on the tray, shoot back to the tables, give them out, and get right back to pick up the rest of the orders. I'm up to my eyebrows in tomato sauce, clam stuff all over my shorts, a band of assorted mess across my middle where I lean the tray, and four french fries in my pocket.

My tables are just getting their main courses and everyone is finishing dessert. I don't know how everyone else is doing it because I can't take even a second to look. I haven't seen Steffi since this all started. She must be so disappointed in me. She recommended a horror.

"How many desserts?" I ask, even though they've just started their veal.

"We're not going to have time for desserts, kids. We have to get to the rec hall before one thirty," Carrie explains to the table. Did you ever try to tell seven-year-olds that they can't have chocolate pudding? There's plenty of grumbling and complaining. It's all my fault, so naturally they hate me. I'm so exhausted I'd rather have them hate me than get twenty-four desserts.

There's a lot of furious eating, more bread, more milk, more butter, another knife, and on and on. I keep running back and forth. Finally, they finish. Just like that, and instantly they're gone. Mine are the last tables to leave. Steffi has already cleaned up hers.

"Victoria."

I can tell from the way she calls my name that she knows how bad it's been. One look at her face and I know it's been even worse than I thought.

"Don't worry," she says, shaking her head and smiling. "It's going to get better. Everybody starts off the same."

"That's not true, Steffi, nobody made a mess like I did. Even Claire was better than I was."

Poor Steffi, she doesn't know what to say. It's all true. I'm hopeless. She makes some noises about how I'll look back at all this and laugh, but I probably won't get the chance since they'll certainly fire me today anyway.

"Torrie, do you want me to help you or what?"

"Aren't you supposed to meet Robbie now?"

"Yeah, but that's okay. He'll understand."

"Thanks, but I think it's important that I handle it by myself. I'll catch you later back at the bunk."

I don't have to convince her, because she's so anxious to spend time with Robbie. Boy, can I understand that. All too well.

All you have to do is take one look at my tables and you know why nobody is fighting to get the little kids' group. It's a rubbish heap. They do more eating on the table than on their plates.

I dive into the job and after what seems like fifty trips

to the kitchen I finally get the tables emptied and ready for dinner setup. No more fancy bird napkins, I'm just happy to get the necessary things on the table. What difference does it make since they hate me already? And I'm not so crazy about them, either. Except for one little boy. His name was Henry, and he looked the way I feel inside now. Very sad. I hate being a failure. I wonder what his problem is?

I drag myself back to the bunk and everyone else is sunbathing outside, giggling and talking. I'm exhausted.

"Victoria Martin?" Liana, one of the women who works in the office pokes her head in the bunk.

"That's me."

"I think you have volunteered for mail delivery."

"Volunteer? I don't think I volunteered for anything yet."

"Nobody really does," she says very apologetically. "They just sort of assign the volunteers, but you don't have to if you don't want to. It's not part of your job. You can explain to Madame Katzoff if you—"

"Explain to Madame Katzoff? Oh, no! I love mail delivery. I really do." I jump off the bed. "I'm ready right now."

"Great. You can pick up the sacks at the front office." And she's gone.

I sink back on my bed. Sixteen-year-olds don't cry, I tell myself, but it doesn't really help much. I know I wouldn't feel so awful if I'd done a better job. And now I have to worry about screwing up mail delivery. Sounds easy, but in my hands it'll probably be a disaster.

I change into my jeans and head over to the office. There are three other "volunteers" there, but they've already got their sacks and started by the time I arrive. The only sack left is the unbunked one. Unbunked means that it's just the camper's name. You have to look up the bunk numbers on the master sheet and then give them out.

This job takes me from two thirty until after four, which gives me about a half hour to get washed up and ready for dinner setup.

"Victoria." That's Alexandra. She's in her bathing suit. "I was just going down for a swim. How about it? I'll wait if you want."

Besides the fact that I'd probably sink right down to the bottom from exhaustion, I can't go swimming, ever—Robbie's there. He's in charge of the waterfront. So that's it. Summer camp without the water. Great, huh?

"Thanks, Al, but I'm beat."

"Sure thing, see you later." And she's off.

The bunk is empty and the quiet feels good. I refuse to allow my mind to go over the horrendous things that have happened so far and I'm not thinking about dinner because that's too terrifying. Of course, I'm not thinking about the Robbie problem or the fact that it's just a matter of minutes before Nina finds my bunk. That doesn't leave much I can think about, which is terrific because I'm much too tired for anything. I sit on the edge of my bed and stare into middle distance. That sounds better than it is because at this second, middle distance happens to be filled with Dena Joyce. She's just breezed into the bunk, a bundle of excitement. At least someone has something to be happy about.

"I've been looking all over for you," she says, with a smile that almost touches her earlobes.

"What's up?" I can't even get past a whisper.

"I want to hear all about it."

"What?"

"Lunch."

I can't believe her. I'm so stunned I'm speechless.

"Where's your sense of humor?" she wants to know.

"Cool it, D. J., she doesn't need that," Alexandra says, following her into the bunk.

Dena Joyce gives Al a killer look, shrugs her shoulders, and wiggles off. "I didn't know we had such a delicate flower among us."

"She can be a real asshole sometimes," Alexandra says, sitting down next to me. "Think of it this way. Now you've got no place to go but up."

"Oh yes, I do."

"Where?"

"Home."

"Come on, Victoria, it's just a bad first day. You'll get the hang of it by tomorrow."

"I don't even know if I can do dinner tonight. Maybe they won't let me. Gosh, that's the first happy thought I've had since lunch."

"You'll see, dinner will be much better."

But she's wrong. Dinner is just as bad, maybe worse. I'm not even going to describe it. All I can say is that creamed spinach is even harder to scrape off than clam chowder. It got on three people's shoulders. The fourth, Anna, my enemy, was so nervous that she made me serve her from across the table. She saved her shoulders, but when she reached for the bowl, she missed. You can't grab creamed spinach; there's nothing to hang on to. Of course I felt terrible, but not as bad as the afternoon; now that I know I'm going home.

I've decided to call my parents as soon as dinner is over and make arrangements to go home. I might even be able to get out before breakfast tomorrow morning.

"Steffi," I tell her, when we're walking back to the bunk alone after the dinner disaster, "I can't do it."

"Sure you can." She starts to give me a pep talk, but I cut her off.

"I'm going home."

She's shocked. "You can't."

"I have to."

"Just because you had a bad first day. That doesn't mean anything. Come on, Torrie. Gosh, I never thought you'd be a . . ."

"A what? A quitter?"

"Hey, I didn't mean that."

"Sure you did, and you're right, but I can't help it. It's just one of the things I can't do. Like play the violin or eat liver. I just can't do it."

"I feel awful. I mean, it was going to be such a great summer, but if you're not here . . . well, it just won't be the same."

"You still have Robbie."

"But that's different. You're my best friend. Besides, we all planned to be together this summer, the three of us, didn't we?"

"I'm really sorry, Steffi, but I just can't do it."

"You could give it a little more time, couldn't you?"

I shake my head no.

I hate to do this to Steffi, but I've made up my mind. I guess she senses that because instead of getting angry, she just sort of gives up, and we walk the rest of the way in silence.

When we get to the bunk she stops, and in a very understanding voice tells me we're still best friends and if this is what I have to do, I have to do it.

The best time to catch my parents home is around ten thirty. Even if they've gone out to dinner they'll be home by then. I try until eleven, but no luck. You're not allowed to use the phone after that so I have to wait until the morning.

It's the first night I get a good night's sleep. Sure, I know it's tough on Steffi and I really do care about her, but I can't hack it. That's all. You gotta know when to stop.

Six

I try my parents first thing in the morning. No answer. It's very strange for them to be out of the house at six thirty in the morning. The only explanation is that they're out on Long Island with friends. My heart sinks when I think that I'll have to stay here another day. Three more meals. Three more disasters. I'll never make it.

To make matters worse, guess who's waiting for me when I get back to the bunk? That's right, El Creepo, the sister you love to lose, and her new friend, Nance. I thought I was too lucky. I avoided her for almost twenty-four hours.

"Hi, Victoria," Nina says, smiling at me as if she were some wonderful surprise.

I control myself.

"Yeah, hi," I say, and start hurrying to get into my waitress uniform.

"This is my friend, Nance. She's in my bunk."

"Hi, Nance." I give her a quick smile.

Everyone is dressed already. I can't take a chance on being late, but I don't want Nina to get suspicious. "Mom didn't say she was going away for a couple of days, did she?"

"Yeah, she did. They went up to see somebody in Woodstock."

"Who?" I try to make it sound like just general curiosity.

"I can't remember."

"Didn't she tell you?"

"Yes, but I forgot. I didn't recognize the name." She's already opening my cubby and checking out my wardrobe. As she opens it, I close it. That doesn't stop her. She opens it again.

"What if I really needed her?" I say, slamming the door. "Why didn't you write it down, dummy?"

"You don't have to call me names. I didn't know you needed it."

"I don't, I'm just curious."

"So?"

"What do you mean, 'so'?"

"So, what difference does it make? Besides, I did write it down."

"Why didn't you say so?"

"You didn't ask."

Nina and I are so wrapped up in this stupid conversation

that I don't even notice that everyone has stopped everything and is just standing there watching us. Somehow my sister brings out the worst in me. I never act this stupid with anyone else.

"Forget the whole thing," I tell her and everyone else. I'm really a little annoyed. Especially at Steffi. She shouldn't be doing this. "Just get the number and forget the whole thing."

"Huh?"

This is so baffling to everyone that they lose interest.

"Did you bring your blue vest?" Out comes the true reason for the visit.

"Of course I did."

"I told you," she says to her friend, and goes right for my cubby. "Wait till you see it. It's fabulous, exactly the same."

"Okay," I say, "so you get the number and meet me at the office."

"What number?"

"The phone number. Where Mom and Dad are."

"You said you didn't need it. Are you going to call them?"

"Did you show Nance the vest?"

"She has one just like it."

"So you want to borrow mine so you can dress alike?"

"Yeah, would you lend it?" Nina doesn't have to look that stunned. I lend her a lot of stuff, only most of the time I don't know I'm doing it.

"Sure. Take it and meet me with the number at the office, right?"

She knows something's up with the phone number, but she's getting the vest so she doesn't push her luck.

"I'll see you in five minutes, okay?" And she and Nancy and the vest rush out the door.

I try my parents at the number Nina gives me, but there's no answer there either. I'll try later.

Somehow I got lucky with the lineup and flag-raising. They didn't miss me so I skip the whole thing and go straight on to the mess hall.

It's true, it's easier to set up the tables today, but then that wasn't my big problem. I'm okay until the people come, then I fall apart.

And here they come, hordes of them. I never thought I would feel so ugly about little kids, but they terrify me now. They are kind of cute the way they rush into the dining hall. It's so important when you're that age to have the right seat. Everyone seems to get his seat, at least the one he wants, except for Henry, the sad little boy from yesterday. He looks like his heart is going to break today.

"Hi, Henry," I say, to try to cheer him up, but it doesn't work.

"Hello," he says, and puts his head down as if he's hiding from sight.

Meanwhile, just as one of the other little boys was about to take the seat next to Henry, a bigger boy whispers something in his ear. They both look at Henry and giggle. This touches off a ripple down one side of the table. Raoul, the counselor, stops it with a stern look at the boys. Too late, it's obvious that Henry is what's so funny, and he sinks deeper into his chair, his face cherry-colored.

The bigger boy, who is obviously the leader, or the bully, puts his fingers to his nose like something smells bad, and the table falls into hysterics. It's obvious who smells. Even Raoul can't stop it this time. In fact, the more he tries the louder the laughter grows. The little rats. Boy, kids really are mean sometimes.

I'm about to go over to Big Shot and drop something on his head. The way I serve, nobody would think I did it on purpose. I'm halfway around the table when Henry jumps up and races across the dining room and out the front door.

"I'll get him," I tell Raoul, and shoot out after him.

He doesn't go far. There he is, sitting on the bench in the far corner of the porch, crying.

"Henry?" I come up and put my hand on his shoulder. He's sobbing so hard I can feel his whole body shaking. "Hey, he's just a stupid bully. You can't pay attention to him."

The same second I'm saying these things to Henry, I know how stupid I sound. He can't not pay attention to him. Everyone else does. Sure, he's a bully and he's a jerk, but so what? It still hurts. I'd cry too.

"Can I help you?" I ask him.

He doesn't stop crying, he just shakes his head no.

"I know how you feel," I say.

That makes him stop crying for a second. He looks up, surprised. "You wet your bed too?"

314

"Not anymore, but there are other things just as bad."

"No, there isn't," and he's back to crying.

"What do you think about a grown-up like me screwing up on a job that everyone else in the world can do with one hand tied behind her back? Didn't you see the whole place laughing at me yesterday when I dropped all those things?"

"I wanna go home," Henry sobs out to me. "Please ask them if I can go home. I don't like it here anymore."

"You're only just starting. It's a great camp and you're going to have a fabulous summer. You've just got to give it a chance."

"I wanna go home."

"You can't let a dummy like that ruin your whole summer."

"I wanna go home."

"Would you like me to talk to him? I can think of a few things that would make him think twice before he bothered you again. Would you like that?"

He shakes his head no, and tears sprinkle all over my shirt.

"What *do* you want?"

"I wanna go home."

"You can't."

"How come, if I wanna?"

"Because that's quitting. And you can't quit before you really give it a try." I sound very adult and reasonable. "For starters," I say, "do you have to wet your bed?"

"Yeah."

"Okay, then we'll have to work around that. Look, Henry, there are other ways to deal with a rat like what's his name. . . ."

"Steven."

"Steven. I really love to nail those people. Don't you worry—I'll help you."

The minute the words pop out of my mouth I remember that I'm not going to be here myself since I'm quitting too. Doing exactly what I'm telling Henry not to do. But of course my situation is different.

So I go on. "You can't let bullies like that win so easily. At least go down fighting. What do you think? You want to give it a try?"

"I wanna go home."

"If you quit now, you'll always be a quitter. That's the way you'll think of yourself."

Suddenly he's stopped crying, and he's looking at me hard.

"I don't want to be a quitter."

I don't either. How come I didn't see what I'm doing until I tell some little kid?

"Neither do I," I tell him, "and that's just what I was going to do too. Just because I had one lousy day and the worst problem imaginable with my best friend that will probably destroy our friendship. I also hate this gross creature in my bunk who always picks on me. Boy, Henry, your damp sheets don't hold a candle to all my problems."

"Then let's both go home."

I guess he's a sensible little boy, but I know that's the wrong thing to do. My dad always says you can't be a quitter.

"I'll make you a deal," I tell him. "If you stay, I'll stay."

He thinks about it for a long minute.

"Come on, Henry, we can beat them. Let's give it a try. What do you say?"

"Okay, but you gotta drop something on his head."

"I can't do that."

"Sure you can, you always do."

He's beginning to sound like Dena Joyce. Maybe he's not so cute. "Okay," I tell him, "you come back into the dining room and I'll see what I can do."

He smiles for the first time. Add no front teeth to the bed-wetting. He's got a way to go.

I motion for him to follow me. "Watch out, Steven!"

"And that gross girl . . ."

"Dena Joyce."

"Dena Joyce!"

And we head into the mess hall, heads high, shoulders back. By the time we hit the table Henry's head is hanging again and everyone is screaming for their food.

I get so busy trying to catch up that I forget to dump on Steven. Lucky for me, I trip over the back of one of the chairs and a fried egg pops off the plate and lands smack on his head. The whole table cracks up. I wink at Henry. It's a small victory.

"Victoria Martin." The gravel voice of Madame Katzoff wipes the smile off my face. "That'll cost you fifty cents. You better shape up. And fast! Or else!" she says as she passes my table.

317

It's not quitting if you get fired. But I can't do that now. I have to stick around for Henry. We made a deal. I apologize, but she doesn't even wait to acknowledge me. Steven's so deep into his fried egg that he doesn't even get the satisfaction of watching me get zonked. Well, it was worth it, and I think it helped Henry a little. At least he knows he has a friend.

Even though I'm still the last one to finish serving, it seems a little better than yesterday's breakfast. Not as much improvement as I think, though, when I remember that I didn't serve breakfast yesterday. My disaster started with lunch.

"Torrie," Steffi says, poking her head back into the dining room, "we'll wait for you on the porch, okay?"

I would love to say no, but there's no way. I can't avoid my best friend every time she's with her boyfriend. She's sure to catch on pretty fast.

"I'll be out in a minute," I call back. I have to pull myself together for this. Just the sight of Robbie shakes me up so much that I'm sure everybody can see. And that would be horrendous—if Steffi knew, I mean.

I can see them through the screen door. They're sitting at the far end of the porch, very close on the wooden bench. And they're talking. It all looks very private, so I decide just to wait. And wait.

Obviously they could do this forever, so I cough a few times to give them warning, groan, shove the screen door open and go out onto the porch.

"Hi, Steffi," I say very up and looking only at Steffi. "Hi, Robbie." Still up and only looking at Steffi. I don't think I can carry this off.

"That was pretty fast," Steffi says, trying to look on the bright side. "You're really getting into it."

Now Robbie tries his helping hand. "It's only ten minutes extra. That's not too bad, you know, ten minutes."

"Yeah," I say, looking over his head. "Ten minutes later than Claire and all the other retards. Great."

"Well, it's only for another day or so, right? When are they going to pick you up or what?"

"They're not going to. I changed my mind."

Steffi jumps up and hugs me. "That's fabulous! Oh, I'm so happy. Now it's going to be a perfect summer. The three of us. That's the way it's going to be!"

Ugh!

"That's great," Robbie says. "Steffi really felt terrible about your going home. So did I."

I don't even look on his side of the porch, for that one.

"What happened?" Steffi wants to know.

"I just thought some more about it and decided that I would give it another chance. One day isn't enough, I guess." If Robbie weren't around I would tell Steffi the truth about Henry and quitting, but with Robbie here I just feel strange. I can't be myself. In fact, I struggle just to speak regular. It's going to be one long horrendous summer.

"Let's all get a Coke, okay, Robbie?" Steffi says.

"I can't, Stef," he says. "I have to be down at the waterfront in about ten minutes. Want to walk me down?"

"Sure," Steffi says. "How about it, Torrie? You haven't even seen the waterfront yet, have you?"

"I'll go down this afternoon," I lie, because I intend never to go. At least not while Robbie's on duty, and that's probably all the time, since he's in charge of the waterfront.

"Come on, Torrie, you've got time."

"I can't." Another lie. "I promised Nina that I would stop by and see her bunk."

Steffi gives me a funny look. That was stupid—she knows me too well.

"Okay," she says, "I'll catch you back at the bunk." And she and Robbie go off toward the lake. I stand there on the porch, alone. I feel terrible. The most important friendship in my life is going down the tubes, and I can't stop it.

Let's face it, I'm just like Steffi—madly in love with Robbie. And something else. Is it my imagination, or is he beginning to give me strange looks? Nice strange. Too nice strange.

What a mess!

I don't want to look like too much of a liar, so I stop by Nina's bunk. Lucky for me it's empty. I take back my vest, which of course is thrown on the floor in true Nina slob way. By the time I get back to my own bunk, good old D. J. is there.

"Lucky you," she says.

"How come?" I say, probably falling into the biggest trap ever made.

"You pulled dock duty for all of next week. Don't look so innocent. You may fool your dear best friend, but I'm a lot smarter."

"Hey, gimme a break, huh? I don't even know what you're talking about."

Just as I say it, I realize what she's talking about. Robbie runs the waterfront. I have to be his assistant for seven days. I can't do it. That's all. I just can't do it.

"If you think it's so sensational, we can switch, then you can be the lucky one."

"I think Mr. Robbie Wagner is absolutely adorable. A real hot ticket. But not worth a week of shivering in a wet bathing suit. No thanks, you keep it."

"Maybe Claire . . ."

"Are you kidding? She hates the water worse than I do. Why don't you ask dear old Steffi? I'm sure she'd love to switch places to be near her boyfriend. If she was smart she would."

"I don't even know why I talk to you about this anyway. You've got such a warped view of everything. Robbie is my best friend's boyfriend, period."

"Sure thing," she says, giving me that sly nasty smile.

I wonder about people like Dena Joyce. She must like being disagreeable. I wonder if there's anyone she would be nice to. So far I haven't seen any sign of niceness. And I'm finished trying to be nice to her—from now on I'm going to treat her like she deserves. Let her say one more thing to me, and I'm really going to sock it to her. Just one more thing.

And she does. "Hey, Victoria, you got the time?"

"Leave me alone, will you?" I answer, just as Claire, Alexandra, and one of the twins come into the bunk. So everyone thinks I'm nuts. So what?

Staying was a stupid idea. It can only get worse. I should have minded my own business with Henry and I would have been able to go home right this minute.

"Anybody want to switch dock duty for anything you want?" I ask generally. Nobody answers. "I'll exchange for anything." I look at Claire.

"Who wouldn't?" Claire says, rolling her eyes. "That's the worst job around."

"Claire's right," one of the twins says. "Everyone's got to do it, so I don't think it's fair for anyone to get out of it."

"If someone wants to change with me, it's my business. Besides, I was just asking."

"Well," twinny says, "I'm saying no."

"Fine. Anyone else?"

Only Alexandra is nice about it, but she loves what she has, arts and crafts, so she doesn't want to change. So far I'm stuck, and everyone thinks I'm just trying to get out of a hard job. Maybe Steffi wants to change. I have to be careful. She'd probably think I can't stand to be near him for a whole week. Boy, is she right, but for all the wrong reasons.

When Steffi and I are walking to the mess hall, I tell her I would be willing to change dock duty next week if she likes, and then she could spend a whole extra week with Robbie.

"Oh, I'd love to but I don't think I can get out of Drama Group. Becky Walker specially requested me for the first week to help organize the summer play. I was very involved last year. I've already said yes, but an extra week with Robbie is tempting . . ." Steffi is really struggling. Finally she says she can't.

Unless I can think of something brilliant over the weekend I'm stuck for dock duty starting Monday.

I make one last try with the other twin on Sunday, but she's not interested either. Somehow Steffi finds out that I've been trying to dump the assignment, and of course she thinks it's because I don't like Robbie.

"That's not true, Steffi," I tell her. "It's just that I'm going to get my period next week and I hate to be stuck in a bathing suit."

She buys it, but that's not great. Now I have to pretend to have my period all next week and pretend not to have it the following week when I really will have it. This whole thing gets worse by the minute. A week of dock duty. Horrendous. I'll never make it.

Seven

Monday morning starts like all Monday mornings—rain. Well, not exactly rain, just slight drizzle. The light gray kind of day that looks like it might clear up any minute. Just promising enough to keep the people on dock duty at their stations.

Alone.

That's just what I needed—to be alone with Robbie. Of course he's very friendly, welcoming me, showing me around and explaining rules like how we handle the safety equipment and all that. I force myself to pay close attention because it's serious business, but half my brain is stuck on thinking how handsome he is close-up and how much I like the sound of his voice. Every once in a while I forget and look up at his face, at his bottom lip, especially, when he smiles. He's got the sweetest smile, with just a trace of a dimple on one cheek. I guess I knew all this from Steffi, but I never knew what it would make me feel like. It makes me feel like I want to reach out and touch him.

And when we do touch, accidentally, the feeling ripples through my body and I get warm all over. How am I going to last seven days? That thought almost makes me want to cry.

I find a little trick that helps. Whenever I get too carried away, lost in the sound of his voice or the sight of that bottom lip, I say, "Steffi." That's it, I just say her name over and over again like it's some kind of magic charm that will break the spell.

When I run out of charms I just clam up. At first he chats with me, the way you would with someone you're working with, but all I can manage are one-syllable answers so the conversation just kind of dribbles away. Then it gets silent, and that's hard to break. It's obvious he thinks I don't like him, but that's the price I have to pay.

One bad thing happens in the morning. The two of us are out there reading, about ten feet apart, when a frog croaks and we both look up at the same instant. For a second neither of us realizes that we're staring at each other.

It's intense, the way our eyes get locked together for that moment. Finally I force myself back to the book, but that's it; I can't read another thing for the rest of the morning.

The afternoon is just as horrendous. At about three, Steffi comes down to visit us, and I feel so guilty I can't even look at her. I haven't *done* one thing wrong, but everything I *think* is horrible.

And she doesn't have much luck with Robbie, either. I guess just sitting around here in this funny kind of gloom has hit him too.

Steffi pulls me aside. "What's up? Are you both in the dumps or what?"

"It's just the weather. It's really depressing to sit around here in this drizzle."

But she doesn't buy my explanation. "Look, I know you're not crazy about Robbie, but at least you could try to be a little friendly. . . ."

"That's not fair, Steffi. It's really hard. Here we are alone all this time and we barely know each other."

"I guess you're right, Torrie, I'm sorry. It's just that it's so important to me that you two like each other. Maybe I'm pushing too hard."

"Yeah, it just takes time."

By now Robbie has finished checking the lines and we're all back together. It's awful-time again.

"What do you think?" he says. "Is it going to clear up?"

We do the weather bit for a few minutes, and then I find an excuse to leave them alone.

They walk over to the end of the dock and talk. I watch them. She loves him: I can see that. I can see it in her eyes, in her face, in the way she moves close to him and touches his arm whenever she can. I hope she can't see it in me.

They talk for a while, then he bends down and kisses her lightly on the forehead. When he straightens up he looks in my direction.

I look away. Why did he do that? There's something strange about his attitude toward me. I'm not sure if it's just me seeing him through my feelings or if he really is acting different.

Finally, after a hundred years, Steffi goes back to her drama group. Great how I love to get rid of my best friend, isn't it?

The rest of the afternoon is spent in serious silence. The weather's getting worse, drippy and chilly, but I'm not even cold. In fact, I'm practically in a sweat.

At five we say good-bye and he goes in one direction and I go in another. Intense.

Tuesday is a total nightmare. Between waitressing and dock duty, my life is a total disaster. We are now, that's Robbie and me, at the point where we don't talk at all. When he comes around to my side of the dock, I smile nicely and walk around to the other side. If he does ask me something, I practically jump out of my skin at the sound of his voice.

By the way, it's drizzling again. All day.

I spend the afternoon in dread of Steffi's visit. That's the worst time. It's very tricky because we both have to come up with all sorts of crazy things that make us look busy. I must have tied the knot on the line to the raft ten times. The last time I do it I'm trying so hard to look involved that I forget what I'm doing, and the minute I turn my back it opens, the rope slides off the dock, and the raft is free.

Nothing to do but go in after it. It may be cold and awful, but it's better than facing Steffi.

It comes to me sometime during the hours I spend sitting, damp and shivering, trying to concentrate on the book I've been staring at for the last two days: Summer camp is like a prison sentence.

And I feel like a criminal, too, trying to steal my best friend's boyfriend. That's the truth. Sure, I'm not doing it outright, but I love him, and inside my heart, I want him to love me, too.

At night I don't take part in any of the activities. I say I'm not feeling well. Steffi thinks I have my period, so she accepts it. Maybe she doesn't accept it completely, but she wants to, so that helps. Besides, she spends a lot of time with Robbie now.

The only one of the other girls I'm friendly with is Alexandra. Liza is okay, but just not my type, and I couldn't care less about the twins. Claire is a dodo and I outright hate and despise Dena Joyce.

"How's dock duty?" D. J. asks every chance she gets. And the way she says it is so nasty that I'm afraid Steffi will notice. For some reason she doesn't. It's like she's oblivious. Why shouldn't she be? Would she suspect her best friend of betraying her? Of course not.

Meanwhile, Ken is around a lot. I don't give him any encouragement, but then I know why he's hanging around. He wants to be near Steffi. She's so dense about anyone but Robbie that she doesn't even notice, except to say how nice he is and how much he likes me.

"Why don't we all go down for a soda?" he asks me, staring at Steffi.

"I'm going to pass," I say. "I'm too tired. Thanks anyway."

"How about you, Steffi?" He's practically drooling.

"Only if Victoria wants to. I'm sort of tired myself."

Now he's got to turn back to me. I never saw so much pleading in anyone's eyes. How can I say no? I'm such a horrendous person lately that I better grab my one little chance to be nice to someone.

"Okay," I say, "I'll go."

He practically kisses me. Naturally Steffi in her great denseness whispers to me that he's out-of-his-mind-happy that I'm going. I don't even bother to tell her the truth.

When we get down to the rec hall, the music is blasting, and it's jammed. Everybody is there.

But not Robbie, thank goodness. For the first time since I arrived, or more accurately since he arrived, I'm having a good time. I love to dance and I'm pretty good at it, so I get asked a lot. Nobody really sends me wild, but it's fun, and I even have a good time with Steffi.

"This is great," she says to me. "You're like your old self again."

"I think I've gotten a second wind."

I dance with Ken a couple of times, but he only has eyes for

Steffi. They really get along pretty well. If Robbie weren't in the picture they'd make a good couple. But Robbie is not only in the picture; when I turn around to get a cold drink, he's also there in the flesh. We see each other and turn away quickly. I'm back where I started. My evening is ruined.

Rather than start making up reasons why I'm suddenly back to gloom-face, I whisper to Steffi that I'm really exhausted and I'm going back to the bunk. She's disappointed but understands. I get out before she sees Robbie, so there's no way for her to connect his coming with my going.

When I get back to the bunk there's a message from my parents asking me to call them. It's still early enough, so I hurry down to the front office and phone them.

"How's it going, honey," my dad asks.

"Great," I tell him.

"What's wrong?"

How can they always tell so fast? "Nothing. It's just it's a lot harder than I thought."

"Maybe I should have told you about the time I worked as a waiter at the Carnegie Deli. What a mess. I dropped a tray loaded with pickles and mustard all over a customer who turned out to be the owner's father-in-law."

"Oh, Daddy, now I know where I get it from. What happened? Did they fire you?"

"On the spot. But I wasn't defeated. Now I could tell everyone I was an experienced waiter. I just left out a couple of details."

"I don't even think I'll be lucky enough to get fired. I'll just end up with so many fines that I'll owe them money at the end of the summer."

"Hang in there, honey. I guarantee you're going to end up loving it."

"Ha!"

"Take my word for it," he says, and then tells me a few more things about his short but brilliant career in the restaurant business. And somehow I feel better. Nothing ever seems so horrendous after I talk to my dad.

Of course, I don't tell him about Robbie. Nobody can help me about that nightmare.

Walking back to the bunk, the air is warm and smells delicious, like the forest after a rain. The sky is clear and filled with stars. It's supposed to be beautiful tomorrow. At least we won't have to be alone again: We have swimming groups all day, plus two general swims with the whole camp.

It's so lovely out that I take off the plastic stuff I had covering the hole in the wall behind my bed. Now I sort of have my own little porthole. I've gotten so used to the country that I don't even worry about animals crawling in and falling on my head. I figure if they don't come in through the windows, they won't come in through this little hole. That's what I figure. If I'm wrong, I'll probably have a heart attack.

Which will cure my Robbie problem, anyway. Everything always comes back to that. Because I've never felt this way about anyone else before. Whenever I think about him, I say in my head, "I love you, Robbie." I say it over and over again. I'm always nervous when I'm with him because of Steffi, but if that situation didn't exist, I would want to be with him all the time. I would want to touch him and have his arms around me. I would want to kiss him, to feel his lips on mine, his body pressed against mine. The whole length of him. But it's not possible. None of it. I can control the outside, but not what I feel inside.

Eight

The next morning is magnificent, just the way it's supposed to be in summer camp. Two days of rain turned everything bright shiny green, and a million flowers bloomed. Even the shrubbery around the slum bunks looks good. Of course, if you know anything about it, you know it's all weeds, but at least they cover the broken shutters and piles of trash.

I don't know why I'm feeling so good today. Maybe it's because of that conversation I had with my father, or maybe because I didn't drop anything big and wet at breakfast. Toast sliding off a plate or a runaway hard-boiled egg hardly count in my case. I'm getting better. I was out in under ten minutes. That's ten minutes after everyone else. I barely had time to think about my fantastic success, because I'm due down at the dock by nine o'clock. First group is junior girls. Nina and her friends.

There are twenty-six thirteen-year-olds. Eighteen of them claim they can't go in the water because they have their periods. They barely have the strength to drag themselves over to the grass, throw down their towels, take out their suntan lotion, and start polishing their nails.

Unfortunately, Nina is one of the well ones, and she and seven others go through the lifesaving lessons. For the next hour she bugs me every five minutes.

"Victoria," she calls out from the water, "is this right?" she says, doing a backstroke. Or, "Are my legs straight?" and fifty other unnecessary questions.

I don't want to look like a bad sister in front of Robbie, so I answer her as sweetly as possible. She sees what's happening and takes hideous advantage of the situation.

I would love to push her head under the water. And hold it there for about a month. All right, two weeks.

Then, right in earshot of Robbie, she asks me about Todd, and before I have a chance to answer informs me that her friend, Lisa, his sister, told her that he is definitely going out with Judy First.

I know Robbie hears that because he looks up at me for a second. Then she asks me if she can borrow my pink sweater. I would like to wrap it around her throat, but I can't seem selfish in front of Robbie, so I say yes. It nearly chokes me.

Finally the end of first activity is announced over the PA, and they all head for their second activity.

"I'll stop by your bunk later for the sweater," Nina calls as she leaves. "Okay?"

I don't answer.

But it's not that easy with Nina. "Okay?" she shouts again.

"Yeah."

And she's gone.

The next group is Henry's. I can see them coming in the distance. They look so cute, walking in double file holding hands.

When they get close enough I smile and wave at them. I love them. They're my table.

They're all surprised to see me and maybe a little nervous. After all, if I save lives or teach swimming anything like I serve meals, they know they're in deep trouble.

Of course I'm friendly, but I try to look sort of professional to build up their confidence.

Robbie is really in charge of the lessons, but I have to keep a watch too. They're six- to eight-year-olds, and you have to keep a sharp eye on them because they're always swimming away on their own or doing something crazy. In the water they're like a lot of little porpoises leaping and playing around.

Robbie lines them all up in the shallow part of the crib. That's a portion of the lake enclosed with ropes where the kids all have to swim unless they've passed their deep-water tests. When they do, they can swim out to the raft. It gets pretty deep farther out in the crib. These kids are so little that they can't stand at the middle of the crib, so we have to be very careful that they don't drift away out of the beginner area. Of course the counselors keep an eye on them too.

Unfortunately, Henry gets put right next to his mortal enemy, the big stupid bully, Steven. I would like to change his place, but I don't want to do that without asking Robbie, and he's busy with a demonstration of the crawl.

It turns out to be okay anyway, because Henry is a better swimmer than expected, so I don't have to worry about Steven pushing him around.

After the lesson Robbie gives them all a free swim period. The crib turns into one big splash with lots of shouting and laughing and plenty of "watch me's." That's what they all want. "Victoria, watch me!" Even Henry is having a good time. At least Steven seems to be leaving him alone.

I'm busy showing one of the younger boys, Timmy Whelan, the dead man's float when suddenly there's a lot of commotion way down at the end of the crib.

Something's wrong! I grab Timmy, toss him up on the dock, and run down to the end of the pier to see what's happening.

When I get there I see a couple of kids have gone under the ropes and are way out in the deep water. And they're shouting. It's serious!

I dive in and, swimming as fast as I can, head for them. It takes forever when you have to move fast in the water, but I finally get there. It turns out to be Steven and one of his little followers.

"What's wrong?" I ask them, trying to catch my breath. "What are you kids doing this far out?"

"Henry. It's Henry," the little one gasps, sputtering with water.

"Where is he?" I ask, looking all around. He's nowhere in sight. "Where is he?" I shout at Steven.

"He was over there." He points to an empty spot a few feet away toward the raft.

"Get back and get Robbie—fast!" I tell them, and dive under the water.

The lake is clean and you can see far down into the tall weeds. Streaks of sunlight cut through the water, making my air bubbles glisten as they race up behind me. There's nothing but silence and stillness and emptiness. I swing around in a full circle. No Henry. A horrendous panic shortens my breath and I have to surface to fill my lungs again. I search the top of the water. Still no Henry. Oh, please, please don't let anything awful happen to him. He's so sweet and so little.

I have to find him fast. If he *is* underwater, even seconds can be too long.

Down I dive again. This time I head toward the wooden raft. If he got into trouble he may have tried to make it to the raft. Then I see him, just off the edge of the raft. For an instant he looks okay, but then I see him sliding away from the raft and sinking down, his arms above his head, bubbles rushing from his mouth.

I shoot up from the water, take a huge gulp of air, and

dive down again. Pushing the water behind me with my arm, kicking furiously, I swim down toward the spot where I estimate he should be when I get to him. I have to go deeper than I thought, and I didn't take in enough air. But I can't go up again. It would take too long. I have to keep going. It's just another couple of seconds and I'll reach him.

A hard pain fills my chest. I have to force myself to keep going down to Henry. The pain is like a steel wire tightening around me. My head feels like it's going to explode. I reach out to try to grab him, but he's still too far away. Please don't let it be too late. One more inch and I won't be able to do it. I can't stand the pain.

And then I get him. I pull him to me, wrap my arm around his body, bend my knees up, and shove my feet out with all the power in my legs. We shoot up through the water together, me holding Henry with one arm while I propel myself with the other, kicking madly all the while.

I see the top of the water . . . another couple of feet and I'll break through. But then I can't! The stopped-up air inside me explodes out and just as quickly a rush of water gushes into my mouth, choking back any air left. In that instant, with all my might, I throw Henry up as far as I can, straight up out of the water, and incredibly, hands grab him from me and then the water floods my brain and I fight for air to stop the choking. I feel myself being pushed up, my head bursts free of the water, but I can't get the air into me. I can't stop the coughing long enough to inhale. All the while choking and coughing, I'm being pulled along through the water. I know somebody's saving me, but all I care about is getting some air into my lungs. I have to breathe. . . .

And then I do. Between the coughs I begin to grab a little air. It turns into choking when it gets to my lungs, but some air seeps in, and through the coughing and gasping, a little more, and some of the panic stops because I'm beginning to breathe again.

I feel myself being lifted out of the water and carried in someone's arms. My arms hang down. I'm too exhausted to even hold my head up. All I can manage is breathing.

Gently I'm put down on the grass and for the first time I begin to breathe normally.

I open my eyes and see his face, inches from mine.

Someplace, way back inside my brain, I knew it was Robbie saving me. Something about the feel of his arms holding me, his chest against my body: I knew it was him.

And now I'm looking at him, caught in his eyes and too weak to turn away. And I see something in his face and I feel something between us, and it makes tears well up in my eyes.

"Are you okay?" he asks softly.

I nod my head yes. "Henry? Is he all right?"

"Yes," he says, gently brushing the hair back from my forehead. "You got him just in time. He's okay."

And now the tears come. I turn my head to the side, put my hands over my face, and cry. Part of it is relief for Henry and for myself, and another part is a terrible sadness for what

I know is happening between Robbie and me. Something that neither of us can help.

He knows it too. And he stays there, hovering over me a moment too long. And then he pulls himself up and others, people I didn't even see before, move in and help me up.

"Where's Henry?" I ask them. "I want to see him."

"He's over there on the bench," one of the counselors says. "Thanks to you, he's okay."

And sure enough there he is, all wrapped in a blanket and he's just fine. I go over to him and grab him up in my arms. Boy, I was never so happy to see any kid in my life.

"You okay?" I ask, squeezing him.

"Yeah," he says, "I'm okay. You saved my life. I would have drowned. Thank you, Victoria." And with that he gives me a huge smacker on the cheek. I give him one right back and everyone laughs.

We're all feeling pretty good.

"What happened?" I ask him. "What were you doing all the way out there?"

Suddenly he gets very quiet. Something's up. He won't talk.

"Hey, you know you aren't supposed to be out of the crib until you pass your test. How come you did that?"

Henry puts his head down, and I can see he's going to cry if I bug him anymore.

"It's okay." I hug him. "But just don't do that anymore. Right?"

"I won't," he says. "I promise."

"Steven made him," Adam Gold pipes up from the back of the crowd.

I turn to look at him. "How'd he do that?"

But now Adam clams up. Suddenly he doesn't know anything. And nobody else does. I might have known Steven was involved. Boy, I could kick that kid! He really is a little brat.

I can see there's no point in trying to get the real story now. First of all, Henry's too upset, and besides, no one is going to spill it in front of a whole crowd like this. But I'm not finished with that little monster yet. No way.

Naturally, after all that, swim period is called off.

"Victoria?" It's Robbie. "Why don't you go back to your bunk and lie down for a while? I can manage okay for now."

"I'm all right, really," I tell him, but he insists, and then the JC gets in too and says I look very pale. Maybe I should stop by the infirmary. He offers to go with me.

"I'll go lie down, but I don't think I need to see the doctor. I'm really okay, just kind of wiped out."

I put on my robe and go up toward the bunks.

Nobody is in the bunk when I get there. All I want to do anyway is fall down on the bed. I'm worse than I thought. And when I think about what happened and what could have happened, I start to get sick to my stomach. I think about Henry and how he could have died. And me too. That's how those things can happen in the water. One minute everything is okay, and you're laughing, and then the next somebody's dead.

Wow! That's the closest I ever came to anything that serious.

I guess I really did save Henry's life. I remember once my parents talking about this old Chinese proverb. I don't remember the words, but it's about how when you save somebody's life, they become your responsibility for always; you're obligated to them because you gave them a new life. You're sort of their mother. Now I really have to take care of Henry.

Wait till I get my hands on that rotten little Steven.

I guess I fell asleep, because the next thing I know the PA is blasting dinner call. They must have let me sleep through the setup. I jump up, throw on my uniform, and race down to the mess hall.

Steffi sees me coming in the door and comes right over to me and gives me a huge hug. "You're fabulous, Torrie. Everybody's talking about how you saved Henry's life. You're terrific."

And then a million other people are crowding around me and hugging me and congratulating me, and it's terrific. It's like I'm a hero. It's great.

Turns out all the waitresses got together and were sharing my tables so I could rest. I look at my tables, and for the first time they're eating at the same time as everyone else.

I thank everyone and take over my station. In a few minutes it's like usual. They're one course behind. They all say they're used to it and besides they like the leisurely pace.

Just before dessert, both my tables stand up and give me a cheer, and then the whole dining room applauds. Boy, am I glad I stayed.

Nine

For the next week and a half I live off the big rescue, but by the end of the second week nobody's talking about it anymore. The high is gone, and I'm back down in the dumps again. Henry too. It's tough for both of us. He's been trying, but he hasn't had much success yet. He still walks around looking like he's just lost his last friend, which isn't possible since he never had any to start with, and he still cries at least five times a day and looks just plain unhappy the rest of the time. Plus he's still king of the damp sheets. In fact, the only success he's had is with me. I stayed because of him. And I hate it. Some success.

Most of the time I feel about as miserable as Henry looks. The big three problems are still big and three—Robbie, Steffi, and pain-in-the-ass Dena Joyce.

My heart is still doing those crazy jumps when I see

Robbie, and I can never carry on a decent conversation when he's around. So mostly I just stay quiet and study him. I'm beginning to see more of the person inside.

A couple of days ago a whole group of us were watching the weekly tennis meets. They had three matches going on at the same time, but almost everyone was watching Robbie and this fabulous player Wally Kramer. Wally is a notorious bad sport with the most horrendous temper; he's the kind who smashes rackets if he loses. And he was really going bananas that day because Robbie was holding his own against him. Every time he lost a point Wally had something nasty to say.

At one point they were neck and neck with Wally serving. He has this fantastic serve that's like a bullet and nobody can ever return it, but this time he overshot the line. Robbie called it out and everybody saw it was, but Wally blew up, threw his racket down, and really got crazed.

By then Robbie had had it. "Hey, Kramer, you got a problem? Say it, don't do a whole number."

"Yeah, well, I don't like your calls."

"Okay, then, let's forget the whole thing," Robbie said, and started to walk off. That's when Wally called after him, something about first you cheat and then you quit, and Robbie turned around, and in two seconds he was over the net and they were rolling around on the ground. It was wild how fast it all happened.

They stopped it before it got very far, but even Steffi was surprised. Somehow you don't think of Robbie as the type to lose his temper like that. It's not that he was really wrong, Wally is definitely a crud, and you can't just go around calling people cheaters and get away with it. Still, Robbie always seemed so cool and under control; it was weird to see him like that.

Mostly I know about Robbie from Steffi, and she never says anything bad about him. I guess nobody can be that perfect, but you wouldn't know it from Steffi's description. She can go on forever about how great he is, and how he just started Stanford and he's at the top of his class already, and how he's a fabulous athlete and so unspoiled even though he comes from this ultra-rich family in Connecticut.

Ken Irving isn't so crazy about him, but that's probably because he likes Steffi. He says Robbie's a little too sure of himself. Maybe he's just jealous. Most of the other guys like him, and the girls certainly do. If it weren't for Steffi, there'd probably be a stampede to get at him.

I guess there are lots of things about Robbie Wagner that are just plain regular person; still, there's a lot about him that's different. He's sort of aloof, and I like that. Like when the other guys are roughhousing and fooling around, he doesn't get involved. They're all about the same age, but he seems more sophisticated. That appeals to me too. Most of the boys I know are still at the goofy stage. It's like he's passed it already, except that fight business. That was really out of character—very immature.

"That was very immature," D. J. says to Steffi and me later in the bunk.

It's okay if I think it, but it bugs me to hear D. J. say it.

"I don't think so." I'm stupid enough to fall for the bait. "Wally Kramer is pure nerd city."

"Jackass is more like it," Steffi adds, "and it's time someone stopped him."

"Oh dear, Robbie and his girlfriends." And with a hideous wink at me, D. J. wiggles off.

"She is such a pain," Steffi says. "One of these days I'm really going to let her have it."

"Forget it, she's just jealous."

"How come you're so nice about her lately? She's such a shit."

"I just tune her out."

What I don't tell Steffi is that I hate D. J. even more than she does, but I'm in no position to start any kind of trouble with her. All I have to do is give her one little piece of ammunition and she'll blow my whole friendship with Steffi to smithereens.

As is, we're only okay when we're alone, and even then there's a tiny something that's not quite right. As long as she doesn't know what it is, it's okay; I can put up with it. I think she thinks I'm just not completely happy here at camp, and since she's the one who talked me into going, she doesn't want to push it too much.

Besides, in a little more than a week the summer will be half over. Not a minute too soon for me. What a disaster!

Actually, it's not a total bomb. For one thing, the bunk

turned out to be okay. Nobody inspects us, so we can keep it the way we want, which means you can't tell the trash heap outside from the one inside. There isn't one neat person in the whole bunk. That's really lucky, because I think she would have killed herself or the rest of us by now.

There never was enough room in the cubbies or the closet in the back, but somehow, in the beginning, everything fit better. Now you can't find the cubbies for all the clothes thrown around. Beds have not been made in weeks, and the sheets aren't changed unless something drastic is spilled on them. Actually, it's heaven. We all love it. It's like living the way you always dreamed. And you don't even have to feel guilty, because everyone else is just as bad as you are.

Only one problem. Don't ever misplace anything, because you will never find it.

There's only one cleaning job we all do. Soda cans. If you don't take them out at night, by the next morning the entire ant population of the Western Hemisphere finds them. And they march right in the front door. The first time we made that mistake, actually it was D. J., she shoved her empty can under Claire's bed. Naturally, she wouldn't do it under her own. Claire, jerk that she is, probably thanked her. Anyway, the next morning there was a six-inch-wide wavy black line moving across the room connecting the door to the soda can. Four billion ants had come for the party.

Alexandra and the twins cleaned them up while the rest of us stood around screaming, squealing in horror and disgust and rushing around shaking out all the piles of clothes on the floor. The poor ants were probably frightened to death.

From then on: No empty soda cans allowed. Anything nonfood can stay on the floor—permanently.

This all proves that our parents are completely wrong. There's no harm in sloppiness. Other than some wrinkled clothes, it's perfectly fine. And if you lose something in the mess, you're bound to find it when you pack to go home.

I've made a good friend in Alexandra. The twins aren't so awful, except they never do anything alone and they agree with whoever gets to them first. Liza is fun in small doses. Claire is hopeless, and D. J. is like a wicked witch in training.

And there's no way to avoid her. She's always watching me, waiting for me to make a mistake. But she's in for a surprise—I'm not going to. All I have to do is stay loose for twenty-six days and I've got it made. It's a cinch. That's what I keep telling myself.

I wish I could really believe it.

Ten

We're all waiting for Color War to break. Color War is a special thing that happens only in summer camp. It's a kind of big competition. The camp is divided into two teams, the green team and the gray. Then you do all the regular field sports, only you play for your team. After three days the team with the most points wins. There are also special events, like play night and sing night. Each team puts on an original musical, and the best one wins a lot of points. Everything is divided into teams, even arts and crafts, and then certain counselors judge the winners.

If you're on the green team you have to wear green all the time. And, except for when you go back to the bunk to dress or sleep, you always stay with your teammates, even when you march to meals or anything.

You can see what a big deal all of this is. It gets to be very important, and you really go all out for your team. Anyway, you never know how Color War is going to break. It's always very exciting. Steffi told me that last year they had a small plane fly over the campus and drop leaflets announcing Color War and giving lists of team members.

One night Steffi, Alexandra, and I are sitting around hanging out when I get this idea, wouldn't it be fun to break Color War ourselves.

At first we're just kidding around, but it begins to kind of grow and before you know it we put together the whole thing. It doesn't sound hard, and it would really be a riot. All we need is some green and gray crepe paper.

The plan is to wait until everyone is asleep, then sneak into the bunks and tie either a green or gray piece of paper to the end of each bed. When the kids get up in the morning, they'll all think Color War has started. It would be fabulous. No one has ever done such a thing before.

I have Thursday morning off, so I go into town to get the crepe paper. We plan to break it just before the weekend.

It's imperative that Dena Joyce and Claire the squealer do not know what we're planning.

This means that we have to hide the paper until Friday night. The best place to keep it is where it belongs. No one would ever look for it there.

We plan to do it around three or four in the morning. The three of us will sneak out of our bunk and each one will take one row of bunks to do.

I get the last row, that's seniors and intermediates, the oldest kids.

Steffi doesn't even tell Robbie, and on Friday night we leave the dance early and go back to the bunk to get everything ready.

Before the others get back we set everything up, hiding black T-shirts and jeans in our beds under the covers so that we can change into them when the lights are out. We each put our supply of crepe paper in the beds too. We cut the strips into short pieces the right size to tie around the metal footboards of the beds. Each one takes a mixture of gray and green.

Alexandra has an alarm watch that she sets for three thirty. She hardly has to bother, since I'm so excited that I can't sleep a wink anyway.

Funny to watch other people sleep. Dena Joyce, the one we really have to worry about, changes positions every three minutes. I've never seen such a restless sleeper.

I keep an eye on my watch, and just before three I wake up Alexandra so that she can turn off her alarm before it goes off.

"Huh?" she says, totally dazed.

"Shush . . . it's time to get up."

Then I wake Steffi, who's just as groggy, and the three of us tiptoe out of the bunk.

"It's pitch-black," Steffi whispers to me.

And it is. It's a new moon, which is no moon at all. I never could understand who made that one up. Why not just say no-moon and not make people crazy? Anyway, it's a no-moon, and the only lights around are the tree lights and there aren't many of those, so we're really in the dark.

It's a little better when your eyes get used to it and, of course, we know our own bunk.

I push open the screen door and it squeaks. We stop dead, but nobody seems to have heard. Quickly the three of us slip out onto the porch. We'd be in big trouble if this wasn't our bunk, but luckily we know how to avoid the broken places in the flooring.

"What do you think?" Steffi asks us.

Alexandra's answer is a big gulping sound. That's exactly the way I feel too. Scared. It sounded like such a fun idea when we were sitting around planning it, but now . . . it's turned scary. If they catch us we're really finished. And there are a million ways for this to go wrong. If somebody wakes and sees us they'll probably scream. I can just see that, one kid screaming and then all the others wake up and start screaming too. What if they think we're thieves? They could even attack us.

"You want to forget it?" I ask them.

"Oh, no," Alexandra says, shaking her head furiously, "absolutely not. No way . . . unless, of course, you want to . . ."

"Uh-uh," I say.

". . . or maybe Steffi?" You can tell she'd love Steffi to say no.

But Steffi says she's not going to be the one to chicken out.

"Me neither," says Alexandra, and then to me, "and you certainly can't since it was your idea."

"I wouldn't dream of it." For the first time I'm not so crazy about Alexandra. It's easy to see that none of us wants to do it. It's funny, but we're all stuck.

"Should we vote on it?" I take one last chance.

"What's the point of a vote if no one is disagreeing?" Al asks.

"I just want to be democratic."

"Okay," she says, "anybody for chickening out?"

We all raise our hands. And then we crack up laughing.

"Come on," Steffi says, "we have to do it. It's such a fabulous idea."

"We've gotten past the worst part already," Alexandra says.

"How's that?" I ask.

"What's worse than Dena Joyce?"

"It's settled," I say, "let's move it."

And the three of us go off into the black night, each one of us heading for a different row.

The minute I leave them my knees begin to buckle. The idea of doing this is scary enough but the idea of doing it alone is absolutely terrifying. Next time I'll keep my big mouth shut.

The first bunk is the oldest girls, Super seniors. They're fifteen. I know most of them because they're sort of in our group. At least, they're invited to our parties.

I get out seven pieces of crepe paper, put my shopping bag down, and carefully and quietly creep up the steps of bunk five.

It's all quiet. I turn the doorknob and gently open the screen door. It's nearly pitch-black. I slip into the room as silently as I can and tiptoe over to the first bed. Carefully I tie a piece of the paper around the metal bar at the foot of the bed. I get the second one ready.

I tie that one on. Nobody wakes up. This must be what it's like to be a thief. It's horrible and I'm a wreck, and this is only my first bunk. I'll never make it.

But I do. At least I finish the first bunk. I have no idea how many of each color I did. It was too dark. But it doesn't make any difference anyway.

By the third bunk I'm like a professional. It's incredible how soundly everyone sleeps. I'm beginning to get excited because it's going to work. Then I start to get giggly. I can feel it growing in the bottom of my stomach, which is ridiculous since I'm all alone, but I can't help myself.

I tie on the first four ribbons, and then a little burp of laughter pops out of my mouth. I stop dead. There's no other sound. Nobody heard. I swallow the next giggle, but it's getting bad, so instead of tying on the last four I just throw them on the foot of their beds and hurry out of the door.

Now I'm in terror of doing the last two bunks. I can't trust myself not to burst out laughing. But I've got to get a grip otherwise the whole thing is going to bomb.

These two last bunks are thirteen-year-olds, intermediates. The very last is the worst because that's where my adorable sister, Nina, is. If she wakes up I'm really absolutely lost.

Somehow I get through the first bunk and now all I have to do is El Creepo's bunk. I take a deep breath, then I take five more, and then three more, and then I know if I don't get started right this minute I'll be taking deep breaths till the dawn.

I count to my special lucky number. It's really mine alone because I'll bet there isn't anyone else in the whole world who uses forty-seven for her lucky number. But it goes too fast. I may change it to 147.

No problem getting into the bunk. I tie Nina's on first because I have to get that over with.

"Could I have a glass of water?" a voice whispers from the bed in the corner.

I freeze.

"Could I, huh?"

There's only one thing to do. I go into the bathroom and hunt around for a glass. It's even darker in the bathroom. I move my hands around on the shelf where they would probably keep the glasses. But I can't find any. This is horrendous. I don't know what to do.

Then I hear somebody getting out of bed. They're coming to use the bathroom. Please don't let it be Nina.

I open the door to the bathroom and stand behind it. The person goes into the toilet. She closes the door. I wait for her to finish and open the door. Then I grab it so she can't close it. She tries but I hold it. And my breath.

She tries twice, then I hear her padding back to bed.

I'm about to try to get out when I hear the voice again. "Big deal, can't you just get me a little glass of water?"

I start searching around again for a glass when I hear the slippers coming back to the bathroom. I jump behind the door again. This time the slippers stop at the sink. I hear the water. It seems like forever until she goes back to the other room.

"Thanks," a voice says, and then the slippers pad over to her own bed. There's a sound of springs as she climbs into bed and then quiet.

But she can't be sleeping. There's no way I can finish. All I care about now is getting out of here without being seen.

I wait a couple of minutes and then I start walking toward the door. There's no sound, and just as I reach the screen door, a very sleepy voice asks, "Where are you going?"

"To the bathroom," I say.

"Okay," she answers, and I slip out of the front door fast.

Once outside I start running back to my bunk. It's beginning to get lighter out and we have to do our own bunks, otherwise they'll know in a minute who did it.

We're supposed to meet outside the bunk. Steffi's already there and Alexandra comes right behind me.

"How'd it go?" I ask them.

"Horrendous," Steffi says. "I couldn't do the last bunk because one of the kids was up with a flashlight when I got to the door."

Alexandra had trouble too. One of the little kids woke up

and had to go to the bathroom, so she took her. She was so groggy she didn't even notice the difference.

Except for a few people, maybe fifteen, we did everyone. Now all we have to do is get back in our own bunk, tie on some papers, and get back into bed.

This is the worst part.

We go into the bunk one at a time, very quietly. I go last. The minute I open the door my eyes shoot over to Dena Joyce. She's dead asleep on her side curled up like a baby. From this side it even looks like she's sucking her thumb. I tiptoe to my bed.

My eyes are on D. J. all the time. Strangely enough, from the other side she looks like she's sucking her thumb too. What a thought. I tuck it in the back of my mind. It would make great ammunition.

Each one of us ties a paper onto the next bed just as planned. It's really going perfectly.

I love doing things like this. It's so exciting. I love an adventure because it's so dangerous. Can you imagine what would happen if Madame Katzoff or Dr. Davis found out?

I'm safely in bed when I hear D. J. move in her bed. I carefully turn around and there she is, thumb out of her mouth, eyes open, staring at me.

"I can't sleep," I say.

She doesn't say anything. Then, after a couple of seconds, she closes her eyes.

She probably wasn't even really awake. That's what I have to think or I'm finished. We're all finished.

I decide I'm simply not going to worry. So for the next hour I stay awake, purposely forcing myself not to worry. It doesn't work.

But I must have finally fallen asleep because the next thing I know I hear voices, not close by, but outside the bunk.

Lots of voices, crowds. What's going on? And then I remember and jump up out of bed. Boy, do I remember.

I'm the first one up, but a minute later the twins get up. Right at the same time, too. And the first thing they notice is the crepe paper and in two seconds they put the whole thing together.

"It's Color War!" Enid shouts. At least the twin in Enid's bed.

"Fantabulous!" Ellen says, jumping out of bed, and then everyone is up.

"Hey, wow!" Steffi says. Boy is she a lousy actress.

And so is Alexandra, who overdoes it horrendously by jumping up and running around the bunk grabbing at the ties on everyone's bunk.

Even though it's fake we still made the teams just the way we want them. Al, Steffi, and I on one team, and the rest of them on the other.

I watch Dena Joyce closely. She doesn't seem so excited. In fact, she doesn't seem excited at all, but then again, she's always pretty cool.

"Fabulous," I join in the excitement, my eyes still peeled on D. J. She's looking funny. It's like she's observing us. "Who's on the green team?" I say, waving my crepe paper. "How about you, D. J.?"

"Right," she says, and without another word leaves the bunk.

She knows.

We're lost.

Al and Steffi both see what happened. She's going to rat on us. And there's no place to run.

The twins and Liza are still jumping around, but the three of us go very quiet.

"What do you think?" Al whispers to me.

"We just have to wait and see," I say.

"But what do you think will happen?"

I shrug my shoulders. We both look at Steffi.

"At best, the worst."

"Now I feel better," I say.

"You want the truth, don't you?"

Meanwhile, the twins and Liza have stopped jumping around. "What's up?" Liza asks.

The three of us trip over each other to say, "Nothing." And then try to look very ordinary. If I do it as badly as they do, we're in big trouble.

"Something's fishy here," Twinny Somebody says, and her shadow shakes her head in agreement.

"Yeah," Steffi says, looking at Liza. "What's up?"

"Right." Al and I jump right into it, taking our cue. "Something's funny."

"I think so too," the other twin says, and before you know it we're all standing around trying to find out what's happening. Except some of us know already, and nothing matters anyway since Dena Joyce *really* knows; and it's just a matter of time before they come with the Dobermans.

"Come on," Liza says. "Let's go find out what's up."

And the three of them go out leaving us unprotected. The minute they leave the bunk we fall into a hysterical laughing fit that's really sheer horrendous panic. And I mean fall, all over the beds, the floor; we can't get our balance.

We're going on like this for I don't know how long when suddenly Steffi stops. "Listen," she says, "listen how quiet it's got."

It's true. Suddenly there's this weird silence. All that excited noise outside has stopped.

"What do you think?" Al is the first to ask, her eyes popping.

"I don't know," I say. "Look out the window."

"No, you look."

"No way," I say. "I got us into this. My job is finished. You both have to get us out."

"Do you think D. J. told or what?" Now Steffi is beginning to look as bad as Al, which is about what I feel in my stomach. "If she didn't it's only because she loves us so much. Come on, we're worrying too much. It was only a little joke; why would they take it so seriously?"

"Are you kidding?" Steffi suddenly gets very sensible. "Color War is heavy stuff."

Alexandra is shaking her head, agreeing, "Everybody really goes all out for it, so when dear old D. J. told them it was all a big trick, they probably went bonkers. Wait till you see, they're going to be furious."

"So what do you think is going to happen to us?" I ask her.

"It's all according to who gets us first."

"Right," Steffi says. "If we can survive the kids, we'll probably just get a good talking to . . ."

"That's not so bad."

". . . by Madame Katzoff?"

"It's horrendous."

We all try to figure what she'll actually do. And we decide that no matter, she can't really do more than just fine us. I mean, they don't have capital punishment in summer camp. At least, it didn't say so in the brochure.

A little more conjecture and we end up in terror.

It's still eerily quiet out there and then slowly, far in the background, we begin to hear sounds. And they get louder, like the sound of a crowd of people in the distance. A big crowd, and crazy, like it's the French Revolution and we're King Louis the whatever.

"I'll choose you for who looks out of the window," I say.

And while our whole castle is being stormed, we do one-potato, two-potato. Steffi loses.

She sort of creeps across the room and peeks out from between the broken shutters. "So?" I ask her when she gets there.

"Holy cow!"

Now Al and I race over to the window. Oh, God, it's awful. What looks like hundreds of camper-type humans are spilling out from behind the last line of bunks and all converging on our bunk. And boy do they look angry. Remember unruly mobs from movies? That's the picture, and they're coming fast.

"Are the gargoyles with them?" Al asks.

"I don't see them," I say.

"Then we're okay."

Both Steffi and I look at Alexandra like she's off the wall.

"Are you kidding? Four million peasants in revolution and you say we're okay. What's going to happen when they get here and they're almost here right now."

"You'll explain," she says.

"Just say it was a little joke . . ." Steffi gets right in there.

"No, *you* say it was a little joke."

It's hard to believe those hordes of people are actually headed here. It's all ridiculous. After all, what are they going to do to us anyway?

And even though I know they really can't string us up or anything like that, still the sight of all those angry kids out there is scary.

"Should we hide or what?" Steffi asks.

"Great idea," I say, and the three of us frantically start to search for hiding places. The crowd sounds are getting louder. God, it was only a little joke.

"This is stupid," I tell them. "Three people can't hide in

this room. Forget it, they'll find us in a minute. Besides, it looks worse. It's like admitting guilt."

"What should we do?" Alexandra asks.

"Stay here and face it."

"Or what?" That's Steffi, of course.

"Or run."

"Let's go!"

And the three of us head for the door. We open it, look out, and slam it shut instantly. It's too late. Half the population of upper New York State is marching on us.

"Out the window!" I shout.

But the stupid broken shutters don't open. Nothing to do but face it bravely. That's probably what courage really is. No other choice.

We can hear the pounding and scuffling of the mob and then footsteps, a lot of them, coming up the steps onto the porch. Their mistake.

Then the shouts, "Watch it!" "Oh, shit!" and other exclamations as the boards crack and sink under their feet. We may have our own kind of moat.

Then the pounding starts.

"Open this door!" someone hollers.

"Shove the cubby in front of the door!" Steffi says, and the three of us slide Liza's cubby against the door. Now the pounding gets even harder and more voices are shouting for us to open up.

"The other cubby!" I call out to Steffi, but it's too late.

They've already got the door partway open and nothing is going to hold it. We're done for. Incredible. This is nuts. Plain old campers don't break down doors. This is a nightmare.

Nothing left but to give up. "Okay," I say, "since it was my idea, I'll go first."

"Right," says my best friend, "you go first."

All the time those nuts out there haven't stopped pounding and now the door is halfway off its hinges and splitting down the center.

We can see the enemy faces squeezing grotesquely into the partly open door. Two more minutes and they'll be in. We've pasted ourselves against the wall as far back as the room will allow. I can't believe this all started from such a little joke.

"They're really nuts," I say to Steffi, and she just shakes her head. She can't believe it either.

"What are we going to do when they get in?" she asks me, and I can see she's scared. I am too.

So is Alexandra.

A couple more slams on that door and it's finished. Al looks like she's going to cry.

I'm beginning to feel that way too.

The shouts and the shuffling and the pounding and now a new sound even more terrifying. A high screeching noise, at first thin, someplace far in the background and then building in power, louder and louder and finally like a siren right in front of the bunk. The squeezed heads begin to pull out from the bulging door to turn in that direction, and the assault falls off a little. The door that was stretched open closes a bit, and the attackers let up. Huge relief.

We all run to the window but there's nothing to see. The crowds are turning in the direction of the rec hall. The siren is still blasting, but now we can hear another sound, like a drum and then a cymbal and then horns, and it's music. The siren is still blaring but dying out as the music comes closer. It's a marching band!

At first a few of the kids from the back of the crowd break away and start heading over toward the rec hall; then a few more leave. The first ones begin to pick up speed and then break into a run, then the others follow and more and more kids are turning and running in the direction of the music.

"What's happening?" Al says.

"Who cares?" I say. "We're saved."

And we are. In no time there isn't a soul left in front of the bunk. They're all running to the music.

"I know what it is," Steffi says, and at that moment it dawns on me, too, what's happening. "Color War, that's what."

"Only the real thing this time."

Alexandra is only now beginning to pull herself together. "Isn't that the weirdest, nuttiest thing? We get saved by the very thing that almost knocked us out."

"Don't count your chickens. We're not finished yet. Not by a long shot," Steffi says, but she's smiling because the worst is definitely over.

"We made it. All they're going to do is fine us or something like that," I say.

But Al is still worried. "Yeah, but what's the something like that?"

"No big deal—I can practically guarantee everybody's going to be too busy with Color War to bother with our little nothing. You'll see, they're going to be laughing about it soon, right, Steffi?"

"She's right, Al. Maybe a fine, tops. Don't worry."

"Hey, you know what? It just hit me that Color War really *did* break. I'm dying to know what teams we're on. Let's see what's happening."

We have to practically drag Alexandra out of the bunk, but finally she comes with us and we all race down to the rec hall.

The whole camp is there. The band is marching around the lawn followed by some counselors dressed in clown costumes, with huge helium balloons stretching up into the air anchored by long strings attached to their shoulders. They have baskets tucked under one arm and with the other hand they're tossing green- and gray-colored balls to the kids. Everybody is scrambling for them. Nobody pays any attention to us. One of the colored balls comes right at us and Al grabs it.

It's shiny, like a tree ornament, and there's something inside. She twists it open and takes out the folded paper inside. It's the team lists.

"Quick," Steffi says. "Open it. I'm dying to know if Robbie's on my team or what."

Me too, only I'm dying to know that he's not on mine. Boy, he'd better not be.

Alexandra goes first since she caught it.

"Green team, I'm on the green team! Here, Victoria, you find yours."

I get it in a second. "Green team too. Great." I hand the list to Steffi. "Fingers crossed you're on our team too."

"Damn," she says.

"What?" I grab the list.

"Gray team. What about Robbie? You look."

I turn to the boys' part, and his name practically jumps off the page.

"I knew it," Steffi says. She's right, there he is, third from the top, on the green team.

"Sorry." And I really am, but it's no big deal. It's not like we're alone; there's at least a hundred and fifty kids on each team.

"That stinks. Everybody good is on the green team." Poor Steffi, she's really disappointed.

"Hey, it's going to be all right," I tell her. "You've got D. J. on your team."

"Gross."

". . . and the twins."

"Both of 'em?"

"Both. And Dracula and the Wolfman and Erica from *All My Children*."

"That's enough," Al says, pulling me close to her. "No more consorting with the enemy."

"Up yours," Steffi snarls.

"Uh-uh, now where's your sense of sportsmanship?"

"Hey!" One of the little kids, maybe a sophomore, comes up from out of nowhere and yanks at my sleeve. "Aren't you one of the waitresses who did that thing?"

I shake my head no, but she's not one bit convinced.

"Oh, yes you are." And then she grabs her little friend and, pointing to me, says, "Isn't she that one from the dining room?"

"You mean The Spiller?"

"Yeah."

"Yeah." The other little one shakes her head. "That's her."

Nice. That's what I'm known as—"The Spiller." I wonder why.

"Boy," the first little one says, "are you in trouble. My counselor is really mad at you."

"So is mine," the other one says. "I'm going to tell her."

And the two of them run off and so do we. We head back to the safety of our bunk, fast. But not fast enough.

"Just a minute, you three." Without turning, we all know we're finished. It's all over. But when we do turn, we see there's still a little hope. It isn't Madame Katzoff or the Doctor. It's only Ginny Fowler, the head counselor. "I'd like to have a little conversation with the three of you. Meet me in my office in fifteen minutes."

And she goes off.

"She's okay," Steffi says. "She's been here for years. Everybody likes her."

Alexandra agrees. "A big talking-to and a little fine. Don't worry, it's cool."

"We just got lucky," I say. "If it hadn't been for the real Color War we'd have been sunk. I'd love to get back at the Dena Joyce gross-out some way."

"It's tough, though," Al says. "It's like she's made of steel. No soft spots."

"Everybody has soft spots, you've just got to find them."

"Dena Joyce?" Steffi shakes her head like there's no way.

But I have an idea. I don't say anything to them because it needs more investigation. But just maybe good old hard-as-nails isn't so break-proof. We'll see.

"Come on, let's get over to Ginny's," Steffi says. "The faster we get this over with, the faster we'll be in the clear or what."

And, as Steffi would say, we all go off to meet our destiny or what.

Exactly as predicted, Ginny gave us the big talking-to, but the fine wasn't so little. We each lost eleven dollars. Still, it was better than being hanged, which would have been better than a chat with the gargoyles; so we got off easy. Steffi said one day we'd look back and think it was a fabulous adventure. I said I had some ideas, too, but she said if I even mentioned one they were going to turn me in.

That was yesterday. Today our mini Color War is starting this morning. From the minute we get up this morning we're no longer just regular people; we're either green team or gray team. And we're all killers.

Everything for the team.

Starting with breakfast. Lineup at the flagpole is done by teams, with me on one side of the grass circle and Steffi and her teammates on the other. It's weird for us to be separated like this. At this moment Steffi has more in common with Dena Joyce than she does with me. Well, I guess maybe that's an exaggeration. Nobody could have more in common with D. J. except for maybe Godzilla.

I'm still not used to these early summer mornings in the country. They're really super-looking, fresh and green, and you get a wonderful feeling just standing there breathing in all that clean air; but it's really cold. I'm always shivering in these little uniforms. It's either the cold or dread of serving. I'm still terrible at waitressing. I can't seem to get the hang of it. But Anna, the counselor I'm always spilling on, is beginning to like me more. She says since she's been here she's lost four pounds. It's a form of eating anxiety. Truth is, I haven't spilled anything on her in almost ten days. She's due.

One of the big problems is all the jumping up and down everyone does. Every two minutes the whole camp rises for some stupid thing or other; sometimes it's just to sing to someone or because they've won something or other. But they're always doing it, and I'm always just passing with my tray. Naturally, it creates a problem—either it's a shoulder under a tray or a head under a tray. Either one is good for a swing from the clean-up squad, now known as Victoria's group.

This morning it all feels different. Exciting. I love the competition. Instead of just walking to the mess hall we march down in our groups singing team songs. We've got a whole stack of them. Most of them are easy because they're set to old tunes everyone knows. Strangely enough, here we are marching across the lawn singing songs with a lot of rah-rah-rahs in them and not feeling like jerks. It's incredible, but I guess you get in the spirit, and besides, when everyone is doing something it doesn't seem so weird.

In the dining room we all still have our regular tables. But now everything counts. Even the way we serve.

We set up the tables and wait for the kids. You can hear them singing "Hats Off" as they march from their bunks. The change is really fabulous.

They come marching into the dining room and take their usual seats, but it's all completely different. It's like they're in the army they're so well behaved. Even my tables are perfect.

I'd looked up Henry's name yesterday and he's on my team, and the terrible bully Steven is on the gray team. Unfortunately, they sit next to each other. Steven is still as unpleasant as ever, and Henry still has his same problems, the big one in bed anyway. He's also not the most popular boy in the bunk. Steven sees to that. I wish I could think of some way to help Henry, but so far the only thing he can do is tough it out, which is very hard for him because he just isn't tough enough.

And I don't think he ever will be, which is probably why I like him so much.

This morning he looks adorable—his shiny blond hair slicked straight back and his neatly ironed green uniform with the green knee socks. He's not the youngest boy in the bunk, but he is the littlest and the cutest. I wish he weren't so unhappy-looking. It's like he's on the brink of tears all the time. And much too quiet for a seven-year-old boy, except when we're alone, then he's practically a chatterbox and very smart, too.

Did I mention that along with Robbie being on my team, to make matters even more perfect, El Creepo is also on the green team? Well, she is. She's such a little snitch, she didn't even waste a second telling my parents about the Color War Fiasco. They happened to call last night, and so naturally she tells them, and naturally they really didn't understand, and my mother said I couldn't stay out of trouble for just one minute and things like that. I didn't need that, really I didn't.

"Victoria, may I please have an egg instead of cereal this morning?" That comes from Fay Miller, normally a seven-year-old monster but this morning a saint. That's what Color War does; you see, if you don't stay in line you get demerits and that comes off the team score. They even count eating. They count everything, the way you dress, neatness in your bunk, the way you march, the way you sing; everything you do is all part of the competition. Normally Fay Miller would either scream when I brought her her cereal or, if she was in a real mood, dump it on the floor. It's weird, I never heard her normal voice before today.

And that's the way it continues throughout breakfast. I'm almost perfect, too. I get everyone's orders right, I don't drop anything, I don't spill anything, and I don't bump into anybody—practically to the end.

Then, just as I'm serving the iced tea, Robbie walks by, smiles, and says hi. That's all it takes. I stop in midair, smile back, lose part of my stomach someplace around my knees, and most of the iced tea around my feet. I also lose a half point for my team. Anna breathes a sigh of relief. Even though she's on the green team, too, at least she's still dry.

Why does even the sight of him make me so crazy? And it doesn't get any better. Something's happening to him, too, I know it. Like yesterday afternoon. It was really hot and a bunch of us were hanging out in the pool when some of the guys came over. Robbie was with them. I don't know where Steffi was, but she wasn't around.

As soon as I saw him I pretended to get very involved helping Alexandra with her diving; but I could practically feel his eyes on me. And every once in a while I would look up, and sure enough, there he was, looking at me. More like staring. Maybe he just thinks I'm an off-the-wall weirdo and he's fascinated, but that's not what I read. I don't want to say what I read, not even to myself.

On the way out, Steven manages to trip Henry. All his little cronies get a big kick out of that.

"You okay?" I bend down to help Henry.

He nods his head yes, and then does a wonderful thing—he doesn't cry. That's an immense improvement for him. I think I have something to do with it, because he sees how terrible things are for me and how I'm holding up. It's like we're in it together.

"Don't you worry, we're going to get him one of these days, you'll see."

"I guess," he says, but I can tell he's not convinced; I'm not either. It looks like he doesn't stand a chance against someone like Steven, but maybe that's the way people always feel about a bully, which is probably what makes bullies so effective.

Not a great beginning for either of us today. Maybe it'll get better with the races. Both teams are meeting at the big playing field for a morning of all kinds of racing, from real track events to crazy things like potato sack races.

I'm a pretty fast runner, so maybe I can make back the half point I lost for my team.

Eleven

By the time we finish setting up for lunch and get to the field everyone else is already there and some of the races have started. In fact, the broad-jumping competition is over and the gray team picked up six points.

Since this is the first day, everyone is very excited and there's a lot of shouting and cheering. Parts of Color War are really annoying, things like Steffi and I not being able even to stand together. We have to stick on opposite sides of the field with our teams. And it means that Robbie has to be over on my side. And there he is.

"Are you in any of the events?" he asks me.

I love you.

I don't say that, I only think it. In fact, I don't say anything;

all I do is shrug my shoulders and make some stupid face that's supposed to mean *I don't know.*

He looks at me with those totally awesome blue eyes that feel like they're seeing right through you. "Do you want to be my partner?" he asks.

Of course I want to be his partner—forever, but that's impossible.

"I can't," I say, and then regret it instantly. It tells too much, so I scramble to fix it. "I mean that you can't choose your partners, can you? At least I didn't think you could."

"You can for the potato sack race."

"Oh, I'd love to, but I have to leave early to set up for lunch. Gee, thank you anyway, it would have been really fun."

Shut up now, Victoria.

". . . I adore potato races, they're really great . . . just terrific." When I get nervous I just rattle on. "They're really fun." And on. "Too bad I don't have time, but I can't be late for setup . . . so I'll catch you later . . ."

"It's now."

"Huh?"

"The race is right now."

"Too soon. My foot will never be healed in time."

I can be very fast when I get desperate.

Of course he's confused. "Your foot? What's wrong with your foot?"

"Just a cut. Not too bad."

"Sorry. You seem to have a lot of trouble with your feet,

don't you?" He's referring to my nonexistent sprained ankle of a couple of weeks ago. I don't know if he believed that one but he looks very suspicious this time. I can't believe he doesn't know what the problem is.

"Right," I say, and I feel a little annoyed with him for pushing me. It's the first time I've felt anything but dumb goofy lovesick about him. He must know we shouldn't be partners. Why is he doing this?

"You've got to get in this race." From out of nowhere, Steffi appears. "I don't care if it is my own team, I can't root for Dena Joyce and Wally Kramer or Claire and that geek Norman. C'mon, you two, are you going to get with it or what?"

"I'm ready, but Victoria's hurt her foot."

"Again?" Steffi says, and just from her look I know it'd better heal fast or we're back where we started two weeks ago with her thinking I don't like Robbie.

"Just a little cut," I tell her. "Nothing." Then to Robbie, "I hope I won't hold you back."

"What are you talking about? We'll kill 'em," he says. "Wait here, I'll be right back." And he runs over to grab a sack off the pile at the side of the finish line.

I give Steffi what has to be the goofiest smile ever sat on a face and say, "Terrific!"

"Is it really or what?"

"Hey, yeah, you heard what Robbie said, we're gonna kill 'em."

"I didn't mean that. I don't know why I keep pushing you

two together. My luck, you'll probably end up liking each other so much you'll dump me."

My heart drops right to my feet.

"Oh, Steffi, that would never happen."

"Take it easy, Torrie, I was only kidding around. I know that would never happen. God, you're my best friend."

Then she laughs, and I do too—at least I try. I actually get a sick feeling just hearing her say that—it's too close for comfort.

I feel I should say something, but the only things that come into my mind are too real and serious, so I settle for easy and meaningless. "Hey, gimme a break."

And then Robbie's back, so we both giggle kind of secretly and of course he wants to know what's so funny.

"You are," Steffi says lightly, poking Robbie in the ribs with her finger. Naturally he pretends to be mortally wounded and doubles over in what's supposed to be horrendous pain. Lover-type people always play those games together. I suppose it's cute to them, but it makes the other people feel stupid and left out.

Suddenly I'm in a funk. I'm tired of always being uncomfortable with people who are supposed to be my closest friends, at least Steffi is, yet all I ever feel is bad around them. Either I'm worried that what I feel for Robbie will show or I feel left out or . . . or I feel jealous. Might as well admit it because that's the truth.

"Hey, Torrie, are you dreaming or what?" Steffi says, pulling herself away from fun and games with Robbie. "Snap out of it, you've got a race to win."

"Let's try it," Robbie says, holding open the sack on the ground. "You get in first."

I step in. And Robbie steps in. And Steffi steps back to watch.

It's awful.

The feel of Robbie standing alongside me, his arm around my waist, mine around his, is almost unbearable. I must be bright red, my face is certainly burning enough. Nothing's happened yet, and I'm in a sweat. What a bad idea.

"Hang on tight," Robbie says, "and count with me so we can jump together." I don't trust myself to do anything more than nod. "Bend your knees and throw yourself forward."

We both bend our knees into an almost crouch and then spring forward with all our might. He lands way ahead of me, dragging the sack and throwing me over so I have to grab on to him to keep from falling to the ground.

"Sorry," I say, and kind of crawl up him to get my legs untwisted from the burlap.

"It's my fault," he says. "I have to keep my jump down to your level. Let's try it again."

"See ya," Steffi calls out, as she heads over to the gray side of the field. "Good luck!"

One of the twins standing by hears her and shouts "Hey, Klinger, which team are you on, anyway?"

"Right. Gray all the way," she says, then calls out to us, "Break a leg."

That's theater talk for good luck, but if Steffi had any idea of the things that are going on in my head she would mean it for real.

Robbie and I are off. It's so hard and such a struggle to just keep up that I practically forget it's Robbie I'm clutching on to, which is funny since this is the closest I've ever been to him.

Then the rhythm gets easier and I begin to think of what I'm feeling. I'm holding his waist and I can feel his body under the T-shirt. It's very warm.

So am I, especially all up and down my arm, the one that's wrapped around him. And every time we jump up the whole side of my body touches his.

"Okay," he says all out of breath, "enough practice. Let's get over to the starting line."

"Okay." My first words since I got in the burlap sack. No danger of me charming him.

We get into the lineup. There are eight other couples in the race, four gray team and four green. We each have to stand next to a couple from the opposing team. Naturally we get next to Dena Joyce, and does she give me a look when she sees who's in there with me.

"Where's Steffi?" she says, leaning over and looking down into our sack.

If I was red before, I just caught fire. Again, I'm speechless. It's all because of the guilt. But Robbie isn't thrown by her. He knows it's a nasty remark, he just doesn't know the history of it.

"What's your problem, D. J., you blind? Don't you see Steffi over there?" he says, pointing to where Steffi's standing. He says it jokingly, but there's an edge you can't miss. She doesn't. And she shuts up because Robbie's no pushover like I am.

He also doesn't seem to feel guilty, which makes me feel good—and a little bad. Maybe I was wrong about him. I guess I was reading something into his looks that really isn't there. It isn't any place but inside my head; and I guess that's where it better stay.

Ginny, the head counselor, announces the race, and we all inch up to the starting line.

"On your mark . . . get set . . . go!" And we're off, hopping, jumping, and falling all over each other, and getting up and jumping again. We're neck-and-neck with Dena Joyce and Wally, and going at top speed.

"Up, down, up, down, up, down," we keep saying in unison. "Up, down, up, down . . ."

We're so busy watching out for D. J. and Wally that we don't see Liza coming up on our other side until she knocks into us and we go flying into D. J. and all three sacks go hurtling one over another.

"Quick," Robbie says, grabbing me under the arms, "get up!"

We lost precious time, and now we're last; we have to catch up to the other five couples.

Up, down, up, down . . . we give it all we've got and we pick up speed. Two other couples bound into one another and go down. Only three more ahead of us.

We're really in rhythm now. We're moving like one person. And fast!

One more couple down and we're third and gaining.

"C'mon," Robbie says, smiling down at me, "we can do it."

Oh, God, I really want to do it . . . for you, Robbie. For you.

Up, down, up, down . . . we're second, right behind Claire and Norman. One good blast forward and we can pass them, but every time we try, they move over in front of us. It's too hard to swing over to the side, we'd lose too much time if we did.

"Straight ahead," Robbie says.

"Can't," I say. "We'll hit them."

"They'll move, you'll see . . ."

Down, up, down, up . . . we're nearly up to them and they're not moving. And then we take one huge leap and they lean out of the way and we shoot past them. We're in the lead! Twenty more feet . . . I can hear them breathing and grunting just inches behind us. I feel like they're going to fall right into us. I have no breath left; one more jump and I'm going to sink into the ground. I can hear the crowd cheering over my own huffing and puffing. I can't see them. I can't see anything except a blur of everything that keeps going up and down with me.

Just as we bend for the down part of our jump, Claire and Norman land on the bottom of our sack, stopping us dead and then jerking us backward onto them, which sends them flying down, tearing our sack as they go.

With one big wrench Robbie frees us, and wrapping the torn burlap around our waists we start off again.

The two other couples behind us are closing in, but we only have another couple of feet left to the finishing line. Everybody is screaming. With one last enormous leap, we throw ourselves over the line, and then down we go and over and over, rolling on the ground. Hands are reaching out to help us, and then they're untangling us from the shreds of the bag.

"We won!" Everybody's shrieking and jumping up and down.

Including Robbie and me. We're hugging and leaping up and down and dancing around, and it's the most exciting thing.

"You won, you rats." It's Steffi, and she's smiling, trying hard to be a good gray-team person but secretly delighted that we won, and probably especially happy because her friends are finally getting along together. It's what she wanted all along. And we are—the joy of winning and something else, something that's been stored up inside me for all these weeks, comes pouring out in the hugging and touching; something that I know I have to control but can't for the moment. Don't want to, but must.

I can't tell if Robbie is sharing any of my feelings. It's better if I don't know.

Twelve

The rest of the races are a triumph for the gray team. With the exception of the twenty points we won in the potato race, all the winning points go to the enemy team. As of the first morning of Color War, the green team is trailing by one hundred and fifty points.

The afternoon doesn't help much. We pick up some points for volleyball and lose points on softball and basketball. By dinner we're very much behind. I serve in a complete daze. They're ordering fried potatoes and I'm dreaming potato sacks. All the progress I've made in the last weeks is down the drain.

At least my tables don't have to wait for their dessert; I bring it first—before the main course. I'm totally dense tonight. The kids love it, but Anna suggests I'd better get my act together or risk losing more points. I try, but every couple of minutes my mind drifts back to this afternoon and the excitement of Robbie. As long as I don't look at Steffi, I can enjoy my thoughts, but the moment I do see her, I feel horrendously guilty.

I'm the last one out of the dining room. No one waits because everyone has too much work to do. Steffi shoots off to work on some secret stuff for her team. I have to get over to the rec hall to help out with the scenery for the musical production. That's the big competition the last night of Color War. It's worth five hundred points, so it can make all the difference.

There are about fifteen people, including Robbie, working on the sets when I get there. I make sure I say a nice hello and then move to the other side of the room. He makes no move to get near me. No repeats of this afternoon's mistakes.

We're doing flags of all nations mounted collage-style on a semicircular backdrop. We don't actually have any real flags except our own and a Canadian one, so the rest have to be made up from scraps of materials painted on canvas. Alexandra and I are working on the ribs, the pieces of wood that hold up the flags. It's just sticks of wood crisscrossed and nailed at the intersection. It's not the straightest-looking semicircle, if that's possible anyway, but it's good enough to give the illusion of something that wraps around.

"I'll sort out more nails," Al says, "and you go get a few more pieces of wood, okay?"

"Sure thing," I tell her, and head across the hall to ask Ginny where I can get more sticks.

"We've got a big pile of them in the little shed around the back," she says. "Robbie, can you stop for a minute and help Victoria get more wood out back? You know where it is, don't you?"

"Sure thing," Robbie says, getting up from his painting job. "Got a flashlight?"

"Use mine," Ned Weiner, his partner in painting, says, handing him a miner's lamp-type light.

I follow Robbie out the back door.

If I planned this it wouldn't have worked. It's so silly that she picked Robbie of all people, that I have to smile, just a little one to myself. My luck, Robbie sees me smiling and probably figures this is what I want to happen. Under regular circumstances I would, but not now. I swear I don't.

It's pitch-black around the back. The shed is about twenty feet behind the rec hall. When we get there Robbie holds the door open for me.

"Can you hold this for a second, please?" he says, handing me the light. "I just want to find the switch."

The room is jammed with all kinds of props for plays and tons of sports equipment. It's hard to tell where the wood would be. And Robbie's having trouble finding the switch.

"Do you think it's behind those screens?" I ask him.

"I've found it already but it doesn't work."

"Should I go back and get another flashlight?"

"That's okay, you just shine it over here and I think I can get to the wood."

We start picking our way deeper into the clutter. Now if I really *had* planned this whole thing, then I would delicately trip over something and he would catch me in his arms.

But I didn't plan it, and besides, I'm so solid on my Nikes it would take a wrecker's ball to knock me over.

"Watch your step," he says, turning to me. As he does, his foot slides off a pole on the floor and he loses his balance, grabs for the wall, misses, and comes crashing down. I catch him for a second and then his weight crumples me to the floor, with him on top. In my hands even the most romantic possibility turns into a mess.

"God, I'm sorry," he says. "Are you okay?"

"I think so, if you can just get up. . . ."

"Right, sorry," he says, picking himself up and trying not to knock anything else over. "Here, watch your head." He bends over me, giving me his hand.

I take it. But as I'm getting up I accidentally tip over a screen, and as it falls he grabs me around the back and pulls me against him out of the way.

I'm in his arms. The wool of his sweater is soft against my cheek and the warmth of his body feels good against mine. He's holding me; my eyes are closed. I feel his face against the top of my head. Then I feel his lips. Somewhere in a far corner of my mind a tiny voice says don't do this, what about Steffi, but I don't move.

"Torrie." Steffi's name for me. Still I stay in his arms. With his free hand he gently tips my head back and his lips come down on mine. Softly, sweetly, his mouth slightly open against my lips that part to match his.

I feel an enormous rush of love for him, so strong I can't stop myself from putting my arms around him and holding him as tightly as he's holding me.

I know I've never felt like this before.

And then he says the very same words that are in my head, that he never felt like this before.

I don't want to think. I only want to feel how good it is. I slide my arms around his neck and his hands trace the sides of my body along the curve of my waist and down to the tops of my thighs. The kisses become harder and stronger—not just his, mine too, and time falls out as we sink down to the floor, still holding each other.

We're side by side and we can't get close enough. His hand moves under my T-shirt along my bare skin; his fingers lightly touch my breasts. It makes me jump, not just from the coolness of his fingers, but because I know this is all wrong.

"Please stop," I say, but I don't move his hands or pull away from him. I feel like I can't, and then his lips press even harder against mine and it's like I'm lost. How could I do this to Steffi? How could I? But I do it, and the harder he kisses me the more I want him to, and when his hands begin to wander down into the top of my shorts I don't stop him. I just keep kissing him as if that's going to drive everything bad away.

I can feel his erection hard against my thigh, and I know I should stop this—not just for Steffi, but for me, too, before it gets out of control. I don't know him. He's not my boyfriend; he loves someone else. I've never been like this before with any other boy, not even if he loved me. I've wanted to be with Robbie since the first day I saw him. And even though I know all these things I still don't stop myself.

But he does. He pulls back away from me. "Torrie," he says, holding me by the shoulders and looking right at me. It's that same electricity that I can't ever get away from. "This is what I felt when I first saw you. You did too, that day, I know it."

"I don't want to feel this way. It's wrong. It's horrendously terrible."

"There's nothing we can do about it. We can't change it."

"Yes, we can."

"How?"

"Like we've been doing. We do nothing, that's all. Just stay far away from each other."

"No way," he says and pulls me tightly to him. "No way." There's a terrible determination in the sound of his voice and the feel of his mouth pressing hard against mine. In a second we're hanging on to each other closer than before, closer than I've ever been to any other boy. I never let myself go the way I'm doing now. I want him to hold me in his arms. I don't want him to stop no matter what. That's what real love must feel like.

We're lying together on the floor, the length of our bodies touching, holding each other tightly, kissing; nobody's in control, not him and not me. I just keep letting things go, getting deeper and deeper and further away from myself. It's really heavy, I know it. I know how selfish it is, how I'm betraying my best friend, how heartbroken she'd be if she knew. I know all those things but the feel of Robbie, the possibility that he could be in love with me, just wipes everything else out.

I've never made love with anyone. I knew I wouldn't with Todd. I just didn't feel that way about him, but it's different with Robbie. It could happen with him, but I don't want it to. I don't want to be in love with him. Right from the beginning I've been fighting it. But if he falls in love with me, I don't know if I'll be able to fight it anymore. I really want him like I've never wanted anyone before.

But the wrongness of it is terrible. And then that thought takes over.

"We're away too long," I say, twisting out of his arms and standing up.

"Wait," he says. "I want to talk to you."

"No." And while I'm still feeling determined, I pick up a pile of sticks and start off toward the rec hall.

"Wait a minute, Torrie." Robbie stops me outside the door. His hand is on my shoulder. I don't turn. I don't want to look at him, we're too close. I want to keep thinking straight.

But he turns me, and even in the semidarkness I can see

enough of him to feel that intense pull again. "It can't be the same, ever. Not with Steffi. That would be a bigger lie," he says.

"She doesn't have to know. Nothing really happened anyway. Nothing that will ever happen again."

He holds my face in his hands and bends down to kiss me. I get an instant flash of that first day I saw him, when he got off the bus. That's what he did with Steffi. Just like that, bending down slightly to kiss her. I remember it. "Please, don't. . . ." I slip out of his hands and start back to the door.

"Victoria, is that you?" A voice out of the dark. I get a horrible sick feeling. That's the worst voice I could ever hear.

I turn around to look in the direction it came from, but I don't see her.

"I thought so," she says, still not coming out of the dark. "See ya around."

"Who was that?" Robbie asks.

"Dena Joyce."

Everyone knows about Dena Joyce. Even Robbie. "Damn," he says, and I can see he's lost his cool. "What do you think she saw?"

"Enough." I feel like I could cry.

"It would take someone really rotten to go back to Steffi with this kind of thing."

"Don't worry, she is."

"Then I have to tell her first," Robbie says. "Now, before her birthday."

"What are you going to say?"

"I'll tell her the truth."

"About this—what happened tonight?"

"No, not yet. That can come later."

"What should I do about Dena Joyce?"

"Speak to her. Blame it on me. Say I came on to you, anything . . ."

"I'll try, but she's such a bitch I don't think it'll do any good."

"Try." Robbie pushes open the door. I hold it while he picks up a pile of wood and carries it inside. He comes back for a second trip. I pick up an armload and together we bring in the rest of the sticks. A couple of people look up at us, but mostly everybody is too busy to bother. It's almost eight thirty. We have been gone a long time.

The rest of the evening is unreal. I'm supposed to be criss-crossing sticks, but Alexandra ends up doing most of the work. I can barely think straight. She knows something's up but she can't ask. Strangely enough, it doesn't feel like anyone put two and two together about Robbie and me—no one but Dena Joyce.

I've got to talk to her tonight.

I know she's been over to the Juniors' bunks helping out with their songs, so I wait for her outside. I get lucky and she comes out alone.

"D. J.," I whisper to her.

"Didn't waste any time, did you?"

"I have to talk to you."

"Wonder what about." And just like that, she starts walking toward our bunk.

I catch up to her. "Look, it's really not what it looked like."

"Heavens no," she says in that really gross voice. "You were just giving him artificial respiration, right?" She's going to make me crawl.

But I'm ready to. I'll do anything, and she knows it.

"All I mean is that that was the first time and it just . . . it just happened."

"Sure thing."

It's hopeless. "Are you going to tell Steffi?" I come right out with it.

"Oh, I don't know. What do you think I should do? After all, she is a friend of mine and I think she should know about her so-called friend."

"It would be horrible if she found out. I would do anything so that she didn't have to know."

"Anything?" She practically licks her chops.

But I really will because, besides losing Steffi's friendship, she would be so hurt it would be horrendous, so I say, "Yes, anything."

"I'll think about it," she says, and dances off into the bunk.

"Torrie." Two seconds later Steffi comes up behind me. "What's up with her?" she asks, motioning as the last of Dena Joyce goes into the bunk.

"Nothing."

"You look upset. Is something wrong or what?"

I tell her I have a headache. "I must be getting my period."

"Again?"

"Maybe not. It's probably just Color War getting to me."

Now it's really terrible, I mean with Steffi. I can hardly talk to her. All I can think about is what a rat I am, how I've betrayed her. And she trusts me so much.

"Come on, Torrie, get a grip. It's not that much of a big deal."

For a second I think she's reading my mind and it makes me jump, then I realize that she's talking about Color War.

"Was Robbie working on the scenery tonight?" Steffi asks me as we walk into the bunk. Of course, Dena Joyce hears and stops in the middle of pulling off her sweater. It makes a great picture, D. J. frozen into a listening position with her head inside her sweater.

"She never looked better," Steffi whispers to me, pointing to her.

I pretend to laugh, but I find myself a little scared to be caught laughing at D. J. Then it hits me what a bad position I'm going to be in with her—all the time. And boy, is she going to use it. I don't know if I can handle it. Like now, I pretend I have to rush to the bathroom. Am I going to spend the rest of the summer running off to the bathroom every time Steffi starts to speak to me?

I manage to avoid my best friend long enough to get undressed and get in bed, and then it's lights-out and I can pretend to go right to sleep. Dena Joyce wishes me a special good night and happy dreams.

Just so happens I have a wonderful dream, all about Robbie and me dancing really close at someone's birthday party. It's fabulous until just as I'm waking up I realize whose birthday it was.

"I would love to borrow your leather jacket," D. J. coos, half in and half out of my dream. I try to squeeze myself back into the dream, but when she repeats herself it's very real and no more cooing, now it's the Wicked Witch of the East and I'm not messing with her.

"On the floor, the pile near the end of my bed."

"Thanks." She's back to cooing.

Later Steffi asks me how come I lent D. J. my good leather jacket. I have to set up something for the future because I think there's probably going to be a lot of borrowing from now on— in one direction, anyway—so I'd better have a good reason to be nice to D. J.

"You know," I say, trying not to choke on such a big lie, "I think she's really changing."

"Yeah," Steffi says, completely unconvinced. "Into what? A toad?"

"C'mon, Steffi. . . ."

"Gag me with a spoon."

There's no way I can pull this off except by changing

the subject quickly. "Did you have your strategy meeting last night?"

"Yeah, how about you?"

"Right after breakfast this morning. I got on the planning committee."

These strategy meetings are for a very important event of Color War. Each team tries to put their flag up on top of Mount Mohaph. The one who gets it up there first wins five hundred points. The only other thing worth that much is the musical the last night of Color War.

It's not a big-deal mountain, more like a little hill, but each team has kids standing guard from early morning until dark. You've got to get past about ten people to get up. It's really hard and usually it turns out to be a big chase; most years nobody gets there.

"You better come up with something great because we've really got a winner. Ken thought it up. He's really smart."

Oh, God, if only she could like him. That would solve everything.

"And very nice . . ."

Maybe she can.

"And I can tell he likes me. *And* he lives in New York." She sounds like she's playing with the possibility so I get right in there with the heavy guns.

"I think he's fabulous, really terrific."

She looks at me sort of surprised. "Do you?"

"Absolutely. He's super."

"Oh, Torrie, now I feel terrible. I didn't know you were

interested. I would never go near anyone you were even the tiniest bit interested in. . . ."

"Are you kidding? I'm not even the slightest bit . . . I mean, no way."

"But you said he's so fabulous."

"For you, not for me. He doesn't appeal to me at all."

"Me neither. Robbie's all I need . . . *ever!*"

"Excuse me, but I think I have to go to the bathroom."

"You *think* you have to go?"

What she says about Robbie being all she ever needs does it for me. Just like I predicted, this is going to be the summer of the bathroom.

"Excuse me, Steffi. I'll be right back." And I rush off.

It's simple to wait in the bathroom long enough for everyone to start leaving the bunk.

"Come on, Torrie," Steffi calls to me. "You want to be late or what?"

Now it's safe to come out.

"What do you think?" Dena Joyce asks me, modeling my jacket, practically drooling with pleasure.

Steffi makes a gag-me-with-a-spoon face, and Edna, the PA announcer, saves me with the waitress call, and we all start the stampede down to the flagpole.

The strategy meeting turns out to be very exciting, and it takes my mind off Robbie and gives me some breathing space. Nance, Nina's friend, has a really great idea. She suggests that we get one of the little kids to dress up in somebody's sheepskin jacket, and then when it starts to get dark, sort of late twilight, pretend to be a furry little animal and crawl up the mountain real fast.

It sounds crazy, but if it's dark enough and the kid was really little he might be able to sneak up through the wooded part of the hill. We all decide it's worth a try. The only trouble is they need the right little kid. I say Henry, but everybody else thinks he's sort of a scared little kid. Everyone knows how Steven pushes him around.

"He's the perfect size," I try to convince them. "I think he's the littlest kid in the whole camp, and he's fast. I've seen him run." But they all have the same feeling about him, that he couldn't pull it off. They may be right, he does let everyone push him around a whole lot and he's always crying about something. Still, it would be so great for him to get a chance to prove himself. Boy, if he could do this, nobody would ever dare take advantage of him again, and he'd feel so good about himself and have such confidence that he might not even wet his bed anymore. Well, maybe.

We spend a lot of time trying to figure out who could do it, but Ronald Benter, the only kid who's really right for it, is too big. I keep pushing for Henry. Finally Alexandra says maybe we should give him a try.

"It's no big deal really," she says, "because chances are it's not going to work anyway."

Then everyone agrees it's such a long shot, so what, let Henry try.

"Let me handle it," I say. "We're good friends. I know I can get him to try. Besides, no one will notice if they see him with me."

They all say okay and one of the boy counselors offers to lend his jacket.

"You better hurry, Victoria," Al says. "We should really have him try to do it tonight. I hear the grays have a super good idea this time."

"I know where he is right now," I say. "See you later," and I hurry off toward the baseball field.

Thirteen

I come up from behind the sports stand and stop just out of sight. Naturally Henry is sitting on the bench. He's a terrible baseball player. No confidence.

"Henry," I call to him.

He looks around. I poke my head out and wave. He comes running over. He really is so cute—if only he would smile more.

I tell him about the plan and how it's a big secret and he's been chosen over everyone else. All he has to do is wear this fur wrapped around him and sneak up the hill with the flag tucked under his arm. It gets his usual reaction.

"I don't wanna."

"Come on, Henry. The worst that can happen is you get caught. So big deal, at least you tried. What do you say?"

"I don't wanna."

"Sure you do. It's your big chance to really win over Steven. You could be the hero of the whole camp. That'd be great, wouldn't it? Huh?"

He's got his head down and he's kicking the grass. He's in his pre-crying position; unless I can convince him fast I won't be able to get to him through the tears. And there's only one way to get to him. It's for his own good.

"Forget it, you're doing it." That's called the Steven-bully method. "I've already signed you up." Combined with a little lie.

"But I don't wanna."

"It's too late. Your name is on it."

"Can't you erase it?"

"No way. Dr. Davis won't let me." I probably didn't need this last thing, but I'm in a big hurry.

"I'm scared."

I tell him not to worry, that I'll be with him and to wear dark pants and a dark T-shirt. "I'll pick you up right after dinner."

When I send him back into the game he's still on the verge of tears, but nobody notices because he's always that way.

I do my regular things for the rest of the day, but all the while I'm trying to work out some sort of plan for this evening. It gets dark at about eight, so it should be just perfect around seven forty-five.

Henry and I will go around to the wooded side at the base

of the mountain, just far enough away so that they can see somebody's there, but not make out who we are. Now, in my head, this is the way I see it. Just before we get there, I wrap the sheepskin around Henry and then just pretend I'm out walking the dog. Forget it that nobody has dogs at camp, if somebody sees me with a dog they're going to figure that somebody *does* have a dog. Seeing is believing, right?

Okay, so I sort of play with my dog for a couple of minutes and then I pretend to throw a ball up the mountain. That's when Henry takes off. He runs up the side of the hill on all fours, supposedly after the ball. He's got the flag folded under his arm. As soon as he gets out of sight he can get up and run the rest of the way normally. Once he gets to the top all he has to do is stick the flag into the ground at the side of the Mohaph flag. That's it; then he just walks down and I'll be waiting for him. Nobody will know anything until the morning.

It's in the bag. Even Henry can manage something as easy as this. Boy, if this works it's going to change his whole life. I just know it.

I work on the plan all the rest of the day, and by the time I'm ready to pick Henry up I've got it down pat. It's practically foolproof. Alexandra thinks so too. At the last minute she lets the guard on our team in on it so they can help out if I need them.

I spend all the time it takes us to get from Henry's bunk to the mountain trying to build up his confidence, but he's nearly hopeless until I put him in the fur jacket. Then, magically, something happens: he turns into a puppy. In two seconds he's scurrying along through the tall grass at top speed with only his little furry back showing; he's not Henry anymore, he's a real-live dog. The transformation is incredible. And when I throw the ball he chases after it and brings it back in his mouth. Nothing to do but pet him, so I do.

Meanwhile, one of the gray-team guards watching calls out to me, "That your dog?" And I know we have it made.

"Yeah," I call back.

"What's his name?" she wants to know.

I can't get involved because I have to get him going up the mountain in the next couple of minutes before it gets dark. The first name that comes to mind is Sport so that's what I tell her. Then she starts calling, "Here, Sport; here, Sport . . ."

Henry is so deep into his dog act that he starts performing for her. Oh, no . . .

"Sport, come!" I shout to Henry, but he keeps making his little circles. If he screws this up I'll kill him.

"Sport, for God's sake, come over here right this minute. You stupid mutt!"

Lucky for us the guard turns out to be Christy Margolies, who is not known for her great brains, but even she has to see that this isn't one of your everyday run-of-the-mill poodle-type breeds.

And she does. "What kind of dog is that?"

I grab the first name that comes into my head, "A whiffle."

"Really weird," she says, stretching her neck to get a better look.

Now I'm getting nervous. Even Christy can't be fooled much longer. Just when I'm starting to lose faith in the whole stupid idea, Henry suddenly stops dead, walks over to the nearest tree and, brilliant kid that he is, lifts his leg.

"Yeah, a whiffle." She's one of those dummies who pretends to know everything. "I think my cousin had one."

"They're great with balls—watch," I say, and throw the ball as hard as I can up the hill. "Get it, boy! Go up there and get it! And bring it back for all of us."

And off he goes up the mountain with Christy cheering him on.

Later everyone had to admit it was brilliant. Henry was fantastic. He went up that mountain, planted the flag, and came down again—*with* the ball. I ran to meet him, scooped him up in my arms, gave him a giant kiss, and nobody even knew what happened.

At least not that night.

The next morning the whole camp went crazy when they saw the green-team flag at the top of Mount Mohaph. We got five hundred points and Henry was the camp hero. It was fabulous. He was carried on people's shoulders all the way down to the mess hall. They made up a special song for him, and overnight he became a superstar. And boy, did he love that.

Steven didn't stand a chance. He was finished. Kids were

fighting to sit next to Henry, to stand next to him—every-thing. He was an instant star.

What a difference it made in that kid. All smiles. No more tears, and probably no more damp sheets either. He really had it made now. That was almost as good as the five hundred points that would go down in camp history.

I get a lot of credit too. Only I'm too nervous to enjoy it. Especially with Robbie turning my stomach upside down, Steffi on my mind, and Dena Joyce on my back.

Fourteen

As of tonight, the last night of Color War, the green team is one hundred and eight point five points ahead. We were trailing badly until Henry's big flag coup. The last major event is the musical, worth five hundred points. All we have to do is pick up one hundred and fifty-eight points and we win the whole thing.

There are two parts to this event, the singing part and the dance contest. I'm a pretty good dancer, but I decided not to enter when someone suggested Robbie be my partner. That's all I need, so I said I was too busy.

Robbie's in it, but he's dancing with Alexandra, who's only all right. Steffi's very good, and she's dancing with Ken. He may be good too, but I've never really seen him do his stuff.

The musical part turns out to be really great. The sets we

made for our team are perfect. It looks like just what it's supposed to be, lots of different flags. Even the ones painted on canvas look real. I wasn't involved in any of the music so it all comes as a surprise to me. I love it; even the gray team has some good songs. It's a hard choice, but the judges give us one hundred and fifty points and the gray team gets only one hundred. We're looking good.

Twenty couples enter the dance contest. The first and second place winners will share the two hundred and fifty points.

Nina is dancing with one of the senior boys. She's not bad. Mostly it's because she's borrowed my style exactly. If she wasn't my sister I would think she was kind of cute. And if she wasn't dressed in my clothes from head to toe I'd like her even better.

Steffi and Ken are terrific. They're really a hot couple together. If only it were true. That would be the answer to all my problems. But it isn't. No matter how good it looks, it just isn't.

The judges are from the dance academy in town so they don't know anybody. Second place is chosen first. It's two seniors on the gray team. Now we *have* to win first place. But it's going to be tough because Steffi and Ken are really grooving and they're fantastic.

I'm torn. I want my team to win and I've really worked hard, but Steffi is my best friend and it would be so great if at least she had this triumph. I guess it's really because I feel so guilty. I want her to win.

They start eliminating couples until they get down to five couples, including my own sister. She's getting terrific, but Steffi and Ken are really standouts. They've got some steps that I never saw before. They must have been practicing a lot lately. Here I go again, trying to make it something it's not just because it would be so neat. Instant problem solving, that's my line.

Now they're down to two couples, two green team Super seniors who aren't bad, but not nearly as good as Steffi and Ken. The gray team's got it.

And they do! It's Steffi and Ken and they carry their team over the top. It's all over and the gray team wins!

The place goes crazy with all the screaming and jumping up and down. Through it all I manage to stay as far away from Robbie as possible. Every once in a while I catch him looking over at me, but I turn away fast. Last time I look he's with Steffi and then the band starts to play "Friends" and everybody joins hands and sings together. Color War is officially over.

I wish camp was.

Or at least Steffi's birthday—in three weeks, which also happens to be the last week of camp. She has great plans for her and Robbie. I'm even included in some of them. The whole thing is horrendous, and I dread it.

Fifteen

I may be wrong, but I think I sense something different in Steffi these last ten days since the end of Color War. She's quieter than she usually is, but it's mostly about Robbie that she's different. Normally she goes on and on about him, but lately she hasn't been talking about him much. Maybe it's just me. I run every time his name comes up. In fact, that's what happened just now. We were sitting around after lunch doing our nails—Alexandra, one of the twins, Steffi and me—when D. J. comes wiggling into the bunk.

"Victoria," says Miss Obnoxious of the World, "I think I'm coming down with a sore throat. Could you do me a huge favor?"

"I guess so." I try to make it as inconspicuous as possible, but everybody hears. They all turn around in unison and look at me as if I just went bonkers.

"If you could just do my mail delivery today and tomorrow it would really help sooo much. . . ." I don't know why she bothers, but she smiles. Maybe she's just happy. I would be too if I didn't have to do that lousy job.

It's too much for Steffi. "Why don't you just take an aspirin? A sore throat is no big deal, you know."

"I didn't ask you." No smiles now. "I asked Victoria. Do you want to do it or not?" she says to me.

"It's okay, I don't mind." Then I turn to Steffi. "Really, I don't mind."

Steffi shrugs her shoulders like, *do what you want*, and I get so nervous I spill the whole bottle of Glorious Pink all over my shorts.

"So." D. J. gives Steffi one of her triumphant looks. "What's up with Mr. Wonderful lately?"

My cue to exit—and fast. "I'll get an early start on that mail." And I'm off and out the door dripping Glorious Pink all the way.

I'm halfway to the main office before I feel safe enough to slow down to a walk.

I have to do something about D. J. She's blackmailing me like in a movie. It's incredible that she knows how to do it so well. I never could—I'd feel too bad for the person. Besides, I'd be embarrassed to do something as dinky as that, but she takes it so naturally.

"Torrie!"

I know without turning it has to be Robbie, the only other

person who calls me by that name. I've been successfully avoiding him for over a week now.

I stop, take a deep breath, and turn. "Hi."

He catches up to me. "I have to talk to you."

"I'm just hurrying now. I have to sort mail and then I've got, uh, I don't know . . ." Suddenly I can't think, but then I decide I'm going to go with the truth. "Actually, I don't want to. It was all a terrible mistake and I'm sorry it happened."

I watch those earnest blue eyes start to squint up in pain while I say these things to him.

"I know what you mean," he says. "That's why I've got to tell her."

"About us?"

"No, not if you don't want me to, but I do have to talk to her about what's happened between her and me."

"What are you going to say?"

"I don't know. I'll just tell her the truth."

"That you don't love her anymore?"

"I'm not sure if I ever did. I think she thought she loved me, but we were apart a long time. Things change in a year. . . ."

"You mean it was different when you saw her again?"

"Yeah, it was, even before you. Sure, I still liked her, but not like before."

It's not much, but it does make me feel a little better knowing it wasn't only me that ruined it. I tell him that, and he says I shouldn't feel guilty. He's the one who let Steffi down.

This is the first time I've ever had any kind of conversation with Robbie where I wasn't running off, or so uncomfortable because of how I felt about him that I couldn't think straight.

He is a nice guy and I can see he feels really bad about Steffi. I'm not sure how he feels about me. I know he's attracted to me, but I don't know if it's any more than that. Maybe that's all it is with me too.

"I think maybe you jumped to conclusions about me," he says.

"How do you mean?"

"Maybe made too much of a simple attraction because you weren't supposed to feel it."

"I've never been so miserable since I met you."

"Me too," he says. "That week when you were on dock duty . . ."

"Wasn't that horrendous?"

"The worst." His face gets very intense with that special look that grabs you so you can't turn away. "There wasn't a minute in that whole week when I didn't know you were there. No matter what I was doing, you were in my head. I kept thinking I've got to quit this. It's crazy." Then his eyes let me go and he shakes off the seriousness with a smile. "One more rainy day and I'd have gone off the deep end."

"You're lucky," I say, and I'm just as happy *not* to have to tell him what I felt, "one more day like that and I'd have pushed you off myself."

He's back to serious. "Why didn't you say something?"

"I don't know. I guess I was still fighting it. Why didn't you?"

"I wanted to, but I kept thinking what if I misread you. What if you *really* didn't like me?"

"I know what you mean. I was thinking the same thing."

"I could just picture it. There I was, your best friend's boyfriend making a pass at you. You'd have probably spat in my eye."

"My problem is I probably wouldn't have."

"What about now?"

"Now is something else. I don't know what's up anymore. Anywhere I turn looks bad." And I tell him how terrible it's been; how it bugs me all the time, every time I see him, and how it's getting so bad that it's even beginning to sneak into my times alone with Steffi. "I have to do something. Make a choice one way or the other."

"I know which way it's going to be."

"Tell me."

"It's not going to be me."

As soon as he says it, I know he's right. And so does he.

"No matter what you decide," he says, "there's one thing I have to do. I have to tell Steffi before her birthday."

"That's horrible. She's been planning this for weeks. Can't it wait until after?"

"No, it can't. I feel like I'm lying to her and that's the worst of all. At least I owe her the truth."

Watching Robbie struggle with all this and knowing how

413

horrible it's making him feel and what it's done to me makes me see something I didn't see before. I try to tell him.

"Somehow talking to you about all this takes some of the scare out of it. I know I like you, I can't pretend I don't, but it's really no good."

Then I tell him how it's not Steffi over him but it's the important things inside that you've got to listen to or everything comes out terrible. When you say honor and loyalty and stuff like that everybody thinks you're talking baloney, but they're wrong. It really matters. And getting something you want by betraying someone important to you just doesn't work. I know Robbie really is a nice guy and he feels awful about Steffi too, and he knows I'm right.

"Did you talk to Dena Joyce yet?" he asks.

"Not yet. But I've got to do something quick. It's terrible."

And I tell him what she's doing to me and he's furious. Still, there's nothing he can do. "Turn the tables on her," he says.

"Are you kidding? She's invincible. She's like made of steel."

"Everybody's got a soft spot, you just have to find it."

"That's exactly what I used to think, but you don't know Dena Joyce," I tell him. "Which reminds me, I better get to her mail delivery or I'm done for."

"Am I going to see you again?" he asks when I get up to leave.

"You can hardly avoid me in this place."

"I don't mean that way."

I look at him, this gorgeous person I've spent the last six weeks agonizing about, and I think that all I have to do is say the right word and I've got him.

"No," I say. "I'm sorry but I just can't." That's really the right word.

"I'm sorry too," he says. "What about letters?"

"What about them?"

"Will you answer if I write?"

"I don't think so," I say, much too fast for any real thinking.

"I'll take my chances," he says, and one look at him and I think I'm starting all over again.

But I'm not going to. "Gotta run," I say, and without looking back, walk—very fast—toward the main office.

I'm practically crying. I feel terrible, but I think I did do the right thing. Damn! It's very hard to do right things.

Sixteen

My head is jammed with so many problems that voluntary mail sorting takes me half the afternoon. By the time I'm ready to deliver the letters, everyone else is finished.

I go through my rounds in a daze. The only thing that wakes me up is Henry's bunk. It's incredible to see what's happened since the flag business of Color War. The new Henry never stops smiling. Unreal.

"Hi, Victoria!" he says, giving me a running leap hug outside his bunk. He's got two little bunk mates in tow. I get hugs from them too. From here on in anything Henry does must be right. And best of all, Steven got his. He's absolutely out. Henry is the new big shot. I love it.

Except there's no end to the dog story. I must have told it four hundred times already and they still bug me to tell it again.

Actually, I love to because it's so great to see how Henry glows.

They drag me over to the porch steps, and with Henry propped on my lap, I do the whole thing for the four hundred and first time.

"Come on, kids," I say, trying to pick them off me, "I got to move it. I'm really late."

"How did Henry know to lift his leg?" Peter, one of his little converts, wants to know.

Of course, I've answered this same question before, still they ask like it's brand-new. "Because he was doing dog thinking. Show them, Henry."

And in a flash he turns back into Sport, and with the other two following every step, he runs off from tree to tree. It's really a gas.

The JC is watching. He doesn't look like he thinks it's so adorable.

"Don't you think it's terrific what happened to Henry?" I ask him.

"Sure, for Henry it's great."

"Then what's wrong?"

"Look at them," he says, pointing to the three kids racing around on all fours. "It's like running a kennel. And the constant barking . . ."

"Still, it's worth it. He's completely cured."

"Are you kidding? It's worse than before."

"You mean he still wets his bed?"

"Every night. But now because he's the big trendsetter, the

other two do too. It's like sleeping in a rain forest. Thanks a million."

I shrug my shoulders, tell him I'm sorry, and beat it out of there. I still think it's totally awesome, and absolutely the best thing to come out of an otherwise horrendous summer.

And speaking of horrendous summers, I have to do something about Dena Joyce. I have an idea. It's really desperate and maybe it's stupid and certainly it's mean, but nobody deserves it more. I got it from what Robbie said about finding a soft spot. I think I've found one. I'm not sure I can pull it off, but I've got to try. Otherwise she's going to tell Steffi everything, I just know it.

And I really don't want Steffi to know about what happened with Robbie. It's terrible enough that he's going to break off with her. If she knew about me it would be the total end of our friendship forever. I just couldn't face that. I really couldn't.

Two seconds after I come into the bunk she's on me—Dena Joyce, that is.

"Honey"—that's the name she uses when she's about to chop off my head—"I think I'll keep your leather jacket for another day, okay?"

"No."

"Huh?"

"I said no."

"Are you sure?" I love to watch her face. She's shocked, but she's cagey; she smells a rat.

"Absolutely."

For a second she looks very surprised, then she begins to freeze up. "Are you sure? That could be a big mistake, you know." Now she's solid ice. I'm almost sorry I started—she's really scary—but I have to do it.

"Positive," I say.

"Okay." Ice smiles, throws my jacket on the floor, and turns to Liza, who's on her way out the door. "Did you see Steffi?"

"Yes," Liza says. "She had to meet Robbie about an hour ago. She should be back soon."

"Thank you," D. J. says, looking directly at me. "I'll wait here for her."

"Sure thing," Liza says, and goes out the door, leaving me alone with Miss Dracula.

"Want to change your mind?" She gives me one last chance.

Now, I've rehearsed this scene in my mind a million times since I thought it up this afternoon. In my head, this is the way it goes. It's the same so far, except now I tell her that I'm not about to change my mind, and, in fact, I was thinking I might like to wear her silk shirt—for the rest of the summer. Of course, she looks at me like I'm nuts, but she's getting a little worried. She knows I've got something up my sleeve, but she doesn't know what. And I play it out. I let her try to guess. I sort of tease her very subtly. I'm really in control and she's beginning to feel it. She begins to get nervous because I'm so cool. Finally she knuckles under. She can just feel my power and I never have to tell her what I know. I really defeat Dena

Joyce, probably the first time in history. That's the way it goes in my head. In real life it's a little different.

She's standing there with her hands on her perfect hips and an annoyed look smeared across her face. It's horrendous to confront Dena Joyce. All my plans fall into the toilet and all I can say is something on about Henry's level. "If you tell Steffi about me and Robbie, I'll tell the whole world you suck your thumb."

"Right," she says without missing a beat, and, cool as can be, picks up my jacket off the floor, carefully places it on the end of my bed, flashes me a Dr. Davis–type smile, turns and leaves the bunk. Totally awesome. Her losing is like anyone else's winning. It's so brilliant that I find myself wanting to run after her and apologize—*with* my jacket. I would make America's worst blackmailer.

But I did stop her. I stopped Dena Joyce. Probably the bravest most fantastic thing I ever did. Only trouble is nobody will ever know.

The minute D. J. walks out the door, Steffi comes in. She looks sick. Her face is dead-white except for her eyes—they're all red and swollen. Of course she's been crying.

"Steffi . . ." I don't know what to do. I have to pretend I don't know. God, I hate these lies between us.

She sits down on the edge of my bed and begins to sob. It's horrible. Heartbreaking.

"What happened?" I have to ask.

Between tears she tells me everything I already know about

Robbie and the breakup, and besides feeling awful I have to pretend to be shocked. I ask her as few questions as possible and just try to comfort her. She knows I feel terrible because I'm crying too.

"I don't know what happened," she says. "I knew something was wrong, but I didn't expect this."

I just keep listening.

She goes on about how terrible she feels and I can see she's really crushed. Then she gets kind of angry. "You know what I really think, Torrie?"

Suddenly I get a very bad feeling that I do know what she really thinks.

". . . I think it's someone else."

"No," I say. Then I say no again because I just don't know what else to say.

But she's convinced. "It's true, Torrie. It's definitely someone else, and I think I know who. What about you?"

My stomach falls about eighteen floors. "No, no, no," I say.

"You don't know who it is or what?"

I can't even get the little word "no" out of my mouth. All I can do is shake my head—and hope it falls off.

"It's Alexandra," she announces.

"Who?"

"What do you mean, 'who'? Alexandra, my supposed friend right here in my own bunk. What do you think of that?"

421

"It's not true," I say, and it comes out somewhere between it's not true, meaning it can't be, and it's not true, meaning it isn't.

She takes it to mean it can't be and says that it is. "It has to be her."

"It isn't."

But she pays no attention to me. "Boy," she goes on, "she really has to be an ass; I mean it. Sure, we're not best friends, but we've been pretty close all this summer. I can't believe she would do such a thing."

"She didn't."

Now she hears me. "Well, who else could it be? He hates D. J. He practically never said a word to Liza, and he can't tell the twins apart either. There's nobody else possible."

Here it is. I've got my choice. D. J. would never tell, so I don't have to be worried about that. Certainly Robbie wouldn't. I'm safe there. Nobody's on my case. We don't even have a week left to camp, and then Alexandra's off to Connecticut and we'll probably never see her again. Nobody ever has to know the truth. Steffi and I can still be best friends.

I can't do it.

I'll probably regret it forever, but I have to tell her. No matter what. So I do. "You forgot someone," I say.

She's really confused. "Who?"

"Me."

I never saw anyone's face crash down like Steffi's does when that sinks in. First she looks at me like I'm kidding, then

I'm crazy, and then, worst of all, like I'm some kind of mon-ster—which, of course, I am.

After that there's nothing more to say. I can't even explain anything because she stops crying, gets right up, and walks out.

She hasn't said a word to me since. This has to be the most horrendous, horrible, gross summer of my life.

Seventeen

That all happened ten terrible days ago. Even though Steffi didn't say anything to anyone, everyone seems to know. I guess it wasn't hard to figure out, what with Robbie and Steffi breaking up and her not talking to me. Gossip is flying around like crazy.

One thing for sure, D. J. hasn't said a word. She's making wide circles around me. I really got her number. Too bad I can't think of any way to use it. Truth is, I don't want to. At least I can say I'm not a blackmailer. I feel like I'm everything else horrible. I don't blame Steffi in the slightest.

I really miss her.

But she doesn't seem to miss me at all. She spends most of her time hanging out with Alexandra *and* Ken Irving.

I know the Ken Irving thing has got to be pure rebound.

Steffi's not about to jump into another intense relationship so quickly after the Robbie disaster; still, they do look great together. He looks at her the way I used to look at Robbie. Which I don't anymore. Not to say I'm cured, because I'm not by a long shot. I'm still horrendously miserable, but it's different now. Before I used to think about Robbie all the time, now I can't get Steffi out of my mind.

I know all about wanting what you can't have and all that, and maybe it was a little like that with Robbie, but not with Steffi. She was my best friend for ten years and now she hates me: that really hurts. Every time I think about it I get sick to my stomach. It's gross.

And the thought of Robbie liking me doesn't help all that much, even if he is going to write to me, which is not absolutely certain anyway. Besides, if he really does write, then I have the awful problem of whether or not to answer him.

It's like I never learn. Here I am agonizing about Steffi and starting all over again about Robbie. It's cuckoo time, that's what, and I'm head cuckoo.

On top of all that I keep wondering how Steffi really feels inside. She's certainly putting on a good show. She's even got friendly with one of the twins. Suddenly she can tell them apart. I think she's pretending, but whatever, she seems to be recovering pretty good. Better than me. Yesterday I even saw her talking to Robbie.

I spoke to him one last time yesterday. He's still pushing for us to get together. No way. I still think Robbie Wagner is terrific, really, but maybe he's not as special as Steffi made him up to be. Maybe nobody can be that perfect. I'll bet she doesn't think he's all that great anymore, either.

It's not that Robbie and I don't speak, it's just that I keep out of his way. No big deal about it, it's just easier that way.

Ending camp is a pretty emotional time. Even for me, and I can't wait to leave. Madame Katzoff and Dr. Davis get up to give their farewell speeches (actually Dr. Davis just nods) but Madame Katzoff wishes everyone a good winter and to come back next year. The whole camp sings the "Hats Off" song and there's a lot of cheering and applauding. I'm beginning to think they weren't so bad after all until they start reading off our accumulated fines for the season.

Out of the $260 salary I walk away with a big $180. A real bomb summer.

Except for one nice thing—Henry. I go over to say good-bye to him. He's just doing so great I feel really proud about how he's changed. That's the best thing that happened this whole summer.

There's lots of hugging and kissing and promises to visit in the winter. He really is a special little boy.

I watch him walk off toward the buses, one arm around his new friend's shoulder and the other dragging his plastic bag with the wet sheets. He's a changed kid—well, almost.

I go back to my bunk and nobody's there. I guess everybody's off saying good-byes. That's okay, I've been keeping mostly to myself lately anyway. I had so much time I answered all my mail for the whole summer, only it's too late. I might as well take them home with me.

I'm just packing the last of my stuff when Nina comes in. Just what I need.

"What do you want?" I ask her. Might as well get it over with as fast as possible.

"Nothing," she says, and sits down at the end of my bed.

"So?" I try again.

She just shrugs her shoulders.

"So what are you doing here?"

No answer.

"Okay, what do you want to borrow?"

"Nothing."

"Come on, Nina? What's up? I got things to do."

She turns bright pink and gets up off the bed. "I just wanted to say that . . ." She starts inching her way toward the door. ". . . that . . ."

"That what?"

"That I really love you and I'm glad you're my sister." All in one breath and she's out the door and gone.

Weird.

But I guess sort of nice. At least somebody still loves me, even if it is only my sister.

When I go over it in my head later, it makes me feel pretty good. I never think of Nina as a real person, but I guess maybe she's starting to be one.

Real nice.

Everyone knew I was in a funk, but she's the only one who actually tried to help me. It took guts, too, because I'm not always so terrific to her. Especially when I'm not feeling fantastic anyway. I guess there may be something to say for family. Maybe it's not so bad to have her around—sometimes.

Just when I'm packing the last of my things I find my blue vest. I've never been so crazy about it, and I hardly ever wear it, so instead of me lugging it home, I drop it off at Nina's bunk. She's not there so I dump it on her bed and leave.

Walking back I get a warm good feeling inside when I think of how surprised, more like stunned, she'll be when she sees it. Warm and good enough to make me smile for the first time in a lot of days.

Eighteen

Now's the time I'm really dreading—getting on the bus. I feel like nobody's going to want to sit next to me. I don't blame them. It's like I'm a little girl again and I'm the last one chosen for some team thing. It's almost tears time.

This is sort of what happens. I get on the bus, go all the way to the back, and find a seat near the window. People start getting on and taking seats. Everybody seems to have someone to sit with. Everybody but me.

I look out of the window and see Steffi, late as usual, walking to the bus with Ken. They're talking and laughing, having a great time. I feel awful. Not because they're happy, but because I feel so sad about Steffi. We've been best friends for so many years, we shared so many secrets, so much of everything, and now it's over. It's one of the saddest days of my life.

I watch her climbing on the bus. I keep my head down. I can't even look up to see her coming down the aisle. I can't because I don't want her to see me crying.

I'm studying the toes of my Nikes and wishing the bus would get started. It's really gross to be sixteen and catching tears with your tongue, but if I wipe them with my hand everyone will know what's happening.

"You want company or what?"

Or what. The two best words in the English language. I don't even have to look up to know that fabulous voice.

"Absolutely." I nod my head and give Steffi one very wet smile. Then I wipe my face with the back of my sleeve, which is really gross, but things like that don't count with best friends.

my mother was never a kid

One

Getting to be thirteen turned out to be an absolute and complete anticlimax. I mean it. What a letdown. You wouldn't believe the years I wasted dreaming about how sensational everything was going to be once I was a teenager. The way I pictured it, the change was going to be fantastic. Overnight, people would stop treating me like some silly little kid. Instead I'd be respected pretty much as a pre-adult, practically running my own life. Sure, I'll still have to live at home, but mostly I'd be making my own decisions. Oh, occasionally my parents would ask me to do something, but it wouldn't be an order—it'd be more like a suggestion.

Hah!

"Victoria, that room is a pigsty. I want it cleaned up immediately, or you can forget about sleepovers for a month." That's my mother suggesting. "And another thing," she says, adding three more little nuggets of friendly advice, "see that your laundry is put away before you empty the dishwasher and don't leave the house without walking Norman." That's our sheepdog. "And, Victoria?"

"Yes, Mother."

"Put on your jacket. It's only May."

Wow! I must have been some jerk. Truth is, nothing's changed except that maybe now I won't have to listen to that rubbish about waiting till I'm a teenager. Fact is, now they use it against me. "That certainly wasn't proper behavior for a teenager." And I'm still waiting. "A bike tour is a wonderful idea, but you'll have to wait until you're at least sixteen." Of course when I'm sixteen they'll have moved all the good things to eighteen, and when I get there, it'll be twenty-one. I'll always be waiting to be old enough for this or that until I'm ninety. *Then* they'll say, "That's something you should have done when you were seventeen or twenty." It seems like you're always the wrong age. What a relief to know that in just three weeks I'll have a birthday. Fourteen has got to be better.

Except, of course, if you have a mother like mine. You wouldn't believe how overprotective she is. Do you know that I'm the only kid in the whole eighth grade who can't go to the movies at night? And then she takes every little thing so seriously. Like what happened yesterday at school. I can understand her being a little upset, but in my opinion she overreacted. After all, it was the first time in my whole life that

I ever got suspended. For practically nothing. And besides, I wasn't the only one involved. There were eight of us, and just because I was the only one suspended doesn't mean it was all my fault. Which, in fact, it wasn't.

Personally, I think it was mostly Mrs. Serrada's fault. (In case you didn't know, she's the grossest English teacher in the Western Hemisphere.) But what can you expect at Brendon School? That's this really uptight private school I go to. The kind of yes-sir, no-sir place where they make you wear these horrendous uniforms every day. You should see them—gray skirts with fat ugly box pleats and a vomity blue blazer with a scratchy gold emblem on the pocket that everybody always says looks like an eagle sitting on a toilet. It's all a terrible embarrassment, and of course I detest it like crazy. A lot of good that does. I've been going there since the third grade. Anyway, back to what happened yesterday. There probably wouldn't have been any trouble if dear old Serrada hadn't picked such a boring movie for our one and only class trip all term. Actually, I've got nothing against Shakespeare; in fact, I think he's pretty okay sometimes. He did a super job with *Romeo and Juliet* (the movie anyway), but *Richard the Second*? Spare me.

Anyway, all we did was sneak up to the balcony, mess around a little, throw a couple of gum wrappers over the railing, and smoke one cigarette. That was the worst. The cigarette, I mean. I really inhaled it deep and it made me so nauseous and dizzy that I thought I was going to fall right into the orchestra. The thought scared me so much that I slid down to the floor and just sat there waiting for my head to clear. Unfortunately, my friend Liza didn't see me, and when she tripped over my leg she grabbed Danielle and she fell too, and then everyone started fooling around and falling down. Well, everybody started laughing like crazy. And we got a little noisy because Mrs. Serrada turned around to see what was going on and spotted me holding the cigarette. And that's when Tina Osborne shot the rolled gum wrapper. Tina swears she wasn't aiming at Mrs. Serrada, but it hit her smack on the forehead just the same. Excellent! You should have seen old Fatso come charging up the stairs to the balcony. We all jumped up and started to scramble down the opposite staircase, but we were laughing so hard we kept stumbling into each other.

I guess the manager must have heard all the commotion because the next thing you know, the house lights go on, and we're caught. What a hassle Fatso made about the whole thing, especially the cigarette. Nickie Rostivo tried to lighten it a little by telling her that one cigarette for eight people wasn't too dangerous. I even pointed out that we were in the smoking section. That did it. That's when she exploded. Normally she's got a very soft voice, kind of sick-sweet, but when she loses her temper she sounds like a lumberjack. It's really weird to hear that big voice boom out of such a small fat muffin of a woman. "How dare you disgrace the school blah blah blah . . . How could you be so rude . . . untrustworthy" et cetera, et cetera, and on and on. By now the rest of the class was jammed half-way up the steps dying to find out what was going on. Even the nosy movie manager squeezed his way through to get a better look. That's when I started to break up—I mean, seeing his bald head sticking up from the middle of all those kids really cracked me up. I tried to cover the giggles by pretending to have a coughing fit, which probably made it sound even worse. Of course everyone turned to stare at me, and of course that really finished me off. "And what, may I ask, is so amusing?" says Mrs. Serrada in snake spit. "Tell us, Victoria, so that we all may enjoy the joke."

Naturally there's nothing funny, but I can't tell her that because I'm laughing too hard. It's so embarrassing. But I can't help it. These laughing fits happen to me at the worst possible times, and once I start I can't stop. Sometimes it happens to me at the dinner table, and it's really awful. Some stupid thing (it can even be really serious or sad) will strike me as funny, and I start to laugh. It doesn't last too long if nobody pays any attention, but if someone, like my dad, tells me to stop, I'm dead. I become hysterical, and of course he becomes furious because he thinks I'm laughing at him, and he'll invariably send me to my room until I can control myself. You'd think by now they'd understand that it doesn't mean anything and just leave me alone to get over it by myself.

Like with the trouble at school. Sure, I know it was a dumb thing to do, but mostly it was just silly and nobody got hurt and Fatso shouldn't have suspended me. Big deal, so I got hysterical. I would have apologized later. I mean, it wasn't so terrible that she had to suspend me. And naturally that brought the smoke rising from my mother's hair when they told her about it later.

Anyway, I wasn't too scared in the theater. In fact, it was all pretty exciting—you know, all of us in it together. Some of the other kids who weren't involved felt sort of left out, and everybody was coming up to us and wanting to know what happened and all that. By the time we got back to class, the story was all over the school, and what a story it turned into! One version had Nickie Rostivo dangling from the balcony by one hand and all the rest of us smoking, and not plain old cigarettes either, and making out like crazy. Since I was the only one who got suspended, naturally I was the star. Actually, it was kind of fun being a celebrity.

Until I got home. You know, it's a funny thing, but I actually thought my mother might, just once, be on my side a little. After all, I'm the one who really got it the worst and I didn't do anything that much different from the others. I don't think it was fair to take it all out on me and I told her so, really and truly expecting her to agree. Hah! What a pipe dream. She was furious with me. What does she care what's fair or unfair? All she wanted to know was whether I thought sneaking up to that balcony was right or wrong. I said of course I knew it was wrong. "Then," she said, "why did you do it?" How come she can't understand that it's not that simple? Doesn't she remember what it's like when all your friends are involved in something stupid, not really terrible, just a little nutty and a lot of fun? What does she want me to do—say no like some goody-goody?

I was dumb to expect any sympathy from her. Still, the worst I thought would happen was that I'd be grounded for a couple of days like everyone else. But not my mother. She had to treat me like some kind of silly five-year-old. First she tells me that I can't watch TV or have any sleepovers for the next month. I don't like that, but it's not the end of the world. Then she says, get this, I'm not allowed to talk on the phone for a whole week. Furthermore, when anyone calls she's going to tell them that I can't come to the phone because I'm being punished. Is that the most embarrassing thing you've ever heard? I'm never going to be able to face anyone ever again. But she doesn't care. She'd probably like it if I stayed right here in my bedroom, sitting on my stupid canopied bed, until it was time for college.

Wouldn't you know it, the phone's ringing right now. I'll bet it's for me. Naturally my mother has to answer on the hall extension right outside my room. She wants to make sure I hear her. Oh, God! It's Michael Langer, a really nice guy from high school, and she's telling him how I can't come to the phone because I'm being punished. How could she? I'm steaming mad, and as soon as I hear her hang up, I stamp my foot really hard and scream, "I hate you!"

The first time I told her that I was very little and she got terrifically upset. Her eyes were all watery and she took me on her lap and we talked for a long time until I finally told her that I really loved her. Since then she's read that all children feel like that sometimes and it's healthy to let them say it.

Now she comes stumping toward my room, saying, "You

just listen to me!" She's angry and just pushes the door open without even knocking. "You're behaving like a four-year-old."

And we start our usual argument. "That's the way you treat me," I say, and she tells me that's because I act like one and I should realize I was wrong and accept my punishment, and it goes on that way with me saying one thing and her saying another but never really answering me. Like I say that I don't mind being punished, but it's embarrassing to have all my friends know about it, and she says, "Well, you should have thought of that first." That's what I mean. What kind of an answer is that? Oh, what's the use, she doesn't even try to understand me and there's nothing I can do about it.

I swear I'll never treat my daughter the way they treat me. I'll really be able to understand her because I'll remember how awful it was for me. I'll never do anything to embarrass her and I'll never make her cry. I'll be her best friend and never lose my temper with her even if she makes mistakes like forgetting a dentist appointment or being late for dinner or getting a bad mark on a science test. I'll just talk to her and try to understand why these things happened, and even if I can't, I'll never get angry with her no matter what, never yell at her and never punish her. Never. Not ever.

I can't believe my mother was ever my age. I think she was born a mother. Or if she was ever a kid, she must have been perfect. Unless maybe things were so completely different in the olden days that kids didn't do any thinking on their own, just did exactly what they were told. I picture my mother exactly

440

like a girl in my class, Margie Sloan, a revolting goody-goody who wouldn't dream of ever sneaking up to a balcony or even handing in a paper a minute late. Everyone agrees that Margie is the most boring person in the entire school, and she's never invited to parties or even just for sleepovers. That's probably the way my mother was. No wonder we can't get along. We're just not the same type.

There's another thing that really bugs me about my mother. The way she talks. "If I have to raise my voice one more time I'm going to blah blah blah." Or, "How dare you? . . . Who do you think you are?" and "If I ever catch you doing that again blah blah blah," and so on. She has about ten of these beauties and they never change. She always sounds like a mother, an angry mother. God, I hope I don't grow up to be like her. And I really despise it when everybody compares me to her. "Oh, you're the perfect image of your mother." Naturally it's always one of my mother's friends who says it. If one of my friends said it I'd kick her in the shin.

The worst part about it is that it's sort of true. We do have the same kind of pushed-up nose and the same color eyes and supposedly we have the same smile, though I really don't see that at all. Actually, I guess it wouldn't be the worst thing in the world if I looked like her when I grow up because she's pretty all-right-looking. But that's it. I mean, I absolutely don't want to be like her in any way.

Boy, did I get stuck when you consider some of the great mothers around. Like my friend Steffi's mother. Now, she's absolutely brilliant. I feel like I can say anything at all to her because she's such an understanding person. And she's fun, too. When Steffi and I ice-skate at the Wollman Rink, I actually don't mind if her mother comes along. I wouldn't hate being her daughter at all. In fact, I'd love it. Beats me why Steffi says she can't stand her.

The phone's ringing again. More embarrassment. Then I hear my mother say, "Oh, hello, Mr. Davis." It's going to be worse than embarrassing because there's only one Mr. Davis I know and that's the new principal at school. He's only been there six months but already nobody can stand him. I think the phone call's going to be a disaster.

"Uh-huh . . . uh-huh . . . uh-huh." That's my mother. He's probably saying a whole lot of vicious, awful things about me and she's agreeing. Even if they're not out-and-out lies, they're certainly horrendous exaggerations because he absolutely hates me. I mean, a hundred people can be doing something wrong and he'll only pick me out. He really has it in for me. I'm not saying he's 100 percent wrong or that I should get medals for them, but they're not that big a deal. Like that time when I got caught playing hooky, Marie and Betsy both said they were going to come with me. And the business with the paint on the blackboard. There were four of us in on that in the beginning and it was only because Tommy Agrasso was absent on that day that I had to be the one to steal the paint from the art class. I admit I thought up the idea of smearing glue on the keys of the auditorium piano, but that evened out because I was the one they made scrub it off. And as for always talking in the classrooms, everybody in the whole world does that and it's too trivial to even mention.

My mother's talking very low on the phone to Mr. Davis, but finally she hangs up and I can tell by the bang that I'm in big trouble. She charges into my room. Not only doesn't she knock, she practically takes the whole door down with her, she's in such a fury.

"Do you know who that was?"

"Yeah."

"Yes," she hisses. In the middle of everything she has to correct my grammar.

"Yes," I repeat because things are bad enough already.

"That was the principal."

"How is he?"

"Don't be smart!"

You see how hopeless it is? I was only being polite.

"You aren't being suspended . . ."

"Oh, wow! Did I misjudge that nice old guy. . . ."

"It's worse than that. They don't want you back at all. You make too much trouble for them. They feel you're—how did he put it—in the wrong learning environment."

Groan. Sickening thud as my stomach drops to my knees. Kicked out!

"They can't do that!" I blurt.

"Why not?" My mother's eyes are practically smoldering. "Tell me why not."

I'm afraid to look at her.

"You apparently think you can do anything in the world that *you* want. Why can't the school? Why shouldn't you get thrown out? You cause nothing but unhappiness and embarrassment and . . ."

Suddenly she kind of sinks down on the edge of the bed and buries her face in her hands for a couple of seconds. I hear a deep, long sigh. Finally she raises her head and stares right into my eyes. I never have the guts to look back, especially if I'm feeling guilty. Instead I get real busy brushing invisible things off my jeans or concentrating on nothing in the middle of my empty palm.

"Victoria," she says after a couple of seconds, "are you deliberately trying to hurt us, your father and me?"

"No." Very small voice.

"Then why do you keep doing all these awful things? Please, tell me."

I wish I could tell her, but all I can do is shrug my shoulders and say, "I don't know." Because honestly, I don't. I mean, these things never seem so terrible when I'm doing them, it's only later, when they get so blown up that I know I shouldn't have done them, but then of course it's too late. But that's me. Always messing up. You should hear me with the boys. I say the dumbest things. Even the way I look is all wrong. I must have spent ninety million allowances on face gook and my complexion is still horrendous, my hair looks dirty two seconds after I wash it, and my knees are so bony that I'll probably have to wear jeans the rest of my life. Oh, what's the use? I could go on forever. The thing is, I'm a mess. Also, it's horrific the way I don't know where I'm supposed to be. I mean, I'm certainly not a little kid like my sister Nina, but nobody lets me be as grown-up as I feel inside. Of course there's no point try-ing to tell my mother these things. She'd just say I looked fine and probably blame it on adolescence, like it was some kind of disease. Maybe it is.

"I hate to keep punishing you," my mother says, shaking her head and looking just a little bit sad. "I wish there were some other way."

"Well, I don't know," I mumble. Why do I always grope like a jerk when I want to say something important? "I guess you could try to understand me a little better." I expect to hear her say, "I understand you perfectly," or something like that. But she surprises me.

"All right, Victoria, I'll try. What is it I don't understand?"

Oh, God, what a question. Doesn't she know there's no way to answer?

"Well?"

"Me."

"Okay. What is it I don't understand about you? This is serious, Victoria, so let's talk about it. Tell me what I'm doing wrong."

Now she wants to talk—when she's got me on the torture rack. That's just like her. How come she always gets to pick the time for these little chats? "You have to tell me what's on your mind, Victoria. I can't do it without your help."

See. It's hopeless. I mean, how am I going to help her when I don't know what's going on either? I finally say, "Well, you don't ever let me live my own life. I'm not a baby, I can take care of myself. But all you do is keep treating me like a child. I'm not a child. I'm an . . . I feel I'm as adult as a real adult."

I really don't want to go on, but she doesn't interrupt and kind of forces me to keep talking. Maybe I'd do it anyway. Sometimes I'm a real motormouth.

"Like, I hear what you and Mrs. Weinstein and the Elliotts and all your other friends talk about when they come over," I blabber on. "The movies, television, why you don't like Mr. Bailey, where the good places are to eat, and things like that. What's so adult about that? Those are the same things I talk about with my friends. I mean, I don't see any difference." I take a deep breath so I can keep rattling on, but the fact is I can't think of anything else to say.

"All right," my mother says. "You have a point. A lot of things you and I do are pretty much alike. I'll even call them adult things. But how about this? Suppose I came home and you asked me what I did this afternoon and I said, oh, I was with the Weinsteins and the Elliotts and all my friends at the movies and we spent the whole time secretly smoking and giggling and running up the aisles and throwing spitballs. What would you think, Victoria? That I was behaving like an adult? Do adults do that? Do they?"

Naturally I'm not going to answer that one.

"So you're not an adult yet, Victoria. And if you think you are, then the misunderstanding's on your part. I'm not saying you're a child, either. You're something in between. It's a difficult time and I'm sorry, but until you're a lot more mature than you are, you need supervision. And that includes punishment when you do very childish and very bad things."

"I don't do very bad things." I pout. "Or anyway, I don't do them on purpose. That's another thing you don't understand. They're just normal nothings that go a little wrong."

"You mean to say that all those things that happen are . . . are what? Accidents?"

"Not exactly. I just mean that I don't cause all that trouble on purpose. Besides, mostly they're just little things and I don't know why everybody always gets so excited about them. Like today . . ."

"A perfect example. Because of your shenanigans today the entire movie was ruined for everyone. Are you going to tell me *that* was an accident?"

"But it was, sort of. I mean, nobody meant to ruin the movie. All we wanted to do was sit in the balcony. You know, Mom, it's really gross the way they treat us like such babies when we go on a class trip. It's positively horrendous when you're almost fourteen to have to march through the streets in pairs. And then in the movie they never let us sit next to our friends and you can't talk and you can't buy sweets. And if you do some little thing like changing your seat without asking, they practically freak."

"According to Mr. Davis, you weren't just out of your seat, you were smoking and creating a ruckus."

"So all Mrs. Serrada had to do was shush us and we would have been quiet. Instead she comes charging up the steps like some bull elephant . . ."

"Victoria!" She doesn't even let me finish. "You were breaking the rules. Can't you understand that?"

Rules. How come adults are always so hung up on rules? Even if I tell my mother that a lot of Mrs. Serrada's rules are really dumb, she'll still say, "That's no excuse for breaking them." Except I think it is. Boy, if they let kids make the rules things would be a lot better. I'd probably never get into trouble.

"Well? Can't you?"

"Huh?"

"Can't you understand that you were breaking the rules?"

"I didn't exactly think of it that way. Anyway, it wasn't my fault."

"Of course not. It's never your fault, is it? It's always somebody else's. The teacher's. Or the principal's. All the complaints they've had about you in school, none of them are your fault, are they? Everybody's picking on you."

See, I told you, no matter how many kids are involved, I'm the one who always gets blamed the most, and it's not fair, and now they want to throw me out into the street, and my whole life is ruined, and maybe I should just run away and make them all feel sorry for what they did.

My mother says: "Mr. Davis is setting up an appointment

for us at school. We will go and see him and you will be very humble and very sweet. I'll try to straighten this whole matter out. I don't know how successful I'll be. Mr. Davis sounded pretty final about not wanting you back. You're too disruptive. But we'll try because the only other alternative would be a boarding school."

"I won't go!" I blurt it out. I know all about boarding schools. My friend Monica's sister Laura had to go away to one called the Barley School someplace up in Maine, and I heard they beat you and make you go to bed at eight o'clock and scrub the floor every morning. I'd rather die. As it is I'm crying like crazy already.

"Come on now, Victoria," my mother says, pushing a couple of wet strands of hair back off my face. "Boarding schools aren't anything like those awful places you see in the movies."

"I'll run away. I will!" Which is what I thought about doing anyway except this time it's real.

"Calm down for a minute and listen to me. Actually, Daddy and I have talked about it before all this, and it might be the best thing that could happen to you. These places are fabulous, like sleep-away camps, only they have classes. You'd probably end up loving it. There's a wonderful school called the Barley School up in New England. Laura Baer went there and she loved it." Of course I know better, but I'm too destroyed to argue.

"I'll hate it," I sob.

"There's no point in discussing it until after we've seen the principal. In the meantime, I want you right here in the house where I can keep an eye on you all weekend. I'm sorry to have to punish you, but you have certainly earned it."

And, just like that, she walks out of the room. Can you believe that? My whole life is coming to an end and she won't even let me talk about it. That absolutely proves she doesn't care one iota about me. None of them do. I suppose my sister Nina does a little. But who wants an eleven-year-old pain in the butt on your side?

Oh my God! "Hey, Mom!" I cry, dashing into the hall.

"What now?"

"The party down at Liz's!"

"I told you. I want you home all weekend. You can forget about going to Philadelphia."

"But, Mom! She's expecting me. My own cousin. That party's practically in my honor."

"Out of the question. Now go and wash your face and comb your hair—Grandma's coming."

I know it's going to be futile, but I've got to try to convince her. I've been counting on going to that party for two months, and my heart would crack right in two if I couldn't make it. Still, for once in my life, I play it cool. I don't say another word. I just head straight for the bathroom like she said and do my best to wash the crying look off my face and even pull my hair tight back with an elastic band just the way she likes it. By the time I'm finished I hear my grandmother in the living room. What a bore!

Don't get me wrong. I'm crazy about my grandmother. She's absolutely the greatest. But you know how grandmothers are, they take everything so seriously. All she has to know is that I've been suspended from school and she'll probably be up all night worrying.

Wait a minute! I don't have to tell her. My mother certainly isn't going to bring it up, so how's she going to know?

"Victoria, darling," says my grandmother as soon as she sees me, "what's the matter? Your eyes are all red. Are you sick?" And she's up in a flash testing my forehead for fever. "I told you she looked a little green the other day, Felicia," she says to my mother, and there's just a hint of accusation in her voice like maybe they're not feeding me enough or something.

"No, Grandma, I'm fine."

"You don't look so fine to me. You look like you've been crying. What's wrong? Did you have trouble at school today?"

I must be the easiest person in the whole world to nail. Nothing left to do but tell the whole gruesome story again. Ugh. I can see that my mother is embarrassed but I wade right in, and just when I'm at the part where it's so unfair that I was the only one suspended, the phone rings. Naturally I jump up to answer it.

"Oh, no you don't, young lady," says good old Mom. "When I say no phone calls, I mean no phone calls." And with the steam rising from the top of her head, my mother storms out of the room to answer the phone. I pray it's not for me.

"Boy, is she mean!" I say to my grandmother.

"Being suspended is a very serious matter, dear, I can see she's very upset." That's one of the beautiful things about my grandmother. She always sounds like she loves me. Like calling me dear and talking so sweetly even if she doesn't agree with me. And we don't agree all the time mostly because she's, you know, sort of proper and old-fashioned sometimes. But she never really loses her patience or gets angry with me.

"Every time I get caught in something the school makes such a big deal about it. They're always suspending me for nothing at all."

"You mean this isn't the first time?"

"Well, not exactly. But you can't really count that other time because it wasn't my fault. I just happened to be there when the trouble started."

"Maybe it wasn't, but you must admit, dear, you do seem to be in the wrong place at the wrong time more often than just about anyone else."

"I guess I'm just unlucky. How come my mother can't look at things the way you do instead of always flying off the handle?"

"I used to do some pretty fancy flying off the handle when your mother and Uncle Steve were children. They could be very irritating at times."

I can believe that about my mother. She irritates me all the time. But Uncle Steve? Grandma has to be kidding. He's the best uncle in the whole world. I can practically talk to him like a friend. He's in the advertising business and knows everybody and he's always getting tickets for us to shows and concerts and everything. Mom has him over to dinner a couple of times a month (he's divorced) and always cooks something special for him. I know she's his sister but I always think of him more as my friend than her brother, if that makes any sense. That's probably because he treats me practically like an adult. You know how most adults don't really listen to kids or take them seriously? Well, he's just the opposite. Boy, is my mother lucky to have him for a brother.

"Yes indeed," my grandmother is saying. "Being a mother can be a very hard job."

"Well, it doesn't look so tough to me."

"But it is. Imagine being solely responsible for another person."

"She doesn't *have* to be so responsible for me. I can take care of myself a lot better than she thinks."

"You seem to have slipped up a little today."

"Yeah, well . . ."

"And the other times?"

"Maybe it's like you said. I was in the wrong place at the wrong time."

"Maybe. And possibly when you get older that will happen less and less. But in the meantime somebody's got to take very good care of someone who's so unlucky, and that, my dear, is a full-time job, with a lot of close watching and plenty of worrying. Believe me, Victoria, that can make even the best mother a little mean sometimes."

"Still, I bet you wouldn't be if you were my mother."

My grandmother smiles and starts to say something, but then my mother comes back so she changes her mind.

"That was Mr. Davis calling," my mother says to me. "Our appointment is for nine o'clock Monday morning. I suggest you think very hard over the weekend about what you're going to say to him."

"Speaking of the weekend," Grandma says, "what train are you taking to Elizabeth's tomorrow, Victoria?" I guess my mother didn't tell her about me not going.

"Mommy says I can't go because of the school thing." I've got the feeling this may be my last chance so I play it big. You know those hound dogs that always look like they're going to cry? That's a giggle compared to my face right now.

"Well, that's a shame," my grandmother says to my mother.

"It certainly is, and I hope she learns something this time."

"Elizabeth will be so disappointed." Now I'm not saying my grandmother winked or smiled or did anything big like that, but I just got this vibe from her that is definitely good stuff.

"I know," says my mother, "and I feel terrible to have to disappoint her. . . ."

"Especially on her birthday." God bless Grandma.

"I don't know what to do about that."

"Oh, why don't you let her go . . . for Elizabeth's sake?"

I've got to not smile. I've got to not smile. I've got to not smile.

"You're probably right. I certainly don't want this to be a punishment for Elizabeth." She looks at me and says, "Why should she suffer just because you don't know the difference between right and wrong?"

I almost leap at my mother and kiss her for letting me go. Instead I give my grandmother a huge kiss and shoot out of the room to start packing.

Two

I'm taking a morning train tomorrow. I can hardly wait. I'm going to get away from this whole grungy scene and visit my favorite cousin, Liz, down in Philadelphia. She's almost a year older than me, but we get along great. I was down there for Christmas vacation and we had a fantastic time. There was this boy David (he's sixteen), a friend of Liz's boyfriend, who really liked me. Of course, he thought I was a lot older than thirteen. Everyone thinks I'm very mature for my age so it was easy to fool him. Anyway, we went to a party at his friend's house, and when they turned out the light, he kissed me. Some jerk turned it on again a couple of minutes later and we were still kissing. It was such a long kiss that I thought I was going to faint from hold-ing my breath so long. But it helps. Holding your breath, I mean. Then you don't think so much about how your lips are squashing into your braces.

I'll never forget one of the girls at the party. Her name is Cindy, and she's fifteen and thinks she's really hot stuff. A lot of the boys do too, mostly because she's very overdeveloped. I mean her breasts are gigantic. Liz says that she has a terrible reputation and that the boys only like her because she lets them go pretty far. I don't think I could ever let a boy touch my breasts unless we were really in love and then it would have to be on the outside of my clothes. Sometimes I put my own hand on myself, you know, just to see how it feels. It's not bad, but nothing special. But that's probably because it's me touching me. A couple of times Steffi and I were fooling around pretending to be movie stars and we'd make fun of a love scene. We always start off messing around and laughing a lot but then it would get kind of serious in the clinches. Don't laugh, but I sort of liked it when she put her hands on my breasts. It felt sort of, I don't know, tingly. That's when we'd stop. I was always a little embarrassed afterward even though she is my best friend and it was only a fooling-around game. I think she felt the same way because we never talked about it and we usually share everything.

David, the boy from Philly, wrote to me when I got back to New York. It was an okay letter, nothing really personal, but he did ask when I was coming down for another visit. I wrote him and told him that I would be down for the weekend of May 17 for Liz's birthday and that he was invited to the party.

457

He never answered, but Liz said she saw him and he told her that he'd be there. I hope so because right now I don't like any of the boys in my class except maybe Nickie Rostivo and he doesn't even come up to my shoulder. He's cute, but I feel like his mother.

And speaking of mothers, here comes mine *click click click* down the hall and (without knocking) into my room to say that she and Daddy are going to drive Grandma home and then go to a movie. That means that no one will be home except Nina and me, so I ask her about answering the phone. "Nina is quite capable of answering the phone," she says, talking in that fancy cold voice she uses when she's angry at me. To me, the only thing Nina is quite capable of is being a huge pain in the butt. But at least she knows I'm the boss, and of course the first thing I do is make her take the phone off the hook. Most of the time Nina does anything I want. I mean anything. Like one time a whole load of kids from school came back to my house and we were sitting around talking and listening to music when one of the boys got the bright idea that we ought to stage a striptease. Of course none of us were about to take off our clothes, so I got Nina and I told her, "Lucky you, you're the star." And you know what? The jerk actually did it. It was really hysterical with her streaking through the house stark naked. Too much. Finally she hid in the hall closet and wouldn't come out until everyone went home. If I told her to jump off the roof she probably would. She's so silly.

Actually, that naked thing was probably a little much. I've

always felt kind of bad pushing her into it like that because I think I really embarrassed her. To tell you the truth, I only hate Nina some of the time. Mostly because she can never keep a secret and drives me batty the way she's always hanging around me and my friends. If I leave my door open even a crack she just sort of seeps in. She's so quiet that sometimes I don't even know she's there, but then I'll feel someone staring at me and ugh . . . she's so weird. She even looks weird. She's got the skinniest, boniest legs, glasses that keep slipping down her ski-jump nose, and stringy red hair. She'll probably be okay when she grows up, but right now she's an embarrassment. For that matter so are my parents. I just hate to have them come up to school or accompany our class on trips. I'm always worried that they're going to do something horrible in front of everybody like take my hand when we cross the street or make me drink milk instead of Coke at lunchtime. It never actually happens, but that's the way I feel so I hardly ever tell them about parent things at school.

My mother is a sculptor and we have her stuff all over the house. I don't mind that so much because she's really pretty good at it. Last year she had two pieces in the Museum of Modern Art. Those are about the only two pieces I don't like: They're not really much of anything, just forms. Mostly she does heads and they usually look very lifelike. She's done four heads of me. The ones she did when I was little are super, but the one she did last year looked more like her than me. I hated it. Another thing about my mother. She's an absolute tennis freak and as far back as I can remember she's been bugging me to take lessons. So finally last summer I said okay and now it beats me why she was so hot for me to learn because she hardly ever plays with me. Naturally when she does, she always beats me without even half trying. Still, I wouldn't mind playing with her a little more. Just for the practice, of course.

My dad's a lawyer. Not the exciting kind who works in court with murderers and juries. The dull kind. He's into real estate law of some kind. Sometimes at dinner he'll tell my mother a whole long story about one of his cases, and you should see how she hangs on every word. She never listens to me like that. Personally I think she's full of baloney—about being so interested, I mean. Really, who could be so fascinated by things like tax shelters and depreciation? It's ridiculous things like that that give me my laughing fits.

You probably think I spend a lot of time talking and thinking about my mother, and you're right. But I can't help it. She seems to be all over my life. Not so much my father. He's pretty okay. Actually he can even be fun sometimes. Like with Coney Island. Every spring he takes us there for the whole day and he lets us go on any ride we want. You know how most fathers are. They just kind of stand off and watch, but not him. He goes on all the rides with us and even into those crazy horror houses. You have to see him, he's really hysterical. We have the best time and he never makes us leave until we're absolutely ready. He can really be pretty nice when he wants to be. But not my mother. She just ruins everything for me, always telling me what I should do and what I forgot to do, and even if by chance I did remember, how it was all wrong anyway. Thank God Grandma came today. I'll have a whole stupendous totally free weekend where I won't have to listen to all that junk.

I don't know about you, but whenever I have something special to look forward to I can't stop thinking about it. Like this weekend and the party. I've been working it over in my head all week, especially at night. I lie awake for hours thinking about what I'll wear, what I'll say and do, and almost every little thing that could possibly happen. Even some impossible things. I create little scenes and play them over and over again like a movie in my head. Naturally I'm the star and everyone is madly in love with me and I look absolutely perfect and my dancing is spectacular (you know the kind where everyone forms a ring round you) and my conversation is the best. With dreams like that, the real party is bound to be a bomb. Most of them are anyway. I mean, like the boys stand at one end of the room messing around, punching each other on the shoulders and laughing like real jerks, and the girls sit on the other side whispering silly things about the boys. The music blasts away, but nobody dances, and it's too loud for conversation. The only time anyone ever gets together is for a kissing game and that stinks too because most of the time you have to kiss gross guys you really can't stand. And even if you do get to kiss someone you really like, it's never as good as you think it's going to be. I don't know why I always look forward to these parties so much. But I do.

Like with Liz's party this weekend. I'm so anxious to get going for Philly I'm up at 6 a.m. It does my head in when that happens, but it does all the time. All I have to be is a little excited over something and either I can't sleep or I wake up at some ridiculous hour in the morning, and then forget it, I absolutely can't go back to sleep. Today it's not too bad because I only have three hours to kill before the train and there's a new hairstyle I want to try where you part it really high on the left and let this big loopy wave sort of dangle over your right eyebrow. I saw it in an old movie poster in Brentano's—some lady named Veronica Lake, I think—and Steffi says I have just the right hair for it and that it's very sexy and I'd look twenty years old or at least fifteen. So I can work on that in front of the mirror and then have some breakfast, and three hours aren't that hard to kill anyway.

The hairstyle is wild. I love it. Liz is going to die when she sees it. It's almost seven thirty and my mother comes into the kitchen, takes one look at my hair, makes a "you-must-be-out-of-your-mind" face, and says, "I hope you're not going to wear that outside."

She says a couple more gems and I end up putting my hair back in a straight old parting.

I really feel like I want to argue about it with my mother but I don't for two very good reasons. One, I'll lose. Two, I can always dump the old way and go back to the Veronica look on the train. But I can't stay quiet about her next "suggestion."

She insists that my bratty little sister come with us to the station to see me off on the train. What for? Who needs her? Is the train going to stay in the station until the engineer gets the go-ahead from Nina?

I say to my mother very reasonably:

"I'll vomit if she comes along."

My mother responds:

"Tell your aunt Hilda I'll call her on Sunday."

I say:

"Why does that ugly little creep have to come with us anyway?"

She says:

"We won't discuss it. You should be pleased your own sister thinks enough of you to want to see you off. It's a compliment."

I say:

"She's just doing it to spite me. She knows I hate every gut in her body and I don't think it's fair for you to drag her along just because she wants to come. What about me? I don't want her to come. How come you always side with her?" Et cetera, et cetera. When it comes to Nina I could go on forever.

"Finish your breakfast," says my mother, who never cares what I think.

That's when I almost go into a tantrum. Luckily, I catch it just in time. The next words out of my mouth are going to be, "If she comes to the station, I'm not going!" And then my mother would say, "It's just as well, Philadelphia is too far away," or something stupid like that and I'd have been skunked.

So I smother the shriek in my throat and ram down the rest of the cereal and the troll is coming along. She'll pay.

You have to understand. There are times when I really don't hate Nina. Like when she falls down and bleeds or some bully at school is picking on her or if she gets in bad trouble with my mother. But most of the time she's a giant pain and a gross liar and she borrows without asking and she never puts back, and if she does, it's always dirty and wrinkled, and she's sneaky and tends to rat on other people just to save her own skin. My general policy in regard to Nina is to consider the spot she's standing in—empty. It never works.

Anyway, she's coming to the station with us, and speaking of the devil, I think I hear the toad slithering into the kitchen now, ten minutes late already and naturally you have to add on seven minutes while my mother makes her wash her hands and face. Now I ask you, who in Penn Station is going to inspect her hands and face?

But at least we're on the move. I do a last-minute check of my suitcase to make sure I've got Liz's present, my English hairbrush, and some sensational new aqua eyeliner Steffi and I found in the ladies' room at Schrafft's.

"Who walks Norman?" my mother asks.

"She does! She does!" Nina shouts, jumping up and down like some kind of a nut.

"I already did, Mom, so tell her to mind her own business." Of course my mother doesn't tell her. She never does anything I want.

We take a cab to Penn Station and Nina doesn't even look up from her love comic all the way there. Beats me why she's so hot to go with us.

While my mother is buying my ticket, I put the touch on Nina. She hoards her money and always has a ton of it. All I want to borrow is five dollars, but when it comes to money she's a miser. I can usually get anything out of her but money. I already know how I'm going to swing it. She's wearing my argyle socks.

"Take off my socks," I tell her when she says no to the loan.

"You said I could borrow them," she says.

"That was two days ago," I remind her. "You were supposed to wash them out and return them yesterday." She puts her nose back into her love comic like I'm not even there. I pull the comic away. "Take off my socks." I have to work fast before my mother comes back. I know she's not going to let me take the socks back now. Nina knows that too, so she starts to take them off slowly, looking around for my mother. She's balancing on one foot, and all I have to do is poke my finger into that skinny ugly chest and down she goes. It's so tempting, but I know she'll howl. Still, it's worth it. I know she's never going to lend me the lousy money so I pretend I'm reaching for the sock and give her a little tap and whoops . . . there she sprawls.

"I'm telling. . . . Mom!" She howls and it's almost all one word. I can see my mother rushing over, ticket in hand. "You're like two babies," she says for everyone to hear. "I can't leave

465

you alone for two minutes blah blah blah . . ." She goes on in the mother voice with the mother words. Nina is crying that I pushed her. I try to explain in a calm voice that I only bumped her by accident reaching for my favorite socks, which she borrowed without asking, and, anyway, I want them back right now.

I admit it's all pretty stupid, but I'm too far into it now to pull out. My mother threatens to return the ticket and call off the whole trip unless we stop "this very instant." That's not fair. Naturally I'm going to stop, but Nina's not going anywhere so she has nothing to lose, and just to get at me, she keeps crying and pulling at the socks.

"Give her back the comic book," says my mother. I toss it at the gnome just hard enough so it shoots past her and lands on the floor. Big mistake. Not throwing it, but letting her see that I'm wearing her charm bracelet.

Too late. "That's my bracelet!" She's practically shrieking. The whole scene is getting very embarrassing because people are stopping to stare at us and by now Nina is even more disgusting than usual with her wet-streaked face and one bare foot. "She took it out of my drawer. Make her give it back right now."

I wish my train were pulling into the station so I could push her under it. *Crunch.* It would be worth losing a good pair of argyles.

Nina is still making wounded-buffalo sounds and by now my mother is furious. "I don't want to hear one more word from either of you! Nina, put those socks on right this minute and meet us over there," she says, pointing to a big round information booth in the center of one wall of the station. We both walk toward it, leaving the sniveling creep sitting on the floor pulling on my socks.

"You call us Sunday afternoon and tell us what train you're taking," my mother says to me, checking the clock over the booth with her watch. It's only a quarter to nine and my train doesn't leave for fifteen minutes so, unfortunately, there's plenty of time for instructions. "Either Daddy or I will pick you up on Sunday night right here in front of the information booth. Now look around and make sure you know where we are." And my mother begins to point out things to help me remember where this one and only information booth right in the middle of two enormous marble pillars is. She's too much. I stop listening when she starts to show me how it's directly under this monster Dupont Cinerama–type advertisement right opposite the escalator. It's not even worth reminding her that I've made this same trip twice in the last year and that they always pick me up in the same spot and that I'm really not a moron or a two-year-old.

By now the troll has joined us and she's ready for action.

"Mommy," Nina says, "tell her to give me my bracelet back. Mom . . ." Nina is the greatest whiner in the country. She has this special way of just letting her mouth hang down and making all the words seem to come directly out of her nose. My mother really hates it when she does that. You can tell by the glare on her face. I love it when Nina is on the other end of that look.

"I don't want to hear another word about socks or bracelets. How many times do I have to tell you, don't lend and don't borrow. You hear me? Now come on. Move." And she leads the way to Track 13.

I can't resist a tiny grin to aggravate Nina. "Mom . . . ," she whines, pulling my mother's arm. "She's looking at me." But my mother's had it and she doesn't even turn around. There are some last-minute moronic instructions and then it's time for good-bye kisses. For my mother only. I'm just about to hop up the steps when Nina, who's probably been busy plotting something horrible since upstairs, announces, "I need my bracelet for Emily's party on Saturday afternoon."

Last week we had the word "smug" on a vocabulary test. Right now it's on my sister's face. I figure the best thing to do is pretend I didn't hear her and jump on the train. Before I can, she grabs my jacket and screams, and I mean screams, "I need my bracelet!" We're obviously everyone's free afternoon entertainment.

My mother says, "Give her the bracelet." I say I want my socks.

Sometimes in the middle of these arguments I think that I must have gone through the same fight billions of times with only one change. Sometimes it's socks, shirts, gloves, or hats. The fight's the same, only the item is different. It's getting late now and everyone else is on the train and I'm starting to get nervous. But there's no stopping now, so we go around again. Nina says she wants her bracelet, my mother says give it to her, and I say not until she gives me my socks. Now my mother is really furious and grabs the bracelet off my wrist and says, "I said give it to her."

It's all so stupid, I don't know why I do it, but I make a grab for the bracelet. I know it's a silly move but I'm angry because it's really unfair. My mother's temper is gone and she smacks my hand.

"Get on that goddamn train right this minute!" she screams at me.

I can see the people looking at us from the train windows. The tears make me practically blind and I can hardly see to grab my suitcase. I trip up the steps to the train. She shouts something else to me but I don't even hear her. I push through the door into the car, where everyone turns to look at me. The tears are rolling over my cheeks as I start down the aisle. Awful luck, the only empty seat is way down at the other end of the car. That means I have to walk past all these nosy people ogling at me. I don't even care anymore. All I can think of is that my mother is the most unfair person in the whole world and I really think she's a B-I-T-C-H and I can't stand living with her anymore. I'm not kidding, I'm really thinking of moving out. I'm steaming mad. I hate my mother and she's ruining my life. I hate her. Hate, hate, hate.

Three

I have two things to say about the party in Philadelphia (I'm on the train home now). One, it started badly. Two, it got worse. In fact, the whole weekend bombed out for me, including Liz. I'm not in her house ten minutes when she breaks the news that she's not going to wear pants to the party after all. Instead she's going to wear this gorgeous silk dress. That's bad enough, but I really start having a nervous breakdown when she tells me that all the other girls are wearing dresses too. Naturally I don't have one with me. And then she swears that she told me on the phone last week that it was dresses, but that's totally untrue because that's something a person doesn't forget. Maybe a school assignment could slip your mind, but not what everybody's wearing to practically the most important party all term.

It wouldn't be so tragic if I could borrow something from Liz, but she's almost three inches taller than me so there I am, stuck wearing my sailor pants and feeling like a real jerk. Wait, it gets worse. Here it is Saturday night and I just looked in the mirror for a last-minute check. I know for sure my skin was super-perfect an hour ago, but now there is the biggest, grossest, most horrendous pimple in the history of the world growing smack in the middle of my chin. Great! Now I'm really going to wow that David. The only five-foot-four-inch pimple dressed in pants and all his.

It turned out that I didn't have to worry about David after all. That's right. He never showed up for the party. No phone call or anything. Just another one in my long line of admirers. I really knock 'em out.

The party was a real nightmare for me anyway. I spent the whole evening sitting on the back porch talking to Annie Gordon, the fat girl from next door who Liz has to invite to all her parties. But that's not even the worst.

Two of the boys who think they're really hotshots lit up a joint right behind us on the porch and start puffing away like mad. Then Liz comes out and she gets right into the action. It hits me that she's being kind of silly, I mean doing it practically right under her parents' noses, but I figure she knows what she's doing, so I keep quiet. Then she sees Annie and me and whispers, "Move closer and I'll give you a drag."

Annie's jaw falls a mile. She leaps up and takes off, clopping down the steps so fast she misses practically half of them.

Actually it's a hysterical sight, except instead of cracking up I probably should have followed her. But you know me, I have to be Miss Cool, so instead I just slide over and join the group. Fatal mistake.

I probably sound like I'm uptight about grass but I'm absolutely not. It's no big deal anymore. I mean, I hardly know anyone, except maybe Annie Gordon, who hasn't tried dope at least once. First time I smoked it was at this big fountain in Central Park where a whole load of kids hang out. They do it right out in the open. Anyway, I took a couple of puffs and it was okay, not outrageous like some kids say, but good enough. Still, I don't think it's worth taking a big risk for, like at Liz's party, smoking on the back porch while her parents are right inside the house. I'm up to my eyeballs in trouble already, so when Liz hands me the joint I tell her, "No thanks, I'll pass this time."

You should have seen the way those weirdos look at me. Like I'm some kind of freak or something. Then the really gross one sitting next to me pipes up with, "Another Annie Gordon." And they all laugh their heads off.

It's really hard not to let creeps like that get to you. I try— for almost ten seconds. Then I can't stand it anymore so I reach out, grab the stupid joint, take a giant drag, and let the smoke out right in Big Mouth's face.

"Perfect . . . ," I say.

"Yeah," he says, real pleased.

". . . for my nine-year-old sister." I zing it to him. "What nursery school did you get this banana peel at?" And before he can stop stuttering I launch into two and a half minutes on the advantages of Acapulco Gold over Panama Red (or is it Acapulco Red and Panama Gold?). Somewhere in the middle of my brilliant dissertation three things happen: Liz reaches out for the joint, I start to hand it to her, and dear Aunt Hilda comes out of the house. I'm not saying I'm wonderful or anything, but even though I have just enough time to drop the butt into Liz's hungry little fingers, I keep the joint myself. I figure, how can I stick her with it right in front of her own mother?

Aunt Hilda is pretty easygoing most of the time, but when she sees me holding that tiny wrinkled-up joint she knows right away what it is and lets out this little shriek and that's it. End of party. End of weekend. End of me. She starts sweeping everybody out of the house, and Liz goes right up the spout, crying and bawling and arguing with Aunt Hilda, but it does no good. The party's over.

Of course there's absolutely no way to convince her that it wasn't all my fault when she sees me sitting there with the joint in my hand, so I don't even try. Anyway, it's just like I said about how a hundred people can be doing something wrong and I'm the one who gets caught.

This time my aunt is angry at Liz, too. But get this, only because she was "careless enough to allow Victoria to bring pot to the party."

It really makes me mad that Liz didn't even take part of the blame. Worse. She was actually teed off at me for getting

473

caught. All she wanted to know was how come I didn't shove it in my pocket or step on it or eat it or something. Can you catch your breath?

Then my Aunt Hilda says that it would be better if I went home because she couldn't let a thing as serious as "smoking a pot" (that's what she actually said. Good thing the guys weren't smoking two pots or she'd have called the police) go by without teaching Liz a very serious lesson. So to punish Liz, she sends me home. Neat logic, huh? And of course she has to call my mother Sunday morning and tell her the whole story. Right during breakfast. They talk for about a minute, then Aunt Hilda calls me to the phone. "I think your mother wants to say a few words to you."

"Mom?" I ask, hoping for a dead connection.

No luck.

"This is the last straw. . . . I've absolutely had it with you. . . . This time you've gone too far. . . ."

"But it wasn't my fault. I didn't bring the dope."

"I don't want to hear another word about it."

"I only took one drag. I didn't start it."

"Of course not, you never do!"

"But I'm not lying. I swear."

"I'm not going to argue over the phone. We'll discuss it when you come home."

"But I didn't—"

"I said we'll discuss it when you come home. There's a nine forty-five. I want you to be on it."

474

"Damn."

"What did you say?"

"Nothing."

"What?"

"I said, I said nothing."

"Put Aunt Hilda back on."

Now my mother goes through a whole long thing with my aunt and my aunt keeps shaking her head with a "tsk tsk tsk" and looking at me. You know how you always read about somebody's stomach sinking? Well, that's mine now. I know I'll never be able to talk my parents out of sending me away to that gross boarding school now. I'm horrendously depressed at the thought of having to spend the next four years in P.S. Prison or whatever they call that disgusting place. Home may not be the greatest place in the world but it has to be better than reform school.

And all that garbage they're going to give me about how it's for my own benefit is just so much baloney. All they want to do is get rid of me and I know it. Do you know how it feels when your own mother and father don't want you? It's the worst thing in the world, that's what.

Rather than stand here and cry I start to get busy putting the dishes in the dishwasher.

"That's okay, Victoria, just leave them," says my aunt, putting down the phone. "You'd better get packed if you're going to make the nine forty-five. I'll get my car keys and be ready in five minutes."

I go upstairs and throw my things in the suitcase and I'm back down in less than two minutes. My marvelous, adorable cousin doesn't say a word. She just keeps eating her waffle. Boy, was I wrong about her.

The train was in the station when we got there so we really had to make a run for it. When it was time for good-byes my aunt kissed my cheek but I didn't kiss back. I was really mad at her. By the time I got to my seat, we were moving. I flopped down without even looking out the window and here I am. Miserable. What a mess. I don't think I'll ever visit them again.

"I promise you, young lady, nothing's that bad." I look up and see that it's the conductor leaning over me. He happens to be wrong. It's very bad, but he's sort of an old man with a nice pink face so I give him a smile while I reach into my jeans for the ticket.

"That's better, Smiley," he says, bending his whole face up into a big crinkly grin. We're practically nose to nose and it's so silly that I smile for real.

As long as I've got the smile handy, I turn it toward the old lady sitting next to me, and she likes it so much she offers to change seats with me and let me sit near the window. I love window seats. I must have had a million arguments with my sister over who gets the window seat. It's the difference between a boring hour and a half and a fascinating experience staring out of the window and getting lost in somebody else's world. I really need to get lost somewhere today.

"Is this your first trip to New York, dear?" the old lady

wants to know. I tell her I live in New York and about my cousin in Philly. Then she says that the first time she made this trip was just before her daughter was born. I really don't feel like talking so I don't listen too closely. I hope she'll get the idea. I would love to say, "Please leave me alone," or just not answer, but I'd never have the nerve so I just keep shaking my head and pretend to be interested.

"Joseph, that's my husband, was truly upset with me but I said to him, 'I'm the one who's having the baby and I simply couldn't be comfortable unless I used Dr. Tuller in New York.' After all, Ethel and I, that's my twin sister, had always used Dr. Tuller and I wasn't about to change now, what with a first baby and all. It took some fancy convincing but I finally said to him, 'When you have a baby you can use any Philadelphia doctor you want.'"

This seems to strike her as positively hysterical. She's too much. I start to laugh too, but not at her doctor story. I've got this wild picture in my head of another little old lady, the spitting image of this one. I wonder if they still dress alike. That would really be weird. Two twin old ladies with the same kerchief, lipstick, and pointy patent-leather shoes all in shocking crimson. I'd love to ask her but she'd probably think I was being fresh. I am.

Luckily, she gives up on me and goes back to her book. That gives me about ninety undisturbed minutes to sit here and work myself up into a panic about what my parents are going to do when I get home. Too bad worrying isn't a subject at school, I'd get straight As. I'm the best around. If I cut myself, I'm sure I'm going to get tetanus. If my parents argue, I worry they're going to get a divorce, and if they get sick, I'm sure they're going to die. I worry about being adopted (I'm not), failing tests, getting spots, robbers when I'm alone in the house, and spiders all the time, even when everybody's home.

No matter what the worry, it always feels the same. It's like somebody opened a trapdoor in my stomach and let in a whoosh of icy wind that practically takes my breath away. And if that's not bad enough, there's a little metal ball that just sits way down in the pit of my stomach. It never moves, but it weighs a ton. As soon as I start to think about my mother's face when she meets me at the station I get all those old symptoms. I really dread that look of anger and disappointment.

My mother always says I look for trouble, but I really don't. Just the opposite. In fact, trouble with anyone, particularly my mother, makes me miserable. I don't remember having problems with her when I was little. In fact, everything was just great then. I think it began to change when I got to be about twelve. We just never seemed to agree on anything after that. We even had an argument on my birthday last year. I don't remember, but it was probably something she wouldn't let me do. I know I've said I hate my mother, but I really don't. It's just that she seems a million miles away from me.

My elbows are probably filthy from leaning on the window-sill and my forehead's going to have a big black smudge from pressing against the pane, but that's my favorite position for train travel. I can just sit like that for hours watching the scenery shoot by. Seems like the whole trip to New York is nothing but miles and miles of split-level houses. Still, I'm not bored. I have a special thing that I do. I pick a house and concentrate on one tiny thing about it. Maybe the way a branch brushes against a window or some missing bricks on the side of the steps, something private that only the people who live in the house would know about. It's like sneaking into their lives for a minute without their knowing it. It tickles me to think that I'm the only person in the whole world looking at the broken window shade on the house that just whizzed by. Then I always think, maybe it doesn't really exist—not just the window shade, the house and all of it. Maybe I made it all up. I remember one time my parents were having a discussion with some of their friends about different philosophical explanations of life and someone described Aristotle's, and it was just like that. I loved it. He said that you were the only real thing that existed in the world and everything else was a creation of your imagination, and if you weren't there, the world was empty.

Like now, all those houses, the people on the train, even the train itself is right out of my mind. I made them all up, including Aristotle and his ideas, and of course, if that's the case, I'm the only one alive and I get to live forever. Cool, huh? It could be possible, except the way I am with science I don't think I could really invent something as complicated as, say, electricity. On the other hand, I certainly could come up with a simple thing like a plug, which is all I ever get to see anyway. No wonder electricity is so mysterious—there's nothing on the other side of the wall. Just like a movie set, it's only what's in front of me that's real. Of course the whole theory collapses when it comes to my mother. With any kind of person to choose from, why in the world would I stick myself with her? Another thought: if I know my mother, most likely *she's* real and I'm just a figment of *her* imagination. Obviously Aristotle was off his nut and there really is something behind the plug on the wall, and with my luck I'm going to have to explain it all on some science test one day.

Suddenly I close my eyes, overcome by a terrible dread. I'm on a train heading home, where I'll never be able to explain away the dope business, and where they're bound to kick me out of school. As sure as I'm sitting here, my folks will send me off to that disgusting boarding school. I don't want to go home. I can't go home. I squeeze my eyes tight and try to will the train to stop. Come on, Aristotle or somebody. Help me. Where are all those great big mysterious forces floating free out there in the galaxies somewhere? How do you get the train to stop? How do you get time to stop? If I could only stop time I'd be safe. Or better, make it go back a little so I'd have a chance to avoid the stupid things that got me in all this bad trouble in the first place. No cigarette up in the balcony. No party in Philadelphia! I'd even be nice to Nina.

Go back, train. Go back, time. Come on, give me a hand. I listen to the rattle of the train as it speeds through the countryside and I feel it's trying to help me. Clickety-clack, back and back. Clickety-clack, back and back and back and back. I lean forward to look out of the window and see if maybe the crazy train isn't in fact going backward, and just as I do the train makes one of those wild sways as it's rounding a turn and my head whacks into the windowpane. It's a good hard bang because there's an instant roar of thunder inside my skull and what feels like a bolt of lightning shooting down the back of my neck and into my spine. Pain. And in the next breath, gone. I'm okay, just a little shaky. Boy, you'd think they'd be more careful on those sharp turns. Even the train lights went out. And we must have hit the tunnel into Penn Station because it's black outside, too.

Four

Now the lights in the train flash back on and I look around the car and everything looks calm. I guess I was the only one that got bumped. It must have been the way I was leaning on my elbows.

Wow! I didn't think ninety minutes could zoom by so quickly. It's only about five minutes from when you go under the tunnel until you get into Penn Station. The idea of going home to face all the trouble I'm in really makes me feel sick. Ugh. I dread it.

I excuse myself to the young woman sitting next to me and squeeze by her so I can reach for my suitcase over the seat. I'm especially careful because she's very pregnant. Funny, I never noticed when the old lady, the one with the twin sister, left and this young woman got on. I guess I was too busy with

Aristotle. Even though I push as far as I can toward the seat in front when I inch past her, I manage to catch her toes under my wooden clogs. She jumps and lets out a loud "Ouch!"

"I'm really sorry," I say, but I have to look away because I'm in danger of cracking up at the sight of her struggling to reach her foot past that gigantic stomach. When she finally succeeds, she takes off the shiniest red pointy shoes you've ever seen, and rubs her toes. Her shoes look like something right out of *The Wizard of Oz*, but funny thing is, I could swear the old lady was wearing the same kind. They certainly look like old lady's shoes, even the wild color. Actually, the pregnant lady's taste is just about as awful as the old lady's with her matching scarf and crazy shoes and, oh my God, crimson lipstick. Bad taste must be catching.

Everyone is moving around, getting their luggage, and making last-minute adjustments. The train slows down to a crawl as we enter the station.

I get a flash thought: Maybe I'll hide and stay on the train until we hit the freight yards and then I'll hook up with some hoboes and never go home. There's one small problem. I'm terrified of railroad tracks. It takes me forever to get up the courage to cross them. One of my big nightmares is that I won't know which is the third rail. I know some trains don't even use them, but I can never remember which ones. Science is just not my field, and neither, for that matter, are messy old hoboes.

Nothing to do but start making my way down the aisle to the door. It's slow moving because the car is packed with kids and mothers carrying babies. I must have been very wrapped up in my own problems because I never even noticed all these babies. And, funny thing, I don't even remember hearing them. Though they sure are noisy enough now.

The pregnant lady is ahead of me and still limping a bit, but she turns and smiles at me, so I suppose everything is all right. Everybody's shuffling along an inch at a time but that's okay with me. I'm certainly not in any big hurry to get to what's waiting for me. When I reach the end of the car, the conductor is helping one of the women. She's weighted down with a yowling baby, an old cardboard suitcase, and a big hatbox from some store called Wanamaker's. He's giving her a hand down the steps when he notices me. I get the same kind of huge happy smile as I did from the other conductor. I guess I never realized how warm and pleasant conductors could be. At least these two are. They must really like their jobs. It's easy to smile back.

"What'd I tell you, Smiley, nothing's that bad," he says, taking my elbow as I jump down the last step. When I hear him call me Smiley, I have to take another look to make sure it's not the original conductor. Of course it's not. This man can't be more than twenty-five, and the first conductor was at least sixty, but they do smile alike. Maybe they're father and son. If it wasn't so noisy and crowded I'd ask, but by now I'm already on the platform and being shoved along toward the steps at the far end.

Meanwhile another train has pulled in on the opposite side

of the platform and people are pouring out and heading for the same steps. I'm snuggled deep inside the moving crowd, just letting myself be carried along. It might be nice to keep going with them and see where I end up. It's got to be better than in front of my mother.

On second thought, as I look around at the people, it might be a mistake. They're a very strange-looking group. You can tell they're all really square. All the women are wearing skirts and the men are dressed in baggy suits and most of them are wearing old-fashioned felt hats. Not even the kids are wearing jeans. In fact, nobody is but me. It's unreal. This has got to be some kind of convention group from Missouri or someplace.

Something snappy like librarians, funeral directors, and Eagle Scouts.

Just as I get to the steps I see this girl I know way back in the crowd.

"Hey!" I wave to her over the tops of some little kids.

She sees me and for a second looks kind of confused, like she's not sure I'm waving at her. But when I motion *Yes, you* with my head, she smiles and starts to make her way toward me.

Big mistake. When I look more closely, I see that I absolutely don't know her. Actually, she looks very familiar, but now that she's almost up to me I can see that I've never laid eyes on her before in my life. How embarrassing.

"Hi," she says right there in front of me, looking sort of blank but expectant.

Nothing to do but apologize. "Sorry," I say, "I really

thought I knew you. I mean . . . it's incredible the way you look so familiar . . . I could have sworn . . ." Mumble, stutter, stumble.

"That's okay. I guess I just have one of those familiar faces." And she smiles wider and I like her right off. "I'm Cici," she says. It's crazy but she really reminds me of someone I know. I mean absolutely.

"I'm Victoria," I say, and we both stand there like jerks. Only way out is to let ourselves go with the crowd, which we both do.

"See you around," she says, and she's gone. What an embarrassment.

We all march up the steps like in an orderly school fire drill, only nobody's pushing or shoving. I thought I came up the staircase that leads to the escalator, but I guess I was wrong. There's nothing here but another steep flight of steps. I'm probably dumb for sticking with this crowd. It's certain they've never been to New York before.

Sure enough, I'm lost. I've followed these hayseeds up some back stairs and ended up in a section of the station I've never seen before. Great. After going to Philly seven times, I get myself lost. Boy, my mother will never buy that one.

It's absolutely amazing that I've never seen this section of the station before. I mean, it's enormous. I don't see how I could have missed it. And it's jammed with people. Oh, gross! I bet I got off at the wrong station.

"Excuse me, sir, can you tell me what station this is?" I ask a

man in a sort of uniform with a red hat who looks like he must work for the railroad. He stares at me for a minute like he's trying to figure out if I'm pulling his leg, then decides I'm serious. "Pennsylvania Station, New York, New York." He booms it out like a conductor and then starts to laugh. "Where'd you think, girlie?" Embarrassing jerk. I don't think it's so funny and I'm about to tell him so when somebody shoves a suitcase in his hand and he hurries off, not even waiting for my answer.

I'm being very calm despite the fact that when I look up at the towering ceiling and at all the gigantic space around me I get an awful scary feeling that something's really gone screwy. Maybe the man in the red hat is wrong. I ask a kind-looking elderly woman and she gives me the same "are-you-kidding" look and then the same answer. Only she seems a little more concerned and I back off and lose her fast.

I'm looking around at this place and the people, and it's all really weird and at the same time—I don't know—kind of ordinary. Now it hits me! It's got to be. There's no other answer. I don't know why I didn't guess right away. Of course! They're shooting a movie! It's a cast of thousands and I'm stuck right smack in the middle. Fantastic. I'm going to be in a movie.

To tell you the truth, I'm relieved. You remember those trapdoors I told you about in my stomach? The icy air, the metal ball, the whole bit? Well, it was beginning to happen. I'm not that hot to be in a movie, but I'm just out-of-my-head-happy that it isn't what I thought it was, which is very peculiar because I really don't even know what I thought it was. Though

I probably won't be all that delighted when I see myself on the screen with my messy hair and the scaredy-cat look on my face. Ugh, I've probably got a dirt mustache where I wiped the sweat off my lip. And, as always, the twinkling tinsel teeth. At least I'll be able to pick myself out easily.

It's amazing the money they spend on these movie sets. They practically have to rebuild the whole station—well, the inside anyway. Will you look what they did to the information booth? It's half the size. You know, I can see how they can make something bigger, maybe add a cardboard wall here or there, or whatever, but I just don't know how they make an information booth smaller. And then if they did figure out how to shrink it, it would still have my mother in front of it. That tiny draft I get in my stomach is turning into a hurricane. Victoria, I tell myself, trying to sound strong like my mother, cool it. But I know it's only me telling me, so it doesn't work. Now I'm having trouble swallowing.

She could be late—my mother, I mean—or maybe the crowds are in the way or something. Just in case, I stand right in the center of the front of the information booth. On my toes with my arms up so she can't miss me. Right now, to tell the truth, I'm dying to see my mother. Even if she's angry. Nina would look pretty good to me now too, so you can imagine my state of mind. But so far no familiar faces.

Except one. Or, to be more exact . . . two. I may be freaking out, but remember the pregnant lady, the one with the pointy red shoes whose toes I squashed? Well, there she is, standing not ten feet away from me. Which is no big deal except that at this very minute she happens to be hugging her identical twin sister. Well, think about it. That's a very weird coincidence— I mean, it must be a one-in-a-million shot for this pregnant woman to be wearing the same shoes, scarf, and crazy lipstick colors and also have a twin sister exactly like the old lady who disappeared (well *I* never saw her get off the train). I think that's pretty odd. In fact, it's so odd that my hands are shaking like some kind of weirdo. I shove them in my jeans pockets so nobody will notice. This is getting seriously strange.

Five

"Victoria?" The voice comes from behind me, but when I turn to look, I don't see anyone. I mean anyone I know. Then way back in the crowd I see an arm waving at me. From where I'm standing I can't see the person attached to it, but I'm feeling much better already because the arm is definitely waving at me and someone's calling my name. Wow! I was really getting worried. I can feel one of those goofy ear-to-ear grins spreading over my face as I watch the waving arm make its way through the crowd.

Forget it. Another false alarm. It's only the girl from the train platform, the one I thought I knew.

"Hi." She's got a great smile—wide, white, and wireless. "Waiting for someone?" she asks.

"Yes, my parents. Well, my mother anyway. Except she's really late, which isn't like her at all."

"I thought you looked kind of worried. Why don't you give them a call?"

"I don't want to leave this spot in case she comes."

"You go and call and I'll wait here. What's she look like?"

"I don't know, sort of ordinary, blondish hair, medium height. She'll probably be wearing jeans and a T-shirt."

"Blue jeans?" She looks really surprised.

"She lives in them."

"Well, that ought to make her pretty easy to find. Okay, don't worry. I'll hold her here if she comes." I feel better already to have someone else involved. "The phones are way over there," she says, pointing across the huge waiting room.

I head for the phones without looking too hard at the people because they just make me nervous. I put in two nickels and start to dial. Right away one of my nickels comes back. I let the phone ring forever, but there's no answer. I try again and the same thing happens with the nickels, but there's still no answer. She must be on her way. I head back to the information booth.

Cici is still waiting in front.

"There's no answer so they must be on their way here."

We stand around for about ten minutes, not doing much talking, just looking around. I think I spot my mother's head, hair, arm, what have you, half a dozen times. But I turn out to be wrong every time. I must be getting jumpy.

"Why don't you try to call them again? I'll wait here." I'm fantastically lucky to have run into Cici. I'd really hate to be alone at a time like this.

It turns out we wait for more than an hour. I call eight more times and still no answer. Now I'm plenty worried. It's just not like my mother not to show. She's never even late.

"Look, Victoria, why don't you come home with me and we'll call from there."

"I don't know if I should. What if she comes after I leave? Then she'll really worry." And probably be mad, if I know her.

Still, it's not such a bad idea. Having her worry, I mean. Who knows, she might get so scared that I've run away or been kidnapped or something horrendous like that that she might have second thoughts about sending me away to boarding school. Like she could realize how terrible it is without me. Well, maybe that's a little much, but still, it certainly would give her a jolt and I wouldn't mind that. Why should I be the only one to suffer all the time?

"Okay," I say, "let's go. I'll call from your house." Wow! Are they going to go mad. I take Cici by surprise. She probably didn't expect me to agree so fast, but she looks delighted.

"Neato!" she says. "Let's hurry. I'm starving." By now Cici has taken hold of my arm and is leading me through the crowd, and dopey me, I'm letting her. We go down two flights of steps and end up at the subway heading for Queens. I guess I should have asked where she lives and things like that, but now it's too late.

It looks like I'm stuck with her. It's not all that terrible because I can tell right off that I'm really going to like Cici. You know how it is, sometimes you just meet someone and bang, you hit it off. Better than that, you're old friends instantly.

We can hear the subway train pulling in as we get to the turnstiles. "Hold it a minute!" I say, and start rummaging through my pockets for two tokens I know I had.

"I've got it," Cici says, shoving what looks like two nickels into the turnstiles. "Quick! The train's here."

Crazy. The nickel things work and we both bolt through, zoom down the steps and into the train just as the doors begin to close. We're out of breath and laughing hard. She's too much. She wasn't even nervous using those fake tokens. I must remember to ask her where she gets them.

We're in one of those real old trains with the woven straw seats. You never ever see them in Manhattan anymore. It's pretty crowded and there are no empty seats so we both grab different poles.

Now, for the first time, with Cici standing far enough away, I can get a real good look at my new friend. She's maybe an inch or two shorter than I am, not skinny but real slim, and I'm happy to say even more flat-chested than me. Her hair hangs a little below her ears and she's got it parted on the side with a big dangly wave that keeps sliding across her right eye. I love it and you know what? It's exactly like that Veronica Lake thing I tried to do that my mother made me change. Shows you what she knows. Anyway, it's streaky blond and a little frizzy, sort of the way mine looks when I don't blow-dry

493

it. I'd call her pretty—in fact, maybe even very pretty. Especially in the outfit she's wearing. She's got on one of those old-fashioned peasant skirts, the kind I'm always looking for—you know, gathered tight at the waist and swinging out real full down to the middle of her calves. Her blouse is great too, with puffed lacy sleeves and a scoop neck. Sometimes, if you're mega-lucky, you can pick up things like that in a thrift shop. Like I said, her clothes are sensational, but you should see her shoes and socks. You wouldn't believe how gross they are. Her shoes look exactly like men's brown loafers, and to top it off she's wearing heavy white gym socks. And if that isn't horrendous enough, she's got shiny copper pennies stuck inside the front slot of each shoe. Ugh. I've got to tell her what a big mistake she's making. Maybe later, when we get to be better friends. Though actually, it feels like we're pretty good friends already. Like I said, sometimes it just happens that way.

Right now, standing here and staring at Cici, it's really beginning to bug me that she looks so familiar. I bet I know her from someplace. Maybe summer camp. I go over to where she's standing and ask her if she's ever been to camp. She says she has and names three camps that I've heard somebody mention—I can't remember who—but when I try a few names on her—Judy Rubin, Cait Clancy, Jill Schwartz—she doesn't know them. And she's never heard of the camps I've gone to. Maybe I don't know her, but she absolutely reminds me of someone I do know and it's going to drive me batty till I remember who.

As I look around, it hits me that the people going to Queens look a lot like the people in Penn Station, who don't look much like the people I'm used to seeing every day. Which makes me think that either fashions change faster than I thought or the people in Queens are about thirty years behind the times. I guess you can see how hard I'm trying to squeeze everything into plain old ordinary explanations. I don't think it's working too well.

The train rumbles on with the lights blinking on and off every now and then. At one point in the darkness, cut off from Cici, a weird scary feeling comes over me that the car is really empty and I'm all alone. Not just here in the subway, but everywhere. It's sort of like that Aristotle thing again, except that when the lights come back on and I look around, I know all this couldn't be my creation. If it was, then I wouldn't feel so out-of-place—and I really do.

I can't explain why I'm getting spooked now or why this all seems so weird. I mean, when you're riding on the subway to Queens, how far out can it be? That's just what makes it so bizarre, when something that should be so ordinary is so unusual. Take these people. They seem like plain old everyday New Yorkers—dressed up in costumes. Which is something even plain old everyday New Yorkers just don't do when they ride the subway.

Even the subway car is different. Very old-fashioned, as I mentioned, but also too clean. There's only one tiny bit of graffiti and it doesn't even make sense. It's a little picture of a guy's eyes and nose peeking over a line with the words "Kilroy was here" underneath. And the advertisements. I've never even heard of half of them. What's Citronella? Where's Luna Park? And now I take a good look around, Cici isn't the only girl in those awful shoes.

The train pulls into Ely Avenue and some people get off. Cici pokes me and points to two empty seats. We sit down and she takes some grimy piece of grayish-white material out of her bag. It's all rolled up in this disgusting ball held closed by a needle with some gray thread. She unravels a tiny corner and starts to sew with the most grotesque stitches you've ever seen. Beats me what that rag could be and why anyone would bother sewing such a thing. I'm about to ask about it, but I catch myself at the last second and instead ask what stop we get off at.

"We gotta go to the end of the line," she says. "Parsons Boulevard. Are you hungry? I'm starving."

I'd forgotten to even think about food, but now that I do, I guess I'm kind of hungry too. "Yeah," I say, "I could eat."

"Terrif," she says. I notice that she uses that word a lot. "We can grab a chow mein sandwich at Woolworth's."

Talk about grossing me out! I love Chinese food, but a chow mein sandwich on white bread toast probably, with lettuce and a pickle, sounds horrific, but I don't want to hurt her feelings so I pretend I'd love one.

"Your skirt is amazing," I tell Cici. "I love it. I've been looking for one like that forever. Where'd you get it?"

"My mother got it for me."

"I bet she picked it up in a thrift shop." Somehow mentioning a thrift shop was a mistake because she looks at me really funny, like either I'm kidding or I'm nuts. For a second she even looks kind of insulted, so I smile to show her I didn't mean anything bad, then she laughs and says, "Yeah."

Something tells me to drop the subject and I do.

An old man sitting next to us beckons with his finger for us to lean over and look at something in his hand. Naturally I pay no attention. All my parents have to find out is that I was talking to some strange man in the subway . . . beautiful. I'd never hear the end of it. Cici surprises me though. She smiles and bends over to look. I think she must be nuts. In fact, I wish she wouldn't do it, because I always get a little nervous in the subway anyhow, with all those rapes and knifings, I mean. I poke Cici and shake my head no, but she doesn't seem to get the message. Now she really looks interested in what he's showing her and pulls me over to have a look. I can't believe how she's not even the least bit nervous about this man.

She's got me hanging over him so I can't not look. Turns out he's trying to show us something on the inside of a peanut. Did you know that if you separate the two halves of a nut, inside is this thing that looks exactly like the face of Santa Claus? I never knew that before. He gives us each a nut. I put mine right in my pocket. You know I'm not about to eat food from a stranger. Though, strangely enough, this time I almost feel I could.

497

Weird, but when the old man showed us the nut thing, the other people around us seemed to lean closer and smile like they were approving. They even seemed friendly. Can you picture people in a subway being interested and friendly? And another thing, you probably think I'm exaggerating, but you know that feeling you get in the subway? Uptight, tense, like something horrendous could happen at any time? I don't feel it here. I actually feel very relaxed, like I couldn't be in a safer, more comfortable place. And if that old man tried anything funny on us, I get the feeling the other people would stop him fast. I must be dreaming.

Cici and I chatter away for the rest of the trip. We seem to have a million things in common. Especially problems. She tells me about how she's always getting into trouble for the littlest, most unimportant things. Just like me. Plus she hates the way she looks, too. I tell her she's crazy because she's really cute-looking, but she says her eyes are too small and close together and she thinks her knuckles are too big.

"But the worst things are my knees. Look." And she lifts her skirt enough to show me perfectly okay-looking knees, and believe me I'm an expert on knees so I know what I'm talking about.

"What's wrong with them?" I ask, because maybe it's something I can't see.

"Are you kidding? They're so bony you could cut yourself just looking at them."

She's nuts. They're fine and there's nothing the matter

with her eyes either. But I know she'd never believe me, so all I say is, "Wait till you see mine."

And then she tells me how she's a social flop with boys, and we compare all the jerky mistakes we've made at parties, and we're practically hysterical because we both do the same stupid things.

I think she's as excited about me as I am about her. She starts to tell me about all the great plans she's got for us today. First we're going to eat, then a double feature (I told her I only have three dollars to spend; for some reason she thinks that's hysterical), then later, after dinner, a big party at some boy's house. I tell her it all sounds fantastic, and she says that as long as I love her outfit so much, I can borrow her other one, which is much dressier and even nicer. Luckily, her feet are mega-tiny, like a size one, so there's no question of me borrowing her gross shoes. I tell her that I think my clogs (would you believe she never even heard of clogs?) would be perfect with the skirt. She doesn't say anything, but I can see that she thinks my clogs are as weird as I think her loafers are.

Still, you can tell that things like what kind of shoes a person wears don't matter to Cici. She's the easygoing type that doesn't try to shove her opinions at you. That's one of the things I like so much about her. You do what you want and she does what she wants. Plenty of room for everyone.

At Parsons Boulevard the train empties and we go up the stairs and out of the subway. We stop in a candy store and I try to phone my house. Still no answer. Cici says we have to walk a few blocks to the main drag, Jamaica Avenue. Everything's there.

At Woolworth's the lunch turns out to be sensational. I eat two gigantic chow mein sandwiches and they're nothing like I thought they'd be. It's a big blob of really great chow mein served with a whole bunch of crispy fried noodles on a soft hamburger bun and it's delicious. Plus—you won't believe this—it only costs a dime.

I don't know much about the price of chow mein sandwiches, but when the girl behind the counter asks for a nickel for an orange drink, I nearly choke. And it's not just what they charge for the food, it's everything—lipsticks, hair junk, school stuff—it's all way less than the regular price. I look around to see if it's a special sale day, but I don't see any signs. I try to think of an easy explanation, but the only plausible one I can come up with (and I admit it's reaching a bit) is that I just wasn't paying attention again. That's what my science teacher is always saying about me. I dream.

Well, I must have been dreaming the day they explained all this. I mean, this whole thing was probably planned in advance as a commemoration of some national event, and the day they told everyone, I just wasn't listening. I was probably dreaming or doodling or something like that, and now here I am stuck right smack in the middle and too embarrassed to ask. Serves me right, I guess.

The other explanation is a lot simpler: I've flipped my lid, gone bananas. All that science homework that Mr. Flynn gives could really make you crazy.

Six

If either of those explanations don't really grab you, I've got another one. Only I can't exactly describe it because it's very far out, more of a feeling than something tangible. But there are three things I'm absolutely certain about: One, all this has nothing to do with any of my real problems (being suspended from school and being falsely and practically accused of dealing dope, which is really horrendously unfair). Two, it started way back there on the train. And three, it's really major stuff. I can tell because the feelings I'm getting are very negative. For a person who gets jumpy just going up in an elevator alone at night, this is off-your-rocker stuff. So far I haven't—gone off my rocker, I mean. But I think that's mainly because of Cici. She's solid and real and I trust her completely; and that's what keeps me calm, sane, cool. Meanwhile, I think I just saw my solid trustworthy friend take the old five-finger discount. That's shoplifting in case you didn't know. Though why she wants something that says "toggle bolts" on the package beats me. For that matter, what is a toggle bolt anyway?

"What did you do that for?" I whisper into her shoulder.

"What?" she says, all innocent.

"Steal the funny-looking bolt."

"Oh," she says, really crushed, "you saw me take it?"

"Sure, you scooped it up your sleeve."

"How about the eraser?"

"I missed that one."

"Aha! It worked. That's my new method. See, what I do is lick my palm and then press it down hard on the eraser and—presto!—it sticks to my hand, and then it's simple to slip it right into my pocket. Watch."

And she goes to work. With a great flourish, she licks her hand and jams it down against a small rubber electrical plug. *A hundred people turn to look.* Including the store manager. She's the worst thief I've ever seen. I try to make crazy motions to her so she doesn't put the plug in her pocket, but she's so carried away with her new method that she doesn't notice my frantic hand motions until it's too late. I never thought being collared meant the store manager comes over and actually grabs you by the collar. But that's exactly what happens to Cici and with me standing there like some kind of jerk not knowing what to do.

Meanwhile the manager goes into a long spiel about how he's going to call her parents, the police, her school, et cetera, and he's going to press charges, and with this black mark against her she'll never be able to go to college or hold a job or anything. After he goes on for about five minutes about how she's finished for life, he says to her, "And now, young lady, what do you have to say for yourself?"

And Cici turns to him and says, bold as brass, "Ohta foeks elitna meonmen ogla."

Right on! I think she must be the greatest girl I ever knew in my whole life.

"Mashconki," she says to me, "wahofa dorma conchi?"

I shrug my shoulder and answer, "Vaggon."

Now she turns back to the manager, who's looking very confused, and gives him a huge Yugoslavian-type smile (whatever that is) and, reaching over to the counter, takes another of those indispensable rubber plugs and with the most heart-breaking of limps drags herself over to me and hands me the plug. Now, obviously in excruciating pain, she makes her way back to the speechless manager and with a hideously lopsided curtsey, mumbles to him, "Absarupa," and shakes his hand.

Taking my cue from her (but with only the courage for a small facial tic), I nod to the manager and also shake his hand and give him a hearty, "Absarupa."

It's all so successful that we turn to the crowd that has gathered and with a humble bow and our warmest smiles, wish them all an "Absarupa." I think I see tears in one old woman's eyes as they answer in unison, "Absarupa."

Hostilely they turn to the manager, who swallows his

embarrassment, stuffs two more plugs into Cici's twisted hand, and gulps, "Absarupa."

Now, for the final touch, Cici contorts her head toward the audience, and with such effort that her whole body trembles, says, "Omerika goot!"

My stomach is beginning to turn, but the crowd applauds, and with one last (I hope) magnificent gesture, Cici hands each person a brown rubber plug. One thing I can tell about Cici already is that she doesn't know when to stop, so I allow her one last "Absarupa," grab her by her good arm, and shove her toward the exit. We move pretty fast, considering her afflictions.

A minor miracle strikes somewhere between the lipstick counter and the front glass doors, and when we burst into the street, she's completely cured. Grabbing hands, we charge down the block, zip across the street and down the next block, yelping with laughter, gasping for breath. With a tug from Cici we go flying slam into the ticket booth of a movie theatre. Still hysterical.

"You're crazy," I tell her between giggles and snorts. "I can't believe we got away with it. He must be some kind of a moron."

"I've got this terrific idea for when we go back later," says my lunatic friend. "I got this thing we can do with our jackets that'll make us look like Siamese twins. We both get into the same jacket. Here, all you do is . . ." And she starts to wiggle out of her jacket.

"Show me later," I say, pushing her jacket back on. "We'll miss the movie."

No question about it, I was right. Cici is sensational, but she definitely doesn't know when to stop. Never in my life will I enter that five-and-dime again. I start fishing into my pockets for my money.

"Did you see these pictures?" she asks, and out comes that rolled-up rag again as she digs into her bag for money.

I study the movie posters. "No, but I think they were on TV."

"Huh?" she says, screwing up her forehead like she never heard of TV or something. "On what?"

There goes that feeling again. "Nothing," I say. "They look super to me. Actually, I've been dying to see them." It's not true, but it seems to satisfy Cici, and besides, something tells me it's better not to go into it now. Then I catch sight of the admission price. At first glance I think it says seventeen cents, then I realized that that must be the tax so I study it closer. It's really weird, but it's not the tax. That's the whole price. Seventeen cents to see *Laura* and *Since You Went Away*. Even if we are in Queens and they are old movies, still, that's the most incredible bargain I've ever heard of. At that price I can afford to be a sport, so I pay for both tickets.

"Hey!" Cici is delighted. "Thanks. That's terrif. I'll buy the candy."

We go in and it's one of those gigantic old theaters that looks like a castle in fairyland. It's even got that funny kind of ceiling my mother used to tell me about. It's fixed up to twinkle. When my mother was little, her brother, my uncle Steve, used to take her to scary movies and she'd spend the whole time staring up at the ceiling trying to figure out how they did it. If she didn't tell me that they run a movie of the sky on the ceiling, I would never know. It's so incredibly real-looking. I didn't think they had this stuff in theaters anymore. Bet this is probably the last one left in the city.

We find two perfect seats right in the center aisle and start squeezing in past the people when somebody flashes a big spotlight on us.

"Just a minute there, girls. Where do you think you're going?" It's a woman's voice. Cici grabs my arm and starts pulling me as fast as she can in the opposite direction, crunching toes, bumping knees, and tripping over people.

"Excuse me. Excuse me," we keep mumbling.

"Hey, watch it!"

"What d'ye think you're doing!" Everyone in the row is furious.

The flashing light circle is bounding over us. Whistles, applauding, and angry shouts come from the rest of the audience. Oh, God, it's like the class trip, only no Miss Fatso. Worse. I catch a glimpse of what looks like a nine-foot-tall Amazon in a white uniform right out of all those women's prison movies. I don't even bother to look where I'm going. I just let Cici lead me.

We dash up the aisle and into the lobby and shoot behind a

huge goldfish pond with a waterfall and a real goldfish the size of a flounder in it. We spot the monster prison matron coming up the aisle hot on our trail, red-faced, huffing, and furious. She goes right over the next aisle and stands there waiting to catch us. Cici starts to wiggle out of her jacket. Oh, please, God, don't let it be that awful Siamese-twin thing.

Now I'm really shaking and I don't even know why. I didn't do anything wrong. I paid for the tickets. I think. Why is that monster chasing us? And why are we running? Now Cici starts to laugh. We're going to end up spending the whole double feature crouched behind the goldfish pond. Maybe that's why it's only seventeen cents.

"As soon as the witch goes down that aisle," she says, giggling and loving the whole thing, "we'll make a run for the end aisle." And she ties her jacket around her waist, the better to run with. Whew. At least it's not the twin trick.

"Why?" I ask her. I mean, this is really getting silly, running and not knowing why.

"Because it's against the wall and she won't be able to see our outline."

"No," I say, "I mean, why are we running?"

"So we don't have to sit in the children's section."

"The children's section! Gross! I'm almost fourteen. Why should I sit in the children's section?"

"Because that thing says so," she says, jerking her head toward the gargantuan matron. "She's in charge of the children's section, and she doesn't care how old you are. If she says you sit there, it's tough. You sit there. Now, are you ready to make a dash for the end aisle?"

"You bet. Nobody's putting me in any silly children's section."

With the matron's back toward us, we shoot for the end aisle. A second before the aisle door, Cici stops dead.

"My dress! I left my dress behind the goldfish pond."

That ball of rags is a dress? No way.

"Leave it," I say. "We'll get it later on our way out."

"No good. Somebody'll take it."

Not unless there's a garbage pickup. I'd really love to know who'd want that thing, but she seems so attached to it I can't ask.

"You want to wait here?" she says.

"Uh-uh." No, sir. I'm not about to take a chance on losing Cici. She may be my last friend in the world.

So we race back. Just as I thought, the dress is rolled up in a ball right where she left it. She's really relieved and jams it into her bag. Here we are again, back crouching behind the fish pond. By now I figure we've missed about one-third of the movie. Cici reads my thoughts. "Don't worry," she says. "I always sit through them twice anyway."

"Okay, now's our chance," Cici says and we fly toward the end aisle. Just as we hit the door, the matron comes out of the other aisle and spots us.

"Come back here this instant."

Oh boy, four huge steps and she's halfway across the

theater. We race through the door and into a wall of darkness. It takes a couple of seconds to be able to focus. I can hear the heavy thud of her feet behind us. Nightmare! Wouldn't you know I don't see any empty seats. Then, just as the light begins to crack through the door behind us, Cici spots two seats a couple of rows ahead. They're not together; one is on each side of a man. We lunge for them. Cici slides in past the man and I take the one closest to the aisle. Just as we thump down into our seats, the ominous flashlight comes bounding down the aisle, leaping up and down the rows searching for the escaped murderers.

I fight down the urge to slide down in my seat. The littler I am, the more I'll look like a kid, so I sit up as tall as I can. Maybe she'll think I'm the guy's wife. Now the other people are beginning to give the matron nasty looks. She's disturbing them. My idea works—she can't find us so she has to retreat. I peek around and see her face in the little window of the door. She's probably going to hang out there waiting to trap us. Well, she's going to have a long wait because we're not planning to move for a good four hours.

I look across the man at Cici and we both smile. We won! We outfoxed the dragon. Nice one. I slump back in my seat feeling very up and ready to enjoy the movie. But something begins to nag at me about the man sitting between us. I think they call it peripheral vision when you see something out of the corner of your eye that you don't even know you're seeing. Well, most of the time you don't notice unless something about

509

it strikes you funny like the fact that the guy is all huddled up in a raincoat when it's as sunny as can be outside and it absolutely isn't raining in the theater. Now, I'm no dope, so I know all about men with raincoats, but I've got my fingers crossed. He could be the exception, you know.

Naturally I can't concentrate on the movie anymore. All I'm doing is waiting for the inevitable. It happens. Or maybe it doesn't happen. That's always the trouble with these things. I could swear something touched my knee. Of course it could have been the edge of his coat brushing against me or it could have been his leg when he changed position or it could have been something someone dropped from the balcony or it could have been his goddamn grungy hand. Nothing I can do but sit and wait and see if it happens again.

It happens again! This time there's no mistake. It's his hand. It skims across my knee. Now, it could be accidental or it could be on goddamn purpose. I'm beginning to perspire something awful. I even feel nauseous. I look behind me and sure enough, the matron's face is still framed in the window of the door. I don't even dare glance in Cici's direction because I have to look past the creep. I'll give him one more chance.

Big mistake. This time it doesn't just brush against me. It stays there. *There's a hand on my knee!* I'm frozen to the spot. Nothing moves on the outside, but inside my head it's all tearing around frantically. There's a hand on my knee! Gross! My eyes are staring so hard I think they're going to pop. Oh, God! I'm trapped between the dragon in the back and this disgusting goon. I want to slam his hand off me and scream, "Get away from me, you filthy old man!" I want to kick him with all my might right in the shin. I want to run out of this horrible theater. I want to go home!

"Get away from me, you filthy old man!" My God, did I say that? No . . . it's Cici and she's yelling at the top of her lungs, and everybody is turning to look, and now she winds up and gives him a bonebreaker kick right in the shin, and he jumps a mile and grabs his leg and lets out a long "Ooooooh . . ."

Believe it or not, I haven't moved a hair. Now Cici pushes past him and grabs my hand.

"Come on. This stinks." And turning to the man who's still rubbing his leg, she says good and loud, "You disgusting pervert."

She really has guts.

Cici isn't finished yet. She pulls me out into the aisle, turns to the man, and shaking her finger just like my mother would do, really chews him out.

"You've got some nerve. I ought to call the police." Naturally nobody in our section is watching the movie anymore, but the rest of the audience is in a fury, whistling, stamping, and shouting for quiet. The old guy has slumped so far down into his seat that he's nothing but a pile of raincoat. Everyone around is grumbling at him and making hostile remarks. Finally he's so shamed that he leaps up and races out, knocking into the matron charging straight for us. There's no place to hide and the only place to run is the emergency exit. The matron or the movie?

We both make the same decision at the same second and shoot right out the door and into the back alley. Well, there goes thirty-four cents down the drain.

"I guess that wasn't such a good idea," Cici says, and she looks really upset. "Sorry you wasted all that money." Sometimes I can't tell whether she's serious or what. Just in case she's not kidding, I tell her it's okay, I'll catch them at home.

"Where?" She says it like I'm nuts.

"TV," I say. In the back of my mind, I'm not sure she'll even know what I'm talking about. But it doesn't make any difference because Cici is already halfway into another conversation and I can tell from the sparks that she's got a new plan. And it's going to be a beaut.

"I still got the other half of our tickets. Maybe I can talk to the guy at the door. I've got the perfect story. All I say is . . ."

Oh, no. I can't believe her. I'd rather go back to the manager at Woolworth's than mess with that matron. Cici really freaks me out, but I love her. I never had a friend who was nuttier or more exciting. She sure is different, except she's not. It's that weird familiarity thing again. Like right now she's gabbing on about her newest scheme and I'm not even listening. I'm just watching her expressions and the way she moves her hands and all, and thinking how she reminds me of someone I know. It's on the edge of my brain, but I can't grab it. And it's going to drive me loony.

". . . and if it doesn't work? So tough. It's worth the try. What do you think? Wanna try?"

I'm so involved in trying to figure out who she looks like that I miss half her plan, but that's okay because the part I did catch was all about some dreaded tropical disease and the life-saving medicine we supposedly left on the seat in the theater, and all I have to do is pretend I'm a blind nun.

"Sounds like a great idea, Cici." I try not to choke too loud. "But I'm really kind of beat, and besides, I'm getting tired of dragging this suitcase around. Would you mind if we passed it up for now?"

"Sure thing. Why don't we dump your things at my house and I'll save the stubs for tomorrow?"

Maybe I'll feel more like a blind nun tomorrow.

Seven

We start walking down the alley toward the street. Of course I have no idea where she lives so I just follow along. When we hit the end of the alley we turn right and we're on the main street again. This time we walk slowly and I get a chance to look around. First store I see is a National Shoe store. I study the window slowly and carefully. Last week I bought a pair of espadrilles in the one around my neighborhood for $14. This store obviously doesn't carry espadrilles, but they do have a whole lot of really gross shoes with little wedgies for prices all the way up to $2.99. That's right, two dollars and ninety-nine cents. For shoes. Not slippers—regular shoes. It's getting harder and harder to keep my cool.

We walk past other stores and it's the same story. All the prices are ridiculously low and the clothes are weird and the people are strange-looking and I'm running out of excuses.

I have to admit that I don't feel as freaked as I did at first. Maybe that's because I'm getting used to it or maybe it's Cici. She couldn't possibly be a part of anything that would hurt me. I just know it. I trust her. Absolutely. Besides, I've got at least two inches and ten pounds on her so she better not try anything funny. Okay, that's settled. Now all I have to do is get my head together and examine this whole thing calmly and rationally. Later I can get hysterical.

Right now I've got to be objective.

If this kind of thing happened to a character in a book I would say it's got to be science fiction, but since it's really happening to me, it's more like science nonfiction. That's a good start, isn't it? And another thing. I'm pretty sure that I'm not on another planet or anything far out like that. I mean, everything is only slightly different . . . like an old movie.

I know it's not like the twenties because I just saw *The Great Gatsby* and nobody was dressed like this, and besides, the cars and the clothes and everything look more like the ones in the beginning of that Barbra Streisand movie, *The Way We Were*. I think that was supposed to take place in the forties. Okay, so just say this is the forties. The forties! I must be out of my head, whacko. I mean, how come? How can I be in the forties, and if I am, what am I doing here and how am I ever going to get home and back to my family in the seventies?

Cool it, Victoria.

This kind of calm rational thinking can really make a

person crazy. Still, I can't beat around the bush anymore. I've got to say it. So here goes.

I think some horrendously screwy thing has happened to me and I got zapped back in time. I know this sounds really far out, but just suppose somehow I fell into a time fault. You know, like those faults they have in the earth in California. Well, maybe there's something like that in time and somehow I got sucked into one and zoomed back thirty years. My science teacher is always saying that nothing is ever wasted in nature, so maybe all those used-up years are still around somewhere, sort of stored way down deep in the center of time. I suppose I better level with you. I got a thirty-two on my last science exam. But just say I'm right. Then that's okay. I mean I'm lucky because I could have fallen much farther, like thousands or even millions of years, and then there would have been dinosaurs or an ice age or something really gross like that.

Okay, so great, I only fell thirty years. Still, how am I going to get home? Or will I have to stay here always? Which is awful because except for Cici I'm absolutely alone here. In fact, it's even worse than that because I've got this outrageous secret and I can't even tell her. Just picture if I did. She'd probably think I was nuts or a liar or just trying to be cute and then she'd stop liking me and I couldn't bear that. I definitely can't let her know.

Another thing that's even scarier. I know you can fall down into something, but I'm not that lousy in science not to know that you can't fall up. In other words, I could be stuck here for the rest of my life.

And if that's true, and it looks like it may be, I'm never going to see my mother and father again. Even Nina. I'll never have to look at that grungy face again. I can feel the tears coming already. Count to ten, jerk, think of your big toe, fine, now think of your little toes, whatever you do, don't cry! Think happy. Hey, no science term paper! No use. Here they come . . . ten, nine, eight, big toe, little toe . . .

"Hey, what's the matter?" Cici's voice is very concerned.

I can't tell her the whole truth, but since she's my only friend, I have to tell her something. "I don't know," I say. "I just feel upset. Maybe it's because I had this really bad fight with my mother before I left and then when she wasn't there to meet me . . . Oh, I don't know, it's so depressing to fight with your mother, especially if you're not going to see her . . ."

"It's better that way."

"Huh?"

"Sure. Gives her time to cool down. Mothers aren't so great, but they don't usually hold grudges. I know mine doesn't. That may be the best thing about her. Actually, she's probably a great mother—you know, cooking, cleaning, not letting you sit in a wet bathing suit and all that, but she's really tough—strict and very serious about being a mother."

"Mine too. I mean serious about being a mother. That's really our big problem. She can't understand me at all because it's like she was never a kid. Like she was born a mother."

"I know exactly what you mean. She probably drove her Barbie dolls crazy too. I've promised myself that when I have kids I'm really going to understand them because I'll remember what it was like for me."

I tell Cici that that's just the way I feel, and we congratulate ourselves on what sensational mothers we're going to make. And you know what? I'm beginning to feel better. Cici seems to have that effect on me. It's her kooky way of looking at things. She sort of tilts everything.

"I live right up this hill and in half a block." Cici interrupts my daydreams and points up a very steep hill.

I've been so involved in trying to get it all together that I didn't even realize we weren't on the main drag anymore. Now we're in sort of a residential area with mostly old wooden houses. Not really like suburbia, more like the city but with private homes, one jammed in right next to the other with little squiggly cement walks like you draw when you're a little kid. Everything looks very neat and clean. In fact, since that funny little Kilroy picture in the subway, I haven't seen one speck of graffiti anywhere.

We pass one of those old-fashioned candy stores and I tell Cici maybe I should try to phone my mother again.

"Sure," she says, "go on. I'll wait out here."

"I'll only be a sec," I say, and shoot inside, practically falling over the newspaper stand. A paper called *PM* slides down to the floor. Now's my chance. I bend down to pick it up and zero right in on the date. I've got to know if I'm . . . oh, wow!

It says May 19, 1944. 1944! I can't believe it! I'm always wrong. How come I have to be right this time?

"You want that paper, young lady?" says the fat man behind the counter. My brain is in a terrible turmoil. What's happening? *How* did it happen? 1944? Somebody—anybody—help! But all I can say to the man is, "No . . . uh, thank you. That's all right. I just wanted to use the phone."

"Right behind you." He points to a wall phone next to the candy counter. And I think, Grandma, you were never righter. Talk about the wrong time and the wrong place! It's even silly to call, I tell myself, but so what, I've got nothing to lose. Have I? Probably there'll be no answer anyway. Still, this whole thing is so nutty maybe there's something else I didn't think of, like just suppose it isn't 1944 all over. I mean, maybe it's only here in Queens. That's no crazier than anything else that's happened, is it? Besides, the fat man is looking at me like I'm a loony so I'd better use the phone before he starts asking questions.

I count to thirteen, which is my lucky number, and start dialing. One ring . . . two rings . . . three rings . . . my God, someone's answering!

"What number are you dialing, please?"

Typical. It's the operator. I'm so nutty. I dialed wrong. I tell her, "Sorry," hang up and dial again. This time I'm very careful.

"What number are you dialing, please?"

Again. I must really be some kind of jerk, but I swear I dialed it perfectly. I tell the operator the number.

"One moment, please."

My luck, it's probably out of order. No wonder no one answered all this time. I should have thought of that. I'll bet they've been going out of their heads worrying about why I didn't call. Oh, boy.

"I am sorry, madam. There is no such number."

"You're kidding."

"I am sorry, madam. We show no such number."

"Hey, wait, I forgot to say that's Manhattan, not Queens."

"Madam, our listings cover all five boroughs."

"Well, you have to be looking it up wrong because that's my own number and we've had it for as long as I can remember, so you see there has to be some mistake. Please look it up again."

"Madam, if you give me your party's name, I will check the number."

"This is silly. I mean, I know the number's right."

"Very well, madam."

"No, wait, please. The name's Martin. Philip Martin."

"One moment, please."

This has got to be the wildest thing. That's absolutely my number. I mean, a person doesn't forget the number they've had practically all their lives.

"I'm sorry, Madam, we have no listing for Philip Martin."

"You've got to. I mean . . ." Obviously I'm beginning to lose my cool, so I take a deep breath and very calmly ask her to check 81 Central Park West for that name. Of course, no matter how silly she is, she's got to find our name at that address. Unless . . .

"Madam, we have no 81 Central Park West."

Help!

"Now, look, operator. You just have to look it up again."

"I'm sorry, madam."

"Will you stop calling me madam. I'm not even fourteen yet."

"Is there another spelling?"

"Of my own name? Do you think I'm a moron or something?"

"I'm sorry, madam."

"I told you, I'm not a . . . oh, forget it."

And I crash the phone down hard. Remind me to change my lucky number. Thirteen stinks. For a change my eyes are all watery. You probably think I cry a lot, but I can't help it this time. I've got this really lost empty feeling, and worse than that, I feel there's no hope anymore. I mean, it's all true. This is definitely the forties and I have no home and no family and I'm going to be stuck here forever. That's plenty hard to take.

Eight

"Hey, is anything wrong?" I didn't even notice Cici come into the store and now she's standing there staring at me. I do a few silly things like blowing my nose and scratching my eyes so she won't see that I've been crying. I'm sure I don't fool her one bit.

"They're not home." I have to tell her something.

"It's still early—don't worry. You can try again when we get to my house. C'mon, let's go. We're almost there."

And we go outside and start walking up the hill.

"Cici! Hey, Cici!"

About fifty feet behind us two girls about our age are shouting to Cici.

"Hey, wait up!" they call, running up to us.

We stop to wait for them, and Cici tells me that they're friends from her class.

"What's buzzin', cousin?" the taller one says when they reach us. Then they both just stop and stare at me.

Cici takes over the introductions. "This is my friend Victoria and she's staying over at my house, maybe for the weekend." That's the first I've heard of any weekend. My own feeling is that I must get ahold of my mother and get back home. I mean deep, deep down I know this is all crazy and that she's waiting for me somewhere. But I don't say anything.

"Victoria, this is Betty," she says, nodding to a skinny girl with short stringy hair that almost looks dirty, "and this is Joyce." Joyce is cute but kind of stuck-up-looking.

I'm sort of surprised that Cici's friends are so gross. I'll have to ask her about them later.

In the most outrageous naa-naa voice, Joyce, Miss Snot, who is really too much, tells Cici that she and Betty have been studying practically nonstop since last night.

"I don't know how you're going to do it with those notes you've got," says Betty with such a giggle in her voice that I'd like to push my hand in her silly face.

Whatever exam they're talking about is really getting to Cici. She starts to squirm and tries to change the subject real fast, but Joyce isn't about to let her.

"You must tell Cici to show you her notes," she says to me. "They're the cat's pajamas." And both she and Betty double over in hysterics.

Obviously Cici's notes are horrendous.

"Wish I could lend you mine," Joyce says, gloating so much

I may throw up, "but I'll be using them all weekend. Sorry."

"Yeah, well, that's okay. I've got a lot of it in my head already and besides . . . uh . . ." Cici is sort of scrambling around for some way to recover. She finds it. "Victoria's going to help me."

No way. Unless she's only getting a D and wants an F. Of course, I don't say any of that. I just stand there trying to look very scientific.

"She's a straight-A science student. . . ."

There she goes. Miss Overkill.

". . . In fact, she's so far ahead that she's already finished all her biology and chemistry and she's started first-year trigonometry."

"Trigonometry?" Joyce announces, real smart-ass. "Funny, I always thought that was math."

"You mean you really thought astral trig was math?" I say brilliantly. "How amusing." There's this magnificent silence while we all watch Joyce's jaw drop down to her knees. Cici is so pleased with me I'm afraid she may break into applause and spoil the whole scene. I feel sensational.

"Hey, look, we're really late," Cici says. "We must get home. See you tonight at the party."

"See you later," I say.

You should see their faces at the thought of an extra girl at their precious party.

"Is she coming?" Betty asks Cici, giving her eyes that "Oh, God" roll.

Cici's not about to listen to any more jazz from these two,

so she tells them straight out, "If you don't like it, lump it." And she gives me a little shove and we start running up the hill.

At the top of the hill we turn onto a quiet street with big old oak trees. On one side are old wooden frame houses, and on the other, the uphill side, are huge fortress-like brick homes each set about fifty feet up from the sidewalk. They're all big and dark and sort of loom over the street. Sounds scary but it isn't. In fact, they're kind of silly-looking because the structures are so gigantic and the property is so tiny that the houses practically have to hold their breath to fit on the land.

Cici's head is down as we walk along the block, and I think she's forgotten all about me. I feel a little uncomfortable because, you know, I'm very dependent on her.

"Hey!" she says, and suddenly the kookiness is back in her face and I know what she's been doing. She's been cooking up a new plan. "Come here," she says, and pulls me into one of the open garages. "Want one?" she says, coming up with a short unfiltered cigarette from some side pocket of her bag. It's a little crushed but otherwise perfectly smokable. There's no point in ruining her surprise by telling her that I hate unfiltered cigarettes. They make me even more nauseous than filtered ones, which do a pretty good job on my stomach.

She lights the cigarette and takes a puff and hands it to me. "Want a drag?" she says.

Naturally I can't refuse. I take the tiniest puff possible, hold it in my mouth for a couple of seconds, and then slowly let it kind of leak out between my teeth. There's got to be a better way. I hand it back to Cici, who takes another drag.

"Do you inhale?" she asks me, trying to be real cool as the smoke pours out of her nose and winds its way right into her eyes. "Ohh . . . that stings."

"That happens to me all the time," I tell her, but she's too busy jumping around and rubbing her eyes. "And it's worse when I inhale. I get so dizzy I think I'm going to fall over."

"Me too. Sometimes after dinner I sneak up to the bathroom for a butt and I get so woozy that the floor tiles start rolling up and down."

"I'm probably not going to be a smoker. It's really bad for you."

"Yeah? Where'd you hear that?"

Cici has this way of kidding with a deadpan face. At first I didn't know when she was joking, but now I think I can tell.

"Except grass." I keep a straight face too. "Now that's really good for you."

"Really healthy," she says, "if you're a cow."

"I mean *grass*, dope."

"Hey!" Suddenly she looks insulted. Oh boy, we're on different wavelengths. She probably never heard of grass or . . . wow! She must think I'm calling her a dope. No way to explain so I change the subject fast.

"I don't think those two creeps, Betty and what's-her-face, Joyce, were too happy about me going to the party tonight."

"Tough. If they don't like it, they can lump it."

"Yeah, those two really turn me off. Did you see what a kick they were getting out of bugging you about that science test? Please."

"Ugh! Don't even mention it. Old Horseface Davis—she's my teacher—said that if I don't get a seventy-five on it, she's going to flunk me and then I won't graduate. Can you just see me left back? Doing eighth grade again? I'd die first."

"Too right!"

"I wish Horseface would. She's such a rat fink and she hates me, which is really unfair because I've been trying very hard lately. I even did a project for extra credit—some dumb thing with an egg and a glass jar. What a flop! How was I supposed to know the egg had to be hard-boiled? You should have seen her face when she tried to do the experiment."

It must have been horrendous because just the memory of it makes Cici crack up.

"And then to top things off, I get hysterical. I knew I was in real trouble and it wasn't funny, but sometimes I get this thing where I can't stop laughing."

"Yeah. I know exactly what you mean." It's always such a relief to find someone as nutty as you are.

"That's when she exploded and gave me the ultimatum about getting a seventy-five on the final. That stinks because, except for her classes, all my other marks are great. Oh, well maybe sewing is a little problem."

"You mean that thing in your bag?"

"Yeah, my graduation dress."

I don't believe it. I mean, I'm in total shock at the thought of someone actually wearing that rag. And for graduation no less. Naturally I don't say anything, but I guess she sees it in my face because she shrugs and says, "I know, I hate sewing even worse than science."

I would say that's pretty obvious, except I don't. All I say is "I wish I could help you, but science is a killer for me, too. The minute someone mentions anything even vaguely scientific, I turn right off."

"Me too. Only I turn so far off that I even forget to take notes. Like now, I'm really up the creek because I'm missing half the notes and the other half is so crummy that I can hardly read them."

"Can't you borrow somebody else's notes?"

"No can do. Everybody needs their own notes. Oh well, you can't go crazy."

That's what my mother says, "You can't go crazy," but I think I would if I wasn't going to graduate. "What are you going to do?"

"I'll figure something out, I guess."

Something's fishy. I mean, she's much too cool. I'm really curious, so I level with her. "How come you don't seem so worried?" One look at her face and I can tell I'm right. She's got something up her sleeve.

"Yeah, well"—she looks at me real hard, like she's deciding something—"I guess I'm not."

"How come?" I'm not letting go because now I'm really curious.

"You won't say anything?"

"Are you kidding?"

"Well, this is really secret stuff. I'm finished if even a word gets out."

"I swear to God and hope to die, I won't breathe a word of it."

"I'm getting the test," she whispers.

"What do you mean?"

"This kid Ted's giving me the test." She's looking over her shoulder like she expects the CIA any second. Then she says, even softer, "His mom's my teacher."

"No way! Wow! I wouldn't have the guts for something like that. Aren't you scared you'll get caught?"

"Plenty scared. Don't even remind me. I start to sweat just thinking about it. Boy, I'd die if anyone ever found out. Of course I'd probably be expelled instantly, but what's even worse, my parents would be absolutely crushed. I know I'm not perfect but I've never done anything like *this* before. It's almost like being a criminal, but I can't help it, I'm trapped. I gotta graduate."

"What if he tells someone—like brags? You know how boys are."

"Yeah, I know, but Ted's no kid, he's almost eighteen, and besides, he'd be in as much hot water as me. After all, he's doing the stealing, right?"

"I guess so, but it's taking a big chance anyhow."

"You don't know how big. I gotta trust Ted, and, boy, is he a crud. For a teacher's kid, he's almost a delinquent. I mean it. He practically dropped out of high school last year, and he hangs around with a real tough crowd. And you want to hear the payoff?"

"Yeah."

"He likes me. Ugh!"

"Is that how come he's doing this for you?"

"Are you kidding? I'm paying him a bomb. That's how come. I didn't even ask him to do it. He must have heard about it from some of the kids because one time about a week ago we were all in Pop Stiller's malt shop and he pulls me aside and says, 'I'll get it for you.' I didn't even know what he was talking about at first so I said something like, 'Yeah, I'll bet you will,' and started to walk away, but then he followed me and whispered that he'd get the science test for me and I nearly fainted."

Cici took another drag on the cigarette and coughed three or four times. She handed it to me. This time I inhaled, and *I* nearly fainted. She didn't notice.

"At first I thought he was pulling my leg, but then when I saw he was serious I said forget it—I'm not going to get involved in anything like that—and I just walked away. Then when I got home I started thinking about not graduating. How would I ever face my family or my friends again? And then I thought about when I was in sixth grade and Harold Klinger got left back.

"He didn't find out until the last day before summer vacation when we all got our report cards. You know how that's the best day of the whole term with everyone kidding around, talking and comparing cards? Except Harold. He just sat in his seat, and his face was getting redder and redder, even his ears, and then suddenly he burst into tears—the real sobbing kind where you can't catch your breath. It was horrible. Then Mr. Bernard, who was a real rat, said to him, no sympathy, nothing, just, 'Harold, I think you'd better step out into the hall until you can control yourself.' Harold was crying so hard he could barely find the door."

The cigarette was burning down. I handed it back to Cici. "He must have been really dumb," I say.

"Yeah, but even so, I felt sorry for him. Everybody did. It was awful what getting left back did to him. He used to be the class joker and very popular, but he didn't make any friends in his new class, and when you'd meet him in the halls, he was so embarrassed he could barely look at you. I finally stopped saying anything to him because it made him so uncomfortable. And that was only being left back in sixth grade. When it happens in eighth grade and you don't graduate and all your friends go on to high school and you gotta come back to grammar school, it's the worst thing in the whole world. That's when I made up my mind. No matter what, it's not going to happen to me, even if I have to cheat. . . . I don't care. I gotta graduate."

Poor Cici. She's probably found the most sympathetic ear

in the whole country. But as bad as my own school problems are, at least I'm not involved in any stealing. Now I feel sort of squirmy for her, so I ask her if maybe there isn't another way out. Like suppose she talked to the teacher. Or maybe took a make-up test.

"With old Horseface?" Cici is shaking her head like I'm nuts. "Not even if I broke down and cried. Her greatest joy in life is the sight of tears. It's hopeless. There's no other way. If I don't get that test, I'm going to fail for sure."

"What if I helped? Suppose we really crammed all night and all day tomorrow?"

"With my notes I could cram for about seven minutes."

"Hey, I got it. Let's Xerox somebody's. It only takes a minute."

"Huh? What's a Xerox?"

Oh, wow! That was dumb. They probably didn't even invent the Xerox machine yet. I have to make up something quick because it sounds like a way out, so she's really curious.

"It's a city word for putting the snatch on something." I could go on and tell how it's named after this famous robber, Jason Xerox, but I can tell she's not interested. So instead I ask her, "What about telling your parents and asking them if they can do something with the teacher?"

"No good. You don't know my parents, especially my mother. I'd never hear the end of it . . . and besides, it wouldn't work. Horseface hates parents worse than kids. There's just no other way, Victoria. I know, because all I've been doing for the last five days is thinking about this thing and I've got no choice. I gotta get the exam and that's all there is to it."

I guess there's no point in telling her what a bad feeling I'm getting just thinking about the plan. She's really trapped. She has to take the gamble, but I'm scared for her.

We're so busy with our conversation that the cigarette burns out before either of us has a chance to really smoke it. Thank God. I hated it anyway. I only do it for effect. I mean, I think I look very mature smoking.

"Let's go," Cici says, picking up her bag. "I live just a few houses down."

We walk down the street about four houses. At the fifth house Cici stops.

"Up here's where I live."

Up here turns out to be a huge square stack of dark red bricks in the shape of a house—you know, the kind you draw when you're about five years old. Two stories high, door in the center, double windows upstairs and down, and smack in the middle of the roof, the chimney. It's not very beautiful, but it sure looks solid. You could huff and puff forever and it'd still be there.

"Hey, look, Victoria . . . uh . . ."

I can see Cici's really worrying, I mean about telling me her secret. Now she's scared I'll let it slip. Of course I assure her it's absolutely safe with me. Cross my heart and hope to die.

"I'm sorry, Victoria, but you're the only other person who

knows and—well, it occurred to me that I really don't know you all that well and . . . oh forget it, that was jerky. I knew the minute I met you that you were going to be my friend . . . my special friend . . . and that I could trust you with anything."

That's the way I feel about Cici too, but I'm not ready to tell her my secret yet. Not until I'm absolutely certain that I'm not nuts.

"Let's go," she says, and starts up the steep flight of brick steps.

"Hey, wait." I stop midflight. "I forgot to ask you about your family."

"Shoot."

"Well, do you have any sisters or brothers?"

"First there's my brother, the meanest, most despicable, lowest form of creepy crud tease in the Western Hemisphere. Then there's my mother. I told you a little about her. She's in charge of the house and the kids—that's me and the creep. She's a regular mother type—you know, tells you when to eat, what to eat, where to go, when to come home, what to wear, and when to breathe. Other than that, you're completely on your own. As for my dad, he's the policy-maker, the great white father. Actually, I love my parents. Until lately, anyway. Now all we do is fight. They just don't realize that I'm not a baby anymore. I'm fourteen and my mother's got to stop hanging over me like I'm a two-year-old."

"Stop. I know just what you mean. My mother does the same exact thing and it really grosses me out."

"I figure she's probably just going through a stage, but I don't know if I can wait for her to outgrow it."

Cici opens the door. Standing in the hall, I can see a large living room on one side and the dining room on the other. In front of me is a flight of stairs leading to the first floor. There's a lot of yellows and golds and oranges, and everything looks solid like the house, neat and clean and homey. Cici goes up a couple of steps and calls out. "Mommy! Mom! I'm home and I've got a friend with me."

"I'll be right down."

Nine

My God! That voice slams into my stomach like a two-by-four. I can't catch my breath. Luckily, Cici is facing the steps and doesn't see me. It's that voice. Oh, God! You won't believe this, but I know it! I'd know it anywhere, anytime. It's so unreal. . . . Oh, let it be a dream. I squeeze my eyes as hard as I can, then open them crazy wide, pinch my hand, and will my mind to wake up. But nothing happens. You know that sort of liquid quality you feel in a dream where everything kind of flows and changes easily? Well, there's nothing flowing or fuzzy or hazy or anything less than dead real here, in this hall, in this house, at this minute.

And there's another thing. This minute. This damn very minute is happening right now thirty years ago. It's the creepiest thing that's ever happened to me, and I'm really shook up because now I know that it's not a dream and soon that woman is going to come down those stairs and I don't know whether to scream or run away or what. I've never been so scared in all my life and nothing's happening. I mean, I'm not crying or running or anything. Only sweating and standing here like an idiot, waiting.

"Come on. I'll make you a malted." Cici's voice startles me. I forget she was even there. Now I stare at her. Who is she, anyway?

"Don't you like malteds?" I guess I didn't answer her. I'm busy trying to work up enough spit for a swallow, to get my tongue off the roof of my mouth and say something. No sound comes out. All I can manage to do is nod my head and follow her through the dining room into an enormous kitchen and stand there like some kind of jerk while she starts making a malted in a real malted machine like they have in drugstores.

"Chocolate ice cream all right?" she asks. This time my head bobs up and down like a mechanical toy and she looks at me kind of funny. I stop the stupid head-nodding, but I still can't speak because if I open my mouth even a crack I know I'm going to burst out crying. I just stand here trying to think of a million other things, but it's no use. Big blobs of tears are crowding my eyes, but luckily Cici doesn't look up from the malteds.

"Hey, listen," she says. "If my mother asks where we've been all day, just say the movies. Forget about all the rest, including the matron and Mr. Hot Pants, okay?"

Before I can answer (which I couldn't do anyway) that voice from upstairs calls out, "Hello, hello."

"Here, Mom, in the kitchen."

There's a sound of footsteps coming down the stairs. At first they're far away at the top and they sound soft, but they get harder and sharper as they clip-clap their way down. I hold my breath to hear better. Now they're at the bottom and the sound of them pounds in my head. She's coming. I panic. And now there's something else reaching for me, something worse, another thought, but I push it away, too frightened to let it in.

"Cici . . . the bathroom. Where's the bathroom? Quick, I don't feel so good."

"Right there." She points to a door right off the kitchen. I rush for it and slam the door behind me just as the footsteps come through the dining room and into the kitchen.

The bathroom is tiny with barely enough room for the toilet, a small sink, and me. The rest of the space looks like it's being devoured by the wallpaper, a gaudy jungle of the biggest orange and yellow mums I've ever seen. There's a tacky little gold-framed mirror straight ahead of me and I stare hard into it. Maybe it'll be like an Alice-through-the-looking-glass thing and if I concentrate hard enough I'll be able to walk right into the mirror and come out the other side, in the seventies in my own house. That's really not so unthinkable when you consider how weird everything else has been. But no luck. Nothing happens, except the dumb face looking back at me is getting blotchier and sweatier and more scared-looking.

I can hear the voices in the kitchen but I can't make out what they're saying. I try not to imagine. I flush the toilet so they don't get too suspicious. I need time to think. I have to get out of here somehow. But the only possible way is through the porthole-size window over the sink. I'm on the first floor so there's a real drop, but I don't know if I can squeeze through. Maybe if I open it all the way. . . . Forget it. There are two large screws on both sides of the frame that keep it from opening any more than four inches.

"Hey, Victoria." It's Cici's voice. "Are you okay?" I try to answer but the most I can do is shake my head emphatically, which of course she can't hear. A couple of seconds go by and she calls my name again.

"Victoria? Coming out?"

I have no choice. I can't stay here forever. I splash some cold water on my face, but I'm still pretty splotchy-looking. I pull up my socks, comb my hair, tighten my belt, smear on some lip gloss, blow my nose, and wipe out the sink where a couple of hairs have fallen. By now my socks have fallen again.

"Victoria?" Oh my God. It's that voice again. "Are you sick, dear?"

I take a very deep breath and start to unlock the door and squeak it open inch by inch. This approach is excruciating, like going into an icy pool bit by bit. The only way to do it is to throw the door open all at once. One. Two. Three. And I do it. Nothing. The door is wide open but there's no one there. Maybe they vanished. Maybe it's all over. Or maybe they're just standing on the other side of the kitchen where I can't see them. I walk the four short steps into the kitchen and . . . there they are.

She's beautiful. Her hair is dark brown with soft shiny curls that almost touch her shoulders. Her cheeks look sort of flushed, they're so pink. She's wearing a silky striped blouse that matches the orangey red of her lipstick. She smiles at me, and her gray eyes sort of squint like they always do when she doesn't wear her glasses. She comes toward me, friendly, welcoming, a fragrant aroma of Arpège, and whoosh—that icy wind shoots through my stomach. I can't stop myself. I back away. In all my life, since as far back as I can remember, this is the first time I have ever been afraid of my own grandmother.

That's who she is. Sure, she's younger and slimmer and all that. But there's no question. I know for absolute certain that she's my grandma. And that has to mean—no! I won't let the thought come any closer. It can't be!

"How nice to meet you, Victoria."

My very own grandmother says that like it's the first time she ever laid eyes on me in her life. And of course it is! I'm completely thunderstruck. If she comes any closer I might scream or, more likely, throw myself into her arms and just hang there for dear life. She takes a step nearer, but I don't budge. I just stay in one spot, a big blob glued to the floor.

Oh, Grandma, can't you see? It's me, Victoria. Why don't you know me, your own granddaughter? Don't you love me? (Dumb. How can she love me when she doesn't even know me?)

"Don't worry, dear, we'll be able to get in touch with your parents. In the meantime just make yourself comfortable and try not to worry too much." She says the whole thing in a kind but formal voice. It's hopeless. She hasn't got the vaguest idea who I am. Then she turns to Cici and says, "I know Felicia is delighted to have you stay with us in the meantime."

Felicia! Not Cici. Felicia! I let the thought in now because there's no way to fight it. I turn and stare at Cici.

"Victoria? Is something wrong?" One of their voices comes through to me and I think I shake my head.

Felicia! Cici! My own mother! Holy cow, am I dumb. It had to be. Unbelievable! I told you she looked familiar. I mean, she didn't really, but there were things about her that reminded me of someone. Not so much the features, but more like the expressions, the way she talked—I don't know what, something, maybe the look in her eyes. I just knew I knew her all along, only I thought she was a friend of somebody's or some girl I met somewhere. That's what threw me. I thought she was a kid like me.

But she's not. She's a woman. Felicia, Cici, whatever she wants to call herself, there's one thing for sure, this crazy nutty kid who isn't afraid to zonk a pervert in the shin, turn Woolworth's upside down, sneak cigarettes in a garage, and probably do a million other kooky things and maybe even some awful things like buying a science test, isn't my friend at all.

She's my *mother*!

Ten

By now you probably figure I've flipped my lid. Well, so do I, but it doesn't change things. Right this minute I'm looking straight at my mother, only she's fourteen years old. I mean, it's fantastic that I'm looking into the very same yellow-brown eyes that I've looked into thousands of times before. I don't know how come I didn't recognize that special look they have. I think I even see it now. Her hair throws me a little. My mother is blonder and curlier now, but I guess a little bleach and some curlers handle that pretty easily. And her chin. It sticks out just like my mother's. Hey, jerk, it isn't *just like*—it *is* my mother's chin.

Well, so far so good. I mean, they're just standing there. Nobody's attacking me so maybe it's not going to be so bad. In fact, I think I feel a little better now. Not so scared. After all, it is my mother and grandmother, and even if they don't know who I am, still, they're not exactly killer monsters. Actually, they're terrific people. All my friends think they're super. Whenever I go to visit my grandmother's country club, everybody is always telling me how sensational she is. And my mother? I told you before I'm the only one who doesn't like her. Except now. Now she turns out to be my best friend. So why am I still shaking?

"Aaah!" Cici says, making a grab for the overflowing malted machine. I jump a foot straight into the air. I guess I'm still a little scared.

"How many times do I have to tell you not to fill it so high," my grandmother says, sounding more like my mother than my grandmother. "Here." She hands Cici the sponge. "Before it drips on the floor."

Cici wipes the counter and fills two glasses with mostly foam and hands one to me. I've got to make myself talk or they're going to think I'm some kind of a moron.

"Thank you," I say. It isn't much but it's all I can manage now in my condition. I really hope my grandmother, or Mrs. Lyons (I guess that's what I'll have to call her now), just thinks I'm shy, not unfriendly. I know she's not going to love me in a day, but I do want her to like me.

"Victoria, would you like to try your house again?" She sounds like she likes me okay.

"Yes, please," I say, squinching my mouth in smile formation, I hope.

"Felicia, let Victoria use the hall phone."

We finish our malteds.

"After you've called, Felicia will introduce you to her brother."

An "ugh" sound plus an "ugh" look is Cici's answer.

"I don't like that, Felicia." That's exactly what my mother says to me when I do something like that about Nina. But what's really incredible is how my mother is about her brother now. I'm talking about the 1970s. I told you how close they are, practically like twins. Uncle Steve can do no wrong. And she's always saying how she would do anything for him and he would do anything for her. In fact, she's always using him as an example of how siblings are supposed to act toward each other. Wow! What baloney. Wait till I tell her . . . What am I talking about? Who am I going to tell? Cici? My fourteen-year-old mother? Sure, I'll just tell her everything. I'll just go right up to her and say, "Hey, Cici, you may not believe this but . . . you're my mother."

"Of course, dear," she'll say. "Now, if you just step over here these nice men with the nets want to have a word with you."

We go into the hall and Cici shows me the telephone.

"Come upstairs to my room when you've finished." And Cici heads up the steps.

I haven't even got the nerve to dial my own number, so I just make up any old number and call it. Lucky for me, there's no answer.

"Victoria!" Cici pokes her head out from the top of the steps. "Any luck?"

"Nope. Still not home."

"They'll probably be home by tonight," she says, coming down the stairs. "You know you can stay here as long as you want."

How's fifty years for starters?

"Anyway," she says, "I was sort of hoping you could stay over for the weekend. I really want you to go to that party tonight."

"Me too." I guess I'm a lousy actress because she looks at me in a funny way.

"Victoria, I think something else is bothering you. Ever since we got home you've been acting sort of—I don't know—scared. Look, you're my good friend, so I'm not going to BS you. You're going to think I'm crazy but . . . uh . . . well, are you afraid of my mother?"

"Afraid of your mother?" I guess I didn't fool her, but I deny it like crazy. "Of course not. I think your mother's terrific, really sensational." This time I really sound convincing, and why shouldn't I? She's my own grandmother and I really do think she's super. "I just felt kind of worried about barging in like this. You know, not invited and all."

"Forget it. She doesn't mind at all. Wow, that's a load off my mind. I really was worried that you hated it here and especially my mother. I know I have some complaints about her, but, gee, she isn't exactly a killer monster."

Where have I heard that before?

I smile and she seems satisfied and we go up the stairs. At the top to the left is what must be my grandparents' room. I follow Cici down a long hall past a small bedroom and then to Cici's room. It doesn't look like her at all. It's really large and elegantly decorated with heavy silk drapes right down to the floor, a delicate crystal chandelier, and, my God, there's my dresser! It's the one from my room at home, the one I've had since as far back as I can remember. The only difference is that on this one the white marble top is in perfect condition. Mine got cracked when we tried to move it a couple of years ago. I've always known it belonged to my mother when she was a kid, but it's so weird to actually see it here in her room. I can't believe my clothes aren't in the drawers.

The room is spotless. I mean absolutely perfect, couldn't be neater. What a disappointment. Well, nobody's perfect. Actually, I should have suspected because my mother's always nagging me to clean my room.

"Here's some space for you to dump your stuff," Cici says, opening the middle drawer of the dresser. The entire inside of the drawer is a mass of rolled-up lumps of clothes jammed together. Gross! I love it. She digs her hands in one corner and shoves them over to make room for my things, only she can't shove much because it's so overloaded already, and the only way I can possibly get my clothes in is to roll them up and stuff them in. Cici holds her things back while I squeeze mine in, and then together we slide the drawer shut quickly, tucking in the hangouts. No problem. I've been doing it for years.

"Nice going," she says, and I'm beginning to feel really comfortable, what with my own dresser and all. The "all" is the mirror. I didn't notice before but that's my mirror too.

"I'd better hide these butts in the secret drawer," Cici says and starts to scramble through her pocketbook while I open the "secret drawer" for her. It's a great hiding place. It's impossible to tell by looking at the dresser that there's a fourth drawer at the bottom because it has no handles and it's disguised as a panel. In fact, you have to slide your fingers underneath to pull it open. Nobody ever knows. . . . So how come I know? Ooh, that was dumb.

"You're the first person who ever knew about that drawer without my showing them," Cici says, shaking her head in amazement. "How did you know it was there?"

No sweat. I tell her the absolute truth. "I have the exact same dresser."

"No kidding."

"Swear to God. It's identical, even has the same round mirror." It feels fantastic to be actually telling the complete truth about something. All the secret-keeping can really make you uptight. "Mine even has that fancy trim on the edge of the mirror."

"No fooling?"

"Right. And those identical tiny little flower things too."

"I'm really surprised . . ."

"It's absolutely incredible, but it's got to be the same exact set . . ."

". . . because it's not a set. We bought the mirror separately."

"Except that my mirror is a lot rounder than yours and smaller. In fact, it's only half the size and the flowers are so tiny you can barely make them out. Actually, they look more like butterflies with extra wings." I'm wishing somebody would stuff an old sock in my mouth or the house would catch fire or something so I could stop. No way. "Truthfully, it's more like a picture than a mirror. I suppose that's why we keep it in the living room."

One of the best things about Cici is that she doesn't get thrown easily. She sees she's dealing with a raving lunatic whose face is probably getting redder and hotter by the second and whose mouth won't stop, so with spectacular compassion and great cool, she just cuts in and changes the subject.

"I gotta get out of these things or they're going to be all cruddy for tonight." And with that she unbuttons her skirt, casually lets it slide to the floor, and steps out of it. The blouse she lets fall in another heap a couple of feet away. I love it! Would you believe my mother, who is forever bugging me to clean my room, is a worse pig than I am? At least I aim for the chair. Of course sometimes the chair gets pretty loaded and a few things might slip to the floor, but that's different.

Cici pulls a pair of shorts and a T-shirt out of the top drawer (we even keep our shirts in the same drawer) and starts to put them on. You wouldn't believe the shorts. They're made of some kind of real sleazy white material with horrendous puckery gathers at the waist and pleats in front and back. Are they gross! I can see her eyeing my jeans.

"If you want to change, I've got a million pairs of shorts, or how about a pair of pedal pushers?"

Ugh . . . I wouldn't be caught dead in those grungy shorts. I don't even know what pedal pushers are, but they sound too cute for words so I pass them up too. Another nice thing about my mother as a kid unlike my mother as a mother is that she doesn't push. No nagging. Whatever I want is okay with her. How did she change so drastically?

Suddenly the door is pushed open by a raunchy-looking guy of about sixteen.

"Knock, you jerk." My mother greets what has to be my uncle Steve, the brother she would do anything in the world for.

"Drop dead, fink," is his loving answer. "Where's my new Submariner?"

"I haven't got the vaguest," she sneers.

"Liar." The natural answer. I'm happy to say this is the first time I'm really beginning to feel at home.

"I am not. You put one smelly foot over that threshold and I'm telling," says my mother.

"Where's my comic?"

"I don't know, and if you don't like it you can lump it."

"It may be true for all we know," he starts to sing a really annoying song, "but it sounds like bull to me . . ."

"Shut up and get out!"

". . . so take your chat to another prat and stop . . ."

"I'm telling . . ."

". . . bugging me."

"Mom!" she screams.

We all just stand there looking at each other. As soon as there's a silence anyplace I always feel like I have to fill it, so I look at Uncle Steve and say, "Hi, I'm Victoria." In the middle of the whole fight I got to be Miss Manners. Naturally he looks at me like I'm some kind of a roach and grunts, "Yeah," and loses interest. I hate him already. I can't believe he's so gross.

"Drop dead," he says to Cici, and starts to walk away. How dare he talk to my mother like that! I'll never forgive him.

"Mom!" she screams and races out of the room and down the hall, shouting for my grandmother in my sister Nina's best I'm-being-murdered voice.

My ex-favorite uncle takes off pretty quickly, and by the time my grandmother gets upstairs he's safely back in his room with the door shut.

"How many times do I have to tell you to stay out of your sister's room?" my grandmother says, opening Uncle Steve's door. And to my mother: "I can't leave you two alone for two minutes without trouble. Aren't you embarrassed to have your friend see you behaving like a two-year-old?"

If she wasn't embarrassed before, she certainly is now. So am I. At least I can see where my mother learned her mother phrases. But, funny thing, my grandmother seems to have forgotten them. I never hear her talk like that now. I just had a horrendous thought. Maybe mother-talk is something you use for a while, then pass on to your daughter, and one day I'll be sounding like that. No way! I swear it.

Now my grandmother studies me closely, squinting even though she has her glasses on this time, and I get the strong feeling maybe she's going to recognize me. Of course that's dumb—how could she? I haven't even been born yet. Instead, she shakes her head and smiles and says, "You know, you two look enough alike to be sisters."

Both of us look in my big mirror above the dresser. Funny, people are always saying I look like my mother, but I could never see it. Now I can. I mean, we really do look alike, almost the same color hair, and we both have oval-shaped faces. I don't know, but for the first time I can really see the resemblance. And it's eerie.

"Felicia," my grandmother says, zeroing in on the pile of clothes on the floor, "don't leave this room without putting your clothes away."

There's only one sentence in the world that can follow those instructions, and it begins, "How many times do I have to tell you . . ."

"How many times do I have to tell you to hang up your clothes when you take them off?" Of course that's my grandmother talking. What did I tell you?

"I said I will," my mother whines.

"Don't let me walk in here and see them on the floor again." I think they're reading from a script.

My grandmother stands in the doorway, hands on her

hips, waiting. With a hopeless shrug my mother bends down and starts to gather up her clothes. Satisfied, my grandmother turns to leave. "I have a Red Cross meeting. I should be home in a couple of hours. If Daddy calls, tell him I'll meet him at the ration board."

The minute my grandmother goes out of the door, Cici rolls her eyes and whispers, "Isn't she the cat's pajamas? Is your mother as bad as mine? I mean, is she always nagging you about how your room should be and things like that?"

Unbelievable! Now my mother is asking me to tell her all the horrendous things about herself. I ask you, does that do your head in or doesn't it?

"Are you kidding?" I'm not about to pass this one up. "Nobody in the whole world"—if she only knew!—"can bug you like my mother. All I have to do is leave one little soda can under my bed and she practically goes berserk. It's her big thing. She's a neatness freak. Of course she's also a homework freak and an on-time freak and a don't-borrow-anybody's-clothes freak and a don't-fight-with-your-sister freak, and that's only the beginning. Honestly, I swear I'm never going to be that way with my kid. How about you?"

"Me? Fat chance. I told you, I plan on being the most terrific mother that ever was."

"How are you going to do that?"

"Easy. Like with her room. It's hers and she can keep it any way she wants."

"You mean that?"

"You bet. Not only that, I'm never just going to barge in without knocking. The way I feel, a person's room is her own private property and that's that."

"Even if it's filled with dirty laundry and old grungy left-over food?"

"Well," Cici says with a tiny hesitation I'm not too crazy about, "maybe then I'd ask her to empty it once a week or something like that."

"What if she forgets?"

"Then I'd remind her."

"Suppose she keeps forgetting?"

"Then I'd keep reminding her."

"Probably she'd say you were nagging."

When I say that she really cracks up. In fact, we both burst out laughing.

"You know what?" she says, still laughing, "she'd probably be right. I can just hear me." And then she turns to me like I was her kid and, hand on hip, finger shaking, and sounding for absolute real, says, "Victoria, this room is a pigsty. How many times do I have to remind you to hang up your clothes, and take that empty Coke bottle out of here this instant!"

"Help! Stop! You sound just like my mother."

"God forbid!" And we both get hysterical again. Except maybe it's not so funny.

"What about other things?" I figure I'm never going to get this opportunity again so I charge ahead. "I mean like curfews and schoolwork and being on time, and what if she accidentally on purpose pushes her pain-in-the-butt sister down in the railway station. . . . What about those things?"

Now she gets kind of serious. "The way I figure, I'm going to take very good care of my child when she's little, but when she gets about our age she can run things for herself so I'm not going to interfere too much. Unless, of course, she needs me."

"My grandmother says that you change your mind about a lot of things when you grow up and have to be responsible for someone else. Especially if that someone is your own child."

"Maybe some people change, but not me. I mean it, I know exactly what kind of mother I'm going to be and I don't see how responsibility is going to make that much difference. Do you?"

"I didn't used to, but now . . . I don't know."

"Oh well, lucky we don't have to worry about it now. We got tons of time before we're mothers, and while we're waiting . . ." The kooky look is back in her eyes. "Wanna see something neat?" She takes out some black-and-white speckled notebooks and a skinny blue pamphlet. "I'll show you the slam books after. First look at this," and she puts the schoolbooks aside and hands me the pamphlet.

I have no idea what a "slam book" is, and the little blue book she gives me looks like just a bunch of dumb cartoons stapled together. The title on the front is "Wally and the King." I flip through and it turns out to be a comic book about a girl named Wally and a guy with a crown on his head and nothing else. From page two on they're having sex. Big deal!

"What d'ya think?" Cici is really anxious for my reaction so I make it big.

"Wow! That's wild," I say, but I don't really think it. Compared to *The Joy of Sex* or a lot of other stuff you can buy in any bookstore, this is a joke. I mean, it's for five-year-olds, but I guess way back in the forties this was real far out. The only thing I can think of is, "Why do they call the girl Wally?"

"Didn't you ever hear of Wallis Simpson and King Edward?"

Now I'm the dumb one so I just shake my head and say, "I guess not."

"He was the King of England who gave up his throne to marry an American divorcée. You know, the Duke and Duchess of Windsor."

"Oh yeah, I've heard of them." I really did but I never knew anything about them. "But I just didn't recognize them without their clothes." I try to make a joke so I don't look so jerky.

"My brother Steve has a deck of French cards in a little metal box but he keeps it locked up. I've combed his room from top to bottom a million times when he wasn't around but I still can't find the key."

Things really have changed a lot since my mother was fourteen. All I have to do now is look on the bookshelves in my own house and I can find all the books on sex I want, and they're a lot more explicit than this silly cartoon book.

555

"And I have something else. Well, I don't have it but Steve does and I've seen it."

Sounds interesting so I ask, "What is it?"

"Did you ever hear of Henry Miller's *Tropic of Cancer*?"

"Sure."

"Well, I know where there's a copy."

Me too. Down the street at the bookstore. But of course, I don't say that because it's such a big deal to Cici, so I pretend I'm really shocked, and that's not easy because I think I'm going to get hysterical in one minute. I mean, this is really too much.

"Nice one. Let's get it."

"Later, when he goes out. Then we'll look for that key, too."

"Cool! Are the slam books porno stuff too?"

Cici laughs and grabs one of the books and shoves it in my hands. "I can't understand how you never heard of slam books. Things must really be different in the city. Here, look through it." And she starts to show me the pages. "See, every page has a heading like cutest, best dresser, funniest, stuff like that. What you do is pass the book around the class and everyone writes in the name of the person they nominate for that category."

"Then what?"

"Then nothing. That's it. It's just fun to see who gets the most votes for anything. Especially the bad things, like who goes the farthest, the fastest, the worst rep—you know, all the awful things."

"Boy, I'd hate to be Janet Foley. She's got her name on all the gross pages. She must be pretty rank."

"You should see her—boobs out to here."

"Felicia! Felicia!" A girl's voice from somewhere outside the house is calling my mother.

"That's Carolanne, the kid from next door," she says, sticking her head way out of the window. "Yeah?"

"I got the carriage. Wanna go now?" Carolanne whoever shouts up.

"I promised her I'd go collecting this afternoon," my mother says to me.

"Collecting?"

"You know, silver."

I don't know silver, but I hate to look too dumb so I say, "Yeah, sure."

"It'll only take an hour or so if we go now."

"I'm ready." No big deal missing the rest of that porno stuff.

Eleven

We both shoot downstairs and you wouldn't believe what's waiting outside for us. There's this dumpy little twelve-year-old pudge who's got to be Carolanne pushing a million-year-old doll carriage stuffed full of rolled-up balls of silver paper. I'm smart enough to figure she's either a freak or a loony so I keep my mouth shut.

"Hubba, hubba," my mother says, and she really looks impressed.

By now she's up to her elbows digging in the mound of silver balls. "You really found the mother lode." Then she turns to me. "Terrif, huh?"

I search her face to see if she's putting me on, but no, she's serious. I figure it's probably safest to play it by ear for now. "Hubba, hubba," I say, just because I can't resist it.

We store the silver Carolanne collected in the garage and start off down the street, pushing this raunchy old carriage. We stop at every house on the block and the people are so nice. They open the doors right away (mostly they aren't even locked, and half the time they're wide open already) and give us tons of silver paper. I guess you couldn't go out and buy silver paper like you can now. You had to peel it off old cigarette wrappers or other kinds of packages.

Some of the people offer us cookies and fruit or a cold drink. It's a little hard getting used to all this trust and friendliness. In fact, I haven't yet. Every time my mother takes a cookie or a piece of fruit I hold my breath waiting for her to chomp on the razor blade.

Little by little it begins to dawn on me that this silver has something to do with the war. I don't know too much about it, but I do know that World War II happened in the forties. It must be going on right now. They probably melt down the silver and use it to make guns or something like that. I notice how concerned everybody is with what they call the "war effort." Wherever you look there are flags and big signs telling you to buy defense bonds or support your boys overseas or even A SLIP OF THE LIP CAN SINK A SHIP. I like that one best. Everyone seems tremendously patriotic.

It's amazing. We're back home with a full carriage in less than an hour. Easiest collecting I've ever done.

"Hey," my mother says, "how about playing a little tennis down at the schoolyard? It's only over at the next block."

I don't believe it. Finally my mother actually wants to play tennis with me. "Okay by me, but I must tell you I'm not too great."

"Me neither."

Yeah, sure.

"C'mon, you can use Steve's racket. Wait here a sec—I'll get the stuff," she says, and shoots into the house.

Maybe I should have said no. I'm crazy about Cici, but I don't know if I'm in the mood to get blitzed at tennis. She's really going to make me look lousy. Oh well, too late. She's back with everything already.

"Let's go," she says, and we jog off down the block.

The court is empty when we get there. Phew. At least nobody will see the massacre. As soon as we get in the court she starts apologizing, giving me a whole load of baloney about how she's only a beginner and she's pretty awful and she has no backhand and she can't serve and all that. For the first time I'm feeling a little negative about her because I hate to be conned. So I don't say much and I just let her serve.

She throws up the ball and I brace myself for her killer serve. It doesn't come the first time. Or the second time or even the third. In fact, you couldn't even call what comes plopping over the net the fourth time a serve. Not only that, she doesn't have a backhand, a forehand, or anything else. She wasn't kidding. She stinks. Wow! I'm totally stunned because I could beat her with my eyes closed. It's almost too easy. I should just take it gently, lob them over nice and easy right in the center court. Give the kid a break. Hah!

I beat her. Three sets, all of them 6–love.

"You're terrific, Victoria. You must show me your serve. It's fabulous."

And so I teach my mother the very serve she taught me last summer. How does that grab you? It grabs me. Naturally I could play all day, but by now some other kids are waiting for the court so we grab our stuff and head home.

There are some kids playing a game called ring-a-levio in the street in front of the house and they ask us to join them. Everybody's a little surprised that I don't know how to play but they show me, and after a while we switch to "kick the can" and they have to show me that too. I'm embarrassed to tell you that we even played jump rope. I haven't played that baby game in years. When that breaks up, Carolanne, my mother, and I play something called comic book. Everyone is a character from some comic. This is obviously my mother's big game because right away she says she's somebody called Sheena of the Jungle. I'm her handmaiden and poor Carolanne gets to be the jungle. It's not exactly my favorite game, and I keep thinking that if anyone saw me playing it, I'd just die. In my time thirteen- and fourteen-year-old girls just don't play games like that. Mostly we do more mature things—like pulling our friends apart, complaining about our parents, polishing our nails, and planning the next party. Maybe we've been missing something because I've been having a fabulous time this afternoon. Kick the can is a great game. So what if it's a little babyish?

"Felicia!" My grandmother's voice comes singing down the street. My mother pays no attention the first five times (temporary deafness runs in the family). There's not too much song left in my grandmother's voice on the sixth, seventh, and eighth yells, and by the ninth it's an angry croak followed by, "If you don't answer this second I'm coming to get you!" That does it.

"In a minute," answers my mother.

"Right now!" The command from my grandmother. It really cracks me up to hear my grandmother giving my mother orders.

"I'm coming," shouts my mother, making no move to end the game. We play for another five minutes or so, then my grandmother calls again and we beat it home. I have to admire my mom. I'd have folded after four yells and no more than two extra minutes at the end.

My grandfather is home when we get there. It's amazing but he practically looks the same as he does now, only with a little less belly. And he's still as funny. I mean, he can really crack me up with his jokes. Dinner is the best, though. We have chicken soup with little tiny unhatched eggs (no shells or white; they just look like mini-yolks) in it. Cici and my uncle Steve spend half the meal arguing about who gets the extra egg. A real Nina-and-me-type situation, the kind that makes you want to throw up if you have to watch it. At one point it looks like my grandmother's going to attack them, but they get the message first and cool it. From the egg argument we move smoothly on to the lost-comic-book fight, then my uncle Steve tells on my mother because she was late for school yesterday morning, and my mother says that my uncle Steve hides his cigarettes under the hall radiator, and he turns purple and calls her a liar, and she says and he says and he says and she says, and I want to cry because it feels so good, just like home.

When my mother and my uncle aren't fighting, my grand-mother is bugging my mother about eating. She can't leave the table until her plate is clean and she has to finish every drop of milk in her glass because everybody is starving in Armenia. My mother is a worse eater than I am, and not wanting to spend the rest of her life at the table, she secretly stuffs her broccoli under the potato skins, her meat into her napkin, and when everyone leaves the table, she feeds her milk to the gera-niums. I have to admit my mother did learn something as a kid. She never bugs Nina and me about eating. She's definitely the type to, because she hassles us about everything else, but I suppose she remembers how terrible it was for her. Anyhow, that business with the potato skins was pretty sharp.

After dinner I pull a fast one on everyone. I pretend I called my mother and that she said I can stay for the weekend. Of course Cici is delighted (sometimes it feels more natural to call her Cici and not "my mother") that I can go to the party with her. Me too. And besides, it gives me an extra day to come up with a reason for never going home. Oh boy, that's going to be a beaut.

Twelve

It takes us almost two hours to dress for the party. We try on every dress in her closet. She wouldn't dream of wearing pants to a party—I mean, we really get dressed up like for a wedding or something. Naturally we end up wearing the same peasant outfits we said we were going to wear in the first place. The rest of her wardrobe is right where it fell on the floor.

At some point my grandmother comes in and suggests we tidy up a bit.

"This room looks like a cyclone hit it." Guess who's talking. "Don't you dare move from here until every stitch of clothing is picked up and put away. How many times do I have to tell you . . . ," and so on and so on.

We work pretty fast and most of the clothes are picked up during the cyclone part of the speech, and by the time my grandmother finishes up with how God forbid some stranger should walk into the room and see such a mess (I suppose it's the same stranger my mother's always warning about in my own life who'll look away in disgust at my torn underwear when I've been in a horrible accident), we've folded everything and put it away. Not only that, we're dressed and ready to go.

We get to the party around eight and almost everyone is there. I get to meet Janet Foley of the big boobs, and of course grungy Betty and snobby Joyce are there, and some absolutely horrendous boys who are even shorter than the boys in my class, which practically makes them midgets. Nice.

We play the usual games—Spin the Bottle, Post Office, and a lights-out-free-for-all. Some joker turns the lights on unexpectedly and a creep named Ralph is caught with his hand under Janet's sweater. She's really too much. She doesn't even look embarrassed. Mostly the boys hang out on one side of the room (everyone calls it a "finished basement") yakking and combing their hair so it stands four inches high off their foreheads, and the girls giggle on the other side. Except for the people, it's exactly the same as all the parties I've ever gone to—a letdown.

One of the boys comes up with the bright idea that we should dance, so they put on one of those old 78 rpm records on the stereo, which is called a Victrola. It's really funky music and you should see the gross dance they do to it. It's called a jitterbug or sometimes a lindy, and it's wild. Looks like the whole thing is how far the guy can throw his partner out, and then as soon as she starts coming back he gives her another shove that either sends her spinning in nice circles or flying through the wall. Definitely not my bag. Everybody dies when Frank Sinatra comes on. Actually, he sounds pretty good if you could just listen. But you've got to dance and that's the worst. I dance with one creep and he holds me so close I think I'm going to end up behind him. It makes you feel very uncomfortable feeling so much of a boy's body. At least it does me. The next one who asks me to dance I tell him I can't because of my hammertoes. I don't even know what this is, but it sounds heavy and it's a sure turn-off.

The weirdest thing, though, is watching my own mother kissing boys, especially this guy Danny. I think she really likes him. I'm not saying he's grotesque or anything like that, but he certainly doesn't hold a candle to my father. Naturally my dad isn't here because they didn't even meet till my mother was twenty-one. It would really be great seeing them both together. But right now, if my calculations are right, he's in this dinky little burg called Ypsilanti. Too bad.

I have to admit it sort of bothers me a teeny bit seeing how much she likes this Danny jerk.

"Hey, Victoria." It's my mother pulling me aside. "What do you think?"

"About the party?"

"Parties are all the same. I mean, what do you think about Danny?"

"That freak? Ugh, he's some weirdo. I mean, he is the

grossest, grungiest, most horrendous creep I've ever seen. Mr. Instant Turn-off." And just so there's not even a pinpoint of room for misunderstanding, I let out with a real Academy Award "Yiiiich!"

My mother's face drops down to her knees and you can see she's really knocked out by my reaction. I know it's a lousy thing to do but I have to look out for my own welfare, don't I? I mean, I am definitely not taking any chances that I'll end up with him for a father. I mean, no way. For one thing, he thinks he's hot stuff, and for another he's probably a real bomb at Coney Island, and for a third, he's much too short.

Cici couldn't have been too crazy about him anyway because she sort of turns off after she hears my reaction. See that? I may have had a hand in my own destiny. Either that or I just blitzed some poor guy's big night. Whatever, the party turns out to be a real downer for me. Except for the big show-offs slinging each other around in this grotesque jitterbug that they do, hardly anybody dances or anything. Just a whole load of kissing games that wouldn't be such a drag if there was someone worth kissing. Which, of course, there isn't. And if that isn't bad enough, there's this little snook, this really jerky asshole, who actually makes an "ugh" face when he has to kiss me. Can you imagine? I mean this nobody, this little acne pimple—God, sometimes I wonder why I expose myself to these silly parties. Always, every time, they turn out to be bombs. So why am I always so anxious to go?

I can't wait for this one to end. Luckily, it's not too long because at about ten to eleven Cici pulls me over to the side and says we have to go home. We thread our way through the kissers and gropers and find our way out to the street.

"Sorry for the big rush," Cici says.

"Forget it. You did me a favor."

"They're always a big letdown, aren't they?"

"You know it!" Will you look at that? It's incredible how much we think alike. What happened to change her so much?

On the way home she tells me the bad news. At least I think it's bad news. She got a note from Ted saying that he has the test and for her to meet him on the corner at eleven thirty tonight. I'm beginning to get very nervous, but Cici looks cool.

The minute we get home she rushes me up to the bedroom. As soon as she closes the door I see that kooky expression come over her face. It's sort of half grin and half trouble, something like a wink, and it means another caper. I don't know if I'm up to a Woolworth-type adventure, but I'm certainly not going to let my own mother risk her neck alone, so like it or not I'm in it. I feed her the right question because I see she's dying to tell me her plans.

"How are we going to get out to meet Ted?"

"It's a snap," she says, and we're off and running. "First thing we do is stuff the beds to look like we're sleeping in case my parents look in. They never do, but you know me, I like to be cautious."

If she's being careful, it's going to be more horrendous than I thought.

"Then all we do is slip out of that window," she says, pointing to the one that leads onto a porch, "and slide down that tree and that's all there is to it."

Maybe it's not so horrendous. From the easy way she makes it sound, she's probably done it millions of times before. I look out of the window but I don't see any tree. It's very dark. I can make out the porch railing and what looks like plain emptiness past that except for a skinny stick poking up in the far corner. Oh, no!

"That thing over there isn't the tree, is it?"

"Right."

I don't know why I bother to ask such a silly question when I know the answer all along. "I kind of thought it would be bigger," I say nervously.

"It used to be when it was alive."

No way to stop these old air vents from opening in my stomach. A dead dried-out stick that's surely going to snap the minute I step on it. I'm probably beginning to look a little green because suddenly my mother is very concerned.

"Hey, don't worry. It makes it even easier to slide down without the leaves in your way. Besides it's only two stories and most of the time you can hang on to the edge of the porch."

Funny thing is most people think I'm pretty gutsy at home, but next to my mother I'm a scaredy-cat. I'm being silly. Like I said, she's probably done it a million times before.

"I'll be all right," I stammer. "It's just—you know, the first time it's kind of scary."

"I understand. Don't feel embarrassed. It's the first for me too and I'm probably just as scared."

"You mean you never did this before?"

"You kidding?"

"But all that business about sliding down and hanging on to the edge . . ."

"Just a matter of all the long and careful planning I've been doing . . ."

I'm relieved. I know for a fact that my mother is a fantastically responsible person. Once she gets involved in a project she can spend weeks just putting together the proper approach. She's highly organized, and I've put myself in her hands many times in almost fourteen years, so I suppose I can take a chance again.

". . . all the way home."

"What 'all the way home'?" I suppose I wasn't listening.

"That's when I worked the plan out."

All the way home! The party was half a block away. I take another look at the tree and it's even skinnier than before. Ah, well, I have no choice anyway. I'm certainly not going to let her meet this creep alone.

"Count me in." The sacrifices we make for our parents.

"Great. Watch, I'll show you how to do the beds." And she starts rolling up a blanket. When it's about the size of a four-year-old, she slides it under the covers, punches a spot in the pillow, and says, "There!" She's got what looks like a full-grown dwarf all squinched up in twenty-degree weather in the middle of December. The fact that it's the end of May and seventy-five degrees could cause a credibility gap just big enough for a grandmother to fall into, but I suppose it's no time to be picky, so I just shut up and start rolling. Besides, the bed is nothing compared to that tree.

Thirteen

"That's perfect, Victoria," my mother says, inspecting my handiwork and sounding strangely like my mother. This whole thing is so weird. Anyway, she opens the window and motions me to follow as she starts crawling out onto the porch. She whispers that it's better if we stay low just in case her brother Steve is looking. One of his windows faces the porch too. I ask, "How far out?" and she answers, "Only about ten feet."

It's a warm velvety night and it feels like you're in the country except for us squeaking our way across the porch. This is about the most terrifying thing I've ever done in my life. I went to summer camps for years and we always used to sneak out at night to meet the boys, but that was different. The whole camp thing was a sort of fake, a let's-pretend world where sneaking out was expected, even laughed at. But this is the real world and what we're doing is no trick—it's dishonest. We're not just fooling around—we're sneaking out to buy stolen property, which is illegal, so that my mother can cheat on a test, which is immoral. And if we get caught, they're not going to just dock us from next week's social. It could be bad news for my mother. Not only won't she graduate but she'll surely get kicked out of school. And maybe worse. I wish I could stop her.

My face is dripping wet just thinking about the terrible things that could happen to her. I mean, the ground seems awfully far away. And that stupid twig of a tree doesn't help either. In fact, the combinations of awfuls is making me very queasy. I wish I had some gum. I have some in my bag but that's in the room. This is getting to be an emergency.

"Cici," I whisper, poking her in the back lightly. "I got to have some gum. Don't move. I'll be back in a sec."

"Wait," she says, reaching into her pocket. "I've got some right here." And she hands me the biggest ball of bubble gum I've ever seen. I pop the gum in my mouth and stuff the paper in my pocket. Just in time. It's almost impossible to chew this enormous glob of gum but it does the trick.

"I'll go first, then I can help you from the bottom," Cici says. "Now remember, hang on to the porch as long as you can. Okay?" And with that my mother leaps over the railing and starts to slide down the tree as easy as pie. The tree bends dangerously back and forth, but she's on the ground before it can break. Besides, I know it's waiting for me before it does its snap, crackle, and plop number. I know I can easily come up with four hundred fantastic reasons for shooting back into the house, but they all fall apart when I think about my mother's terrible predicament and that I'm probably the only person in the whole world who can help her. I don't even know how I can do that, but I know I have to try, so I kick off my clogs and start to climb over the rickety wooden railing. A splinter cuts into my palm and a sensible voice inside my brain reminds me that I am not, after all, my mother's keeper. But it's too late. I'm already on the skinny outside rim of the porch and not about to risk climbing back over the rail again. Besides, I think it's my brother's keeper anyway. Without loosening my grip on the railing, I wrap my legs around the tree branch and it starts zinging back and forth like a rubber band. I can feel it's going to snap if I put all my weight on it, so I let my hands slide down the spokes of the railing as far as they can while I lower my legs down the tree. It's still too high for me to jump. My mother is encouraging me from the ground in whispers.

"It's okay, you can let go of the porch now, and just slide down. I'll grab you before you hit the ground."

It's not okay because I can't let go. My legs keep slipping down the tree, stretching my body till it feels like my arms are going to pull right out of their sockets. Still, it's like my hands are welded to the porch. I can't make them let go.

Suddenly there's a wrenching sound of wood splitting and I go hurtling down the tree. In the blur I see my mother making a grab for me but I'm going too fast and too hard. In a whoosh my bare feet whack into the ground and I go sprawling. We both hold our breath and wait for lights to go on and windows to open. But nothing happens. I think I'm okay; at least I can move everything. Incredibly, the tree is in one piece, but I'm still clutching part of the railing in my hands.

"Wow, you really came flying. Are you hurt?" My mother helps me up, prying the spokes out of my hands and brushing off the twigs and dirt.

"Uh-uh. Just a splinter in my hand and some scrapes, but I made a mess of that railing. I'm really sorry."

"Forget it. Nobody ever uses that porch anyway. Are you sure you still want to come with me?"

"Absolutely." Anything is better than going back up that tree again.

"Okay, then let's go. Ted's going to be waiting on the corner. Hey, your shoes!"

Forget it. I wouldn't go back for my feet, much less my shoes. But I don't want her to think I'm a complete coward, so I tell her that I left my clogs because they're too noisy.

"Good idea," she says. "Let's go," and she leads the way. We tiptoe along the side of the house, silently, hunched over like cat thieves. My mother goes down the front steps to the street and I follow behind her shadow. Even from the middle of the block we can see Ted's car (my mother calls it a "hot rod") parked at the corner. There's enough light from the streetlight to see that he's really gross, especially his hair. The length isn't so bad, but he has this big high loopy pompadour in front and then the hair laps over at the back of his head. Gorgeous.

Right away I can see he thinks he's too cool for words. Funny thing about my mother. She's certainly no jerk—I mean she really knows her way around and nothing seems to scare her and in most ways I feel very dependent on her, but still she sometimes seems a little naive, much too trusting. Like with this creep. I wouldn't trust this worm nohow. One look and you can see how spaced out he is.

First thing Ted says when we get up to the car is "What'd you bring her for?" Meaning me.

"Why shouldn't I?" my mother says, giving him sneer for sneer. "She's a very good friend and besides I told her everything."

"Dumb broad," he says. Oh, I really love this guy. "Get in," he says to my mother, motioning to the seat next to him. "You"—pointing to me—"get in the back."

"Just a minute." When my mother uses that tone—watch out! "Who do you think you're pushing around, Mr. Hot Shot?" Yeah, *Mom*! "Why do we have to get in your stupid car anyway? Just give me the paper and I'll give you the money. We're not looking for a joyride, especially not with you."

"You want the test? Get in the car."

"What for?"

"'Cause I have to get it, that's what for."

"Why didn't you bring it with you? Look, jerko, I'm not supposed to be out now. If my parents find out, they'll kill me."

"That's your tough luck. You didn't think I'd be dumb enough to risk getting caught with the goods."

I may be wrong but I think this jerk sees too many movies. Either that or he's got something up his sleeve.

"It's not exactly the Hope diamond," says my mother fairly reasonably. "It's just a little science test that nobody but me cares about. So why don't you just get it now and let's get this thing over with."

"I just finished telling you I don't have it with me."

"Oh, damn! Come on, Victoria, let's go with Humphrey Bogart or whoever he is, or we'll never get the damn thing tonight."

And we both get in the front seat. Humphrey Bogart isn't too happy with the arrangement. It's obvious, now that the door is closed, that a lot of his spaced-out look and great gangster style is plain old beer. The car reeks of it.

"Where are we going?" I ask, because I can't sit like a dummy, and besides I want to make sure he's awake.

"None of your business." What a charmer.

We drive around for fifteen minutes, and even though I don't know where I am, still I get the impression that we're going in one big circle. All the time we're riding, Ted doesn't say a word, but you can see he's very busy planning something. Finally he seems to make up his mind and pulls over to the side of the street in front of an iron gate. I'm certain we passed this same place a few minutes ago. I give my mother a tiny poke in the side and whisper, "What's up?" But she just shrugs. So we sit and wait. Obviously Ted has something on his mind but he doesn't seem to have the nerve to do it. Finally he reaches into the backseat and comes up with a bottle of beer, gulps down half of it, and offers us the rest. We both say no thanks. He's annoyed and polishes off the rest of the bottle and tosses it out the window. Pig.

"Your friend gets out here," he announces. Obviously that's what he was working up his nerve for. Well, he wasted his time. He must be nuts if he thinks I'm going to let him put me out in the middle of nowhere at midnight.

"Forget it," my mother snaps back. "She stays with me." Wonderful mother.

"I'm not turning over anything with a witness. You want to forget the whole deal?"

"I told you she knows all about it, so what difference does it make if she sees it?"

"It makes a difference to me. You don't like it? Lump it."

"Look, I gotta have that test."

"Then tell your friend to get out."

"Hey, wait a minute!" I thought I'd never open my mouth. "You can't shove me out like that. I don't even know where I am. How am I going to find my way home?" I probably sound like I'm whining, but I don't care.

"Nobody said you had to find your way anywhere," the freak says, capturing my whine perfectly. "Just get out of the car and wait here while we drive around the block and close the deal."

"How long will it take?" I don't know why I ask. Twenty seconds would be too long.

"I don't know—give us ten, fifteen minutes."

"But it's not safe to stand here alone." I turn to my mother for support.

"It's all right," says my wonderful mother, the rat traitor. "Nobody's around."

That's just it. Nobody's around. What's the matter with her, anyway? People don't just stand on empty streets late at night all alone. Especially a girl my age. What's happening? At home she goes berserk when I want to take a bus after dark.

"Come on, you're holding up the works," says Mr. Vomit, who obviously can't wait to get my mother alone in the car.

But I can't bring myself to move.

"Don't worry." My mother tries to reassure me. "I'll make it fast. You'll see, we'll be back in less than five minutes."

I'm trapped. I can't ruin everything for my mother just because I'm scared of the dark, so I have no choice. I open the door and sit there staring out.

"Move it!" This is so grossly unfair, but what can I do? I get out of the car, slam the door, and before I can even turn around I hear the car screech away.

Here I am, totally alone, not just on this street but in the whole world. I back up against an iron gate. It's pretty dark, but if I stay perfectly still maybe they'll think I'm just a big lump in the gate. They, of course, are the stealers, rapers, muggers, and murderers that my mother has been warning me about since before I can remember. Those same monsters she's throwing me out to tonight.

It's absolutely silent on the street and, with the trees tunneling the entire block, inky black. No cars pass. I wait, straining my eyes to catch a glimpse of Ted's car coming around the corner. But there's nothing but dark emptiness down there. Then something, maybe a cat or a squirrel, darts out in front of me and the lump on the gate leaps a mile. A dog howls somewhere in one of the houses down at the far end of the block and the numbness in my head begins to subside enough for me to make out some night sounds, crickets and things like that. There's a slight breeze that rustles the leaves and carries the pleasant odor of fresh-cut grass. My mother's probably right. I'll be okay. Things were different in the forties, much quieter and safer, and you didn't have to worry about being out alone at night.

In fact, I'm probably safer alone in the street right now than she is in the car trying to fight off that moron. It feels like at least five minutes (more like five hours) have passed and they should be coming around the corner any second. By the time I count to forty-six (my new lucky number) the glare from their headlights should be visible. One, two, three . . . I'll close my eyes and open them at forty-six . . . 45678910111213141516 . . .

Oh my God!

There's a man. I can just make him out way down at the end of the street! And he's coming right toward me. I can't tell if he's young or old but he looks big—I mean huge, tall, and fat. I can't let myself jump to conclusions, but the odds are against me. I mean, sure he could be a plain old nice man, or he could be a mugger, stealer, rapist, or murderer. That's what I mean, there's only one little chance in four that he's okay. It's four to one against me. I'm in big trouble. He's walking pretty fast. I've already jumped to conclusions, so now I've got to make up my mind. . . . If I run I've still got a good head start. But where am I going to run to? I don't even know where I am, and then how will my mother find me? Maybe if I stand perfectly still he won't see me. That's dumb. He'd have to be blind not to spot me. I've got to stay cool. Oooh, I think he just spotted me. He hesitates for just a second, and now he's walking slower than before.

Now that he's closer I can see that he's certainly not a priest. If that car doesn't come by the time he gets up to the tree about fifteen feet away from me, I'm going to start screaming and running and pounding on doors and everything. I don't care. He's got another ten seconds.

Where is that car!

But it's still black down at the corner, and now he's right smack in front of me. He stops. My fingers squeeze around the rungs of the gate behind me. It's too late to run. I'll just hang on to the gate and scream and kick—

"Hello, young lady."

"Hello," I say before I can stop myself. Would you believe how well trained I am? I'm even polite to my own killer. He smiles and I can feel my face freeze in terror.

"Is there anything wrong?" he asks, trying to pass himself off as a terrific person just interested in my welfare.

"My, what's a young lady like you doing out this late?" He's still pretending he's not a killer, but I'm not fooled. It's just a matter of time before he attacks me. I've got to do something!

"Are you lost?"

"No, sir. Absolutely not. The soldiers are right around the corner."

"Soldiers?"

"Out collecting silver. Hundreds of them. Pushing their doll carriages."

Where *is* that car!

He looks at me hard for a moment. "Well," he finally says, "I'm sure the soldiers are watching out for you. But look, I live just up that block, in that white house over there. Why don't you come home and my wife will make some cocoa and we can call your parents and they can come and pick you up."

Me? Go in that house with this old smoothie? No way. Then I see it out of the corner of my eye. The car. It swings into the block and here it comes.

"Speak of the devil," I blurt to the man. "Here come my folks now." The car pulls up and Ted and Cici peer out. "Hi, Mom," I practically yell as I pile into the car. "Step on it, Dad, the general's waiting." As the car pulls away, I wave at the man and shout, "Remember the Maine!"

"What was all that about?" Naturally they're both really confused. Then my mother says, "Am I supposed to be your mother?" I just shrug my shoulders and laugh. I mean, what do you do with that kind of question?

Then I tell them about my narrow escape. But all Cici does is say, "You're loony. This is the safest neighborhood in the world." She gives Ted a hate stare. "On the street, anyway. It can get a little dangerous inside a car." I start to argue and rattle on about knifers and muggers and all, but Cici's not really listening, and I can see she's upset about something so I lean over and whisper to her, "What's up?"

"Fink over here," she says good and loud, "decided that two dollars isn't enough, especially since he found out there are no fringe benefits."

"Fringe benefits?"

"He expected me to put out," she says, really zinging it to Ted, whose ears turn a brilliant scarlet. Suddenly he gets very busy staring straight ahead and concentrating so hard he could be driving on a tightrope. "And when I smacked him," my mother continues, "he called the whole deal off."

I glare daggers at him. Propositioning my own teenage mother! I could kill him right then and there.

"Ten bucks," he suddenly says, "that's the price. Take or leave it." He pulls up in front of my mother's house.

"Cici," I poke my mother. "I want to talk to you for a sec."

"Sure thing, Victoria, right after I tell this bum a few little things that are on my mind."

"Forget it. The deal's off, period." Ted snarls. He's hot to leave.

"You probably never even had the blasted test anyhow."

"That's what you think," he says, and reaches into the glove compartment and pulls out what looks like a mimeographed page.

"Well, it doesn't make any difference, I haven't got ten dollars nohow."

"Cici." I'm pulling at her sleeve, trying to get her out of the car so I can talk to her before she starts to unload on Ted, which she is going to any second.

"First thing you can do"—she's so close she looks like she's going to bite his nose off—"is drop dead! Then . . ."

"Cici . . ." Now I'm practically dragging her out of the car. "It's important."

"I'm coming." But she's not, so I whisper that I can lend her some of the money. That makes her practically jump out of the car.

"You can! Neato! How much?"

"I have six dollars"—it's the emergency money my mother gave me, so in a crazy way it's hers already—"and with your two that's eight. Ask him, maybe he'll settle for that."

"Wait a minute. It's really terrif, but I don't know when I could pay you back. It would take me forever to save six dollars. I get thirty-five cents allowance, and even if I save the whole thing plus babysitting—I have this steady job two hours a week, that's fifty cents, plus things like deposit bottles and—"

"Forget it. I don't need it back for ages."

"You're really sensational, and don't worry, 'cause I'll pay you back even if it takes a year. Gee, thanks a million. Really, I . . ."

"You better ask the creep if he'll take eight instead of ten. You never know with him, he's so gross."

"Okay, wait here." And she goes over to the car and leans in the window. I can hear him giving her a really hard time. That's a lot of money to turn down, considering he's already done all the risky work—and stealing it, I mean. I've got a feeling something's fishy. After a couple of minutes my mother comes back, really dragging.

"He says no dice. Ten or nothing."

"What are you going to do?"

"There's one last thing, but I hate to . . ."

"What is it?"

"A charity box. Oh, God, it's just terrible even to think of such a thing."

"You mean like a church?"

"Not exactly. It's the USO. You know, they entertain the troops and things like that."

"That doesn't sound much like a charity. I mean, it's not something serious like cancer or starving children."

"But it's the war effort, and I've collected from a lot of people, and besides, the soldiers really need it, and I don't know . . ."

"How much have you got?"

"Oh, probably four or five dollars. I don't know exactly—it's in a sealed box."

"You only need two dollars. You can pay that back in a month." I know I was the one who was against the whole idea

585

from the beginning, but now that I'm really into it I see we have to go all the way. After all, nobody wants to see their own mother go through the disgrace of being left back. Worse than that, not graduate. Especially when your mother's such a terrific person. That's heavy stuff—not graduating, I mean. When I weight that against some junky old song and dance routine, I mean, like there's no choice. So here I am, trying to convince my mother that it's all right for her to steal from a charity box to buy answers from a moral degenerate to a stolen test. Super. Next thing you know we'll be holding up gas stations. Of course, I do have an advantage. I happen to know that even without that two dollars, we won the war and there's still a USO.

"All you do is send the money in anonymously. Nobody will ever know." I guess I'm pressing, but I want her to pass that stupid old test. Turns out that she doesn't need much convincing.

"Okay," she tells Ted. "I'll give you the ten dollars." And it's really weird, but I think he looks a little disappointed. I told you I think there's something screwy. "Except," she says, "I have to get the money from my room, so in the meantime you give the test to Victoria to hold and you can hold the eight dollars."

Reluctantly Ted folds the test tightly in half, then in quarters, and hands it to me.

"Thanks, sport." I can't resist the dig.

"C'mon, Victoria," my mother says, grabbing my arm. "Let's go."

"Hey, wait a minute!" The would-be defiler of my mother's purity grabs my other arm. "Where's she going with that test?"

"She's got to come with me. I need her help getting up the tree."

"What tree?"

"The one to the porch. That's the only way I can get back into the house."

"Yeah, well, I'm coming too."

"Suit yourself. C'mon, Victoria." And the three of us sneak up the front steps and around to the back of the house. The thought of going back up that tree, especially barefooted, turns my stomach. I don't know how I'm going to get back in, but I'm not going to worry about it now. Of course, my mother makes it look like a snap the way she shimmies up the tree and with one flying leap skims over the railing and lands silently on the porch. Even jerko is impressed. She ducks down and crawls along the porch and into the open window.

Fourteen

Watching her now reminds me how once about two years ago we were on a picnic with two other families in some park on Staten Island, and I don't know why, but everybody (the adults anyway) was kidding around and daring each other to do all sorts of crazy things like swinging from monkey bars and climbing trees. I remember that my mother climbed higher than anybody else, so high that I began to get a little worried. Everyone else thought it was hysterical, but it seemed kind of peculiar, even a little embarrassing to me. Now that I consider it, I guess it was kind of unfair of me to be embarrassed. After all, just because you've got children doesn't mean you're nothing but a mother. I'm hopeless when it comes to my mother. Everything about her is either embarrassing, irritating, or just plain confusing. I don't know why I can't just say she's a great climber and let it go at that.

Anyway, here's Ted and me waiting around for her, kind of kicking the dirt and not talking. By now he knows I can't stand his guts and I'm sure he feels the same way about me. He probably thinks I screwed up his big chance with my mother. Little does he know he never had one.

It's very quiet except for a funny scraping sound every few seconds. It seems to be coming from the house. There it goes again. I've heard that sound before but I can't think where. It's kind of like when you shake . . . of course! She's shaking the charity box, trying to get the coins out. I should have told her to stick a knife in the slot and let the coins slide out on it. It always works on Nina's piggy bank. The sound stops and I catch a glimpse of my mother's head coming out of the window. She's across the porch and at the railing before I can tell her to get a knife. She clears the railing and fairly glides down the tree and lands with a clink of the coin box.

"I've been shaking this thing like mad and all I got out is fourteen cents. At this rate it'll take me all week." She's still shaking the box furiously.

"Take it easy," I say. "I can do it. All I need's a knife."

"They'd hear me for sure if I tried to get into the kitchen," my mother says.

"How about if we break it?"

"No good. It's metal."

All this time the creep has been real quiet. Finally he says,

589

"Well, looks like we'll have to forget the whole thing." And he starts to walk away.

"Hey, wait a minute," my mother says, grabbing him by the sleeve. I still can't get over how anxious he is to drop a ten-dollar deal. That really throws me.

"What do you want?!" He sounds really mean now.

"Your pocketknife."

"Who says I have one?"

For a second my mother doesn't answer. She just narrows her eyes and stares at him real hard. Just exactly like she does when she catches me trying to hide something. "I do." And she's practically tapping her foot. He hasn't got a chance and he knows it!

"Let's have it," my mother commands, and Ted reaches into his side pocket and takes out one of those gigantic Boy Scout knives.

"Gimme the biggest blade you've got." I try to sound like my mother. He opens the knife instantly and hands it to me. Obviously he's one of those jerks who responds automatically when you give him an order. I wish we had known that before. Could have saved ourselves a lot of trouble. Anyway, I get to work pushing the knife's blade into the opening at the top of the box, and after a couple of experienced shakes the coins start to slide down the knife and into my lap. It couldn't be easier and in less than three minutes I've got exactly two dollars in front of me. My mother is really pleased.

"You're really a pro, Victoria. You saved my life. Thanks. I'll never forget you."

That's the nicest thing my mother ever said to me. And right this second I think I love her more than I ever loved her in my whole life. I'm so glad I could do something so important for her. It makes me feel so puffed up I could explode. Now if only I didn't have to climb back up that tree, life would be close to perfect.

"Okay," my mother says, handing Ted the two dollars in change. "That makes ten bucks even, right?"

"Yeah."

"The deal is closed, right?"

"Yeah," the submoron grunts again.

"In that case, I'd like to tell you something."

"Don't bother."

"You're a number-one pig."

"Up yours."

"Drop dead!"

And he starts to leave. It's a waste of time to insult jerks like Ted. Like talking at a toad.

"Hey, wait a minute," my mother calls after him. "You've got to help Victoria up the tree."

"Fat chance. Why should I help her?"

"Because," my mother says, "if you don't we'll never get back, and then we're certain to get caught, and if we do, guess who's going to get found out too. That's why."

Obviously the reason is good enough because he comes

back. My mother scoots up the tree and over the railing.

"Victoria, you start up the tree and I'll grab you when you get close to the rim of the porch, okay?"

I know I've said a million times how terrified I feel about climbing that tree, but this time the vibes are overpowering. I just know it's going to snap. I know it, but what can I do? I have to get up to that room or I'll blow the whole plan. Mr. Obnoxious puts his hands together to make a step for me. I've never been terrifically graceful, but in terror I'm a complete klutz. It takes me four tries before I can even get on to the tree. Now I have one foot wrapped around the trunk and one foot still on Ted's hands. I get the sinking feeling that I may stay this way forever.

"C'mon, Victoria, just a little higher and I can reach your hand." My mother is trying to be encouraging, but I can't get a firm hold on the tree in my bare feet, and that splinter in my hand is killing me, so I can't get a good grip on the branch. I try to take my foot out of Ted's hands and for a second I do, but then panic hits when he starts to move away and I kick out and my foot lands in his face.

"Hey!" he says pretty loud. "What're you doing!" And he shoves my foot hard and my whole body goes swaying to one side and the tree goes with it and . . . aiii . . . it's . . . "Help!" I scream as the tree snaps and I go sprawling all over Ted, who's knocked down under me, luckily breaking my fall. Two dollars' worth of change goes flying all over the ground.

"Victoria!" my mother shouts from the porch. "Are you

okay?" And she leaps over the railing, lowers herself onto the edge of the porch until she's hanging by her fingertips, then she lets go, dropping at least ten feet. She hits the ground lightly and rolls over to where I'm still flat out on top of Ted.

Suddenly, from no place, bright searchlights blast us from all directions, bouncing and leaping over the three of us. In panic we all roll in different directions and scramble to our feet, trying to jump away from the blinding glare. One of the lights lands on me and I stop dead, pinned in the center. I can't see who's at the other end, but I can see that they've nailed my mother too. I don't see Ted.

"Okay, you kids, don't move!" It's a man barking out the command in a no-kidding voice. We don't kid around. In fact, we don't move an inch. At the sound of his voice lights go on all over my mother's house and the house next door. Now the searchlights come closer and I can make out two men. I think to myself: Damn! They're policemen and they've got guns and—you won't believe this, but they're pointing them at us!

Fifteen

"Please, Officer, don't shoot. We live here," my mother says, reaching out and taking my hand like I was her child and she was going to protect me. Unreal!

"What are you doing here?" one of them says, and this time it's more of a real question than a command, and before we can even answer they put their guns back in their holsters and lower the lights from our faces.

"We didn't know it was so late . . . we were just . . . well . . . we were . . ." My mother's stumbling so I jump in.

"Camping out."

"Yeah, that's right, you know, in the great outdoors, under the stars and all that . . ." She's wasting her time because by now the whole family's out of the house along with all the next-door neighbors, and even the people two and three houses down have turned on their lights and opened their windows.

The jig's up, but that doesn't stop dear old Mom. She just rambles on and on about the virtues of life on the prairie. (I think she said prairie but it doesn't make any difference, I'm the only one listening.) All the while the two policemen are looking around, examining the money on the ground and the charity box propped up against the tree. That's when I spot the test paper. It's only about three feet from me. Nonchalantly I sort of slide over to the spot and reach down to pick it up, but one of the cops, a big fat guy, is too fast for me. He grabs it first.

"My God! What happened! Felicia, are you all right? What's happening?" By now my grandmother is out of the house and rushing toward us, grabbing this way and that way at her half-on robe.

"It's okay, Mommy, I can explain." But nobody gives her a chance. My grandfather and grandmother are all over us in a second, all concerned, asking a million questions like, "What's going on? What happened? Are you hurt? Did you fall? Why? Who? What?" And no stopping for explanations, which is just as well because the only explanation we have isn't so hot.

Cici keeps saying that we're all right, we're fine, nobody's hurt, and all that. "I can explain if you just wait a minute, I'll tell you the whole thing."

But that still doesn't seem to calm my grandmother. "I don't understand," she says. "It's the middle of the night. What are you doing in the backyard? Why aren't you in bed?" And she turns to my grandfather like he knows the whole story. "What's going on here, Ned?"

"We'll find out as soon as we let the girls get a word in, dear, and I suggest we do it inside." My grandfather sensibly takes charge, just like he always does. "We'll all go in the house and sit down calmly and talk. Come on, girls." And he starts to lead us into the house.

"One minute please, people." One of the policemen stops us. "We've got to straighten a few things out first. We got a call on breaking and entering from a Mr."—the cop checks his notebook—"a Mr. Owens of 108-67 Eighty-Eighth Road."

"That's me, officer," says one of the neighbors, looking very embarrassed as he pushes his way through what now must be a crowd of about ten or so curious neighbors. "I made that call. Sorry, Ned," he says to my grandfather, "but it looked like robbers to me."

"You did the right thing, Tom. Thank heavens it was only the girls. But thanks anyway. We appreciate your trying to help." And my grandfather shakes Tom's hand just to show that he really is grateful. My grandfather's good that way. He always tries to make people feel they've done the right thing, made the right choice. He's always been so wise.

The police take down some names and unimportant things like addresses and such, and then one of them says to my grandparents, "Looks like you people can handle this yourselves." And my grandparents agree and thank them, and it's all so nice and pleasant that I almost forget that we're about to have our heads chopped off or something equally horrendous when they find out what really happened.

Just as the police turn to leave, the fat one hands my grandfather the test paper. "You better take a look at this." Then my grandfather does a weird thing. He hands the paper to my mother without even unfolding it.

The police leave and the neighbors, seeing that the show is over for the night, start to drift into their houses. And then it hits me. Where's Ted!

I look behind me and all around but he's not there. I see the surprised expression on my mother's face and I know that she's thinking the same thing. The rat's disappeared. He must have slipped away in all the confusion. And with our eight dollars, too! Typical!

"Maybe you girls had better pick up that money before you come in," says my grandfather. Meanwhile my grandmother switches on the outside lights so we can see better. They wait until we've retrieved most of the two dollars, then my grandfather tells us to come inside and we can get anything we've missed in the morning.

"We're missing almost twenty cents." My mother is trying to stall. "Maybe I should get my flashlight and we'll look around a little longer." Something like about three or four weeks is probably what she has in mind, but my grandfather's not buying it and picks up the charity box and says he wants us both in the living room this minute and that's that.

It really freaks me out to hear my grandfather giving orders like that. I mean, when he's my real grandfather, years and years from now, he hardly ever gets angry at anyone, especially my mother or me. It's a part of him I never saw and it really makes me nervous. Everyone troops into the house after him. He leads me right into the living room, and I can see that my mother's even more nervous than I am and I don't blame her. Boy, it's really all over for her. I wish I could help her, but I can't think of any way.

My grandparents, looking very glum, take the two big easy chairs, and my mother and I squeeze together as close as possible in the center of the gigantic couch directly facing them. Uncle Steve plops himself down on the floor between the four of us so he doesn't miss a thing. Nice to know someone is enjoying himself. I'm making a mental note to really hate him in the future or the past or whatever.

"Well, go on, what happened?" Uncle Steve says, practically drooling at the mouth.

"That'll be enough, Steven. If you want to stay, I don't want to hear another word out of you. Is that clear?"

Hooray for you, Grandma!

And she snaps out another few mother phrases that shut him up instantly. I think he'd rather die than miss this.

"All right, Felicia," says my grandfather, and you can see he's bracing himself for the worst, which is only about half as bad as he's going to get. "Start at the beginning."

There's a terrible silence for about thirty seconds, then my mother says, "Uhhh . . . ," takes a deep breath, and looks at me.

Oh my God! I have to do something. She's counting on me.

"It was my fault." I leap in. "I mean, well, I met this boy at the party and I was . . . I was sneaking out to see him, and then Cici . . . I mean, Felicia . . ." I don't know what I'm saying, but it doesn't matter because nobody's buying it anyhow.

"Thanks anyway, Victoria." My mother gives me the tiniest of smiles, "but I want it to be over . . ." And then, practically pleading, "I can't stand how awful it makes me feel."

I should have known. The way she acted at the time it didn't seem to bother her that much, but I should have guessed how much agony she was going through just from how sick it made me feel inside.

"Mom." She turns to my grandmother, and you can barely hear her. "I've never been so ashamed of anything in my whole life. It's terrible . . ."

Now she buries her face in her hands, and all I want to do is put my arms around her and hug her tight. But then, all by herself, she sort of pulls herself together, and you can see she's determined to get it over with once and for all.

And she does.

Even Uncle Steve takes it seriously. As for my grandparents, they look positively crushed. That's the worst part, the look on their faces. Oh, my poor mother, what's going to happen to her? I mean, I know nobody's going to beat her or anything like that, but how is she ever going to get their trust again? I know not graduating is horrible, but hurting your parents that badly and destroying their faith in you is worse, the worst thing in the world.

My grandmother doesn't say anything. She'd be the one hollering if it was just a small bit of mischief, but this is too serious, and she looks at my grandfather, who always takes charge when a big crisis comes along. Finally he says, "I'm thoroughly ashamed of you, Felicia. So is your mother. I never thought you'd do anything dishonest. That's what's so disappointing—your dishonesty."

When my grandmother hears that, tears come to her eyes. She doesn't shout or even seem to be angry, but she looks crushed, like her heart is really breaking apart. She pulls her handkerchief out of her robe pocket and pretends she's not really crying, just blowing her nose. Nobody gets fooled.

"I can't believe it, Ned." She's almost pleading with my grandfather. "There must be some other explanation. There has to be . . . I know my child and she couldn't do anything like this. I just know it. . . ."

"Felicia?" My grandfather turns to Cici, and you can see he's hoping my grandmother is right.

"It's true. . . . I wish so hard it wasn't. But it is."

"Oh my God . . ." Now my grandmother isn't even trying to cover her tears.

"Please, Mom, don't," Cici says softly. "I know apologies won't help anything, but I'm sorry. I've never been so sorry for anything in my life." Then her voice gets stronger and calmer. "And I'm going to go to school and tell them the whole story. It's the only way I can make things right with myself and with you."

"No, you can't do that," says my grandfather. "You'll have no chance of graduating if you do that. Take your chances on the test. It may have been your intention to cheat, but you haven't yet. I don't think we need to make this a wide-open scandal. Maybe your mother and I can get the test postponed for you for a few extra days. We'll talk to your teacher on Monday morning."

"Please don't, Daddy," Cici says. "It's not just the test I'm thinking about. It's even more important than that—it's—I don't know, I suppose it's my honor, or whatever you've got that makes people trust you. I have to prove that I still have it. Even in the beginning I knew this was more serious than cutting a class or some of the other crazy things all the kids do. This wasn't kid's stuff, and now that it's all blown apart, I can't duck it like a kid." And then she turns to me and says, "I mean you have to start taking responsibility sometime."

All this time she's talking I'm thinking that she certainly doesn't sound like a kid. She sounds like a mature adult and really intelligent, and I'm very proud that she's my mother, even if she is only fourteen.

My grandfather studies her a minute. "This is a pretty grave affair," he says. "Are you sure you understand the consequences?"

"No, I'm not sure," says Cici. "But I suppose it's time for me to start learning."

My grandfather and grandmother exchange a glance. There's just the tiniest bit of a smile on my grandmother's face,

601

and I see my grandfather nod his head. "Okay, Felicia," he says, and his voice is softer now. "Everybody makes mistakes. Even grown-ups. Admitting them and correcting them is what's important and you're doing a very brave thing."

"That's the way I feel too, Felicia," says my grandmother as she stands up and holds out her arms. My mother rushes into them and turns to be embraced by my grandfather.

"Just remember we're in your corner and we'll help you any way we can," he says. "And I think right at this moment both your mother and I are pretty proud of your decision."

Even Uncle Steve, who hasn't said a word, looks kind of impressed. And so am I. I don't know why there's a little lump in my throat, but there is. I know it's very bad, what she did, but still, to confess the whole story to the teacher because of her honor—it takes more guts than I would have, that's for sure.

"I'll go with you if you want, Cici." That's me speaking. Right now I'd do anything in the world to help her.

"Would you, Victoria? I'd really appreciate that." And she sort of smiles and I feel sensational.

"Do you realize what time it is?" There goes my grandmother sounding like a regular mother again. "It's almost two a.m. and these children are still up. All three of you, into bed this instant."

"Boy, she really screwed up my whole night and I've got an important ball game tomorrow morning. How am I going to pitch without any sleep?" Uncle Steve is back in action again.

"Same as usual—lousy," says Cici, and my grandmother says the usual things, and we seem to be back to normal. We all go up to bed, and I can see that it's not really back to normal at all. Cici's got this horrendous thing hanging over her head, and on top of that she's headed for eighth grade all over again. What a nightmare!

As soon as we get into her room she starts to change into her pj's, all the time looking away from me. I guess she's crying. I wish I could say something that would make her feel better, but I can't think of anything that isn't silly or obviously baloney.

Without turning toward me, she hands me the folded test paper. "Here, you keep this. I don't ever want to see it again." Then, still hiding her face, she snaps out the light.

"Good night, Victoria. I'm sorry your visit turned out so badly." Even in the dark I can tell she's still crying.

"I really liked being here, Cici, I just wish there was something I could do to help you."

"Thanks. You were really keen the way you tried to take the blame. I won't forget that ever . . . ever. Victoria?"

"Yes?"

"I know this is nutty, 'cause I've just met you, but right now you're the best friend I have in the whole world. I feel I could tell you anything."

"Me too," I answer, but it's not true because I know that I can't tell her the most important thing. I just can't. So I don't say anything else and neither does she, and after a while my mind begins to quiet down and just as it starts to turn gray outside, I drift off to sleep.

And I dream. Long, involved, endless chasing nightmares. Running-away stories where I hang on to cliff edges, window-sills hundreds of feet above the street, and airplane wings until finally, agonies later, the light of the sun streaming into the room pulls me out and into the warm quiet midday. A second before I open my eyes a thought shoots through my head. Where will I be? And I pray it'll be in my own bed at home, but even before I look I know I'm not. The feel of the sun on my cheek and the brightness on my eyelids—that doesn't happen in my room no matter what time it is. My room is in a court and sunlight like this never comes in. So there's no point in the guessing game, I open my eyes. Sure enough, I'm just where I was when I fell asleep, across the room from Cici, in my mother's bedroom in 1944. I know I'll never get home anymore.

Sixteen

Just from the feel of it, I can tell it's afternoon. There's a little white radio clock on the night table between our beds, but it's facing my mother's side. I turn it very carefully, avoiding the globs of gum stuck to the top. Obviously this is where my mother sticks her gum before she goes to sleep. That's not bad except when you play the radio the top gets hot and then it melts down the sides and . . . ugh. My mother would flip if I did that now. I wish people didn't have to change so much.

I'm right, it's almost three o'clock. I suppose we've managed to use up most of the day already. Just as well, it's sure to be a gross one anyway. I slide out of bed as silently as I can, trying not to wake Cici. But she opens her eyes.

"It's okay. I was awake anyway. I just didn't feel like making it official by getting out of bed. But—well . . . you can't go crazy." And with one swoop she swings her legs up and out and lands standing next to her bed. Then she plops down again on the edge and just sits there, staring at nothing. I try to look very involved in getting dressed. Then, just like that, she snaps out of her trance and says, "I'm calling her. Right now."

"Who?"

"Horseface Davis. And I'm going to do it this minute before I change my mind." And she bolts out of the room and heads down the hall, I suppose to the phone. While she's gone I get dressed. Eventually I'm going to have to do something about these clothes. I mean, I can't wear the same thing every day forever. But where am I going to get the money to buy new ones?

"I did it. I called her." Cici has come back into the room, looking pretty deflated.

"What did she say?"

"Nothing much, just that she can't see me till tonight. I'm supposed to be over there at eight thirty. That's a long wait. . . ."

"Felicia!" my grandmother calls from downstairs. "Felicia, Victoria, breakfast!"

"We're coming right down!" my mother leans out the door and shouts. Then she turns to me and shrugs. "Might as well." And we go downstairs to the kitchen, where my grandmother is making her super blueberry pancakes. Fabulous! I love them!

"I hope you like blueberry pancakes," Cici says, helping me to a couple. "These are really keen." That word "keen" always makes me want to giggle.

"Are you kidding? I love them. These are the best I've ever had."

They both look at me kind of funny because I haven't even tasted them yet. Little mistake, but easy to wriggle out of. "They have to be because I've never had homemade pancakes before. All we have at home are the frozen ones."

"Frozen pancakes? I never heard of such a thing." Now my grandmother is really interested. "Where do you buy them?"

Here goes nothing. "Actually, my father picks them up in a commune in New Jersey." It's my policy to tell stories so odd that people can't find anything to hang a question on. All they can say is a polite "Oh, of course," and let it drop. That's just what my grandmother says now. I see from her face that I have to be more careful. They probably think I'm a little strange already—I mean, what with my jeans and clogs. Especially the clogs. I can see my grandmother staring at them, but I'm prepared. If she says anything I'll tell her they're orthopedic. In fact, why wait?

"They're orthopedic."

"I beg your pardon?"

"My shoes. They're orthopedic."

"Oh, of course." What'd I tell you.

"Foreign orthopedic." I know that's a little heavy, but I might as well pick up a little sympathy while I'm at it. From the way she shakes her head, I can see that I'm getting some. I finish the pancakes and tell her that they're sensational, and she gives me two more, and I think she's beginning to like me a little more. Still, how much can you like one of your daughter's friends when you only met her a day ago? It's very hard getting used to not being loved by your own family. Sometimes in the past, I mean the future, I used to think that nobody loved me. Well, now that it's really happened it's completely different. I'd never make that mistake again.

I'm so busy devouring my pancakes I don't even notice that my mother hasn't even touched hers. In fact, she's looking absolutely miserable. When she catches me looking at her, she gives me a tiny smile and then she excuses herself and leaves the kitchen. My grandmother doesn't say anything, just takes her plate off the table and makes herself busy putting things away. I finish up the last of my pancakes pretty fast and take my plate to the sink.

"That's all right, dear," says my grandmother. "I'll do that. Why don't you go upstairs and keep Felicia company? I think she needs someone to talk to."

"Sure thing, Mrs. Lyons." Wow, that's funny, I mean, calling my grandmother "Mrs. Lyons." "And thanks for the pancakes—they were the best I've ever had." She smiles and I know I'm making headway.

I go upstairs and my mother is sitting on her bed sewing her grungy old graduation dress.

"Hi." I try to sound casual.

"Sorry I deserted you, but I guess I'm not so hungry."

"Hey, don't worry about me. Really, I understand."

"I knew you would." And she gives me a nice kind of

confidential look. Then, motioning to the dress, she says that she's just killing time so she thought she might as well try to get the placket in, and just as soon as the words come out of her mouth she remembers that she probably won't even need the dress and, like it was on fire, she shoves it off her lap.

"Well, that's one crummy thing I won't have to do."

"You really think she won't let you graduate?"

"Absolutely. When I tell her what I tried to do she'll probably even expel me."

"You think so."

She just gulps and shrugs her shoulders.

"What about Ted? She can't expel her own kid."

"She won't have to 'cause I'm not going to tell who the other person is."

"But he's such a . . . pig."

"Still, I'm not going to rat on him."

"But he doesn't deserve to get away with it like that."

"Maybe not, but I'm not doing it for him, I'm doing it for me."

"How come?"

"It's just . . . promise you won't laugh?"

I promise absolutely, because I could never laugh at my mother now when she's in such terrible trouble.

"Well, you may think this is really jerky after all the crazy things I've done, but squealing is against my ethics. For that matter, so's cheating on a science test." And she waits for me to laugh or something, but I don't because I can really understand how she feels. It's sort of like what happened with me and Liz at the party in Philly. I could have stuck Liz with that joint easy, but I didn't because it would have been like squealing, and come to think of it, that's against my ethics too. Maybe I'm a lot more like my mother than I thought. Right now I kind of hope so.

Anyway, Cici goes on. "Going against your ethics makes it sound like it's religious or something, but for me it means just not doing things that make you feel ashamed inside." For a split second there, I thought she was putting me on, but I can see she's not. Talking very seriously like this makes me a little uncomfortable so I don't make any comment. I just listen. "When you're little, there's always someone to take care of things like that, someone to tell you, no, don't do that. But when you get older, like us, you have to start taking the responsibility yourself. I was still acting like a kid. I suppose I just didn't realize that it was time to stop being a kid and start growing up."

It feels weird hearing her say those things because suddenly she's hitting pretty close to home. You could say that's my problem too—I mean all that trouble I'm always getting into in school. So I tell her I think she's really got it together and that in a funny way she's helped me too. That seems to make her feel a little better for a while anyway. I feel very close to her now and I can tell she feels the same about me. Maybe my grandmother's right about responsibility changing you. Cici sounds different already.

For the next few hours we just sit around the room chatting about all kinds of different things. Mostly we're both trying to not think about what's going to happen. I don't know about my mother, but it doesn't work for me. All I can think of is that soon it's going to be eight thirty and we're going to have to go over to that teacher's house, and from the sound of her, she's horrendous. My teacher, Mrs. Serrada, is a horror, but apparently she's Mary Poppins compared to this gnome. My mother says that Horseface is even meaner in her sewing class than she is in science, if that's possible. Nothing she loves better than to get some poor schnook up there in front of the whole class and make her cry while she rips out seams that took forever to put in. According to Cici (who I suspect knows from firsthand experience), one crummy little mistake and Horseface practically tears the whole dress apart. Oh boy, I dread this confrontation. Still, I suppose that's nothing compared to the consequences. My mother must be worrying about the same thing because right at that moment she turns to me and says, "I'll never live this down. I'll always be that freak girl who didn't graduate. All my friends are going to be in high school and I'll have nobody to talk to in my class. I'll be just like Harold."

"Hey," I say, "that's not true. People forget quickly, you'll see." But she doesn't buy it for a minute and she's right. They're going to point her out like she was some kind of weirdo.

"And then I'll never be able to go to college. But there's no college in the whole world that'll take me with this on my record. My whole life is probably ruined. . . . I wish . . . I wish so hard it never happened. How can I stay here and face next year? I just can't. I can't face it." And she squeezes her eyes tight shut for a second and then she says suddenly, "I'll leave first."

"You mean run away?"

"Right."

"But you can't just take off like that. I mean, there's got to be another way."

"There isn't. Besides, I've made up my mind I have to go."

"Right now?"

"Yes."

Oh, no. I can't let her do such a horrendous thing. "Cici, I think you're making a grotesque mistake."

"Look, Victoria, I only told you because you're my dearest friend and the only person in the whole world I would trust with this kind of secret, but there's no way you can talk me out of it so don't even try."

"But it's dangerous."

"It doesn't matter. I told you I made up my mind so let's not talk about it anymore. Okay?"

"Sure," I say. "I didn't mean to bug you." But all along I'm thinking that I'm not going to let her run away. No matter what.

"Forget it. It's okay."

No way! Now I'm really freaking out because I've made up my mind too. I've got to come up with some way to stop her.

I mean, she's my mother and she's my best friend and I'm not going to stand around doing nothing while she screws up her whole life. Damn it!

I count to forty-six slowly and then . . . "Cici?"

"Yeah?"

"What about all those things you said—you know, the stuff about not being a kid again?"

She looks surprised and then annoyed. Considering she's my only friend in the entire world, I'm probably taking a big chance going at her like this.

Without even answering me, she grabs down an old suitcase from a shelf in her closet and starts throwing clothes in it.

"All those things you said to your parents? Just a load of BS, huh?"

"You know it wasn't, Victoria, but I . . . I just can't go through with it."

And the way she looks at me I feel sick to keep pushing her like this, but I have to stop her . . . any way I can.

"So instead you take the kid's way out. Boy, Cici, you're really too much. Your parents are going to be off the wall when they find out. Don't you care?"

"Hey, cut it out!"

"Plus, now *they're* going to be stuck with the responsibility of straightening out *your* problems for the ninety millionth time."

Now she's furious. "What's it to you, anyway!"

"A lot. You fooled me like everyone else, only worse because it was like you were talking about me and doing what I should be doing—you know, taking responsibility for myself—and it made sense and I really got sold. Big story, huh?"

From the way she stares at me, I think maybe I'm beginning to reach her a little.

"You're wrong, it wasn't baloney. I meant it," she says, "when I said it."

"Then, damn it, stick to it."

She doesn't answer, but she's not packing either.

"C'mon . . . I'll help you. I swear." I'm practically begging her. "I'll stick with you every single minute."

She just stands there staring at the half-packed suitcase, not moving, as though she's trying to decide, and then just like that she flips the top closed and shoves it out of the way. Now she looks up at me. There are tears in her eyes, but she's not crying. "I knew it all along," she says. "Growing up stinks."

And then she smiles at me.

I hope I did right. But I don't have much time to worry because suddenly, from nowhere, the scream of a police siren freezes me. Instantly my mother jumps up. Her face snaps into life as she shouts, "It's an air-raid alarm!"

"What? An air raid?"

"Wait here!" she says. "I must turn off the lights downstairs. Be right back." And she flies out of the room, knocking the stupid test paper off the dresser as she passes.

"Hey, wait for me!" I shout, but she's gone. I pick up the test paper and just sit on the bed staring at it and listening to

that crazy siren wailing like it was right outside the window.

Funny, all this fuss about the test and neither of us really even looked at it before. So I look and—you're not going to believe this, but that creep fooled her. The paper says 1943, but this is 1944 so that's last year's test he was trying to sell her. No wonder he was so hot to call it off. I told you there was something fishy about his attitude. He was ripping her off. What a creep! I shove the paper into the secret drawer. Wait till I show Cici.

"Turn those lights off," a man's voice shouts from the street. I look out of the window and everything is dark so he must mean me. I leap to the switch and turn it off. I can't believe this whole thing. I mean, I keep forgetting we're at war. I know it's only a drill, but what if it's not? A bomb could drop any minute and I'm busy worrying about some dumb test paper. I must get my head together. I just can't sit here in total darkness on the bed like some kind of jerk waiting to be blown out of the roof. But what should I do? Hide under the bed? Fat lot of good that'll do.

"Cici! Cici!" Waste of time trying to shout over those sirens. Well, I'm certainly not going to wait up here. Any jerk knows you're supposed to go to the basement. At least it's more like an air-raid shelter down there. Where is my mother? How could she just go off and leave me like this?

"Cici!" Oh boy, my voice is getting screechy. I'm really losing control. "Cici!" I can't help it, I'm scared, really terrified. I've got to find my mother. "Mommy!"

It's black in the house and there's no light coming from the outside so I just feel along the wall until I get to the door of the room. That hall is like the inside of my eyelids, but at least I know where the steps are so I just creep my way along the hall. If those sirens would only stop. I run my fingers along the wall and accidentally hit a small picture, and it slides off the hinge and falls to the floor. Naturally I manage to clump right on it, crunching the glass and snapping the wood frame all in one step. I'm not about to stop for anything now, so I kick it behind me and keep going. I must be near the end of the hall by now, so I walk more carefully, slowly feeling around, making little circles with my foot, hunting around for the beginning of the stairs. I think the railing was on the right, but I don't remember. And now I can't find it. It must be farther down the hall. I have to hurry. Even if the planes were right overhead you couldn't hear them over the sirens.

"Mommy!" Stupid to call her—she couldn't possibly hear me. Ohhh, my toes are over nothing, no floor, hurtling me forward. I grab out for the railing, for anything, but there's nothing but flat wall. My hands slide, my body falls forward and down, and I'm going through the air, banging my shoulders against the sides of the wall, slamming my hands against the steps, sliding down on my palms over the edges of the stairs, knocking, bumping, and then crashing boom against a solid wall with my forehead. Lightning strikes and painful colors push me farther and farther down until I'm spinning, pulling, pushing, then suddenly falling free and easy. Arms far out, flying gently, floating through tingly red soup, lying back and feeling numb, but good, kind of smiley stupid good. We're hanging there, the red soup and me. Far away I can make out some blue spots slowly swimming around. Blue lima beans? Hello, purple noodles, and way far up at the tippy-top, something white. The top of the pot? The something white is getting bigger and bigger as I get closer. It's round and spreading and it's bright and glaring and yellow and I'm heading right for it, and now my head bursts through it and out into the open. . . .

Seventeen

"What happened? The bomb! Did they drop the bombs?"

"It's all right, girlie." A gentle voice with a big pink sweaty face is leaning over me. "Just take it easy, nobody dropped any bombs, just a short stop."

Ooooh, suddenly my head pounds with pain and I put my hand up to rub it and there's this gigantic bump right between my eyebrows. Wow, is that sore.

"What happened?" I ask again, and the pink face pulls back and now I recognize it. It's that old train conductor, the one who was so nice to me on the trip from Philadelphia, the first one with the big crinkly smile. And that's just what his face does now as he tells me about how the train made a short stop just at the mouth of the tunnel into New York and I must have fallen forward and banged my head against the seat in front. He says that I look okay to him except for that big red mountain growing out of the center of my forehead. Lucky me, I was the only one on the whole train who got hurt.

"Be a good idea, honey, if you tell your mother to take you to the doctor when you get home," says the lady in the next seat.

I look at her to say that I will, and it's that same old lady with the crazy red lipstick that matches her scarf and shoes, the one I thought got off the train ages ago. The train! What am I doing on the train? Where's Cici? The house? The air raid . . .

"The air raid!" I shout. "What about the air raid?" I can't quite get my head together.

"Ain't no air raid, girlie, you must have been dreaming," the conductor says, and looks at the old lady, who shakes her head in agreement.

"Take it easy, honey, everything's all right, you just got yourself a little confused from being bumped on the head. Now, you just sit back and try and relax some." And she pats me gently on the arm and there's a little jerk forward and the train begins to move again.

"She'll be okay now," the old lady says to the conductor, and he winks at me and starts to move on up the aisle.

I sit back quietly in my seat like the lady says, and try to relax. But I can't because my mind's crazy like a bowl of spaghetti, all messy tangles and slippery loose ends. So I end up not thinking, just blinking my eyes like I'm some kind of slide projector and waiting for the picture to change. But it doesn't. I keep getting the same shot of me on the train heading for New York, just like way back in the beginning, which must mean that it's like the conductor says, I was unconscious. Of course, that makes the explanation very simple. While I was knocked out I dreamed the whole thing—Cici, my grandparents, the test, the weekend, and because I'm so brilliant, 1944 and World War II. Uh-uh . . . no way! Listen, I'm not saying I'm a dummy, but I couldn't do it. I mean, I could never put together anything as real as that. How could I? Outside of the movies, I swear I don't know a thing about the forties. So how could I do it, I mean, with the clothes and the people and the war and . . . unless it was all wrong. Suppose it didn't look at all the way I pictured it, then I guess it could have been a dream. But it seemed so real and it took so long and so many things happened and . . .

The loudspeaker announces Penn Station, New York, and people all around me start gathering up their belongings. The lady next to me smiles over the top of a lapful of shopping bags, and I remember shoving my suitcase on the shelf over the seat so I say excuse me and slide past her to get it. While I'm reaching for it, I look around at the people. Most of them are standing. And you know what? They're people, I mean grown-ups—all those kids and babies are gone. And their clothes—well, they're regular—you know, some jeans, some dresses, no hats—regular. I still can't believe it. It seemed so real, so absolutely true. It zonks me to think it was only a dream.

Hey! What am I thinking? This is great. I'm home! All that time, back there in the forties, all I wanted was to get home and see my family, and now I'm here and I can.

Maybe. All I have to do is take one look at the information booth. If my mother's there, then I'll know I'm really home.

I really want her to be there . . . badly.

It's always slow getting off trains and up crowded staircases, but this time it's taking forever. But so far, everything's right, I mean the station looks the way it always does.

The main floor is jammed. I put my head down and burrow into the crowd and with a lot of "excuse mes" push and shove my way through. I'm so afraid to look up because if she's not there . . .

I'm practically on top of the information booth, so I sneak my head up a little just to peek. She's there! Fantastic! And she even brought Nina. Excellent!

"Hey, Mom! Mommy!" And I go charging for her and practically leap into her arms. At first she's stiff, like I really stunned her, which I probably did, because I can't remember the last time I gave her such a greeting. Then she starts to hug me too, and this is ridiculous, but we both stand there hugging and kissing each other like we've been away for years. Boy, am I glad to see her. Even Nina. This is a terrible embarrassment, but I have to tell you that somewhere in all this loving and stuff I get so carried away that I even kiss Nina. I may never live that down.

Now my mother pulls back a little and, wouldn't you know, the first thing she sees is the bump.

"My God! What happened?" And she starts examining and fussing and throwing a million questions at me. So I explain about the short stop and she's all concerned and she doesn't even ask me about anything else, just grabs me and we go whizzing out of the station. Once in the car, she makes me sit back and not say anything. Naturally we drive directly to the doctor, who isn't exactly out of his mind with joy to do business on a Sunday, but he says it's not a concussion and I'm probably going to live. The way my mother takes me home and puts me to bed you'd think she didn't believe him. Nobody's allowed to bug me in any way. And it's lovely just to creep into my very own bed. I didn't realize how tired I was, but practically the minute I hit the pillow, I'm asleep. And best of all, no dreams.

I open my eyes slowly . . . slowly, barely peeking out from under the squint. It feels like my own room, but so far I can't see anything much. I take it very slowly because I'm not up to any more surprises. I open a tiny bit more and then I see it—beautiful gray gauzy nothing. Hooray! I'm home! I told you I've got this corner room in a court that only gets sun at two o'clock in the afternoon, and even then it's used. I mean, it's reflected off a window in the next apartment house and only about four inches of it slices into my room. Anyway, right now it looks like five o'clock on a rainy afternoon in February, so I must be home.

My ecstatic joy lasts about four seconds and then all the awfuls come flooding back—the school problem, the meeting with the principal, the dope hassle down in Philadelphia. Looking from the most optimistic angle, my situation is horrendously gross and getting worse. Maybe I should pretend I'm in a coma. That could happen easily from a bump on the head. Nah, it's hopeless, I could never pull it off. One look at Nina or someone like that and I'd surely start to laugh. Besides, comas are bad news. I mean, you can't even scratch yourself. On the other hand, amnesia is perfect. You can do anything you want and nobody can blame you for anything. It's like starting all over again with no black marks against you. It'd take me ten years to accumulate all those minus points, and by then I'd be almost twenty-four and out from under. I mean, what do you say to a twenty-four-year-old who smokes dope or makes a little noise in the movies?

"Victoria!" Like they say in the confession magazines, it's the voice of truth. Actually, it's only my mother.

"Victoria!" It's coming closer. You know what? I swear it sounds a smidgen like Cici, but of course it was my dream so I probably gave her my mother's voice.

"Victoria!" I'm beginning to get vibes of slight concern in her voice. She turns on the light. "What's the matter?" Heavy concern, working into big worry, bordering on panic. "Victoria!" She rushes to my bed.

"Yeah." I can't do it. I'm too chicken for amnesia.

"Are you deaf?" All that deep beautiful concern is

immediately replaced by plenty of angry impatience. "What are you waiting for? Don't you know we have an appointment with the principal at nine? Aren't things bad enough? Do you want to be late on top of everything?"

She rattles off eight more questions on the same order. All of which I answer by oozing slowly out of bed and reaching for my clothes. I'm not too chicken to rub my bump a little, even though, my luck, there's no trace of it left. If it were a pimple, it'd be there for a week. The little rub works good enough anyway. In fact, too good—now she's starting to help me dress. All almost-fourteen-year-olds just love to be dressed by their mothers. I never win.

Breakfast is strange, not terrible, just different. It's just my mother and me. My father's already left for the office and Nina's gone to school. My mother doesn't even make me eat breakfast, and she doesn't say a word when I don't take milk or anything. The four-block walk to school is weird too. Total silence. Nothing. Not even some helpful hints about how I should behave with the principal or threats about what's in store for me if he doesn't take me back. She doesn't even hassle me about the dope business at Liz's party. Not one blessed thing. I'm beginning to feel very creepy. I mean, I was nervous before, but now . . . it may be more serious than I thought. I've got this bad feeling about my mother. A terrible feeling. Like she's given up on me.

Eighteen

By the time we get to the school, classes have started and the halls are deserted. Everybody's where they're supposed to be, except me. I'm the strange one and I don't like the feeling. I wish I hadn't done all those silly things. I wish I had been more like everyone else. Even the dope thing, if I hadn't always landed into all the other trouble, nobody would have thought to blame me for that. Maybe it's like Cici said: I'm getting too old for this kind of stuff. Sure I know I'll never be a goody-goody like Margie Sloan, but it may be time to cool things a bit. I mean a couple of fun nutty things once in a while is okay, but three times a week was too much. I can see that now. Naturally it's too late. To tell you the truth, if I could get out of this whole thing right now, I'd be so perfect I'd make Margie Sloan look like a junkie.

Miss Olerfield, the principal's secretary, looks out of her head with joy to see me bringing my mother. She knows it means trouble and she's hated me since the gum-on-the-seat incident from the fourth grade. I can't understand people like that who hold a grudge forever.

"Mrs. Martin," she says, "Mr. Davis is waiting for you." And then to me, "I think we can manage a little tiny greeting now, can't we, Victoria?"

"Sorry, Miss Olerfield, I was watching the roach climbing into your purse."

Demented squeals, leaps, and lunges as she flings the entire contents of her bag all over the desk and floor. I want to stop to help her pick it up, but my mother grabs me by the arm and leads me into Mr. Davis's office before I can even offer. From the way she grips my arm, maybe she hasn't given up on me completely.

Mr. Davis gets up from behind his super-neat absolutely empty desk (nobody's ever figured out exactly what a principal does except maybe aggravate kids and their parents) to greet us. He's a real winner, tall and skinny and twelve months pregnant. At least that's what his belly looks like. He's always dressed in dusty brown suits, even when they're blue. He's musty, dull, and tacky. I'm crazy about him.

"Mrs. Martin?" He puts out his hand to my mother. "I don't believe I've had the pleasure."

"Mr. Davis?" my mother says, then suddenly stops dead. And so does he.

"Ted . . . Ted Davis?" My mother looks stunned.

Ted Davis! I don't believe it! Like in my dream. It can't be.

"Cici? Are you Cici Lyons?" His eyes are practically popping. "Don't tell me you're Cici Lyons. I don't believe it."

Lucky they're not looking at me because I'm totally astounded.

I mean, it was only a dream.

It can't have happened. It was only from the bump on my head.

But Cici and Ted? How did I know? I couldn't have unless—*unless I was there.*

"My, my, what a lot of years." Mr. Davis is shaking his head in disbelief.

"Thirty years? No, more, my goodness," says my mother. "All that time. But I swear, you look almost the same. You do."

Of course she's lying; I'd never have recognized him. Then he gives her some line about how she looks the same too, and then they go into a whole long thing about what this one is doing and how that one got divorced three times and that one ran for Congress and someone else moved to Alaska and on and on and I don't recognize any of the names yet.

"I can still see Pop Stiller's malt shop."

I know that name. I'm sure I do. I think my mother mentioned it when she told me about how Ted offered her the test the first time. I know she said she was in some malt shop and I could swear it was Pop somebody's. I think I'm going bananas because maybe I really was there.

627

"It's been gone for years. They tore down the whole block and built a huge apartment house."

Who cares about that? Get to the test thing.

"What about the school?"

"Gone too."

The test. What about the test!

"I have some pretty grim memories of that place," says my mother.

I know one for sure.

"Don't we all."

If they don't get to that damn test, I'm going to ask them myself. I swear I don't care, I have to know.

"You know, Ted, I've never forgiven you for that thing you pulled with me."

Suddenly I'm afraid. Up till now I was dying to know, but now I'm afraid. But it's too late to stop them.

"I know that was awful and I felt terrible afterward, but . . ."

"I could have killed you."

"I never should have run off and left you like that . . ."

"Ooooh . . ." That was me. I didn't mean to, but it just slipped out. They both look at me.

A pinprick of silence, then Mr. Davis goes on. ". . . at the party."

Party? What's he talking about? He wasn't even at that party.

"At the party?" My mother's shaking her head and looking

straight at me. "Oh, yes," she suddenly says. "The party. Deserting me at that miserable party to come home all by myself at midnight. My parents were furious."

He didn't leave her at any party. What are they talking about? Don't they remember? He ran off . . . when we all fell trying to get back into the house . . . the police, the test . . . the whole thing.

"I should have taken you home. I'm really sorry."

They're lying. They don't want me to know. They were going to say it, then they noticed me and they changed the whole story. The party business is baloney. I know it . . . I know it . . . I know it. . . .

"Victoria, please, dear, don't cry . . . it's all right."

My mother is holding me and I can't stop sobbing and shaking. Now they're both fussing over me. I wish I could control myself but I can't. . . .

"It's all right. . . . Everything's going to be okay." She's still hugging me, and even though it feels good, I can't seem to stop sobbing. "Victoria's not herself today. She had a slight accident on the train coming from Philadelphia yesterday. Just a bump on the head, but I think it upset her."

It's not that. It's just such a huge letdown. I absolutely convinced myself that it was all only a dream, and then this stuff happens with my mother and Mr. Davis and I start going mad all over again. I guess it's because I wanted so hard for it to be true—I mean, about how it was with my mother and me back then. We were so close and it felt so good and now it's all gone

629

and she's just my mother again and we're right back where we started . . . a million miles apart.

"Poor child." Mr. Davis puts his head out the door and asks Miss Olerfield to get me a glass of water. While we're waiting for the water, Mr. Davis, never one to miss a chance to kick someone when they're down, starts right in on me. He pulls out my records and begins reading off all my crimes. What seems like four days later, he's still reading. Lucky they don't have firing squads in schools. A lot of the things I can't remember. On the other hand, a lot I can and some of them are beginning to strike me funny, which can be very dangerous. All I need now is to be struck by the laughing bit.

"As you can see this presents an impossible situation," Mr. Davis tells my mother. "We're simply not equipped to deal with these kinds of disruptions and still give the other four hundred students the education they deserve. We must eliminate the incorrigibles."

At least, I didn't think they had firing squads.

"And I'm afraid your daughter qualifies as an incorrigible. We have tried to deal with her time and again, but don't seem to get through to her. She is a constant troublemaker. Not only does she create problems for herself, but she leads the other children astray. We cannot have that kind of influence in our school."

Okay, so maybe I am a troublemaker, sort of, but still I don't think I influence anybody else except maybe jerks like Tina Osborne—and practically anybody could influence her.

"One minute, Ted." Up till now my mother's just been listening. "I agree we're dealing with a difficult situation here, but you must admit most of the incidents are more childish than dangerous. When you talk about leading other students astray, you make it sound almost evil. My daughter's actions are certainly foolish, but hardly immoral."

"A foolish child often becomes an immoral adult."

"I don't think that follows at all."

"It's been my experience—"

"It's been my experience that all children are foolish at times. Don't you agree?"

"Well . . . it's true that children can be foolish, but in this case it's constant."

It looks hopeless. I'm sort of surprised to see how my mother's really coming on strong for me, but still I think he's made up his mind to throw me out and that's that. But, boy, it would be so great if she could only get me out of this mess . . . just this one last time. Actually, I probably used up my last time about five hundred times ago. Wait a minute. It just hit me that I'm acting like a kid, waiting for my mother to fix everything. This whole business is a lot like when Cici wanted to run away and I talked her into staying and taking responsibility for dealing with her own problems. That was fabulous advice considering I never even tried it myself. Maybe it's time I did.

"Excuse me . . ." I practically whisper it, but they both stop talking instantly and turn to me. "Uh . . . I know saying I'm sorry won't change things, but . . ."

"It certainly won't," says Mr. Davis. "It's much too late for apologies. You'd have done well to consider your actions before you took them and not hope to get by with apologies later."

"But—" He's so gross he doesn't even let me finish talking.

"People like you always think you can get by without paying the piper—well, you're going to learn, young lady, that you've got to pay and the price is high."

God. Cici was right. Growing up stinks; still, I make one last try. "I know, Mr. Davis, but—"

"No buts about it . . ." And he's off and running.

"Ted." My mother interrupts in her shut-your-mouth-right-this-minute voice.

It works.

"Why not let the child finish her sentence?"

"Of course, Victoria, go right ahead." He says it like it was all his idea.

"Uh . . ." That's me again, the groper. "Uh . . . I only meant to say, you're right, Mr. Davis. There's no room in this school for someone who does the dumb things I do." Suddenly I have tears in my eyes. "And I really want to stay in this school so I'm not going to do them anymore." I'm swallowing hard.

Now even my mother looks surprised. Still, neither of them make any comment so I bring in the big guns. "I've outgrown it, that's all. Making that kind of trouble is kids' stuff and I'm just too big for it now." I hold my breath and wait.

My mother recovers first. "Victoria, that's the best news I've had in ages." And she looks like she really means it.

"Well, now—" Mr. Davis doesn't seem all that convinced. "Of course, that's easy to say . . ."

But my mother is. "No, it's not, Ted. It's really quite difficult. And I'm very proud of you, Victoria." That makes me feel super. And then to Mr. Davis: "I really think she's come up with the perfect answer to the problem. Don't you, Ted?" She's really pushing for me.

"Well, I don't know. . . ."

"Well, I do, especially when I think of all the mistakes we made as kids. . . . You do remember your mistakes, don't you?" Now she sounds like the Godfather.

And it works. He's remembering. "On the other hand, it does sound like a mature decision. . . ."

"You certainly have a point there," says my mother, egging him on.

"Yes sir, it seems to me we may have come up with the perfect answer to our problem."

"I couldn't agree with you more, Ted."

"In my judgment, and remembering that all children are prone to mistakes at some time . . ."

"You think Victoria deserves another chance." My mother's not taking any.

". . . I think Victoria deserves another chance."

Fabulous! Excellent! Fantastic!

"What do you think, Victoria?" Mr. Davis asks, sticking his head toward me like a giant turtle.

Unbelievable. I mean, what does he think I think? I'm

tempted to give it to him a little and say, "Hey, no, don't give me another chance," but that would be slipping back to the baby stuff, so I catch myself and with great maturity mumble, "Gee, thanks."

Now my mother jumps in with another couple of tons of baloney about what a wise decision he's making and how he's probably responsible for redirecting my whole life. She stops just before she buries us all, and with a whole string of wonderful-to-see-you-agains and we-must-get-togethers, we leave, colliding with Miss Olerfield, who's finally come back with the lifesaving water, which naturally goes flying all over the front of her dress.

"Oh, dear," my mother says, "we're so sorry. We didn't see you."

"It's nothing," Miss Good Sport snaps, practically biting my mother's head off.

"Don't bother getting me another glass, Miss Olerfield," I say sweetly. "I'm feeling much better now."

You can see her mentally adding this to the gum on the seat.

"And, Miss Olerfield?" You can't expect me to resist every temptation. "I hope you find that roach in your bag."

My mother has me down the hall and out of the building so fast I never even got to see Miss Olerfield's reaction. Well, next time. Except now, maybe there isn't going to be any next time, what with the new me. Growing up may be harder than I thought.

Once outside the building my mother lets out a "whew!" of relief and just leans back against the school wall. She looks really beat.

"Am I glad that's over," she says. "I don't think I got two hours' sleep this whole weekend worrying about that meeting."

"But I was the one who was in trouble."

"True. But I happen to be responsible for you, so it's as much my problem as it is yours."

"I didn't think of it that way."

"That's because you're not a mother. Sometimes when I'm dealing with one of your endless arguments with Nina or some god-awful new trouble in school or reminding you for the four billionth time to clean your bedroom, I think I'm not either. Times like that I feel more like a prison matron than a mother. And it makes me very disappointed with myself."

"I suppose maybe I am a lot of trouble. . . ."

"I don't know. Maybe I just don't have the right approach. You won't believe this, Victoria, but when I was your age I was convinced that when I grew up I was going to be the most fantastic mother in the whole world. I would really understand my kids because I'd remember what it was like for me. But things change and I don't know—I suppose you forget."

"I kind of think you did a little."

"On the other hand . . . you certainly can be a terror."

"Used to be. I've absolutely changed completely. Almost."

"Well, you were pretty terrific this morning, and even if the 'new you' doesn't make it all the way through the whole afternoon, it's still encouraging, and it certainly does wonders for my memory. Which reminds me, Ted Davis is a fink creep."

"Huh?" For a second I thought my mother called the principal a fink creep.

"Fink creep. Always was and always will be."

Wow! She did. I turn around to double-check because it sounds just like Cici. And she smiles at me and says, "I think he's one big jerko." And then in a perfect imitation of Mr. Davis's voice, "What do you think, Victoria?"

I think I may be losing my marbles, but this opportunity doesn't come every day, so I take advantage of it. "Absolutely gross!"

"Not bad. How about geek?"

"Perfect. It sounds foul."

"It is. Now I was always partial to goofball for Ted."

"What about grubby freak?"

"Very nice. Although I think I'd throw in wisenheimer, too."

"Okay then, how's grungy, disgusting, raunchy, horrendous, horrific, outrageous—"

"Jackass loser!" And she says it so loud two old ladies passing by stop to give her a dirty look. Imagine if they knew she was talking about my principal. She doesn't seem to care at all. In fact, she smiles and grabs my hand tightly.

"Ouch! That hurt."

"What's wrong?"

Oh my God, the splinter from the tree! "I have a splinter in my hand," I say feebly.

"Let me see." And she examines it closely. "Where'd you get that?"

I got that, mother dear, the night we sneaked out to meet Ted to buy your science test with stolen USO money. You must remember, that was the night Ted—or should I call him Mr. Davis?—tried to get you to "put out"—of course, that was before the police caught us. I could say all that and more, but for once in my life I'm going to play it smart. I'm keeping my mouth shut. Besides, nobody wants to hear about anyone else's dreams. As for the splinter, I could have had it for days and not noticed and then it just worked its way into my dream. That happens, you know, if you hurt your foot for real, you can go limping around in your sleep. And Ted's name? Why shouldn't I know it? Everybody knows their principal's name. Even all those other things I seemed to know about my mother—well, she could have told me them over the years, like I always knew my dresser was a hand-me-down and that she lived in a house, not an apartment. Besides, I would be a real jerk to ruin what I have going now. This started out to be the worst day in my life and now it's looking great. Not only did good old Mr. Davis, the freak creep, redirect my entire life by saving me from boarding school, but my mother and I have never had it so good.

She nearly flipped me out the way she stood up for me with Mr. Davis. And now, walking home, we have it together for the first time—we're really hitting something special. Neither of us said anything much, just that fooling around calling the principal names, but I know we both felt it. Comfortable and easy and liking each other, just the way it used to be with Cici and me. . . .

"Just soak it."

"Huh?"

"The splinter."

"Oh, yeah."

"Or you can wait for Daddy. He's great with splinters. All he needs is a needle and one two three, it's out."

"I'll soak it."

"I thought you would." And she smiles a nice smile at me. When we reach home, she says, "You must be starving. What can I make for you?"

"Blueberry pancakes." I swear it just slipped out.

"You're in luck. I happen to have a box of fresh blueberries."

"I was only kidding. You don't have to bother."

"My pleasure, kiddo."

"Great! I'll be back in a minute—just let me throw on my jeans." And I shoot into my bedroom. I'm practically on the ceiling, I feel so high. Everything in my room looks fabulous. I love everything and everybody, my dresser, my mirror, my mother, everything. I slip my skirt off and pick up my jeans (did you think they were hanging up?) and jump into them. Even the girl in the mirror isn't so bad. I must have hit the one day in the whole year when there isn't even a sign of a pimple. At least not from ten feet across the room, and I'm not pushing my luck by going any closer. A zip and a snap and I'm ready. Looking very spiffy, Victoria, except for that gorgeous cigarette burn right in the middle of your T-shirt. Just big enough to ruin everything. Well, nothing to do but change it. Naturally, all my other shirts are in the laundry for a change. Fortunately, I still have my friend Steffi's shirt I borrowed three and a half months ago when she borrowed my suede jacket, which she practically lives in, so I don't feel so bad about never returning her shirt. It's stuffed away back in the corner of my secret drawer and when I pull it out a paper comes up from under the drawer lining. So I take it out.

And I unfold it.

And I'm blitzed! I mean, absolutely wiped out! Here it is, black-and-white proof, except my hands are shaking so hard it's more like a gray blur.

Look at me going on like some kind of nut. You don't even know what I'm talking about, unless you guessed already. I wish you did, then I wouldn't have to say it, because . . . forget it, I'm saying it anyway.

Right smack in front of me is a 1943 science test!

"Victoria! It's ready. C'mon while they're hot."

For the last three days all I kept doing was to try to pull myself together. Now here I am, trying again. This time there's nothing to do but go inside and eat the blueberry pancakes that I've just lost my appetite for. Fortunately, you can't tell by looking that my mind has just been practically totaled.

I'm pretty good at hiding things when I want to play it cool.

"My God, Victoria, what happened?"

Well, not so much from my mother. "Nothing. I'm just happy that I don't have to go to boarding school."

"You look more shocked than happy."

"I suppose I am. I really thought I was a goner."

"I'm glad it worked out. I like having you home."

My appetite may be picking up a bit. Imagine fresh blueberry pancakes twice in two days.

"They're every bit as good as Grandma's."

"I was worried that I forgot how. I haven't made them for such a long time." Then she looks at me. "I'll have to make them more often."

I think I may be in love.

"Mom?"

"Mmm."

"What really happened at that party?" I could never leave well enough alone.

"Nothing."

"But Mr. Davis said—"

"I thought we agreed what Ted Davis was."

"Right, but—"

"So do I look like the kind of person that would date a gross wisenheimer jerko?"

Boy, it really is just like being with Cici. Remember, back there when I said how fabulous it would be to have someone like her for a mother?

"Absolutely not," I say.

"Actually the whole story is completely different, but I think he was too embarrassed to say it and I don't blame him. It's not exactly a great reference for a principal. I'll tell you if you're ready to accept the fact that your own mother wasn't exactly a perfect child one hundred percent of the time."

"I think I can handle it."

"Hang on to your hat. I once tried to cheat on a science test."

"No kidding?"

I suppose I played it too surprised because now she wiggles out a little. "Of course, I was much younger than you are."

"How much?" I nail her because I know I'm never going to get this chance again.

"Let's see—it was 1944, I think—" She kind of giggles. "A month and half. Actually I've managed to block most of what happened because it really was a very unhappy experience. But I can't block out the fact that I did try to buy a science test from guess who?"

"Mr. Davis."

"The freak creep himself. Only I got caught and he didn't and it was awful because I thought they wouldn't let me graduate."

"What happened?"

"I went to see the teacher and told her the whole story, all except the part about her own son, Ted, being the person who stole the test to sell to me. She kept asking me who it was, but

I wouldn't tell. I had this thing about squealing. Anyway, it paid off because somehow she knew all along that it was Ted and she was very impressed with my sense of loyalty, plus the fact that I had come forward and confessed voluntarily. Maybe it helped that Ted lied and tried to get away with it. Whatever the reason, she let me graduate, but she really fixed old Ted's wagon. He got shipped off to one of those oppressive military academies. I haven't thought of that incident in years, but today seeing Ted Davis brought it all back. I remembered for the first time in too long what it felt like to be thirteen and in trouble. That's why I wanted to make sure he gave you another chance."

"I appreciate it."

"I know just how you feel. This time I really do." And she pops a kiss on the top of my head.

"I found this." And I give her the paper because now I have to see it through to the end.

She unfolds it and looks at it. Then she stares, stunned in absolute shock. And her face starts to get blotchy red and fills with fury.

Why did I show her that stupid test?

She looks up at me hard like she's seeing right into my brain. Now I've ruined everything.

"Where did you find this?"

How can I tell her? It's too bizarre and maybe she'll hate me for it, for being there and seeing all those things she wants to forget. Or she might think I was lying. . . .

"I found it in the secret drawer in my dresser. Way far in the back."

"Of course, that was once my dresser."

"I'm sorry." Here come the tears.

"Oh, honey, not you," and she gives me a big squeeze and laughs, not really so angry anymore. "It's that Ted Davis. That rat fink cheated me. This paper says 1943! He tried to sell me a year-old test paper. Can you imagine, cheating a cheater! How do you like that?"

Of course, I forgot she didn't know. She never saw the paper because I put it in the secret drawer during the air-raid alarm.

"I think maybe I'll send him the test and ask for my money back."

"He'd really freak."

"On second thought, I think I'll save it as a reminder. Sometimes it's useful to remember what it's like to be a kid."

I'm feeling super-good now because I know there really has been a change. Things are going to be better from now on. Mostly I suppose because of Cici. Probably every mother has a Cici somewhere deep inside her if you can only find it. Unless, gross thought, when you do it turns out to be a Margie goody-goody Sloan instead. What a nightmare that would be. Well, for sure no Margie Sloan ever got within a hundred miles of my mother.

I'm just standing there lapping it all up with this big dumb smile on my face.

"What's so funny?" my mother asks.

"Nothing. I just feel good."

"Me too." And her smile is almost as dumb as mine. "How about running across to Schrafft's and picking up some hot fudge and we'll make sundaes?"

"Great," I tell her, and she gives me two dollars and I head for the door.

Nineteen

"Mooo-ooom . . ."

That wasn't me. The troll is home.

"Where are you going?" She always has to know everything.

"Out."

"Mom, where's she going?"

Of course my mother has to tell her, and naturally she just can't wait to have some, and there goes what was going to be a perfect day. Even hot fudge tastes like boiled liver if you have to sit at the same table with the grunge. PS, she's still wearing my socks.

"You'd better walk Norman before you go," she announces.

"It's not my turn."

"It is too. I walked him for the whole weekend while you were away."

"So what? You were supposed to. I walked him before I left on Friday, and Sunday was my turn but you owed me a time so you have to walk him today."

"I don't owe you any turn."

"You do too. Remember Thursday I walked him for you when you said you sprained your finger and you told Mom you couldn't hold the leash."

"I couldn't, and besides, it was your turn anyway."

"Wrong again, creep, Wednesday was my turn."

"But Mom took him to the vet on Wednesday."

"So . . . lucky for me."

"That's not fair."

"Tough."

"Bugbreath." I don't know where eleven-year-olds pick up that kind of language.

Norman is basically a wonderful dog and I love him to pieces except that mostly he's incredibly lazy and stupid and like everyone else in this house (except me) he overreacts, so when he hears the word "out" he goes berserk and starts barking and throwing himself at the door. Naturally my mother hears the pounding and comes in from the kitchen to see what Norman is making such a fuss about.

"It's because Victoria won't take him out," Big Mouth says.

"It's not my turn, Mom."

"Somebody, *anybody*, walk him *please*."

"Not me," Nina says.

"Me neither," I say, and I explain very logically why it's

Nina's turn. I'm not coming on like a baby, it's person-to-person stuff, and my mother is listening, and I can feel it's our new relationship, and she keeps shaking her head, and I can see Nina's dying. Things are really going to be different from now on. I can tell. If only Norman would stop yowling.

"Victoria, dear . . ."

Good start, Mom.

"I'm sure you understand that this isn't the time for a long discussion. . . ."

That's reasonable.

"The dog must go out right now."

On cue Norman lunges for his leash.

"And since you were away all weekend, you take him out."

"But it's Nina's—"

"Now."

I can't believe she could do this horrendous thing to me after all we've been through.

"It's not fair." So what if it sounds baby.

"I said *now*."

It's useless. Hopeless. Nothing's changed. I have no choice. I hate to do it, but I have to. . . . "Make her take off my socks."

With terrifying calm my mother silently holds the door open for me. Then she turns to Nina and quietly says, "Empty the dishwasher."

"It's not my turn," Nina practically whispers.

"And set the table. And Nina?"

"Yeah?"

"TAKE OFF THOSE SOCKS RIGHT THIS MINUTE!" Then she turns to me with a smile, a different look, and says, "I haven't forgotten our hot fudge . . . or anything else."

"I'm on my way," I say happily, and Norman and I start out of the door.

"Victoria?"

"Oh, oh . . ."

"Put on your jacket, it's only May."

"Ah, Mom!"

"On second thought, you decide."

"Sure thing, Mom," I say good and loud. And then, very soft, "Thanks, Cici."

READ ON FOR A PEEK AT
FRANCINE PASCAL'S

FEARLESS

GAIA

Losers with no imagination say that if you start a new school, there has to be a first day. How come they haven't figured out how to beat that? Just think existentially. All you do is take what's supposed to be the first day and bury it someplace in the next month. By the time you get around to it a month later, who cares?

When I first heard the word *existential*, I didn't know what it meant, so I never used it. But then I found out that no one knows what it means, so now I use it all the time.

Since I just moved to New York last week, tomorrow would have been my first day at the new school, but I existentialized it, and now I've got a good thirty days before I have to deal with it. So, like, it'll be just a regular day, and

I'll just grab my usual school stuff, jeans and a T-shirt, and throw them on. Then just like I always do, I'll take them off and throw on about eighteen different T-shirts and four different pairs of jeans before I find the right ones that hide my diesel arms and thunder thighs. Not good things on a girl, but no one else seems to see them like I do.

I won't bother to clean up when I'm done. I don't want to trick my new cohabitants, George and Ella, into thinking that I'm neat or considerate or anything. Why set them up for disappointment? I made that mistake with my old cohabitants and . . . well, I'm not living with them anymore, am I?

George Niven was my dad's mentor in the CIA. He's old. Like fifty or something. His wife, Ella is much younger. Maybe thirty. I don't know. And you certainly can't tell from the way she dresses. Middle of winter she finds a way to show her belly button. And she's got four hundred of these little elastic bands that can only pass for a skirt if you never move your legs. Top that with this unbelievable iridescent red hair and you've got one hot seventeen-year-old. At least that's what she thinks. We all live cozy together in Greenwich Village in a brownstone—that's what they call row houses in New York City. Don't ask me why, because it isn't brown, but we'll let that go for now.

I'm not sure how this transfer of me and my pathetic possessions was arranged. Not by my dad, He is Out of the Picture. No letters. No birthday cards. He didn't even contact me in the hospital last year when I almost fractured my skull. (And no, I didn't almost fracture my skull to test my dad, as a certain asshole suggested.) I haven't seen him since I was twelve, since . . . since—I guess it's time to back up a little. My name is Gaia. Guy. Uh. Yes, it's a weird name. No, I don't feel like explaining it right now.

I am seventeen. The good things about seventeen is that you're not sixteen. Sixteen goes with the word *sweet*, and I am so far from sweet. I've got a black belt-in kung fu and I've trained in karate, judo, jujitsu, and *muay thai*— which is basically kick boxing. I've got a reflex speed that's off the charts. I'm a near perfect shot. I can climb mountains, box, wrestle, break codes in four languages. I can throw a 175-pound man over my shoulders, which accounts for my disgusting shoulders. I can kick just about anybody's ass. I'm not bragging. I wish I were. I wish my dad hadn't made me into the . . . thing I am.

I have blond hair. Not yellow, fairy-tale blond. But blond enough to stick me in the category. You know, so guys expect you to expect them to hit on you. So teachers set your default grade at B-minus. C-plus if you happen to have big breasts, which I don't particularly. My friend from before, Ivy, had this equation between grades and cup size, but I'll spare you that.

Back in ninth grade I dyed my way right out of the

blond category, but after a while it got annoying. The dye stung and turned my hands orange. To be honest, though (and I am not a liar), there's another reason I let my hair grow back. Being blond makes people think they can pick on you, and I like when people think they can pick on me.

You see, I have this handicap. Uh, that's the wrong word. I am hormonally challenged. I am never afraid. I just don't have the gene or whatever it is that makes you scared.

It's not like I'll jump off a cliff or anything. I'm not an idiot. My rationality is not defective. In fact, it's extra good. They say nothing clouds your reason like fear. But then, I wouldn't know. I don't know what it feels like to be scared. It's like if you don't have hope, how can you imagine it? Or being born blind, how do you know what colors are?

I guess you'd say I'm fearless. Whatever fear is.

If I see some big guy beating up on a little guy. I just dive in and finish him off. And I can. Because that's the way I've been trained. I'm so strong, you wouldn't believe. But I hate it.

Since I'm never afraid of anything, my dad figured he'd better make sure I can hold my own when I rush into things. What he did really worked, too. Better than he expected. See, my dad didn't consider nature.

Nature compensates for its mistakes. If it forgot to give me a fear gene, it gave me some other fantastic abilities that definitely work in my favor. When I need it. I have this awesome speed, enormous energy, and amazing strength all quadrupled because there's no fear to hold me back.

It's even hard for me to figure out. People talk about danger and being careful. In my head I totally understand, but in my gut I just don't feel it. So if I see somebody in trouble, I just jump in and use everything I've got. And that's big stuff, and it's intense.

I mean, you ever hear that story about the mother who lifted the car off her little boy? That's like the kind of strength regular people can get from adrenaline. Except I don't need extra adrenaline because without fear, there's nothing to stop you from using every bit of power you have.

And a human body, especially a highly trained one like mine, has a lot of concentrated power.

But there's a price. I remember once reading about the Spartans. They were these fantastic Greek warriors about four hundred something B.C. They'd beat everybody. Nobody could touch them. But after a battle they'd get so drained they'd shake all over and practically slide to the ground. That's what happens to me. It's like I use up everything and my body gets really weak and I almost black out. But it only lasts a couple of minutes. Eventually I'm okay again.

And there is one other thing that works in my favor. I can do whatever I want 'cause I've got nothing to lose.

See, my mother is . . . not here anymore. I don't really

care that my dad is gone because I hate his guts. I don't have any brothers or sisters. I don't even have any grand-parents. Well, actually, I think I do have one, but she lives in some end-of-the-world place in Russia and I get the feeling she's a few beans short of a burrito. But this is a tangent.

Tangent is a heinous word for two reasons:

1. It appears in my trigonometry book.

2. Ella, the woman-with-whom-I-now-live-never-to-be-confused-with-a-mother, accuses me of "going off on them."

Where was I? Right. I was telling you my secrets. It probably all boils down to three magic words: I don't care. I have no family, pets, or friends. I don't even have a lamp or a pair of pants I give a shit about.

I Don't Care.

And nobody can make me.

Ella says I'm looking for trouble. For a dummy she hit it right this time.

I *am* looking for trouble.

THE POINT

Don't go into the park after sunset. The warning rolled around Gaia Moore's head as she crossed the street that bordered Washington Square Park to the east. She savored the words as she would a forkful of chocolate cheesecake.

There was a stand of trees directly in front of her and a park entrance a couple hundred feet to the left. She hooked through the trees, feeling the familiar fizz in her limbs. It wasn't fear, of course. It was energy, maybe even excitement—the things that came when fear should have. She passed slowly through a grassy stretch, staying off the lighted paths that snaked inefficiently through the park.

As the crow flies. That's how she liked to walk. So what if she had nowhere to go? So what if no one on earth knew or probably cared where she was or when she'd get home? That wasn't the point. It didn't mean she had to take the long way. She was starting a new school in the morning, and she meant to put as much distance between herself and tomorrow as she could. Walking fast didn't stop the earth's slow roll, but sometimes it felt like it could.

She'd passed the midway point, marked by the miniature Arc de Triomph, before she caught the flutter of a shadow out of the corner of her eye. She didn't turn her head. She hunched her shoulders so her tall frame looked smaller. The shadow froze. She could feel eyes on her back. Bingo.

The mayor liked to brag how far the New York City crime rate had fallen, but Washington Square at night didn't disappoint. In her short time here she'd learned it was full of junkies who couldn't resist a blond girl with a full wallet, especially under the cover of night.

Gaia didn't alter the rhythm of her steps. An attacker proceeded differently when he sensed your awareness. Any deception was her advantage.

The energy was building in her veins. Come on, she urged silently. Her mind was beautifully blank. Her concentration was perfect. Her ears were pricked to decipher the subtlest motion.

Yet she could have sensed the clumsy attacker thundering from the brush if she'd been deaf and blind. A heavy arm was thrown over her shoulders and tightened around her neck.

"Oh, please," she muttered, burying an elbow in his solar plexus.

As he staggered backward and sucked for air, she turned on him indignantly. Yes, it was a big, clumsy stupid him—a little taller than average and young, probably not even twenty years old. She felt a tiny spark of hope as she let her eyes wander through the bushes. Maybe there were more . . . ? The really incompetent dopes usually traveled in packs. But she heard nothing more than his noisy X-rated complaints.

She let him come at her again. Might as well get a shred of a workout. She even let him earn a little speed as he barreled toward her. She loved turning a man's own strength against him. That was the essence of it. She reversed his momentum with a fast knee strike and finished him off with a front kick.

He lay sprawled in a half-conscious pile, and she was tempted to demand his wallet or his watch or something. A smile flickered over her face. It would be amusing, but that wasn't the point, was it?

Just as she was turning away, she detected a faint glitter on the ground near his left arm. She came closer and leaned down. It was a razor blade, shiny but not perfectly clean. In the dark she couldn't tell if the crud on the blade was rust or blood. She glanced quickly at her hands. No, he'd done her no harm. But it lodged in her mind as a strange choice of weapon.

She walked away without bothering to look further. She knew he'd be fine. Her specialty was subduing without causing any real damage. He'd lie there for a few minutes. He'd be sore, maybe bruised tomorrow. He'd brush the cobwebs off his imagination to invent a story for his buddies about how three seven-foot, three-hundred-pound male karate black belts attacked him in the park.

But she would bet her life on the fact that he would never sneak up on another fragile-looking woman without remembering this night. And that was the point. That was what Gaia lived for.

About the Author

New York Times bestselling author FRANCINE PASCAL is one of the most popular fiction writers for teenagers today and the creator of numerous bestselling series, including Fearless and Sweet Valley High, which was also made into a television series. She has written several YA novels including *Ruling Class* and the Victoria Martin trilogy. Her latest novel is *Sweet Valley Confidential: Ten Years Later.* She lives in New York City and France.

SiMON TeeN

Simon & Schuster's **Simon Teen**
e-newsletter delivers current updates on
the hottest titles, exciting sweepstakes, and
exclusive content from your favorite authors.

Visit **TEEN.SimonandSchuster.com** to
sign up, post your thoughts, and find out what
every avid reader is talking about!